MEG SPIED A PARTICULARLY VIBRANT PATCH OF BLUE.

Intending to point out plant tidbits, she abruptly ceased her steps—only to have Mr. Wilberforce slam into her and knock her off kilter.

He braced his hands on her shoulders to keep her from toppling into the wild sorrel that grew alongside the trail.

Beneath his breath he said, "Miss Brooks, you sorely tempt me."

Turning her head, she whispered, "I do?" Her heart beat so fast, she could barely put a coherent sentence together—short as it might have been.

This close, his eyes were defining shades of summer green and the gold hues of fall sunsets. Breathing became an effort.

The weight of his hands on her shoulders felt deliciously strong and protective. "You're a very enchanting woman and any man fortunate enough to hold you in his arms would be hard-pressed not to take advantage of the situation."

He held his face over hers. "Did you stop because you wanted me to kiss you?"

Meg sucked in her breath. No man had ever asked her that. "It hadn't been my intention . . ."

She got no further. His lips came softly over hers as he kissed her startled mouth.

Critics Declare Stef Ann Holm Is a Winner...

HARMONY

"The most warmhearted, heart-stirring romance of the season."
—*Romantic Times*

"*Harmony* is filled with frolic, mischief, and passion. Holm has a great sense of humor that shines through her characters."
—Laurel Gainer, *Affaire de Coeur*

"It will touch your heart. . . . A captivatingly delightful tale that will inspire, amuse, and move you. The comical exploits of the characters will have you laughing while finding reality tucked between the lines."
—*Rendezvous*

"Stef Ann Holm has developed a wonderful sense of the time. Scott Joplin, Susan B. Anthony, and ragtime music are beautifully woven into the story."
—Linda Mowery, *The Romantic Reader Online*

"When Stef Ann Holm is on, no one has a more lyrical, beautiful and unique voice than she does. Ms. Holm is one of the best at writing an emotionally intense historical romance that leaves nary a dry reader's eye anywhere."
—Harriet Klausner, Amazon.com

"The fun begins with the first stroke. . . . An amusing read."
—Annie Oakely, *Denver Rocky Mountain News*

"When the romantic relationship eventually matures, it does so with heart as Holm champions the need for women to be educated and permitted to combine work and marriage."
—*Publishers Weekly*

"A classic. . . . A fun and delightful read."
—Cathie Linz, author of *Husband Needed*

"Tender and heartbreaking with touches of fun. . . . To celebrate the book, I cranked up my grandmother's Victrola and played a 78 of the Maple Leaf Rag."

—Joyce Dixon, *Painted Rock Online Reviews*

"Holm launches her Brides for All Seasons series in fine form with this warmly humorous, homespun tale. . . . Nicely rendered with Holm's typical charm and wit, this lightly sensual romance provides an accurate sense of time and place."

—*Library Journal*

"Ms. Holm did a beautiful piece of work with her witty characters and humor. Fantastic! 5 BELLS!!!"

—Donita, *Bell, Book, and Candle*

AND BOOKSELLERS AGREE

"Truly enjoyable. This was very good."

—Henrietta Davis, Waldenbooks

"Easy read, nicely written, but ended too soon! Her characters were great!"
—Gracie, Gracie's Book Nook

"It was lovely."
—Merry Cutler, Annie's Book Shop

"By teaming a prim and proper pseudo-spinster with a finicky feline and a rugged outdoorsman and his hungry hound, Stef Ann Holm has another winner."

—Ruth Corbin, Paperback Place

"What great fun! Can't wait to read the next book in the series."
—Sharon Murphy, Paperback Trader

"Ms. Holm has skillfully crafted a wonderful story. Characters that come to life, a lot of laughter and a few tears make *Harmony* a keeper. . . . A great book."

—Margaret Stilson, Paperback Exchange

Books by Stef Ann Holm

Hooked
Harmony
Forget Me Not
Portraits
Crossings
Weeping Angel
Snowbird
King of the Pirates
Liberty Rose
Seasons of Gold

Published by POCKET BOOKS

STEF ANN HOLM

Hooked

SONNET BOOKS

New York London Toronto Sydney Tokyo Singapore

An *Original* Publication of POCKET BOOKS

A Sonnet Book published by
POCKET BOOKS, a division of Simon & Schuster Inc.
1230 Avenue of the Americas, New York, NY 10020

Copyright © 1999 by Stef Ann Holm

ISBN: 0-671-01941-4

First Sonnet Books printing May 1999

10 9 8 7 6 5 4 3 2 1

SONNET BOOKS and colophon are registered trademarks of Simon & Schuster Inc.

Cover photo by Koichiro Shimauchi/Photonica
Tip-in illustration by Gregg Gulbronson

Printed in the U.S.A.

For my agent, Meg Ruley—the real Meg,
who came up with this book's imaginative title
in under a minute while talking to me
from a pay phone at Kennedy Airport

❧ *Acknowledgments* ❧

With special thanks to my friend, Linda Francis Lee, who saw this book the way I wanted to write it, and helped me figure out how to make that story come to life. And also to a most excellent pal, Rachel Gibson, who read several drafts of this novel, gave me insightful critiques and never fell asleep. At least not to my knowledge.

Hooked

❧ Prologue ❧

It was *him*.

U.S. Deputy Marshal Ben Tweedy's hand shook as he read the identification in his prisoner's billfold. Sitting at his desk in the jailhouse, Tweedy shot the man behind bars a quick glance, then tossed the wallet onto the clutter of paper before him. He opened the top drawer, rifled through the article clippings, and found the one that had started it all.

Ladies Cultured Artists Society Likes It in the Buff
By Matthew Gage

Imagine this reporter's surprise when I was approached by a young man in the bar of the Embarcadero Hotel and was told a story so fantastic, I didn't believe it at first. The cream of San Francisco womanhood taking men out of their drawers for the sake of art. Those refined ladies of the Cultured

1

Artists Society hiring virile men to pose
in the nude and perform such tasks as
lifting weights and serving tea in nothing but their skin.

I know firsthand the classes were
falsely concocted as a way to look at
naked men because I posed for them.
And not a one got my face right . . .

Once again, Tweedy gazed with wide eyes into the
cell and the man lounging next to cold steel with one
foot crossed in front of the other.

Godamercy, it *was* him!

Matthew Gage. In the flesh. The renowned stunt
reporter for *The San Francisco Chronicle*. When
Tweedy had arrested him at the Palace Hotel a half
an hour ago, he never would have guessed he'd just
cuffed the notorious newspaper columnist.

Gage had caused so much ballyhoo with the exposé
he'd written on the San Francisco Ladies Cultured
Artists Society, that the story was known as far away
as Bozeman, Montana. One of the upstanding ladies
in the artists society had been none other than the
San Francisco mayor's wife. And now the mayor demanded the newspaper fire Gage for spoiling his wife's
good reputation.

But the reporter had gone into hiding at his editor's
request. A big to-do about it had been printed some
months ago. The real humdinger was that the society
artists article had doubled *The Chronicle*'s circulation
and Gage had taken his undercover work on the road.

As the reporter blended in across the countryside,
his stories came into the paper's office with regularity.
Gage exposing a corrupt charity in Denver that pock-

eted money intended for the poor. Gage inditing six lawmakers in Reno for improperly introducing a bill in the state Senate. Gage posing as a striking railroad worker with the nation's biggest railway system in Wichita.

Matthew Gage's sensationalist style had become the novelty of the day. Readers couldn't get enough of it. Nobody knew what story would be printed in the next edition of *The Chronicle* or, more importantly, where the reporter would turn up.

Nobody knew except Ben Tweedy. The deputy marshal had the reporter locked up in the city jail on a charge of disturbing the peace. Imagine that.

"As I live and breath," Tweedy said in awe.

Contemplation lit the depths of the prisoner's gold-green eyes, and a glint of something else—perhaps mild amusement over his entrapment.

On occasion, Ben had tried to imagine what the man looked like who could con people, talk them into believing anything while charming his way through whatever situation he came across—all just to get his stories.

Gage's tall and well-muscled frame barely cleared the jamb of the jail cell's doorway. He sported a full head of hair, ink black in color, neat and barber-trimmed. His shoulders were wide set; his legs long. Gage's dapper pin-check suit probably cost a whole month of Tweedy's salary. And yet the reporter wore the attire with lazy indifference.

Given the brawl Gage had gotten into tonight, barely a scratch marked him—just a tiny tear in the right shoulder seam of his fancy coat. Mr. Gage had licked Walter Toomey but good.

Godamercy! Deputy Tweedy wanted to slap his

hand on his thigh and shout a praise to the man high up in the sky. Matthew Gage, right here in the jailhouse!

"Say, Gage," Ben addressed as he lit a cheroot and waved out the match, "is it really true those blue-blooded ladies of Nob Hill only pretended to be artists? While, in reality, they just wanted to look at men modeling nothing but their smiles?"

Folding his arms across his chest, Gage replied, "It's all true."

"Hot damn on a tin roof!" Tweedy settled into his lumpy chair. "What about the corruption in Denver? And the Wichita railroad scandal?"

"True."

"Even the six lawmakers in Reno?"

"The lobbyist gave me a thousand dollars to pay off six assemblymen." Gage relaxed his stance, putting one hand in his hip pocket. "He bragged to me that he'd gotten up to ten thousand to pass or kill a bill."

"Godamercy," Tweedy breathed, "you've heard it all, haven't you?"

The other prisoner in the jail threw his tin drinking cup into the steel bars, kicking up a noisy ruckus. "You haven't heard it all from me, Deputy."

Tweedy switched his stare to that of Vernon Wilberforce, who occupied the cell next to Gage's. Unlike the savvy Gage, Wilberforce didn't have the brains of a beetle. "Be quiet, Wilberforce."

"Spare a smoke?" Gage said to Ben. He nearly missed the question, his attention having shifted to Wilberforce.

Ben abruptly rose to his feet, feeling like somebody important because the big newspaperman Gage had hit him up for a cigar. After all, men like Matthew

Gage didn't ride into Bozeman everyday and get into fights with the town's ugliest sumbitch, Walter Toomey, and walk away with only a few pulled threads in his coat seam.

Handing Gage the cheroot through the bars, Ben struck a match and lit the smoke for him. Gage nodded his thanks, then sat on the plain wooden cot in his cubicle. Leaning his back against the brick wall, he bent one leg and stretched the other out as if he were settling in. With a smooth motion of his wrist, he removed his bowler and rested the hat crown on the tip of his shoe. A shoe polished to a sheen, Ben noticed. That black leather had nary a scuff on it. Much like the man himself.

Ben Tweedy gawked, his mouth hanging open until he realized what he was doing. Then he went back to his desk and sat.

The deputy said, "You really are a sly impersonator Matthew Gage."

A succession of smoke rings came off of one puff on Gage's cheroot. As he watched the tiny gray spheres float toward the ceiling, Gage mildly stated in a matter-of-fact voice, "I'm not an impersonator. I'm a journalist."

"But you pretend to be somebody just to get your story." Tweedy sat forward, eagerly anticipating Gage's remark to that one.

Gage made no comment.

Sitting back into his seat, Tweedy grinned. *The truth was the truth.*

The deputy tapped his ash onto the floor. "So, Gage, what was it really like to shuck down below the navel to be sketched for the sake of a story?"

Rolling his thin cigar casually between his thumb

and forefinger, Gage shrugged. "No different than posing as a gambler to report on the city's illegal pool rooms."

Tweedy took a puff, gazed at his cigar, then manipulated his fingers to roll the smoke like Gage. Only Ben didn't have Gage's flair and he promptly dropped his cigar onto the desktop. Embers sparked up a stack of warrants and as Ben slapped at the fire with the butt of his revolver, he made his documents smoke more than a wet wood fire.

The cigar mishap under control, Ben's cheeks grew warm. He called himself a fool for trying to emulate a man who was larger than life. Only Gage could be Gage and get away with it.

Without preamble, Wilberforce announced, "Are you going to waste time talking to him all night? What about me? I've got to get out of here."

Tweedy frowned. "You're not getting out, so shut up."

Wilberforce went on. "My wife will have my hide if she finds out I've been arrested . . . especially if she hears what I've been locked up for."

Tweedy sagely advised, "You shouldn't have tied a rope around Miss Beaulah's Kinetoscope and attempted to steal it."

The silver-plated machine in Beaulah Belle's Bordello played fifty decadent frames of Miss Mabel doing a strip tease. Every man in Bozeman had bought a peek. Vernon vehemently denied taking the movie machine for the nickels inside. Claimed he had a love-tooth in his head for Miss Mabel and had to have her all to himself.

Ben propped his big booted feet on the desk. "Vernon Wilberforce, you are some piece of work thinking

6

you could steal Beaulah's pride and joy. That movie machine is the only one of its kind in Montana and she's damn possessive of it. You're a lucky man she didn't up and shoot you in the chestnuts while you dragged the machine across her velvet carpet."

Wilberforce woefully declared, "I've got to be in the town of Harmony the day after tomorrow. It's imperative I'm there."

"What's so important in Harmony?" Gage asked, leisurely stretching out his leg.

Tweedy grew resentful of Wilberforce luring the newspaper man into a conversation. The deputy could only hold Gage for the night on the charge he'd been arrested for, then he'd have to let him go. While he had the man captive, he wanted to hear all about the makings of his scandalous stories. But he couldn't exactly do that with Wilberforce yammering his woes.

"Wilberforce, I'm telling you to shut your yap," Tweedy warned.

"I'm a contestant in the twelfth annual fly-fishing tournament," Vernon said, ignoring Tweedy.

Large in the body and short in size, Vernon pressed his wide forehead against the bars to look into Gage's cell. "First prize is one thousand dollars. If my wife finds out about me being in here, she'll never forgive me."

Ben interjected, "You should have thought about *that* before you went and lassoed the movie machine."

Wilberforce stared a hole in the floor. "I just couldn't help myself. I've never seen a woman as beautiful as Miss Mabel."

"Probably ain't never seen so *much* of a woman, is more like it," Ben snickered.

"Next time you get an itch," Gage drawled, "maybe you ought to pay for a woman."

"I'm not that kind of man, Mr. Gage." Wilberforce sat taller and put on a somber expression. "And I've had many opportunities. I'm in the traveling business. Bissell carpet sweepers. I sell them. The whole line. Your baby sweeper, child sweeper, grand rapids, prize and regular grand. I'm pretty good at it, too. I've got a wide territory. Bigger than most who work for the outfit."

"Put a lid on it," Tweedy growled, but Wilberforce brushed him off.

"You see," Vernon said, "I've got my catalogue case with me. Was planning on making some rounds while I headed over to Harmony. But . . ." His voice quivered and trailed, then, "but I'm in an awful jam, Mr. Gage. Biggest mess I've ever been in if I don't have some proof that I was in Harmony for that fly-fishing contest. Because if I don't, the missus will want to know why. And what can I tell her? The truth? It would break her heart."

"You're getting me mad, Wilberforce."

Wilberforce pinned his stare on Ben. "I keep trying to tell you, I'm not an offender of the law—aside from that one time I sold a dozen Bissells to a hotel line and charged them for thirteen. But the missus was carrying our fifth child and I needed a little extra. You know how it is. You have a wife and family, Deputy Tweedy?"

"No."

Vernon then asked, "What about you, Mr. Gage?"

Crossing his legs at the ankles, his bowler still teetering on the tip of his shoe, Gage responded without emotion, "No."

8

"That's a shame. Behind every good man, there's a good woman. My Violet, she's a good woman. She can't find out I've been arrested. I shouldn't have had them two shots of whiskey. I temporarily lost my head. I don't know what I would have done with that machine even if I'd've made it out the door. Couldn't exactly put it on the train with me."

The deputy broke into Wilberforce's lamenting. "Gage doesn't want to hear your hard-luck story. Save it for the next fellow to occupy his cell. Because you, Wilberforce, are going to be here for a while." Through a snort, he announced, "If you're let out at all. Stealing in these parts can be a hanging offense. It'll be up to the circuit judge to decide. And he won't be back through here for another month."

Wilberforce blanched, grabbing hold of the cell bars and staring at Ben. "You don't understand! My life is over if you don't let me out. I have to send my wife letters from Harmony so she won't suspect anything is wrong. I'm already registered in that fly-fishing contest, and Violet is counting on me winning the thousand dollar first-prize purse. If she finds out I'm in jail, she'll take the children and move in with her mother."

The reporter continued to blow smoke rings from puffs of his cigar, but added nothing to the conversation—confirming to U.S. Deputy Marshal Ben Tweedy that he wasn't interested in Wilberforce's dilemma.

And why should he be? After all, Gage had duked it out with Walter Toomey. Bozeman's biggest blowhard.

From what Ben gathered through the night clerk's ranting, both men had wanted the continental suite at the Palace Hotel and had arrived to ask for it at the same time. Toomey had brought a lady friend with him. Gage had been alone, which made Ben admire Gage all the more. The man had so much class, he sprang for a high dollar room just to get some shut-eye.

Toomey had thrown the first punch. But Gage had gotten in the last. Now Walter was getting his cut eye sewed up at the doc's.

"Everybody knows that contest is rigged," Tweedy said dryly. "Look what happened last year. That high-brow young fellow won. He shouldn't have. Something real fishy went on. Everybody knew that Stratton boy had it in the bag. He was the best ever." The rub of denim against the leather of a chair fused through Tweedy's comment as he shifted in his seat. "Or so I heard he was the best. I wasn't there. Rumors. You know how they are. When there's a lot of money at stake, you've got gall and wormwood if all the marbles don't roll into your corner."

"Deputy Tweedy," Wilberforce enunciated, "I don't care if you think that contest is rigged. At this point, I don't even care if somebody illegally wins that thousand dollar prize. Because if my wife doesn't receive letters postmarked Harmony, Montana, my life is ruined."

Tweedy unsympathetically laughed, thinking Gage would do likewise.

But when Ben looked at the reporter, his expression wasn't so bored anymore. In fact, he was thoughtfully puffing on his cigar while staring intently at Vernon Wilberforce.

Chapter

❖ 1 ❖

Meg Brooks was going to get married if it was the last thing she did.

Marriage hadn't been her cause until recently. What she'd really wanted to do was go into the hotel business. After all, her family owned the Brooks House Hotel and she knew more about it than anything else. She'd assumed, *expected,* to be able to contribute to the hotel's operation once she graduated from finishing school.

But when she'd approached her father, he said she was too young and inexperienced to take such a responsibility on. She wasn't asking to run the hotel by herself. Merely to improve it. She tried to explain to Father that by giving her a chance, she would gain the experience. And when she pressed on and spoke her suggestions, he thought her ideas on lobby renovation were silly.

Silly.

The word still hurt.

George Brooks's decision had been final. Too stub-

11

born to accept defeat, Meg had written letters of quali-
fication to hotels in the area. The responses were all
the same: No thank you. So Meg had to accept that
her dream of eventually running the family hotel
would never come to pass, and she had to pin her
hopes on something else.

That something else was a man.

On her mother's insistence, Meg had enrolled in
Mrs. Wolcott's Finishing School, formerly Edwina
Huntington's Finishing School. Miss Edwina's lessons
on propriety and proper feminine protocol had proved
to be so well-founded, Miss Edwina herself had landed
a husband last year.

A fact that Meg's mother never missed an opportunity to point out.

For most of her life, Meg had fought against being
like Iris Brooks. Refined and stuffy and no fun at all.
Meg had been a terror as a little girl, doing whatever
she pleased; usually boy things because she tagged
along with her brother, Wayne, and his gang of mischief makers. She'd been fearless and fancy free.

It was only after sitting through several of Mrs. Wolcott's classes, that Meg realized in order to gain a
potential husband's attention, a woman must act like
a suitable wife. The three Cs: cultured, civilized,
charming.

Three things that eluded Meg—she had to pursue
them.

This past fall and winter, Meg had attended the finishing school but she hadn't put her heart in it. She
hadn't wanted to wear her hair in a high twist. She hadn't
wanted to have to remember her gloves. She didn't want
to know about proper teatime conversations. To learn
what to say and when to say it.

Meg had just continued to be, well . . . Meg.

Now that she had distanced herself from the rebellion against her mother's idea, she saw that Edwina Wolcott was blissfully happy. As was Crescencia Defresne, a former student who had married last December. With marriage, and the love of a man, perhaps Meg could find her own contentment.

So she'd recently reformed and turned herself into a lady. What had worked for Miss Edwina and Crescencia could work for her. Meg was now Margaret, the Sophisticate. Polished and poised. She could succeed at this. After all, she'd gotten the wardrobe down pat. Well, almost . . .

"Margaret, why do you insist on displaying your petticoat?" This came from Ruth Elward, Meg's longtime friend. Her white-blond hair was artfully braided in a twist beneath her hat. Dark brown eyes grew inquisitive as she awaited Meg's reply.

"Yes, why?" The second query was uttered by Hildegarde Plunkett. A pretty girl with a round face and slightly ungainly figure.

To an observer, the three young women in spring-colored dresses, with gloves and open parasols, strolling along Birch Avenue looked the epitome of fashion and refinement. Except for the small detail that Meg Brooks didn't keep in tune with the others' footsteps. With a springy bounce to her step, she kept getting ahead of them.

Meg momentarily gazed at her feet as she walked. The insteps of her silk-vested top shoes barely showed because indeed lace flounce fell a half inch below her skirt hem.

Raising her eyes, Meg replied, "It's a fashion rage. I read about it in *Harper's Bazaar*. The article said a flirt of underskirt is considered vogue and is supposed to do wonders in catching the attention of the opposite sex."

Hildegarde twirled her parasol. "My mother would say, if it takes a peek of petticoat to catch a man these days, then you're trying to catch the wrong type of man." Then she wistfully paused. "I read the same article. I wanted to take my petticoat hems down too, but my mother wouldn't let me."

"Margaret, would you please slow down," Ruth chided.

"Yes," Hildegarde seconded, walking even slower, "you're making us look like we're in a hurry."

Meg *was* in a hurry. Her two friends kept a pace as slow as a snail's. Today Meg had something very important to do, just as she had the past few days. Ruth and Hildegarde knew full well why she was excited to be on her way, but they didn't see her short-term involvement with the hotel as anything special.

"What's all this about not having the attention of a man?" Ruth asked. "Have you forgotten about Harold Adams?"

Meg *wanted* to forget about Harold Adams. He'd taken a sweetheart's interest in her only recently—as soon as she'd "conformed" and given up her old ways, he'd come knocking on her door.

With a sigh, Meg clarified, "Harold Adams isn't the type of man a woman envisions herself married to."

Ruth asked, "What's wrong with him?"

Meg lowered her voice, "Don't you think his Adam's apple sticks out too far?"

"I hadn't noticed," Hildegarde offered.

"Oh, you're just trying to be nice," Meg insisted, picking up her pace once more. With her swifter stride, she nearly tripped on the low hem of her petticoat; she even faltered a little but quickly caught her step. "You can't help noticing the way it moves up and down when he talks. It hits you right in the eyes. I try not to stare, but sometimes I can't help it."

Meg exhaled her frustration. "And to make matters worse, he had to go and have the last name Adams just to remind everyone. I know the girls in class call him Harold Adam's Apple."

Reluctant nods were her answer.

There. She knew it.

Thankfully they'd reached the hotel and Meg didn't have to talk about Harold Adams anymore. But it wasn't that thought that put a lightness in her walk. For the next month or so, while her parents were away in Niagara Falls on an anniversary tour, Meg was in charge of the hotel lobby.

In reality, her grandmother had been left to oversee the operation of the Brooks House Hotel; but dear Grandma Nettie trusted Meg to change whatever she felt needed improving. For that, Meg was extremely grateful. She wished Grandma Nettie lived with them all the time, not just when her parents were away. Even though, Grandma was a bit . . . militant.

Meg and her friends said their good-byes and parted company. As she took the hotel steps, Meg forgot to hold her skirts up and she felt a tug on the waistband of her petticoat. Discreetly hiking the elastic up through the soft fabric of her shirtwaist, she entered the lobby and confidently strode to the registry counter where her grandmother stood.

Meg's grand spirits momentarily faltered when she saw what Grandma Nettie was doing.

Spry for her age of seventy-two, she rearranged the

two-foot length of bicycle chain with self-locking shackles and bronze metal lock, in a long spill across the front of the counter—smack next to the guest book.

After a soft bite on her lower lip, Meg hesitantly asked, "Grandma, do you have to set that out?"

Grandma Nettie's fingers fiddled with the chain until its links were perfectly straight. Meg watched. Even though her grandmother had told her she was going to put the bicycle chain on exhibit, Meg had wished she hadn't.

Of course the old Meg was intrigued, but the new, improved Margaret was supposed to be appalled. Especially because Grandma had been telling every last guest exactly what it was for.

"Don't you go getting delicate on me, Margaret, like your mother."

"I'm not," Meg assured, then suddenly realized that once indoors, she should have closed her parasol and removed her gloves. Such a nuisance to remember every little detail.

With a tug, she collapsed the circular canopy and deposited the parasol into the umbrella stand next to the front door. Then she pulled her gloves off and tossed them carelessly behind the registry.

"Don't get me wrong," Grandma went on. "I love your mother as if she were my own daughter, but she can be a tad . . . *too* delicate."

"A tad?" Meg said with exasperation. "She's a good deal more than that. Mother calls a chicken leg the limb. And the breast a bosom because she won't say breast at the dinner table, or anyplace else for that matter. She'll say to Father, 'Papa, slice me the bosom.' Honestly."

"Honestly, is right." Wizened smoky blue eyes lifted to view Meg over the narrow lenses of Grandma's spectacles. "And in answer to your question, I most surely do. This chain represents the militant movement that I intend to personally bring to President McKinley's attention. That is, as soon as your parents get back from Niagara Falls."

Meg asked, "But do you have to chain yourself to the White House in order to make him notice you? Couldn't you simply write him a letter?"

"This is the fighting age, Margaret. Women have to get themselves arrested to attract attention to the cause. A letter won't get me thrown in the hoosegow. My fellow sisters and I plan to convene on the steps May the eighth at noon. We have it on good authority that's the hour the president takes his lunch on the State Floor in the northwest dining room."

As Meg listened, she asked herself what right-minded gentleman would want to marry into such a family?

A proper lady would never consider doing such a thing as getting arrested for making a public fuss. Although there was an appealingly brazen and defiant ring to causing such trouble.

No! Meg determinedly squelched the flash of excitement over the prospect of being put in jail.

Grandma Nettie forged on. "Our intentions are to ruin his meal by locking ourselves on the ornamental iron fence along the north facade. Mrs. Gundy is even going to swallow her key. I'm hiding mine down the front of my corset. Let it be said, that the man who dares try and retrieve it will be sorry he ever laid a hand on my person. I know how you incapacitate a man with physical force. Have I told you how, Margaret?"

"Yes."

"Good. Don't be afraid to do it if the need arises."

"I won't."

Grandma Nettie's limber arm rose into a position much like the Statue of Liberty's. "We shall fight for equality and the right for all women to have the vote."

"But I don't want to vote," Meg replied.

"Margaret, of course you want to vote."

"No I don't."

"Why with your intelligence, you could be anything you wanted to be." With robust enthusiasm, she declared, "I think you'd make a fine first woman president."

"I'd rather be a hotel proprietress. Or, at the very least, irresistible to men."

At this rate, she'd settle for agreeable to one man— any man, as long as he was tall, dark, and handsome. *Oh, all right,* she recanted. As long as he didn't have an Adam's apple that stuck out too far or sweaty hands, and didn't wear too much pomade in his hair.

A voice called out, "Good afternoon. Welcome to the Brooks House Hotel," as the porter, Delbert Long, opened the double front doors and escorted a guest inside.

"We'll continue our talk about this another time, Margaret." Grandma left the desk to greet the new arrival.

In spite of her resolve, Meg pondered Grandma Nettie's words. *Our intentions are to ruin his meal by locking ourselves on the ornamental iron fence along the north facade.* By doing that, her grandmother was going to throw Washington into chaos. The operative word was going to be *scandalous*. Meg hadn't done anything scandalous in far too long. She'd never thought about seeing the White House up close. Maybe she could . . .

No. She couldn't possibly. She was through with misadventure.

Tamping the wayward thought, Meg walked toward the cabinet where she kept cigars. When she'd entered the lobby, she'd noticed the silver tray on the conversation table had been nearly empty of Pilsens. As her special touch, she'd purchased cigars for the men and a cuspidor, placed by the front door *on the outside*—Meg didn't abide indoor spitting. She'd arranged for tea and scones to be brought over in the afternoon for the ladies. Fresh flowers on the fireplace mantel brightened the area every day. And when she could manage it, a violinist for evening enjoyment.

Although Delbert Long was the only violinist she knew—and really, it wasn't a violin he played; it was a fiddle. But beggars couldn't be choosers.

Meg had gotten no farther than five or so paces when she heard an ominous rip. Wide-eyed, she stopped dead in her tracks and slowly looked down. She could feel the damage before she could actually see it.

A silky slippage of material passed her hips and thighs as the snapped elastic and torn waistband began to make its embarrassing descent.

She felt through the fabric of her skirt, grabbed what she could and sidled her way back to the counter. Reaching over the registry, she fumbled for the room keys that were kept on individual hooks. She took the first one her fingers touched, then lifted herself on tiptoe to view the inside of Grandma Nettie's sewing basket. Spotting a safety pin, she stole that as well. With the loose gathers of her petticoat around her hips, and her skirt riding high above her calves, she shot up the stairs without a backward glance.

Knees knocking together, Meg half-walked, half-ran across the carpet runner in the hall. She glanced at the circular tag on the key ring. Room thirty-two. In her haste, she hadn't noticed if two keys had been on the desk hook. One meant the room was occupied and two meant it was vacant. The hotel would be full by this weekend when all the fly fishermen arrived in Harmony for the tournament. A few already had registered and were in residence now. Thankfully, none were in view.

Almost stumbling to keep her underskirt from falling past her knees, Meg started skimming the numbers on doors.

Coming to room thirty-two, she bunched her skirt in her left hand and inserted the key with her right. Before she turned the knob, she rapped twice on the door and waited to the count of fifteen.

No answer.

Letting her breath out, she slipped inside the room and shut the door behind her.

Meg made quick inspection of the furnishings. Not a single piece of luggage or any personal effects in sight. Thank goodness. Spring sunshine spilled in from the window and made a pattern on the floor that stretched to the closed bathroom door. After tossing the key onto the bed, she relaxed and her petticoat fell to her ankles. Opening the safety pin, she held it in her mouth, then wadded her Manchester cloth skirt to her waist and bent to hoist her petticoat over her ankles and knees to her hips.

With a wiggle, Meg brought the torn waistband to its proper place.

Not the best seamstress, Meg realized after the fact, her stitches were too far apart. Tightness and neatness her mother always said when making a seam. Well, Meg was too impatient for that. She'd revamped all five of her petticoats in under an hour flat, and was rather proud of herself for her speed.

Just as she matched the raveled edges of waistband, caught the elastic, and was about to take the pin from her mouth, the bathroom door opened and Meg's head shot up. Shock flew through her as a man—half *naked*—stood in the doorway.

"Oh my," she exclaimed. The starched white muslin in her grasp fell, and the entire petticoat collapsed in a pile around her feet.

A towel was wrapped around his lean middle, and she couldn't help staring at his navel. Coarse black hair swirled there, very lightly sprinkled. And against a belly so flat she could iron a shirtwaist on it and not have a single wrinkle. Upward . . . a chest like a washboard and shoulders wider than she'd ever noticed on a man.

Tall and muscular, with wet hair the color of midnight, a slight growth of beard, bushy brows tapered just enough to be utterly handsome, a set of eyes too dreamy a green for words. And the nicest shaped mouth she'd ever seen.

"Where did you come from?" His voice, so manly and . . . deep, sent a delightful shiver through her body. Not to mention, his gaze ran over her hotter than her hair curler when she forgot about it on the lamp. She could almost feel the sizzle in the air, as he lowered his eyes to her stocking-clad legs.

Mortification shot through her like a dart and she dropped her skirt.

Other than that modest gesture, she couldn't move. She was too stunned to do anything more than keep her lips together in an effort not to swallow the safety pin.

"Hello," she managed, through the pin in her teeth.

"Who are you?" Aside from his question and the furrow in his brow, the man seemed undaunted to find an uninvited female in his room.

"Ah . . . Miss Mah-eg Bah-rooks." She spit the safety pin into her hand. "I'm Miss Meg Brooks." *Uh-oh. She'd introduced herself wrong.* She should have said *Margaret,* not Meg. Flustered, she'd forgotten she'd changed her name to sound more sophisticated. But there was no taking it back now without looking like an idiot. So she just kept talking. "My father owns the hotel."

He showed no outward discomfort—being nearly nude in front of her, and all. She, on the other hand, felt the onset of dizziness. For all her talk about wanting a man to notice her, here she was face-to-face with one, and she had an overwhelming urge to run and hide.

Only she was frozen to the spot.

Greenish-gold eyes narrowed. "What happened to you?"

Trying to keep a modicum of dignity, she said, "I had a bit of an . . . accident. You see my . . ." Her mother's stern warning sounded inside her head. She was told a young lady never mentioned an article of clothing to a man—ever. Even if he was her husband. So a straightforward explanation was out of the question. "I, that is my . . ." Meg's voice trailed. Why couldn't she just say the word *petticoat* in front of him and explain what happened? Had all the lessons in deportment finally sunk in?

Meg gazed at the layers of petticoat covering her shoes that looked a lot like ripples of untoasted meringue, then lifted her eyes. At length, she took the coward's way out and hoped he wouldn't notice she didn't give him a definitive answer. "Are you finding your accommodations here sufficient? Is there anything you require?"

He took a few steps, and she noted his stomach never flinched in the least. It stayed just as taut and hard when he moved. Even though her skirts covered her legs, her petticoat stuck out like a red flag. He gave it a glance, then slowly lifted his eyes to her face. Studying her. Intently. Meg swallowed.

Giving her a crooked smile, he said, "Have you come to turn down my bed?"

Meg wasn't sure if she'd heard him correctly. "W-what?"

"You asked me if I needed anything."

"Yes, well . . . I can have . . . Delbert . . ."

"I don't imagine Delbert is as pretty as you."

Pretty? He thought she was pretty.

Meg felt a warming shiver across her skin.

He took a step toward the bed and she got an eyeful of his broad back. Wide and rippling with muscles. Then he turned to face her and Meg's gaze fell on the tuck in his towel, thinking that it didn't look very secure and could fall off at any moment. Her throat went dry.

He said, "If you haven't come to turn the bed down, have you brought my bags?"

Guiltily flashing her gaze upward, she said in a rush,

"You have bags?" *Why hadn't he taken them up with him?*

"When I left the train station, I did. All I have with me is my case."

That explained it. A haphazard check in. "Oh . . . then I'm certain Delbert will get them for you."

Think, Meg! She had to get out of here. If anyone found out she was in a hotel room with a half-naked man, she would be ruined. The image of the cultivated lady she'd worked so hard to portray would fizzle. To think, she'd just been contemplating a scandal. Well, if this wasn't scandalous behavior, she didn't know what was.

Escape was the operative word here. But not until she could walk without tripping on her unmentionables. How did one make herself look a lot more at ease and calm pulling up her muslin and pinning it while a man watched? She just couldn't. Not even the old Meg had that much nerve.

The heat on her cheeks burned hotter than a stove. It took every bit of self-reliance she could collect to plan her retreat—a retreat she wasn't sure she wanted to make. After all, he was gorgeous. Positively the most attractive man she'd ever seen nearly naked. Who was she fooling? He was the *only* man she'd ever seen nearly naked.

Miss Edwina's words drifted to her: *When a woman is approached by a man she hasn't been introduced to, she must ask for his calling card to ensure he has "Mr." in front of his name and has listed his street and number.* Meg was certain her man in the towel didn't have one on him. Bother it anyway, she had to leave or else face consequences she couldn't repair.

Stepping out of her petticoat, she dipped down and

bunched it in her fists. "I have to be going now." She pressed the stiff cloth against her breasts, keeping her arms crossed and covering as much fabric as she could.

"If you need anything . . . don't, ah, hesitate to ask at the front desk." With a backward walk, she managed to get to the door and clutch the knob. Turning with what she hoped appeared to be a polished gracefulness, she opened the door. Checking first to see if the coast was clear, she hadn't taken a single step out of the room.

Grandma Nettie came down the hallway escorting the new arrival to his room while Delbert Long rolled the second-story bellman's cart right behind them *and* directly toward her.

Meg slammed the door and pressed her back against it, the petticoat still at her breasts—only one-handed now. The other hand was like a vise on the doorknob.

"Another accident?" the man queried. A single brow rose in a wry arch.

Panic welling in her throat, Meg couldn't reply.

The sharp reverberation against her shoulder blade as the wooden door panel was knocked on, made Meg jump away as if she'd been scorched.

More knocking. Then: "Porter, sir," came Delbert's announcement.

Standing in the middle of the room, looking helplessly from one end of the bed to the bureau and fireplace and the bathroom door, she didn't know where to hide. And when the man proceeded toward her with that damp towel looking ready to fall off, she squeezed her eyes closed and took in a deep breath. Certainly no help for the situation, but if that towel unwrapped from his middle and exposed him, she didn't want to see. On the other hand, she could look through the fringe of her lashes and he wouldn't be the wiser . . .

Precariously close to her ear, and in a whisper so deliciously low and baritone it caused her to literally gasp, he bade, "Go into the bathroom and close the door."

Her bearings crashing in on her from the deepness of his voice, her eyes flew open. Through the repeated knock on the door, she said, "I can't hide in there. You don't know Delbert."

Having no choice, she made a dash for the bed and scrambled down. She tucked herself beneath the mattress frame, making sure the full width of her skirt hem had been pulled in and hidden with her. Scooting into the middle, she roused the dust bunnies from the floor. The flying tufts of lint made her think she had to sneeze. She buried her nose in the wad of her petticoat and peered over the cloth.

She couldn't see the man's feet. He'd gone to the door. It opened and Delbert gave a hearty greeting.

"Good afternoon, sir. My apologies for the delay in fetching your luggage. As you can see, the matter has been rectified. I'll put them where you like."

The porter entered the room and came straight to the bed and stopped. Meg stared at his shoes. Lace ups. Calf-skin bluchers. In need of polishing on the right heel.

"Criminy sakes alive," the man declared in a put-out tone, "I wondered if my luggage had been left on the train and was headed for the nether parts of the region to be seized upon by vagabonds."

Meg's mouth fell open.

"Not to worry, sir," Delbert assured. "Where shall I put your things?"

"The bed will be fine, my good fellow," the man directed. She couldn't see him. He must have remained by the door.

What happened to him? His words had just shattered her illusion of his perfect manliness. Mr. Oh-So-Wonderful suddenly had the speech of a mildewed scholar.

Meg's nose itched. She rubbed it in the muslin.

Delbert walked away, then returned once more and set articles on the bed; it creaked some. The springs were slightly worn.

Two bare feet came close, then disappeared into the bathroom. He came back and stood by the bed once more. She studied his masculine toes. Nicely shaped. The nails clean with perfect trimmed whites. Some dark hairs over the tops of his knuckles. Low arches. She thought they were very beautiful for being feet.

She must have not heard him correctly before. Any man with feet like these wouldn't say "criminy sakes alive."

"Thanks," Mr. Wonderful said as a jingle of change exchanged hands.

She couldn't possibly be so lucky Delbert would leave without giving his full routine. Not him.

"Sir, allow me to show you the features of this room."

Meg's forehead lowered and bumped quietly on the floorboards. Nope. No luck for her.

"This is one of our better rooms. You'll notice the bed is quite comfortable, it being of the iron brass frame variety rather than solid oak, which can tend to warp." Delbert walked on. His shoes were buffered by the large rug in front of the mantel. "We keep wood for the fireplace year-round in case of a cold spell. With this being late March, one can never tell. The temperature drops quite considerably at night."

"I'll remember that. Thank you for telling me." Bare feet walked by the bed and toward the door once more. "If I need anything else, I'll call on the front desk."

"But, I haven't shown you the bathroom features. Modern plumbing—just a year old. I can see you've tried out our shower bath. Was it acceptable?"

"Dandy."

Meg held onto a frown. *Dandy?*

She just couldn't put that vocabulary together with the looks and sound of the man. But then again, the men of Harmony had trouble putting charm and culture together with her.

Thuds sounded as the porter went to the bathroom, undaunted by the man's dismissal. Delbert Long was never put off. "This way, sir, and I'll demonstrate in case you overlooked anything."

The man must have sensed Delbert wouldn't leave until finished, so he went with him. Hot and cold water faucets turned on and off. Then the shower curtain slid on its hooks. The opening and closing of the cabinet. A flush from the toilet, or as her mother would say, the necessary.

At last, they exited the bathroom.

Meg turned her face to see if she could find a snippet of the porter's shoes. As she did so, she practically choked on a bouncing puff of linen fuzz. Her sneeze came through her nose before she could stop it.

"What was that?" Delbert asked.

"I didn't hear anything."

Meg held her breath as Delbert's shoes filled her view once more. She began inching her way farther back to the bed's headboard. As she did so, her up-swept hair caught on a coil and tugged. She bit her lip hard to keep from crying out, but a small squeak escaped her.

"There it is again," Delbert declared. "A sneeze before and now a yelp."

"There's nothing of the kind." The man walked Delbert to the door and opened it. "I'm sure you have other guests to see to. Thank you again."

As Delbert wished him a pleasant stay, the door was closed midway through his oft-repeated sentence.

Meg didn't readily move. Her scalp throbbed where her hair had caught. If she could have, she would have lifted her arms to undo herself, but space didn't permit such a maneuver.

"You can come out now. He's gone."

"Ah . . . yes, I know. But I can't."

"What do you mean, you can't?"

"I've had a slight . . ." She couldn't finish.

"Let me guess." He lowered again and stuck his head beneath the bed. She gave him her bewitching smile, the one she practiced in the mirror after brushing her teeth. Unfortunately it didn't have the affect on him she'd hoped. "You've had another accident."

Frowning her disappointment that he didn't find her divinely captivating, she mumbled, "Yes, I did. My hair is stuck and I can't get out. You have to get me free. My hands won't reach the springs."

She thought she heard him mutter an expletive as he stood. And it wasn't anything close to "criminy sakes alive."

The towel fell on the floor in a clump, then more

shuffling inside bags until a pair of worsted trousers came into sight and first one leg then the other slipped into the dark blue trouser legs. He lowered himself to his knees again, then laid on his belly and crawled in toward her.

This close to him, and in such a confining space, the scent of his bathing soap filled the air. *El Soudan's* coconut oil. She'd know it anywhere. The traces smelled so good, she could almost taste him.

She got that giddy feeling again when he reached for her and his fingers tangled in her hair. Explosions of tingles ran down her spine when he sifted through the hair and pulled out pins in order to take down the high pile. Her gaze remained fixed on the floor until she mustered the nerve to look him in the eyes. When she did, her breath caught and, at the same time, his hand stilled. He looked right at her . . . as if he were going to . . .

She didn't know. She'd never seen that kind of fire in a man's eyes before when he gazed at her. That kind of passion and fire she read about but had never experienced. Could he tell she'd discovered paradise in his simple touch?

As he resumed his task, his knuckles brushed her cheek. On purpose? She dared to hope that he had. He was very gentle. A few more carefully orchestrated pulls that separated strands of hair, and she was free.

But neither of them moved. The moment seemed to be etched in time. She would never forget it. Whatever happened, she would always remember this as her first truly sensual encounter.

In his eyes, she saw a war of conflict as if, despite his best intentions, he wasn't thinking honorably. That she, Meg Brooks who had barely turned over a new leaf, could make a man have dishonorable thoughts . . . well, all those hours in finishing school were paying off.

He brought his fingertip slowly down the curve of her cheek. Clearly no accident. She grew pleasantly flustered, liking the sensation.

"You can get out now. If you want," he said in a deep whisper giving her the choice of staying. She couldn't possibly stay hidden beneath his bed; the complications were simply too wicked to think about.

"All right."

With those two words from her, he nodded. Had there been a flicker of regret in his green eyes? He backed away and extended his hand. It was big and inviting.

First a little hesitant, she relented and laid her fingers in his. Smooth palm with no calluses. No sweating either.

His grip wasn't that of a loafer; she was acutely conscious of his impressive strength. She slid from under the bed, petticoat still balled in her fist. He assisted her to her feet. As he did so, her hair tumbled into her eyes, around her shoulders and down to her waist. She'd never liked the color. Copper. So . . . so vivid and . . . coppery. She stuck out like a sore thumb throughout school. Well, maybe not only herself. Crescencia Dufresne's hair was red-orange. Meg supposed copper was better. But not by much.

The man stared at the burnished red waves of hair surrounding her as she made a part in the thick curtain so she could see him in return. He gave her a look over but she couldn't tell what he thought of the copper-color. He probably thought it too much.

"Thank you. I have to go. But . . ." Now Meg had

her hair to contend with as well as the petticoat. She couldn't reappear in the lobby in the state she was in. She had to fix herself up before she left this room.

He reached for her and lifted her hand. She felt her pulse beat unevenly at the base of her throat. He pressed her hairpins into her palm, as well as the safety pin she must have dropped on the floor. Then in that husky voice of his, "Go into the bathroom and put yourself together."

If he hadn't nudged her with a light push of her shoulders, she doubted she could have moved. She'd been transfixed by the play of light from the window that reflected in his eyes.

Once she snapped out of her trance, she strode into the bathroom and made short work out of repairing herself. In the process, she took in the items strewn on the floor. An expensive suit coat, vest, starched white shirt, trousers, and a twist of white drawers. In the corner by the bathtub lay a traveling case, its clasp not fastened. Barely discernable from the opening was the pearl-grip of a gun.

A gun. A mix of fear and curiosity tattooed with Meg's heartbeat. Who *was* he?

With a parting glance in the mirror, she poked the last hairpin home and returned to the bedroom apartment once more.

The man had slipped into a shirt in her absence, although he hadn't buttoned it. A wedge of chest showed through the opening. That tantalizing glimpse of short and forbidden masculine hair.

She paused at the bed, stared at the mound of luggage and fishing gear, then picked up the key she'd tossed earlier. "Well," she sighed taking short steps to the door, "thank you for everything. I'm sorry for the inconvenience I caused you."

He made no comment; merely stared, making a leisurely study of her lips, her eyes, her hair. He looked at her in a way he had no business doing, but his gaze held her still. Her skin grew very warm. It felt as if he were touching her without touching her.

Gun or no gun, she couldn't leave. Not yet. Not until she knew his name. She was utterly smitten by him.

"Well, thank you again Mr. . . . ah . . . ?"

A heavy frown marked his forehead, as if he'd become quite annoyed about something. Then: "Wilberforce. Vernon Wilberforce."

Chapter

❦ 2 ❦

Apricots.

Her burnished red hair color reminded Matthew Gage of a bowl of ripe apricots sitting on a tabletop with early morning sunshine pouring coppery hues over them.

Smiling blandly, he mentally chastised himself. *Gage, you horse's ass, you're turning as poetic as that slob, Phineas Wolf, who writes a corn column for* The Metropolis.

Meg Brooks was the first woman Gage had seen in a long time who interested him. And he'd had to introduce himself as Vernon Wilberforce. The image produced by the sound alone conjured up bedroom disappointment in a big way. Not that he was thinking about tangling the sheets with the pleasing-to-the-eyes Miss Brooks. In spite of her lost underwear, he didn't think she went around flinging her petticoat over headboards.

Even so, her standing before him with her hair cascading down to her waist had put ideas into his head.

Curls of copper hair contrasting against the soft white of a pillow. Thick lashes lowered for his lips to caress. Her figure was not voluptuous, but he hadn't judged her on what she lacked; it was what she had that captured his attention. The creamy-pale color of her skin. Slender wrists and fingers. Faintly rosy mouth.

The ideas that had formed in his head no doubt went against the grain of her morality. Still, there had been that undefinable moment, the pair of them beneath the bed, when she would have yielded him a kiss. Her heavy-lidded eyes had glittered as if she'd been moonstruck. Gage knew better than to start something that would never be finished; and yet, he'd had to touch her cheek to see if it was as soft as it looked.

She had been.

When he'd found Meg Brooks in his room, he'd been so distracted by brown eyes, a full mouth with a little definable bow to the upper lip, and a shapely set of black stocking-covered legs—he'd pitched his cover out the window. *Stupid.*

Gazing down, Gage noted the few glistening strands of reddish-bronze hair still caught in his fingers. He took a step away from the bed, unwound the fine hair and set it on the bare desk.

"Christ almighty," he muttered. Either he was growing sentimental or foolish. Both unnerved him.

Gage couldn't let a woman detract him from his story. He had a roll to play. He hadn't used his Professor Fophead vernacular in a long while. The stodgy old goat was appallingly prudish and talked like he'd been born a century ago. Actually, Gage couldn't take the credit for inventing the jack-a-dandy phrases. He'd based them on an editor he'd once worked for. Louis

Platt. A pantywaist of a man who'd asked his journalists to write slice of Americana stories. Gage had never caught on and left that newspaper for another.

Now *The San Francisco Chronicle* had him.

He was the best stunt reporter *The Chronicle* had ever employed. It had been a fluke he'd taken his column on the road. Posing in the nude had had its rewards. That cultured artists piece had put Gage's name in every household. His undercover whereabouts had turned into a game. So much so that even rival newspapers ran headlines such as: "Where's Gage?" and "Who Will Gage Be Next?"

Not even Gage knew who he'd be from one day to the next. He most certainly hadn't planned on being Vernon Wilberforce. He'd never once assumed the identity or borrowed the name of a real person. Each of his aliases had been his own creation.

But Wilberforce's predicament had fallen into Gage's lap. Wilberforce needed to be in Harmony or his wife would leave him. And Gage needed a new place to hide as soon as Ben Tweedy had unmasked him. If that was all there were to the pieces, Gage wouldn't have come this far. What brought him to town wasn't Wilberforce's woes. Actually, it had been what Tweedy said.

A fly-fishing contest that was rigged. One thousand dollars paid out to the wrong winner. Rumors or fact.

There was nothing like the underdog to get Gage's blood stirred.

Muckraking. It was Gage's bread and butter. He championed those who were less fortunate. He had his reasons; they were buried deep inside him. Only his editor, David West, knew the truth behind the byline. And it would stay that way.

Gage recalled the dawn hours in his Bozeman jail cell listening to the uneven snores of the deputy—Gage had kept the lawman up most of the night telling him about some of his most wild adventures.

As soon as Tweedy's chin dropped to his chest, Gage had given Vernon a long stare, just to unnerve him and see if he'd flinch beneath his gaze; see if he was indeed telling the truth about having to be in Harmony—or if he'd made it up just to get the deputy's sympathy. The Bissell salesman hadn't batted an eyelash.

"Tell me all you know about this fly-fishing contest, Wilberforce," Gage had said.

Wilberforce began talking and didn't stop until Deputy Tweedy woke up and broke things off between them to give Gage his walking papers.

Now Gage was in Harmony, posing as a man he'd only known for six hours, and running on his instinct to uncover things.

The town had no local paper that he could read and dissect. A newspaper told a lot about a place—especially one with a small population like Harmony. They printed the kind of things dailies ignored in their search for bigger headlines. He wanted to examine folksy, newsy, personal stories like who was visiting relatives, who got arrested on Saturday night for intoxication, and who baked the best cake for the church fund-raising raffle. He could have read commentaries on the upcoming fly-fishing contest and gained some insight.

Since Gage couldn't nose around the local rag, he'd have to do all his digging from scratch. He figured he'd better get to work.

Starting with: How in the hell do you fly-fish?

Whenever Gage wanted a trout, he told the waiter.

Gage left the desk and went into the bathroom to retrieve his journal case. Afterward, he returned to the bedroom, slipped the leather buckles free and dumped the contents onto the bed. Rifling through his belongings, he momentarily paused at the bundle of envelopes bound by string and all addressed to his . . . *wife*. Or, rather, *Mrs. Vernon Wilberforce*. Gage grimaced. He had to remember to mail the first one tomorrow or the plan would be made into hash.

Moving on, he gathered his pencils so that he could take notes, a lot of them. Then he shuffled through several tablets and finally reached the item he sought. A simple, blue-cloth covered book, thoroughly battered, its flyleaf stained with coffee cup rings from the former owner: *New American Fly-Fishing Manifesto*.

With a shove of his arm and a total disregard for the mess on the bed, he got most of the stuff out of his way—enough so he could lean back and arrange the two pillows to prop his back against. Crossing his bare foot on top of his knee, he opened the book and became oblivious to his surroundings as he began to read up about his latest stunt.

Meg let the screen door to the house on Elm Street whack closed in her wake, etiquette forgotten—along with her parasol and gloves at the hotel; she had left the premises with her head in the clouds.

The rich aroma of a pot roast wafted to her nose as she entered the vestibule. Mr. Finch had started dinner.

Grandma Nettie had given him a position while Meg's parents were away. His duties were those of a domestic: clean, cook, wash, and iron. He may not have been the right gender for the job, but he actually *liked* doing women's work. And since Meg didn't care to spend her time in the kitchen or polishing the furniture, she thought of Mr. Finch as a temporary godsend. But she did have a difficult time thinking of him as a hired girl.

To her friends, she'd introduced the bowler-wearing man who emptied their rubbish into the bin behind the house as Mr. Finch, the butler. Even though he rarely answered the door, and he wore a white string apron like a housemaid.

Meg heard Mr. Finch's British accent coming from the dining room. "Is that enough ink, Mrs. Rothman?"

"I think it will be fine, Mr. Finch. All I have to print up are these last few. Thank you."

Walking through the parlor and beneath the arched doorway with its ornate spindles and woodwork, Meg found Grandma Nettie at the dining-room table. She pressed a large rubber stamp on a pad of ink, then smacked it in the middle of a flyer. Meg didn't take the time to read what the stamp said.

"Margaret, you're home. I won't be able to have dinner with you this evening. I've got an engagement."

"What kind?"

"It's best you don't know."

A sinking feeling weighed on Meg. She didn't want to tell her grandma not to do as she pleased. But by the same token, if she caused a big fuss Meg didn't want to lose the ground she'd been working so hard to gain.

"Grandma," Meg began, glancing at the paneled doorway that led into the kitchen to make sure the revolving door was closed. She didn't want Mr. Finch to hear. "I have to tell you something."

"What's that, dear?" her grandmother asked, eyes leveling on Meg with a hopeful gleam "Have you decided to become the first woman president?"

"No." Meg pulled out a chair and sat next to Grandma Nettie who had stopped what she was doing to give Meg her undivided attention.

"It's important. I can see it written all over your face."

Unbidden, Meg blushed. "Well, yes it is rather important." She toyed with the fringe of the table's center scarf. "I had an accident today. I . . . I lost my petticoat."

Grandma Nettie didn't flinch. "Is that all? Heavens, once while I was on a crusade march for the Female Suffrage Act, I lost my best lace-up shoes. I threw them—one at a time—at a copper. Did you throw your petticoat at somebody, Margaret?"

"I wouldn't dream of it!" Meg blurted. "Given your situation, you had to throw your shoes, but a lady would never take off her petticoat and throw it at somebody."

"I might if I thought it would get my message across." Grandma shook her head. "I think you're taking this lady business a little too far, Margaret. I knew you before you were a lady and I liked you just fine."

"Thank you, Grandma. But before I quit doing 'rambunctious public displays' as Mother called them, I never had the attentions of a man. And now . . . well, I do." Meg lowered her voice. "And it's not Harold Adams."

Her grandmother's brows rose, then she lifted her gaze to Meg's hair—which hadn't been pinned up very tidily.

Meg felt the need to explain. "I got my hair caught under somebody's bed."

"Whose bed?" Grandma gasped—even she had her limits on liberalism.

It sounded much worse than it was as Meg admitted, "A bed at the hotel."

"What were you doing under a bed at the hotel?"

"Hiding from Delbert because I stepped on the hem of my petticoat and it fell off."

"If your mother heard this, she'd faint dead away," was all Grandma Nettie said.

"I know," Meg dismally agreed, thankful that she didn't have to tell her mother—not that she would have. "But it was an accident. Honest. I really did get trapped in a room while trying to repair the damage. And with a man. The most handsome man I've ever seen."

Her grandmother's pale blue eyes grew bright with amusement. "How intriguing. What was his name?"

"Mr. Wilberforce."

"Room thirty-two. I remember him. I checked him in at noon. He came to town on the eleven twenty-five train. I did think he was very handsome. His name doesn't fit his appearance."

"Well, I do suppose that a woman would want the most handsome man she's ever met to be named something more . . . handsome, but," she quickly went on, "he can't help the name he was born with. And Wilberforce does go nicely with Vernon."

"It does at that."

Meg leaned closer to her grandmother, "Mr. Wilberforce had a gun."

"Really?" Grandma Nettie whispered, setting her

ink stamp down; her gaze held a sparkle of mischief. "What kind?"

"I wouldn't know the model. But it had a pearl-handle."

"The Feds carry Peacemakers. I wonder if he's a Federal agent? This is all very interesting, Margaret." Straightening, Grandma Nettie sighed on a wistful note. "As you know, I loved your grandfather in our forty-eight years together, but after he passed on and I made it my life's work to fight for my sisters, nothing out of the ordinary—like losing my petticoat and hiding beneath a man's bed—has ever happened to me."

She held up her forefinger in pausing thought. "Unless you count the time I went to jail for twenty-four hours for burning my corset and refusing to apologize to the city of Mud Willow Flats when the local granary caught a spark. Land sakes, you could smell popcorn for five miles. I suggested the good ladies in town melt some butter, bring large bowls, and shakers of salt. That's when the sheriff arrested me. He had a Peacemaker."

"You never told me that."

"Oh, I don't like to speak of such things when your mother is around. I might make her faint." Grandma picked up a flyer and studied it. "I make *you* faint, Margaret, now that you've changed."

"It would take a lot to make me faint, Grandma."

"Good."

Grudgingly, Meg said, "I should be working on my journal now." She would have much rather talked with Grandma Nettie about men, but Meg was already late turning in her first assignment.

Meg was still enrolled in Mrs. Wolcott's Finishing School, but Mrs. Wolcott had allowed her a leave of absence in order to help Grandma Nettie at the hotel. On one condition. Meg was to complete various writing assignments and keep a journal on her experiences in the business world. Meg had to present her opinions on the running of the hotel to Mrs. Wolcott at the end of the term in order to graduate.

"Tomorrow I'll be a little late coming to the hotel," Meg added. "I need to buy a new cigar clipper. The one I set out is missing. Stolen, no doubt. Some of those traveling men, you just can't trust them."

"Yes, I know. That King Merkle in room—"

The front door bell cranked.

Grandma Nettie turned toward the parlor and suddenly said, "I forgot to mention—your friends Ruth and Hildegarde called while you were out. They wanted me to tell you that Johannah Treber wore her engagement ring to school. A *diamond,*" her grandma dramatized. "I was supposed to tell you it was a diamond because in class Mrs. Wolcott explained about the origin of the diamond as an engagement ring. She said that a diamond originated in the fires of love, and therefore a diamond is the only *true* engagement ring, signifying love and happiness throughout life." With a soft *humph,* she went on, "Not my words. Theirs. Frankly, any ring given with love is all that a woman should require."

The chime of the bell sounded once more, and Mr. Finch's footsteps could be heard through the foyer.

"Margaret, it just dawned on me. Mr. Wilberforce could be a diamond salesman. It makes sense, you know. Johannah shows off her ring just when he comes to town. And he did have a gun. He has to protect himself from jewel thieves."

"It's a possibility." Then she remembered what Mr.

Wilberforce did have sprawled across the bed in his room. "He brought a fishing pole and tackle. I'll bet he's here for the contest."

Mr. Finch came into the dining room. "Miss Margaret, there's a Harold Adams come to call on you."

Meg groaned. *Harold Adam's Apple.* Once a woman had been stuck in a hotel room with a man as good-looking as Vernon Wilberforce, the Harolds of the world paled in comparison. "I really don't want to see him . . ."

Grandma Nettie put her ink-smudged fingertip to her lips. "We'll let your mother handle this."

Confused, Meg frowned. "What do you mean?"

"Mr. Finch," Grandma Nettie said, "please tell Mr. Adams that Margaret has a sick headache and she's not receiving callers. Thank you."

"Very good, Mrs. Rothman." He departed, leaving Meg to ponder the credibility of the excuse. Whenever Mother said she had a sick headache, Father didn't bother her. Sick headaches warded off unwanted attention.

Sharing a smile with her grandmother, Meg realized this was the first benefit she'd encountered since becoming a proper lady.

Chapter

❧ 3 ❧

Matthew Gage had a weakness for a good cigar and chewing gum.

In the time it took for him to smoke a Havana and read through his notes, he organized his thoughts for a story and pulled together a summation of what he wanted to say before he sat at the typewriter.

He felt lost without his beat up Williams Rightwriter. The curved keyboard was worn by his fingertips, and some of the letters were undecipherable, but he knew where to find them in order to hunt and peck the words with his large fingers. He could make that typewriter sing while his stories came to life; when he got going, the typebar looked like a gang of grasshoppers were attacking the page.

The model he had, had a top platen so he could always see what he was writing—not like that ancient American II he used to type on. Five years ago, he won a Silver Press award for his series of articles on corrupt lobbyists and used part of the prize money to buy a new writing machine.

As he walked Sycamore Drive, he felt the light-weight small tablet in his breast pocket. He was a tried and true list maker. Lists for what he knew. Lists for what he wanted to know.

On his arrival into town, the stationmaster had made a comment about the fishing gear in Gage's grasp.

"So, you're going to try your luck," he'd stated while adjusting the visored cap on his head.

"Yes, sir," Gage replied in his Wilberforce voice. "I most surely am."

The stationmaster had nodded. "The best to you. Hopefully this year's competition won't be tarnished."

"You know," Gage said scratching his temple, "I did hear about some sort of trouble. Just who won last year?"

Gage's knowledge about last year's tournament was like a puzzle without all the border pieces connecting. He had some of the filler parts matching up, but there were too many small fragments missing to make up a readable whole.

In the jailhouse, Wilberforce had talked up a blue streak about Stratton and the relevant facts about him: He was eighteen last year and a ditch digger for the gasworks in a town outside of Harmony; Wilberforce didn't know which one. He'd also rambled on with his opinions on the various entrants he'd heard were competing this year. Another subject that had him flapping his gums was his fishing prowess. He'd gone on so much about everything else, that he hadn't told Gage who the scoundrel was who'd won.

Just when Gage's patience had been sapped and he'd asked him, Deputy Tweedy had inconveniently chosen that moment to unlock Gage's cell and release him.

So it wasn't until Gage was standing on the Harmony train platform that he had another chance to ask.

"Last year's winner is somebody I don't like to talk about, mister," the stationmaster had replied. "He was a good boy. Nobody saw him doing anything wrong. In fact, ask anybody at his fishing spot and they'll attest to the fact that they saw him catch all those fish. So I'd rather not aid the speculation of foul play by speaking his name."

Gage had left things at that.

No sense stirring up suspicion by pushing for an answer. Somebody would tell him who'd won. In a town this size, names and conversations about them were things people constantly tripped over.

Gripping the doorknob to the tobacconist shop, Gage let himself inside. The store was filled by the rich scent of exotic leaves, some delicate, almost floral. The mix of tobacco flavors in the air were those only a true cigar connoisseur could appreciate.

Gage strolled to the glass counter and leisurely gazed into the case. He had the outward appearance of being in no particular hurry. Like he was the chatting sort of fellow who had all the time in the world, when in reality, if he didn't find out what he wanted to know here, he'd be antsy to move on to the next business.

With a cultivated eye, he skimmed the names on the decorative and colorful boxes, and waited for the clerk to finish with a customer. He was surprised by the variety of smokes. From Sumatras to Te-Amo to Upmann red bands.

As he took in an engraved silver holder, the door opened behind him.

Being a newspaper man, he was naturally curious. He had an innate ability to see news and story potential in everything around him. The best place to start a column was by getting to know people, making himself real friendly and approachable. So he turned to see who had entered the store.

The moment he did, Gage's false smile froze and he was struck with an invisible punch to his gut. *It was her.*

Meg Brooks.

He'd spent a long night with his mind wandering to her instead of staying focused on fishing manifests.

She looked exactly as he remembered her. Pretty was too simple a word for her. Tantalizing was more like it. Sunlight from the window came in to illuminate the dress that hugged her every curve.

Yesterday, he'd used the better part of his thoughts on the provocative nature of her stockinged legs—even after she'd put her skirt down. Today, she had her hair done up in a smooth roll, anchored beneath a large hat that tilted at an alluring angle. If he didn't already know the color of her eyes, he wouldn't have been able to make them out. The brim of her hat kept part of her face in shadow; her rose-colored mouth remained in full view. Such an unwittingly seductive appearance had Gage's every nerve ending focused on her.

"Why, Mr. Wilberforce," Meg declared. "Imagine my running into you here."

"Imagine." The word sounded rough to his ears, with the promise that "imagine" could be a whole lot more. Then he remembered he was supposed to be

Wilberforce and he inwardly cursed. "I'll be a ring-tailed polecat. What a coincidence." He cringed at his ridiculous speech. But Meg didn't seem to notice he sounded as stale as week-old bread. She beamed as bright as the sunshine outside.

"Yes, this certainly *is* a coincidence."

If only for his perverse amusement, Gage said, "Great Scott. Don't tell me you smoke cigars, Miss Brooks."

"Goodness, no." Then her delicate brows furrowed with inward panic. "Why do you ask?" A stain of pink colored her cheeks with an obvious implication: *She'd tried smoking cigars before.*

In a lowered tone, she ventured, "You don't think it's sophisticated for a woman to smoke cigars, do you?"

Gage spoke before he thought. "I think anything a woman does that's daring can be highly alluring." Then he caught himself before he went too far with *his* opinion. Wilberforce had his own ideas. So Gage grew equally as hushed and added, "But it all depends on the woman. Hussies smoke cigars, or so I've been told. I did hear of a woman who was called Madame Cigar by her customers. Of course I've never met her."

"No. Certainly not. I'd never imply that you had." Clearly nonplused, the dash of nutmeg in her brown eyes lightened. "It's just that my brother, Wayne—he's in college—he wrote me a letter and said it's all the go for the ladies on campus to smoke cigars. Well, not all of them. Just some. Those who aren't stuffy. So there might not be anything wrong with a lady smoking a cigar."

Unable to help himself, Gage commented, "Then you really are here buying yourself a box of cigars."

"Oh, no. I should clarify. Yes, I'm in the store to buy cigars but *not* to smoke them. Why, my goodness, if it looks like I'm here for personal enjoyment, I'll have to have Delbert purchase the cigars from now on." Then she grew contemplative. "If you had seen this Madame Cigar—which you haven't—you don't suppose I would look like the type of woman who smokes cigars, do you, Mr. Wilberforce? Without being cheap, I mean."

Taken aback by her rationale to be an accepted cigar smoker, he took in the fit of her dress: the white blouse waist that clung softly to her small bosom and the narrow nip of her waist in a fashionable skirt. An edge of petticoat lace showed. Her attire said she considered herself à la mode—a real modern woman. And she was. He recognized the cut of her clothing as being the rage. The only reason he was up to date on the current state of fashions was because he always read *The Chronicle* from cover to back.

He could picture her with a cigar between her fingers and her mane of copper hair down, wearing nothing but that petticoat she liked to tease the boardwalks with and a pink satin corset.

After a moment, he lied. "No. I don't believe you do."

She grew crestfallen, as if disappointed by his answer. But her reply voiced the opposite. "Oh, thank goodness."

Gage couldn't help saying, "You could always defy appearances and take the habit up." He gave her a slight smile. "I'd even recommend my personal favorite."

"You would?" Then she blinked. "I mean, you shouldn't. I couldn't consider smoking."

"Why not?" he drawled.

She stared at him, and for a few seconds, he allowed himself to explore the many facets of her gaze: the feminine length and curl of her eyelashes, the arch of her curved brows, the soft glint of expectation in her eyes, and the slightly expanded pupils that were a dark contrast.

"Because I . . ." She gave him no concrete reason why. "But even though I don't smoke, I do know about cigars." She added, "I have to. I'm a businesswoman."

"Indeed?"

Her gloved hands clutched her pocketbook handle quite primly. "I buy three boxes a week. And not those Jamaican brands, but real Cubans. Pilsens. Four dollars and thirty-five cents a box."

Gage couldn't resist removing his square-crowned hat with its short brim like a derby's, and tucking it beneath his arm while nodding. "By gum, you do know your cigars, Miss Brooks. My apologies."

She looped her handbag through her arm, then fidgeted with the buttons on her gloves. "Tell me, Mr. Wilberforce, are you a jewelry salesman?"

However she got that notion, he couldn't guess. "No."

"Are you a traveling man? Do you sell things?"

He sold human interest stories. Articles that got a rise out of readers. Pieces that made him the hot topic of the day and the words of his column on the mouths of people—whether they agreed with him or not. He couldn't recall what it was like not to be a journalist; he couldn't imagine doing anything else.

But she wasn't asking about him. She was asking about Wilberforce.

Gage knew enough generalities about Wilberforce to fill a scrapbook. He'd had to memorize everything he could about the man he was impersonating.

Biting back an oath, Gage revealed, "Bissell carpet sweepers." He'd cursed more than once that Wilberforce sold Bissells. Why couldn't he have had another occupation?

"Carpet sweepers?"

"The whole line," he said without so much as a pause. "Baby sweeper, child sweeper, grand rapids, prize and regular grand."

They didn't have the chance to say anything further, as the clerk came over to them just as the other customer exited the store.

"I'm sorry for the delay, sir." A large handlebar mustache took up his entire upper lip like one of the many cigars he sold, but his voice was pleasant. Not too gravely. Gage noted his fingernails as he slipped currency into the cash register tray. They were clean; suit and tie hands. Gage noticed everything. Always. A habit too old to break.

Then to Meg, the clerk nodded his recognition. "Miss Brooks."

"Mr. Farley."

Farley tossed his glance from Meg to Gage. "Do you two know each other?"

Gage observed her hesitation; a slight gnawing on her lip. He could all but read her thoughts: *How did a lady confess that she'd met a gentleman in his hotel room without her petticoat on?*

"Yes, we do," Gage supplied when Meg remained stone silent. "We met yesterday. Quite by accident."

Then to her, he gave her a smile bordering on wickedness. "I hope you haven't lost your handkerchief again."

"My what?"

Gage let his gaze slide down her breasts, waist, and hips . . . straight to her toes where a tease of petticoat dusted the tops of her shoes. He almost could have sworn she shivered. "Your handkerchief."

Her eyes followed his; then she let out a nervous laugh. Raising her gaze she put a hand to her throat. "Oh, my . . . yes. My handkerchief. No, I haven't lost it today. Thank you again for helping me . . . um, find it."

He fought the temptation to burst out laughing, but it had been so long since he had laughed, the effort was too rusty to release. He fit his hat back on his head and gave it a tap on the brim for good measure. Such a ridiculous gesture, but it went with the act.

Turning toward Farley, he extended his hand. "How do you do? Allow me to introduce myself. I'm Wilberforce. But call me," the word gritted past his teeth, "Vernon. I'll be in Harmony for the next few weeks. I'm here for the fly-fishing competition."

Farley took his offering. Strong and sure grip. A regular fellow. "L. Farley. I own the store." He broke away and tucked one hand into his vest pocket. "What can I do for you?"

"Do you sell Ybor's?"

"Yes I do."

"I'll take five."

Farley nodded. "And for you, Miss Brooks? The usual?"

"Yes, Mr. Farley," she replied in a voice that was self-assured. "And I also need a cigar clipper."

While Farley put up their orders, Gage remembered something. "You said you were a businesswoman in need of cigars. Could you elaborate for me, Miss Brooks? I find few women in business for themselves."

She flushed. "Why, I'm not exactly the owner of my own business. As I said, my father owns the hotel and I'm helping out in his absence."

Farley came to the counter with three boxes of Pilsens, then set off again for the Ybor's.

"The cigars are for the gentlemen," she said without so much as a blink of an eye.

He shouldn't have cared who she was buying the cigars for. But she said "gentlemen" so casually, he couldn't dispel the wryness from his tone. "The gentlemen?"

"Yes, the gentlemen." Meg gave an airy wave of her hand—quite a dramatic show of savior-faire. "They're for the hotel. You see, I'm in charge of the lobby, Mr. Wilberforce. It's mine to do with as I please. Thus, the cigars for the gentlemen and the tea and scones for the ladies."

"I see." For some strange reason, Gage was relieved.

Farley returned, and Meg said nothing further on the subject.

"Would you like me to put the twelve seventy-five on the hotel account, Miss Brooks?"

"Yes, please."

Farley wrote up the order in a book, then handed Miss Brooks her parcel as the door opened and a ruddy-cheeked young man wearing an open down the middle calf-length coat came into the store.

His ears didn't lay flat against his head, although they didn't stick out so far they were the first thing a person noticed about him. What Gage zeroed in on was his bold as brass fine attire. He wore his hat at a jaunty angle that didn't suit him; the shoulders of his coat were padded; watch charms hung from the chain looped in his checkered vest.

A definite highbrow. Was he the winner of last year's contest?

"There you are, Margaret," he called. "I've been looking all over for you."

Clearly Meg Brooks hadn't wanted to be found. Dread shone in her eyes and she colored fiercely. Facing him, her greeting contained the doom of a felon facing a firing squad. "Hello, Harold."

"I need to talk to you about your grandmother. She's done it again."

Gage noted the man's Adam's apple bobbed quite noticeably when he became excited.

Meg stood straighter, as if taking on a defensive pose.

Turning to Harold, she said, "Harold, I think you should wait for me outside and I'll talk with you there."

"But, Margaret, she's gone and pasted flyers on the front of the Blue Flame Saloon that say women should be allowed to go inside for spirits. Lynell Pickering told me she did it last night under the cover of darkness." Young Harold ruefully shook his head. "I can't explain away that kind of behavior to my father. I know it's not your fault, but she's your grandmother."

"Yes, I know she's my grandmother," Meg challenged. "And whatever she's done . . . well, she's done. That's all. She must have really thought it was a good idea."

Gage smiled. Bully for Meg. Bully for the grandmother, Mrs. Rothman. He'd liked her when she checked him into the hotel. As a matter of fact, he thought her bicycle chain made quite a statement. There was no reason a decent woman shouldn't be allowed into a saloon if she wanted to sip on some suds.

But Harold was an imbecile for calling Meg on it in the company of others.

Tamping the urge to revert to his true personality and back the squealer into a corner, Gage had to say in his foppish voice, "Jiminy Christmas, Master Harold, you look too young to be patronizing a beer hall."

Brows raised, Harold gazed at Gage with a puzzled crease in his forehead. "Who're you?"

"Vernon Wilberforce." Gage didn't hold out his hand. Even Wilberforce had his limits.

Harold scrunched his pug nose. "Margaret, do you know this man?"

"Yes I do, Harold. He's a guest at the hotel."

"Oh." Drawing himself taller, he tried to look as intimidating as possible for a pencil in a suit. "Are you finished in here, Margaret?"

"Yes," came her soft reply. "But wait for me outside. *Please.*"

With a parting look at Gage, Harold left the store.

Meg remained silent a moment; then she picked up the string-tied package. "Good-bye, Mr. Farley." She glanced at Gage. "Good-bye, Mr. Wilberforce. I'm sure we'll be running into each other now that you'll be in town. If you need anyone to show you around, please feel free to call on me."

"I'll keep that in mind."

"I live on Elm Street," she hastily added and retreated a step.

"I'll remember that."

"Second house from the corner."

"A good location."

"The house with the Old Gold trim," she elaborated further.

Gage wanted to grin. He liked her candor just about as much as he would have liked to call on her. But he wouldn't. Couldn't.

"Well then . . . I suppose I should go." Moving toward the window, she stood there a moment, the sun reflecting through the glass to light her profile and hair in ·golden hues. The red ribbon bow pinned to the ornaments in her hat shimmered scarlet. A curl fell softly against her cheek, shining like a new penny.

Her hand grasped the doorknob. She gave Gage a smile of departure. Then she was gone.

Farley stayed behind the counter and shook his head with a chuckle.

Gage said nothing. He hated to admit it, but he was still focused on the image of her profile as she turned toward that window and the sunlight caught on her face.

"She's an eager woman," Farley commented.

"Good grief, I detected that."

"She's got good intentions."

Farley took the money Gage had placed on the counter.

Gage didn't readily leave. He selected one of his newly purchased cigars and gestured to the clerk. "Mind?"

"No, no. Light up."

Farley even struck a match for him.

As Gage lounged next to the counter taking a few

puffs, he asked in what he hoped sounded offhanded, "Are you entered in the fly-fishing competition?"

"I am this year. Wasn't last."

Lucky for Gage, Farley elaborated without prompting. "There was a bit of a to-do over last year's contest. Rumors and accusations of stocking the tributary off the lake. The fellow who engaged that spot for himself won. But nothing's ever been proven. He's an upstanding citizen from a highly respectable family here in town. Besides which, witnesses saw him reel all those fish in. So who's to say? Just because a fellow wins doesn't mean he cheated to do so. All the same, I'm glad I didn't enter because I would have been madder than a wet hen by the controversy surrounding the outcome."

Gage politely listened while he smoked, taking mental notes, gathering information like eggs in a basket.

"Harmony's contest is well-known in the fishing circles," Farley continued. "With a purse of one thousand dollars, you could say that ours is the best of the best. So when a title of great prominence is at stake in the fishing world, I suppose a man will do anything to attain that kind of glory. And money. Too bad. But again, I'm not saying he cheated. In fact, I happen to like last year's winner."

"Is he entering again this year?"

"No." Farley shook his head and toyed with a gold cigar band that laid on the countertop. "He's too busy spending all that cash he won. I suppose it's a shame, but I expect there's going to be some tongue-wagging. It'll all be stirred up again."

As Gage exhaled a curl of smoke, he asked in a leisurely manner, "Does his family live in town?"

"You were talking to one of them today."

Gage knew it. Harold the Horse's Ass.

Farley tossed the band into the wastebasket and then straightened. "Nice young fellow. He's off in some fancy Eastern college now," Farley said, then shook his head with a tsk. "Shame about everything. Yep. Wayne . . ."

Keeping an unaffected air, Gage took a puff.

"Wayne Brooks—Meg's brother."

It was then that Gage's cool faltered and he nearly choked on his smoke.

Chapter

❦ *4* ❦

At 6:45, Meg looked out the window for the last time; then she swore to herself that she wouldn't go toward it again. She found it very discouraging to pace away her Friday and Saturday evenings in front of the window waiting for Mr. Wilberforce to come calling.

Perhaps he hadn't taken the hint. Perhaps she shouldn't have given him a hint. Margaret wouldn't have. Meg had.

Regardless, how could Mr. Wilberforce have taken her seriously with Harold Adams talking to her as if she were an infant? Meg had told Harold she wasn't receiving visitors on Friday and Saturday night because she would be "indisposed"—another word learned from her mother when Mother didn't want her lady friends to come over unexpectedly.

Resigned to the fact that Mr. Wilberforce wasn't coming, Meg went upstairs to put on her nightgown and robe.

She paused by Grandma Nettie's door, which was cracked open, light spilling into the hallway.

"Come in, Margaret, I want to talk to you about the saloon."

Meg wasn't upset about that. What had bothered her more was Harold insisting he show her the damage done to the Blue Flame. Meg had seen for herself the flyers pasted on the front of the building. If Harold thought *that* was a big deal—Grandma Nettie chaining herself to the White House would be a capital offense.

Chief Officer Algie Conlin of the Harmony Police Department had come over this morning to write Grandma a citation. Mr. Pickering of the Blue Flame wasn't pressing charges. He simply wanted the mess cleaned up and since her grandmother had refused, she had to pay a fine and the cost of hiring somebody to take the papers down.

Grandma Nettie sat on the sateen bed quilt, and she patted a spot beside her. "Sit down, dear."

Meg walked into the bedroom that belonged to her parents and lowered herself on the edge of the bed.

Grandma still wore the oyster-colored blouse waist and crow-black silk skirt she'd had on at the hotel. "You're upset with me because of the saloon."

"I told you, it's not that, Grandma. I don't like how Harold thought it so awful he had to broadcast the news right in front of Mr. Wilberforce."

Grandma pulled several of the pins from her gray hair and unwound her thick bun. "If Harold feels it necessary to call you out in public because of something I did, then he needs a dosing of sulphur and molasses."

"I'd be happy to give it to him."

"Margaret," Grandma Nettie said, taking Meg's hand. "I'm likely to have considerably more notoriety in the future."

"What are you planning?"

"More flyers. Only this time I won't paste them up. I'll pass them out on the streets to my sisters." Grandma Nettie's expressive face changed; a bright spark of purpose held her features captive. "As long as women accept the position assigned to them, their emancipation is impossible. I have to make them understand that having the vote is the best way to be heard."

She took Meg's other hand into hers. "You could be quite an asset to the sisters, Margaret. Let me know if you're interested."

"I can't . . . ladies don't do such things."

Meg liked the feel of Grandma Nettie's silky thin skin next to her own. She laid her head on her shoulder and snuggled against the woman beside her. Meg loved her Grandma Nettie dearly. She did things Meg used to do on a smaller scale. Oh, not fighting for the suffragette cause; but hoydenish things. Trifling behavior that Mrs. Wolcott told her was above her now that she had converted to true refinement.

Whispering into the crook of her grandmother's neck, her Colgate's cashmere perfume smelling comforting to Meg, she whispered, "Grandma, I think that you're the bravest person I know."

"Oh, Margaret." Her arm came around Meg and the two women embraced.

In that shared moment, Meg was so proud of her grandma, she wished that she had the courage to defy decorum again, too. Because the real Meg Brooks was suffocating under a self-imposed exile.

* * *

An hour later, Meg went downstairs. She should have taken up needle and thread and repaired her petticoat but she didn't relish the thought of sewing. She simply had no patience for it. So she'd stuffed the damaged underwear beneath her bedstead. After all, she did have four more.

At eight, the clock chimed.

Meg sat sideways in one of the velvet drawing room chairs, teasing the silk fringe on the padded arm with her fingertip as she kept her nose in a book. She wore her house gown—a threadbare old thing whose pale blue crepe de chine had lost its luster long ago.

She'd put Mr. Wilberforce from her mind and she was actually enjoying herself with a good book and a box of caramels that was just shy of heaven. Of course the curl papers in her hair and liberal application of Secret de Ninon on the bridge of her nose for freckles weren't all that great. But a woman had to do what a woman had to do.

The tips of her felt slippers dangled off her stockinged toes. As she turned the page, she plucked another candy and popped it into her mouth.

In the kitchen, Mr. Finch was finishing for the evening. Dishes rattled every now and then as he stacked them. Grandma Nettie had retired to a bath.

Letting the caramel slide over her tongue, Meg absorbed the words that were leaping out at her from the novel. This was an especially juicy story, one where the heroine had been swept away by a band of thieves in the Arabian desert. She was just about to be saved by the hero, a dashing sheik astride a black charger. His tan face scowling down at the rogues . . . he raised his sword—

"Miss Margaret!"

Meg crinkled her nose. "Huh?"

Mr. Finch's stern British voice bellowed from the kitchen once more. "Miss Margaret, somebody is ringing the bell. Aren't you going to answer it?"

Brrrrinnnggggg!

The door chime cranked, jolting Meg from the chair. The book plopped onto the floor. She shoved the caramel into her cheek, keeping it from her tongue with her teeth so that she could say in a mumble, "I'm coming."

Then a distasteful thought wrinkled her nose: *Harold Adam's Apple.*

But he wouldn't come this late. Nobody would unless there was something wrong at the hotel.

Meg opened the door with the expectation of finding the night manager, Mr. Beasley, on the stoop.

Instead, she instantly froze.

"M-Mr. W-Wilberforce!" she squeaked, nearly choking on the candy.

He took a step backward, his gaze wide as it traveled across her in a very brief examination, but she hardly noticed as she took in his towering presence.

The cigar clenched in his teeth was so masculine. His block-crowned derby rested atop his head in a debonair manner. The arm cuts of his coat were filled out perfectly with his broad shoulders, and his vest was red—a dashing contrast to the white of his shirt. His shoes were the latest fashion—black calfskin stitched with celluloid eyelet. He'd really spruced himself up to come calling.

He'd come to call!

Automatically, both hands rose to her hair—all those horrid curl papers. She patted her head as if that would make everything disappear. Then she remembered her freckle cream.

With a mortified gasp, Meg slammed the door in his face.

Think!

The vestibule grew deadly quiet; then the bell rang. She jumped. There was no help for it. She simply had to answer the door and pretend that nothing was out of the ordinary. A lesson that Mrs. Wolcott taught her popped into her mind.

A lady never lets a man know he has caught her at a disadvantage.

Very well.

The door rang a third time. Meg swallowed her caramel.

With a regal grace, she swept the door inward.

"Mr. Wilberforce," she greeted.

He stared at her face.

The cream!

Before she realized what was happening, he'd reached into his pocket, produced a handkerchief, and began to wipe off the white lotion. Gently. With small strokes. Very slowly. Very deliberately. So much so, that Meg shivered.

"I like a woman with freckles," he said close to her ear, evoking a gasp from her.

Meg didn't move when he came closer to rub the last traces of Secret de Ninon from her nose. She could smell his cologne, quite subtle. So subtle, she could still detect his coconut bath soap. "You do . . . ? Really like a woman with freckles?"

Leaning toward her, he replied in a low voice, "I really do."

That did it. She was going to throw away that jar of expensive cosmetic.

When he'd removed the freckle cream, he took a step backward and looked at her. "Much better."

Much better? Even with her hair curlers? But she wasn't going to remind him of that. He might want to take them out . . . and she just couldn't stand here while he did. She'd faint. Yes, faint. This was the "a lot" she'd told Grandma Nettie it took to make her faint.

"Why, this is such a surprise." That was all she could manage until he said something else.

"I hope I'm not disturbing you."

"No. Of course not."

"I would have come at a more appropriate hour, but I was detained," he said, then added, "Business."

The unlit cigar clamped in Mr. Wilberforce's teeth caused him to talk from the corner of his mouth, drawing further attention to his lips. His voice came across in a bourbon-smooth drawl. "I was wondering if you'd be able to accompany me tomorrow for a row on the lake."

Meg's stomach flip-flopped. "I'd be delighted."

"Splendid," he replied. "I'll be by at one. Is that all right?"

"It's perfect."

"Good." He put his fingers to his hat. "I'll see you then."

With a smooth turn, he left the verandah and disappeared into the night, leaving Meg breathless with anticipation.

Sunshine filtered through the network of treetops, while songbirds called from the branches of cottonwoods knobby with swollen buds. A brilliant blue sky stretched high and cloudless. The temperature was slightly cool, but was made comfortable by the warming rays of sun.

A woodsy scent floated on the air, a smell unfamiliar to Gage. In his world, life stunk—almost to an overwhelming literal sense. It was his job to reveal the garbage to his readers. Few of his assignments took him out into nature. He was used to the cloying density of population, choking automobile exhaust, the corrupt odor of ink amid volumes of court documents, and the tarnished taste of political brass.

As a detective journalist, his state of mind usually bordered on being cynical, suspicious, and nongullible. But right now, with a light wind skipping over Fish Lake and stirring the fragrance of wildflowers he couldn't name, he found his basic distrust of life less heightened. There was a certain tranquility here that seeped through his citified clothing and relaxed him.

His motives had been to bring Meg to the scene of the supposed crime her brother had committed.

As Gage dug the paddle into the water, the lake's surface rippled. He glanced at the woman across from him. Her face was partially shaded by a flounced white sun parasol—the kind with an orange duck bill for the handle and a dangling gold tassel. She wore one of those long-waisted dresses in pale pink. The front panel, which stretched from throat to hem, had a lot of tucks and the entire dress was lace-trimmed.

Her hat of choice today was what Minnie Abbott, who wrote the fashion column in *The Chronicle,* called a turban. This one was braided straw with a rosette and two wings—both flying toward the left, leaving the right side appearing cockeyed. Appearing . . . more alluring than it should to him.

Gage forced himself to disregard the fact that he'd asked Meg to join him under false pretexts. There was no room in a journalist's life for guilt. Nerve. He had a lot of it. He produced stories that disturbed the accepted view of things. Many people were angry at him at any given day.

Someone had to expose the seamier side of life, and he did the job well. Reporters weren't necessarily objective truth-seekers. Gage certainly wasn't. He had definite opinions as to what was right and what was wrong. Without that ability to make sharp judgments, he would never be able to suspect that the official story was inaccurate.

In this case: Wayne Brooks winning a thousand dollar purse away from Ollie Stratton of Alder when Stratton had clearly been better qualified at fly-fishing.

This story had all the necessary elements. From L. Farley, Gage had found out where the young man lived. Worse yet, Stratton cared for an aged mother. A heart-tugger. Before Gage went to Alder, he had to learn all he could about Wayne. And Meg was his best source.

"Miss Brooks, you must tell me all about yourself," Gage suggested, steering them toward a small dock.

"I'm completing a term at Mrs. Wolcott's Finishing School," she said. "I've learned a lot of things, mostly how to be a lady." With an arch of her brows, she hastily added, "Not that I wasn't one before."

"I can't imagine you not being a genteel lady, Miss Brooks."

"Thank you."

She straightened and rested the parasol against her shoulder. "Tell me about you, Mr. Wilberforce. Where are you from?"

Without thought he said, "Battlefield, North Dakota." *A far cry from San Francisco.* "Do you like small towns, Miss Brooks?"

"Do you?" she returned.

"It all depends on the town." Gage couldn't let up. "Have you lived here all your life?"

"Uh-huh." She cringed. "I mean," then in a refined voice, "yes."

"Your family?"

"Since my parents married. They used to live in Des Moines. That's where my Grandma Nettie's from."

"Any brothers or sisters?"

"One. A brother. Wayne. I mentioned him before. He's at the university. Cornell," she said with a fair amount of pride.

"Attending Cornell is ambitious."

"Yes, well, Wayne can have his good points and ambition is one of them."

Ambition enough to rig a contest? Gage wondered. It took brains and a lot of dough to be admitted to the prestigious New York State campus. One thousand dollars in prize money could see a person go far.

"What kind of ambition does he have, Miss Brooks?"

She frowned. "He doesn't write to me very much. He's very busy on campus. You know how it is. There's so much going on at any given day."

Gage sensed she didn't really know what her brother wanted out of Cornell.

"Do you have plans to go to college, Miss Brooks?"

"Me? Why, nobody's ever asked me that before."

"Is it something you've thought about?" This didn't mean squat to his line of questioning. Gage was purely curious. More than he ought to be.

"Not really. The requirements for a hotel proprietress don't include a college education. I had a mind to manage a small establishment, much like my father's, but things didn't work out."

"How so?"

"My father wouldn't hire me."

"Why not?"

"He said I lacked experience."

"How could you get experience unless he hired you?"

"Exactly." She smiled at him, quite becoming. "I tried to get a position at another hotel, but I wasn't successful. I found out nobody takes a 'Miss' seriously. If you're a woman, you have to have 'Mrs.' in front of your name and your husband be dead in order for you to gain any respect."

Gage cracked a smile at her unintended humor. "So now what?"

Her brown eyes grew soft as she gazed at him. "So now my plans have changed."

"How so?"

"I'll do what ladies my age are doing. Follow my mother's footsteps and get married." She said the words with certainty. "What about you? Do you have designs to marry?"

Gage abruptly cut the motion of the oars and rested the handles in his lap atop the black and brown suit coat he'd shrugged out of earlier. The boat coasted on its own, but he didn't readily notice the course.

Marriage? He never thought about getting married. Frankly, because he'd make a wretched husband. What woman would want him?

He kept abominable hours. He had a passion to exploit crime, scandal, and shocking circumstances with the spirit of a crusade. Then he delivered his clever words in a way that some called sensationalist.

"I haven't devoted much thought to the subject."

Without further ado, Gage prodded himself into action and rowed the boat toward the shady side of the lake where a covered mooring was located.

The dockage's roof had been recently repaired. Last year's fall leaves dusted the older section, but the new gave off the pungency of fresh wood with its caramel-colored lumber. Lattice made up the sides, while the lower part of the housing was boarded with a platform that ran in a half square.

Gage bumped the edge of the boat on the dock ramp. Clutching his suit coat, he stood and got out. With a careless toss, he discarded the expensive coat onto one of the boathouse benches.

"Hand me that rope, would you, Miss Brooks?"

Meg plucked the damp hemp between two fingers as if she were picking up a dead cat's tail. Holding just enough to remain "delicate" as she stretched her arm out to him. He took the rope and secured the rowboat to the docks, then extended his hand to help her up.

She kept her decorous manner as she rose, and he could have sworn he heard her murmur, "Mrs. Wolcott would be proud."

Then she moved in a fluid way filled with deliberateness—as if she weren't used to such a maneuver. Lifting her foot to the boat's bench seat so that she could step up, her modest air lasted just long enough for her to snag the bottom of her petticoat with the tip of her shoe. Her eyes widened as she swiftly looked down, then yanked her hand out of his with such a jerk, she went reeling backward before he could prevent her from falling overboard.

The last thing he saw were two drawer-covered legs sailing upward amid a festoon of white petticoat ruffles.

Then the bob of hat feathers—minus the head that the hat should have been on. In that instant, Gage dove into the cold lake.

At least she hadn't lost her petticoat.

As soon as she'd stepped on her hem by accident, she'd pulled away from Mr. Wilberforce so she could feel her waistband and make sure the elastic was still in place. Everything had been as it should, but in her attempt to keep appearances she'd fallen overboard in the most unbecoming fashion.

She probably should have let the darn thing fall off. It wasn't as if he hadn't seen her without it before. Clearly, she wasn't cut out to be the wearer of the latest fashion rage.

Her hat . . . the lovely satin straw braided number with wire frame and shirrings of taffeta silk, wings, and dashing rosettes, was drowned. Just as drowned as Meg herself. With each step she took, her shoes squeaked and sloshed.

But as Meg walked the narrow trail that wound around the lake, she thought perhaps it had been fate. Because even though the water hadn't been but four feet deep, he'd rescued her. His strong arms around her had felt wonderful as he'd pulled her out of the chilly water and brought her to shore.

She didn't want to go back to the rental dock. And in spite of their wet clothing, neither did Mr. Wilberforce. In fact, he kept staring at her. To the point where she felt like she should have *insisted* they return to town even though she didn't want to go.

A true lady would have been mortified by the wet fabric clinging to her legs and outlining the shape of her bodice. But her self-consciousness wasn't enough to make her leave.

With teeth chattering and soggy hat in hand, Meg declared, "I know of a nice sunny spot where we can dry out."

"Put my coat on," Mr. Wilberforce insisted as he draped the wool coat over her shivering shoulders. His hot gaze swept across the column of her neck and to the delicate edge of her neckline; her skin burned in spite of the cool water running down her collarbone.

"Thank you." The Allard-Lee & Co. coat smelled faintly of Mr. Wilberforce's cologne. Meg never realized just how comforting something like that could be. She'd never worn a man's coat before.

As Meg trudged along using her closed parasol as a walking stick, she wished Mr. Wilberforce would say something. He had been inexplicably quiet since her . . . accident.

With each step she took, she felt his gaze skimming over her. As if he were pondering just what kind of woman she was. *Or,* if she dared consider a shocking thought, wondering if he were looking at her in a way that no gentleman would consider.

The very idea pulled at her composure. She didn't want to dwell on such a thought because she didn't know how to cope with it. Instead, she kept her thoughts on a safer subject.

He must think her a feminine disaster. To her credit, she'd only had these little accidents since forcing herself to remember ladylike maneuvers. The old

Meg could run in a skirt without so much as a falter. Margaret had too many trappings: gloves, parasol, hat, silk-vested shoes with dainty heels that did more to trip than aid in walking.

"It's not much farther, Mr. Wilberforce," Meg called over her shoulder, looking into his face.

A mistake. Her step faltered a little when she observed what he was doing.

His slow gaze traveled over the tender skin above her mouth. Then her mouth. Beneath his searing examination, a gasp parted her lips.

She really should have said they should go back . . .

But the very idea of spending the afternoon with him was too dazzling to forgo.

"I'm with you, Miss Brooks," he replied in a soft drawl—as if he weren't doing anything at all other than walking.

"Yes . . . I see that."

Meg faced forward and forced her thoughts to quit racing. She had to stop being so foolish. Remember who she was, wanted to be. The three Cs: cultured, civilized, charming.

Never mind about hot gazes and glances at her mouth as if he wanted to . . . well, enough of that. She had to remain steadfast in her efforts to win a man over with her new and improved self.

Since she'd failed in the etiquette department, she decided to charm him with her knowledge of the local flora. Flowers she knew. She'd studied that particular chapter in her deportment book thinking it was one of the more interesting ones. Bouquets made up of ivy, snowdrops, and maiden's blush roses had their own language. The ivy signified friendliness, the snowdrops hope, and the roses secret love.

Ladies waited to be sent flowers with such sentimental messages. But, frankly, Meg preferred yellow daisies, which meant shared feelings. She longed to find a man who shared her same ideals without her having to change her appearance or thoughts.

Regardless, she'd received neither type of bouquet from a gentleman caller.

Meg spied a particularly vibrant patch of blue.

With the intent to point out her knowledge of local plant life, she abruptly ceased her steps—only to have Mr. Wilberforce slam into her and knock her off kilter.

He braced his hands on her shoulders to keep her from toppling into the wild sorrel that grew alongside the trail.

Beneath his breath he said, "Miss Brooks, you sorely tempt me."

Turning her head, she whispered, "I do?" Her heart beat so fast, she could barely put a coherent sentence together—short as it might have been.

This close, his eyes were defining shades of summer green and the gold hues of fall sunsets. Breathing became an effort, collected thoughts became a struggle.

The weight of his hands on her shoulders felt deliciously strong and protective. "You're a very enchanting woman and any man fortunate enough to hold you in his arms would be hard-pressed not to take advantage of the situation." Mr. Wilberforce lowered his face over hers. "Did you stop because you want me to kiss you?"

Meg sucked in her breath. No man had *ever* asked her that. Not even Harold. Not that she had ever been kissed by him. Not that she wanted to be. "It hadn't been my intention . . . but if you want—"

She got no further. His lips came softly over hers and he kissed her startled mouth. Catching her up in his arms, he brought her close to his chest and deepened the kiss. He kept her snugly against him, and she began to relax. Until he traced the seam of her mouth. Such an intimacy . . . it left her reeling.

"Miss Brooks," he spoke against her lips, "have you ever been kissed before?"

She shivered; he held her tighter. "Yes, of course." The lie came easily enough.

"Then you don't mind if we kiss some more," he said after a spell.

And kiss her he did. Slow. Thoughtful. Kisses that left desire racing through her. His touch was a delicious sensation she had never imagined possible. Her fingers came to rest lightly on his shoulders—her hat nearly dropping from her grasp; she needed the support or else she would have . . . swooned. Like a real lady in a fit of the vapors. Completely unlike her. She'd thought such a thing ridiculous. And yet . . .

"I need to sit down," she said in a rush. "I find I'm feeling quite . . . quite unlike myself."

"You feel quite nice to me." His words melted her senses. She might have fainted dead away but she stubbornly refused to miss a second of this bewitching moment.

Pulling her thoughts together, she willed herself to gain a clear head. In order to do so, she had to talk. Talk about anything. The weather. The sky and lake. The flowers.

"I was going to show you that meadow of blue camas when I stopped," she blurted. "Doesn't that look like a puddle of water? But it's not. That bit of yellow beside it, that's marsh buttercup; it has yellow petals. And over there is false Solomon's-seal, and . . . and right here is trout lily. In spite of its name, it doesn't smell like a dead fish. Although I wouldn't be sending a person whom I harbored a token of affection for a bouquet of trout lily. The more suitable choice would be . . . would be . . ." She lost her train of thought when he stared at her like that. His mouth offering a little comma of a smile as if he thought she were a true beauty. "Oh, never mind."

At that, he half-laughed—as if he didn't want to but couldn't help it. A rich and warm sound that provoked shivers up her arms and across the nape of her neck where his delicious coat caressed her bare skin.

"You were going to show me a place where we could sit in the sun." He released her—she missed him immediately—and she instantly chilled as air circulated around her wet clothing.

Meg gripped the edges of her hat so tightly she nearly broke the braiding. "Yes. It's where the tributary of Evergreen Creek runs right into the lake. Beside it is a quaint meadow, where all around, the timber has fallen to keep the spot nice and bright with sun."

Meg moved forward, rather automatically. She heard Mr. Wilberforce follow behind her.

The meadow came into view and Meg stepped over a decaying tree. Off to the right, came the sound of water as it trickled from the creek, flowing over rocks and sun-bleached boulders. A blue jay sat atop one of the tree stumps with a nut in its mouth, then flapped its wings and flew away.

Finding the perfect fallen pine amid the ground blanket of grape ferns and leafy maidenhair, Meg selected a tree and sat down. Her skirts clung to her legs. She laid her hat on the rough trunk of the lodgepole. Then she folded her fingers together and rested them in her lap. She would have done something with her hair if she could have managed without being dreadfully obvious. Instead the dark copper length dripped down her back.

Mr. Wilberforce took a seat beside her, the cuffs of his trousers hiking a good five inches above his ankles. My goodness . . . he was shrinking. That was to say, his wool pants were from the dousing they'd received. Meg bit her lower lip. She was the Queen of Wool Shrinkage. Even when she used that guaranteed no shrink wool soap from Sears & Roebuck.

She hoped he wouldn't notice. Things were going so well.

"Is this what you'd call high?" Mr. Wilberforce asked.

Meg swallowed and glanced at his shortened trousers. "They're not all that high. Why, I'll bet you could let the hem down and nobody would ever be able to tell what happened. I'd offer to do that for you, but I think you'd be much better off with a professional."

He gave her a sideways stare. "I was referring to the stream," he clarified. With a flicker of a frown, he took a glimpse of his worsted trousers. "I know that my pants have become abbreviated. And I thought about tossing you back into the lake because of it."

If he hadn't grinned when he said it, she would have feared he'd been serious. She smiled along with him.

"Do you fly-fish, Miss Brooks?" he asked.

"I did when I was younger."

"Not anymore?"

"Well . . . nothing I would admit to."

He lifted a brow. "You're good at it?"

She didn't want to admit she was an excellent fly caster. Better than her brother, Wayne. In fact, better than most men in Harmony. Surely Mr. Wilberforce wouldn't find a woman interested in fishing very appealing. She should play down that part of her past. After all, she hadn't taken up her rod and reel for weeks now.

"Not all that good," she replied at length. "How about you? Do you think you have a chance at winning?"

"It depends on the competition. Do you know any of this year's contestants? Are they worth my worrying over?"

She watched his lips move as he spoke and it took her a moment to digest what he asked. With a half shake of her head, she thought about his question.

She knew a few of them. Sloppy casters. And that Ham Beauregarde. He was a real show off. Meg's shoulders slightly slumped as she thought over Mr. Wilberforce's question. She almost forgot herself and plopped her elbows on both knees and rested her chin in her palms. She did her best thinking that way.

The words of Mrs. Wolcott's deportment book came flooding back to Meg. She should use due discretion when on a topic that could wound a man's ego. "Well, I'm sure you'll see them practicing and you can form your own opinions." She plunged ahead with, "Yes, Mr. Wilberforce, the stream is high."

"Is the Evergreen the only creek to run into Fish Lake?"

"There are a few smaller tributaries, but they mostly trickle. They don't run in the way the Evergreen does."

"So this is the main waterway that feeds the lake fish."

"Yes."

"Any hatcheries around here?"

"One. In Waverly."

Mr. Wilberforce nodded, as if he were happy about that. How could he go from kissing her to talking about fish? She could hardly keep her mind on what he was saying. She kept reliving that kiss . . .

"What kind of fish do they raise?"

Fish? What was so fascinating about them?

With an inward shrug, Meg replied, "Brown trout. That's the second commonest trout in the state. It's the same fish you'll find in Fish Lake or anyplace else around here. Although rainbows are more prominent."

"Go on."

Imagine that . . . he was actually listening to her as if he were hinged on her every word. "Well, rainbows are smaller than steelhead, brighter in color, and they have larger scales. They take a strike with hardly any coaxing."

"So it's the most rainbows caught in the contest that makes a winner?"

"The judges count any fish."

"Tell me all about how a contestant chooses a spot from which to fish."

"Well, it's by lottery. Everyone puts their name in a hat and they're pulled one by one. The first picked, picks the first spot and so on."

"So you can pick which spot you're going to fish— in advance?"

"Yes. Two days in advance. So you can get to know the water."

Mr. Wilberforce said in his deep voice, "This subject is so fascinating, Miss Brooks. You have me enchanted."

"I do?" So much for another stolen kiss.

"Of course. Your knowledge of fish is remarkable."

Remarkable? She didn't think knowing the difference between rainbow and steelhead was all that remarkable. But if he wanted to think she was fascinating and enchanting and remarkable, she would let him. "You're too kind."

"And you're too modest. You haven't once bragged about your brother winning the contest last year. Mr. Farley told me."

She should have known.

Meg grew dismayed. She wondered if Mr. Farley had also told him about the ensuing outrage surrounding the Brooks name. Oh, what had she expected? Her brother's name was bound to resurface this year, but she would never say anything sordid against him or about his winning all that money.

"Yes . . . Wayne won."

"You must have been proud of him."

"Very." She wouldn't cower if Mr. Wilberforce pursued the matter in a less than flattering way to her brother.

But Mr. Wilberforce remained quiet.

A long moment later, he was kind enough to let the subject go. "Go on about the fish, Miss Brooks." He gave her an encouraging smile. "You're a true pillar of knowledge on this subject."

Relieved, Meg settled against the tree trunk for a long chat, unmindful to the fact that she was wet, her hair in a mess, and her hat waterlogged. And in spite of all that, she had Mr. Wilberforce rapt. Imagine that.

All this time she had been honing her feminine qualities and playing the modest lady to hook a man, when all it took was to talk about fish.

Chapter

❦ 5 ❦

The following day in his hotel room, Gage was distracted by a kiss that should never have happened. But seeing Meg Brooks, her hair falling freely to her waist, her bodice molded softly against her breasts, and the curve of her hips as they flared from her wet skirt—they had all gotten the better of him.

He'd wanted to kiss her, actually, from the first moment he'd laid eyes on her in his room. And even when she'd stood in the doorway of her house wearing that ridiculous freckle cream.

He had to remind himself that she was just part of his job. A source of information; not a source of temptation.

This morning, his thoughts should have been hammered by questions.

Was Meg Brooks protecting her brother? Did she know what exactly had happened? Had she helped him cheat? Did he in fact rig the contest?

She hadn't mentioned Wayne on her own. He'd had to lead her to the question of his win by discussing the contest, hoping she'd brag about her brother. She hadn't. When he brought Wayne up, she hadn't been anxious to talk about him.

In Gage's racket, silence more often than not meant wrongdoing.

The next logical thing he needed to know was what kind of fish had Wayne Brooks caught the most of. Rainbows would be in his favor; brown trout would be condemning. The latter could possibly be traced by a visit to the hatchery in Waverly.

Gage flipped through his notepad and read the notations he'd made when he'd returned to his hotel late yesterday. With irritation, he squinted at several places trying to decipher what he'd written. Gage didn't have the neatest penmanship. Normally, he immediately sat at his typewriter and transcribed his notes. That wasn't the case now since he was without his Rightwriter.

He'd seen a Smith Premier II in the window of the second hand shop. One of the newer models, not but four years old. The price had been reasonable. Hell, he should go buy it. He needed to get out of this hotel room. He couldn't keep his thoughts together.

Leaning back in his chair so that the two front legs lifted, Gage thumped his stockinged feet on the desk's edge and cradled the base of his head in his hands. He could go for a cigar; a smoke made him think better. But Mrs. Rothman had spelled out the hotel rules clearly when he'd checked in. No smoking in the rooms. Only in the lobby.

He mulled over the idea of going downstairs. The possibility of finding Meg there was enough to make him seriously contemplate the action. And not for reasons Gage would have assumed.

Yesterday's rowboat ride had been unlike any he'd ever had. Gage knew a lot of beautiful women. Some would say they flocked to him because it was safer to be on his good side than his bad; a person never knew when they'd become the subject of one of his articles. Better to be painted in a flattering light than slandered.

But to be fair, Gage only slandered those who deserved it.

Leaning forward to make out his words on a jagged piece of paper by his knee, Gage read: *Holding water. High water. Low water.*

Beneath each heading were descriptions.

Gage's mind wandered from streams to the woman who'd given him the flood of information on them.

He liked her strong sense of purpose. Though that staunch purpose had some conflict to it. Gage wondered if she was pretending to be somebody she wasn't. Usually he could sum up a person's personality in one conversation. Meg Brooks somewhat baffled him.

One minute, poised and polished. The next minute, slouching on a log giving Gage the distinct impression she wanted to prop her chin on her hands. Refinement and informality. They seemed to be clashing within her.

Gage understood that. He wanted to be a good journalist, but many of the things he did to get his stories went against the grain. A grain that was becoming rough and hard for Gage to continuously repeat.

Everyone thought Matthew Gage didn't have a conscience. But he did. It ate away at his stomach—literally. He couldn't remember the last time he ate a meal without it burning up his insides. He'd seen a doctor once. More like a castor oil artist who'd suggested Gage give up the cause of his ailment: the evils of his occupation.

An occupation he was hard-pressed to stay focused on yesterday when kissing Meg Brooks. She seemed to like him. Hell and back. It wasn't *him*. It was Wilberforce. Or what parts of Wilberforce he showed her. With Meg, he hated to use that stodgy vernacular of "Indeed" and "Splendid."

Gage never used words like that. He was too savage.

Give him a piece of paper, put a pen into his hand, and tell him to write out five character attributes he had and he would draw a blank. Tell him to write up five faults, and he could easily fill the amusements and entertainments column of *The Chronicle*.

Lowering his feet, Gage walked toward the bed with disgust. His trouble was he wasn't thinking rationally. And that annoyed him. He prided himself on having a mind that thought with absolute clarity morning, noon, and night.

He sat on the bed's edge and shoved his feet into his shoes, laced them, then stood and grabbed his hat and coat. Snagging the key from the dresser, he pocketed it and let himself out.

Taking the stairs down to the lobby, he was struck by the festive decorations. He even had to pause a moment to make sure he was seeing things right. But there was no mistake.

In spite of spring having been ushered in for nearly two weeks, the lobby was decorated with mistletoe and imitation holly. Banners of red and green and gold. Holiday candles and paper snowflakes.

Gage left the banister and headed toward the registry desk. Mrs. Rothman greeted him with, "Merry Christmas, Mr. Wilberforce."

His gaze fell on the garland of evergreens swagged over the front edge of the desk—right below the heavy length of chain. "Is it?"

"Not really," the elderly woman replied with a helpless lift of her hands.

He gave her an easy smile.

"It's Margaret's idea," Mrs. Rothman said, then pointed to the invitation on the desk counter.

Gage read the script that was painstakingly capped with ink-drawn snow:

If for fun you've any thirst,
Come to my party on April 1st;
There'll be tea and fun galore—
So put on youre best, and come at four!

Gazing at Mrs. Rothman over the paper's edge, he hated to admit that Meg had pulled one over on him. He'd forgotten today was April Fool's. "Very clever."

"I thought so," she replied, then said: "She's a lot like me."

Gage couldn't readily match up Meg Brooks to Mrs. Rothman, who, with her bicycle chain and quick wit, was clearly a rebel. "Is she?"

"Yes. But she doesn't want anyone to know." The elder woman leaned forward, lowering her tone. "Much like yourself, Mr. Wilberforce."

Going still, Gage said nothing. He merely arched his brows and waited for her to elaborate.

"I find it interesting that you change your vocabulary to talk with the porter, Delbert, and the house maid, yet you don't put on nearly as colorful a display for me. I know how you talk to them because I overheard you once when I was walking down the hallway. You and I have conversed twice now—once when I checked you in, and this our second encounter. You may drop a few words here and there, but only when you remember." She tapped a weathered fingertip on the registry book in the exact place he had signed *Vernon Wilberforce*. "Who exactly are you, Mr. Wilberforce?"

Gage would have laughed if he wasn't smarting from the woman's keen insight. He looked into her eyes. Deceiving her wasn't easy, but he would never reveal to her his true identity. "I'm a Bissell salesman," he remarked in an even tone, "who is good at what he does."

"You are good at something, Mr. Wilberforce," Mrs. Rothman said while straightening. "But I have yet to determine what that is." Her clear blue eyes filled with speculation, then a protective devotion. "My granddaughter is very special."

"I know that."

"She told me about your rowboat ride yesterday."

Gage wondered if Meg had told her about their kiss. He couldn't tell by the expression on the woman's face.

He took a moment to fully appraise the lobby, scanning the few patrons who sat in chairs. A cluster of gentlemen smoked, while several ladies sat near the window and drank tea.

Mrs. Rothman intruded on his search. "She's not here."

"But she will be."

"Of course." Then in a pondering voice, she mentioned, "It's not just any man who'll jump into an icy lake to save a woman from water not much deeper than a bathtub."

On that, he frowned. "Are you suggesting that I should have left her to her own devices?"

"Nothing of the sort. I like a chivalrous man. But he should know when to use his gallantry and when to let a woman save herself."

Gage thought with a wry smile: *Just like a reporter should know when he's met his match.*

Meg stared into the teacup in front of her. She, Ruth, and Hildegarde sat in Rosemarie's Tearoom. A lace tablecloth covered the round table and chintz seat covers made up the chairs. They were quite uncomfortable; made more unbearable by having to sit stiffly in her straight-fronted corset.

Looking at the untouched tea once more, Meg noted tea leaf sediments had settled on the cup's bottom. In an effort to make the bitter brew more palatable, she reached for the cubes of sugar and creamer. Dumping five lumps in with a healthy amount of cream, she stirred. And stirred.

She would have preferred a sarsparilla.

But their days sitting on the stools at Durbin's Ice Cream parlor were long gone.

The hour neared three in the afternoon. Muted sunlight came in through the big windows; crocheted lace curtains covered the glass giving the teahouse a matronly feel. Meg had met up with Ruth and Hildegarde when they'd been let out of Mrs. Wolcott's class for the day. Meg had waited for them at the school and given Mrs. Wolcott her essay on outdoor spittoons. Her next assignment was to write about the April Fool's party and how one's imagination could be used as a benefit in business.

"You should have come five minutes earlier, Margaret," Ruth said stirring her soda with her straw. "Doctor Teeter came for Johannah."

Meg took a polite sip of her tea and squelched a grimace. "I've seen him before."

Ruth enlightened, "He wore opera-toed alligator shoes."

Hildegarde added, "They looked ghastly."

"They were so new, the leather squeaked when he walked." Ruth daintily put her napkin to the corners of her mouth. "We all tried not to notice, but we couldn't help staring at his feet."

"He's got big feet, too," Hildegarde commented after a small taste of her tea. "Bigger than mine. My mother says that I've practically got the biggest feet of anyone in all of Harmony. If I were a man, I'd wear a size eleven."

Meg thought about Mr. Wilberforce's bare feet. She hadn't told Ruth or Hildegarde how she'd actually met him. Only that he was a guest in the hotel, and he'd come to call on her and take her out for a rowboat ride.

Ruth spoke up, "We forgot to tell you the most important thing."

"Yes!" Hildegarde's smile bracketed her mouth. "The most important thing."

The pair glanced at each other, then Ruth declared, "He called her sweetie cakes."

Sweetie cakes? Meg would much rather drink tea than be called such a syrupy endearment. "That's nice for Johannah," Meg eventually remarked.

"Margaret," Ruth began, stirring a squeeze of lemon juice into her tea and continuing in a slow voice, "you haven't mentioned your Mr. Wilberforce once today. In fact, you haven't shared much at all. Why, when you told us about him after Sunday's church services, you downplayed the whole thing. Is he that ordinary?"

Extraordinary was more like it. But Meg—who all during her girlhood shared the intimate details of her crushes with her two best friends—didn't feel comfortable elaborating on the new feelings that Mr. Wilberforce evoked in her. A woman didn't discuss such things as kisses and discovering that a man could make her heartbeat race with just one look. It didn't seem dignified to Meg.

"What is it that he does for a living?" Hildegarde's question intruded on Meg's thoughts.

Sitting straighter in her chair, Meg refused to be anything but proud of his occupation even though it wasn't one that evoked community respect. A traveling man was often thought of as less than noble. "He's a Bissell carpet sweeper salesman."

"My mother says carpet sweepers are the bane of her existence," Hildegarde supplied while itching the bridge of her nose. "The bail on ours is broken and all the dirt gets redistributed around our parlor rather than being caught inside the case."

"Maybe you should tell your Mr. Wilberforce to pay a call on Hildegarde's mother," Ruth suggested.

"I didn't know he was *her* Mr. Wilberforce."

Meg toyed with the edge of her napkin, wondering

about that herself. One afternoon at a lake, discussing fish of all topics, didn't constitute a man's belonging to a woman. But he had kissed her. That had to mean a lot. Unless he'd been trifling with her. She hated to think that, much less have it be true.

With Mr. Wilberforce, she felt blissfully happy and fully alive. It didn't matter that she forgot herself at times in his presence. He didn't seem to notice. In fact, he openly admired her—something Meg wasn't used to from men.

As if by Meg thinking about him, precisely at that moment Mr. Vernon Wilberforce walked by the tearoom.

Meg's mouth fell open when he paused—as if he caught a glimpse of her through the lace curtains—and to her utter surprise, he stared right at her.

"Margaret!" Ruth whispered loudly. "Who is that man?"

"He's a man all right," Hildegarde seconded.

She found her voice and calmly said, "That's Mr. Wilberforce."

The two girls gasped.

Hildegarde talked behind her hand. "Oh, Margaret, he's divinely tall and divinely dressed and divinely handsome and he's just plain . . . divine."

With the pretext of dabbing her mouth, Ruth spoke into her napkin. "Did you ever! I didn't know a carpet sweeper salesman could be such a knight of appliances. No wonder you're carrying a torch for him, Margaret. He's dreamy."

"And he's coming inside," Hildegarde noted.

Even though Meg felt an intense pleasure as Mr. Wilberforce walked to their table, she tamped down her enthusiasm as she'd been taught. With a calm she didn't feel, she pretended she hadn't noticed him and took a sip of her awful tea.

"Miss Brooks." His masculine voice evoked an awareness through her that she could almost tangibly touch.

Looking up, she casually returned, "Oh, hello, Mr. Wilberforce. What are you doing here?"

It took all her effort not to longingly sigh at the sight of him. His chin sported the slightest bit of dark shadowed beard that made him all the more appealing. The easy smile on his mouth had her wanting to be kissed by him again. And those eyes with their intensity and coloring seemed to smolder as he gazed at her. *Or did she imagine they did?*

"I was out for a breath of fresh air and I saw you through the window. By thunder, a coincidence if there ever was one."

Words failed Meg for a moment; the ridiculous language he had barely used yesterday in her company was back. Pushing aside her disappointment she recovered and said, "I didn't notice you were standing outside."

Ruth cleared her throat and prompted Meg.

"Oh. These are my friends Miss Ruth Elward and Miss Hildegarde Plunkett." Then to the two girls who sat opposite her with their jaws practically hanging open, she made the proper introduction. "This is Mr. Wilberforce."

He put a finger to his hat brim. "Ladies."

Mr. Wilberforce leaned over first Hildegarde's, then Ruth's, hand and brushed a light kiss over their gloved knuckles. Meg watched in stunned silence as he moved to her and took her fingers in his. She hadn't had the good grace to leave her gloves on and his mouth touched her warm skin, seemingly searing her with just the faintest contact.

Her eyes locked with his and she grew breathless, nearly forgetting her manners and herself.

Then Mr. Wilberforce let her hand go, and she lowered her arm to her lap without even being aware of doing so.

"I won't keep you," he said. "I just wanted to say that I'll see you at your party. It sounds splendid."

Meg had hoped, fervently *wished*, he would come. "I shall see you there," she remarked in her most dignified voice when she really wanted to say, *"It wouldn't have been any fun without you."*

He departed, leaving Meg so full of expectation, she could barely think.

An electrified silence hung over the table for a full minute before anyone even moved.

Then Ruth pushed her teacup away and set her napkin in front of her. "My heavens," Ruth said in an awed tone. "There goes a real man."

"He was a man all right," Hildegarde murmured.

Meg had quite a few words about Mr. Wilberforce. But she would never admit she'd written about him in her diary.

Hildegarde put her cup to her lips and absently drank, even though it held no tea.

The girls sat for a while in compatible contemplation.

"Well," Ruth said at length, "come on, Hildegarde. If we're going to make any kind of impression at all at Margaret's party, we'd better get home so we can prepare ourselves."

"My mother says a cucumber paste face mask isn't worth the effort to put on unless you leave it on for a full half hour," Hildegarde commented as she adjusted her pink tea hat and sheer veiling, then smoothed unseen wrinkles from her best jersey gloves.

Ruth followed suit and the two of them put themselves in apple pie order.

Such a bother, Meg thought. All this to be a lady. She used to be able to leave the house in under a flat minute. Now it took her at least fifteen at the mirror above the hall table to fix and fuss.

Meg stood, pondering the idea of a cucumber mask for herself. But she didn't have time to spare. "If I don't leave now, I won't have everything set up by four."

"I hope there will be some men there as handsome as Mr. Wilberforce," Hildegarde said, standing. "I'd even settle for mildly handsome if he said he had a chance at winning that thousand dollar prize."

Ruth rose to her feet. "A wife could fill a home with comfort using that kind of money."

"See you at four," Hildegarde said.

Ruth popped her parasol open. "Good-bye for now."

The look of unabashed hope on their faces stayed in Meg's mind as she left the tearoom. Each of them was pining for a beau—knowing that if they didn't find a man by the end of summer, it was all over. They'd be the next Crescencia Stykems of Harmony.

Cressie had gotten married at the age of twenty-two, but such a thing was so rare . . . a girl *had* to believe she'd be married by twenty.

Or else.

Chapter

❧ 6 ❧

A man wearing a collapsible brown fishing hat that had a huge round brim like a sombrero pumped Gage's arm in a firm handshake. "Hamilton Beauregarde. My friends call me Ham. Gurney hot water heaters and radiators. Got a house that needs heating, I'm the man to see. No job too big or small. Ham's seen it all."

Gage gave him a mild reply. "I rent."

"Damn shame!" he shot back in a voice that boomed, causing Gage to dislodge his hand and take a step backward. "Sir, that's the trouble with the country these days. Too many people want to do things on a temporary basis. What happened to material prosperity? Buy and own your own home. Have a wife and passel of kids. Even get yourself a good hunting dog. A man's all set when he's got himself a good hunting dog and a missus who sets a fine table."

Half listening to Ham, Gage scanned the hotel lobby—rather, the guests who occupied the room. His gaze sought and fell on Meg as she stood by a table that had been decorated in green and white. In the center sat a bowl of live goldfish with a dozen or so miniature fishing rods dangling over the crystal rim. At the end of each rod, a narrow green ribbon line extended across the table—one going to each plate. Partygoers were supposed to pick a plate attached to the line as a souvenir. Some had celluloid fish or small fishing baskets filled with candy. Gage had to admit, the scene was clever as all hell.

The fiddler, on the other hand, should have been embalmed. Every note he struck sounded dead. Gage recognized the man—the porter. Even though he couldn't play a decent melody, the musical touch made for a lively, if not conversational, atmosphere.

"Mr. Wilberforce, there you are."

Gage turned to the sound of the woman's voice and recognized Ruth Elward from the tearoom this afternoon. She looked like a big bloom of pink begonias. From her hat to her dress to her shoes. Trailing behind her, Hildegarde Plunkett, another hothouse flower looking ready to wilt. She gave him a demure smile and a slight wave.

"Hello, Mr. Wilberforce," Hildegarde said as she came to his side. "We're delighted to see you once more."

Ham Beauregarde panned his gaze over the pair, then let his eyes linger on Ruth. She was the fairer of the two. Gage didn't find either woman particularly attractive, but he remained pleasant while being assaulted by their clouds of clashing perfumes.

"Ham Beauregarde here," the salesman said with the brassiness of a tack. "And who might you two lovely ladies be?"

In spite of her cool exterior, Hildegarde tittered. Ruth glared at her and made the proper introductions.

The trio's conversation drifted away from Gage as he looked across the room once more and saw Meg. He thought her very relaxed and self-assured as she went from person to person and engaged herself in small conversation before moving on. Once she glanced at him, smiled, and turned away.

Gage hadn't spoken to her since the tearoom, which he wouldn't have even passed if he hadn't been on his way to the secondhand shop to buy that Smith Premier and sneak the typewriter up to his room.

He shouldn't have gone inside Rosemarie's. He had to remind himself that Wilberforce was married. Only Calhoon at the Harmony post office knew about the letters. As a favor to Wilberforce, Gage mailed a letter each day to a wife in Battlefield. When handed to him through the delivery grate, the postmaster had never looked twice at the daily envelopes.

"Do you know many of the gentlemen at the party, Mr. Wilberforce?" Hildegarde asked with a wide smile.

"Ah, no, Miss Plunkett," Gage replied. "I dare say, I haven't met any of them but Mr. Beauregarde."

"I know them all, Miss Plunkett," Ham supplied while pointing to a portly gentleman. "That's Orvis Schmidt. Ohio Electric Works—need a necktie light, he's got them. Got your battery table lamps, electric belts, and fan motors." He moved on to the lean fellow who stood by the window. "That there is King Merkle. Rubifoam—liquid dentifrice for the teeth." In a lowered tone, Ham added, "Get a load of King's choppers. Dentures if you ask me. So much for keeping his teeth with that poison he peddles."

Ruth's laughter sounded forced.

Ham straightened and panned his arm around the room, neither giving Gage or either lady the opportunity to partake in the conversation. "The rest of these bums are territorial. Stay in one spot. Your bankers and merchants, and other such city dwellers. Not suitcase men like me and Mr. Wilberforce. They don't know how to talk and bicker. And they believe in the never-never plan." He snorted. "Installment buying, buying on credit—I say if you don't have the moola, don't buy the merchandise. I only do business cash on the barrelhead. You do the same?"

Not allowed the opportunity to answer, Gage listened as Ham kept right on with his rachet jaw.

"You know what's wrong with America today, ladies? There's too much get up and go. Time's are changing. Automobiles, you know. Can't say as I like them. Trains. That's the way to travel." Then out of the clear blue to Gage: "What's your line, Wilberforce? Never mind. You don't have to tell me. I'll guess. Bissells."

He chortled, then winked at Ruth. "Bissells are fine if you like dirt. I'm in the radiator business. Gurney. The best you can buy." He fingered the inside of his trouser pocket and produced a calling card. "You ever need a dependable heating appliance, look me up."

Ruth nodded, taking the card. "I'll do that." She tucked the paper into her purse, then traded glances with her friend. "Well, we should see if Margaret needs our help."

"Yes, we should." Hildegarde stepped beside Ruth and the two went on their way. Clearly not interested in Hamilton Beauregarde. Gage couldn't blame them.

"Neither appealed to me," Ham said in a low

breath. "Well, maybe the blond. But I prefer a different sort of woman." After a short moment, Ham fastened his gaze on Meg and gave her an appreciative appraisal. "You want to know how I knew you sold Bissells, Wilberforce? The girlie told me you were in the sweeper line." Then with barely a breath, he continued to flap his chops. "Top notch, those Bissells. Been around. What's your territory?"

Gage folded his arms across his chest, waiting for Ham to breeze right along. When he didn't, Gage glanced at him.

For the first time, Ham paused for Gage to reply. Only Gage didn't have the answer. He had no idea what cities comprised Wilberforce's territory, other than Wilberforce had said it was bigger than most other sweeper salesmen's. Not using an alias and impersonating an actual person was posing complications Gage hadn't had to deal with before.

"You know, Ham," Gage began, "I'm not one to discuss business at a party. Good grief, if we did, we'd be in a dither over who had the biggest territory. Criminy sakes alive, it's bad enough we're all competing against one another in this fishing tournament. I'll bet you sure know a thing or two about flies," Gage said. "So tell me, how did you fare in last year's contest? I haven't heard any scuttlebutt other than that talk about Wayne Brooks winning over that Stratton boy."

Ham's expression soured; his tone lowered as if taking Gage into his confidence. "I don't like to speak ill of those not present, but that Wayne Brooks is a sly fox. Don't know how he pulled it off, but he did. Damn trouble is, everybody saw him catch all those fish."

Just as Gage had heard. If he didn't come up with any contrary evidence soon, he was going to believe Wayne's win had been pure luck.

He glanced at Meg. She was engaged in a conversation with a big fellow. A real bruiser. He could crush an ant just by his gaze. Yet the eyes he had for Meg were as soft as butter.

Gage barely heard Ham as he droned. For the first time ever, Gage succumbed to the facts staring him straight in the face.

He could be jealous.

Gage didn't want to believe he might be. There was no room in his life for jealousy, but he'd like to have thought that she'd reserved all those blushes and shy glances for him. But clear as day, her cheeks had just colored that pretty pink over something the big man had said.

"What I wouldn't have given to be a fly on the end of Brooks's hook." Ham's nasal voice intruded on Gage's thoughts. "I wonder if he had himself some kind of special bait? I heard canned corn kernels are a hell of a lure at certain times."

His stare on Meg, Gage automatically replied, "Good thing for us he's not entered this year. We'll catch some of those rainbows for ourselves."

Snorting, Ham declared, "That tributary is known for its rainbows—not that you don't have your browns. It's just that for somebody to catch mostly browns, it just doesn't add up the way it should. And Wayne Brooks caught mostly browns."

At the moment, Gage didn't give a fig. The information had just further implicated Wayne Brooks, but Gage didn't want to think about Meg's brother or damning him in the newspaper.

Ham rattled on and on in a tone that grew irritating. All Gage saw was Meg Brooks and another man making her laugh.

Gage didn't like it. Couldn't explain why with anything remotely resembling a credible reason. Simply, he just didn't like it.

Without a glance at Ham, Gage said, "Excuse me."

He went directly toward Meg and left Ham to his own conversation.

Meg could barely keep her eyes off Mr. Wilberforce when Hildegarde and Ruth went over to him. Her two best friends, laughing and standing close to him. Why it was enough to make her . . . jealous.

She barely heard a word Gus Gushurst was saying to her. Then before she knew it, Mr. Wilberforce was coming toward her. She couldn't help smiling at him, paying no mind to Mr. Gushurst's latest comment on the success of her party.

"Miss Brooks," Mr. Wilberforce said in a low voice. "You've done a fine job."

"Mr. Wilberforce," she began, beaming with pleasure inside, "I'd like you to meet Mr. Gushurst."

Mr. Wilberforce extended his hand to the boxer. "Gus Gushurst."

"Mr. Gushurst is the president of the Woolly Bugger Club," Meg explained. "They sponsor the fishing contest."

"Nice to see the town has a fly-tying club, Mr. Gushurst."

"No need for formalities. My friends call me Gus," he returned.

"Then call me Vernon."

Meg would have liked to call him Vernon, too. But

she didn't dare take the liberty. He might think she was forward.

Gus folded his arms across his wide chest. "So, Vernon, Miss Brooks tells me you're entering the contest."

"Indeed."

"Good. Good. Can always use some new competition." Mr. Gushurst put his hands on his waistband and tugged his pants higher. "That Ham Beauregarde who runs at the mouth always insists he's going to win." Bushy brows wiggled in contemplation. "He might have had a chance at second place if Oliver Stratton hadn't come in at it. Last year there was a bit of a . . ." His words trailed as he looked apologetically to Meg. "Dispute. But the winner was found deserving so let's not dwell on it after the fact."

After an awkward pause, Mr. Gushurst stated, "Well, if you two will excuse me. I've got to circulate. Wouldn't want it to be said that I'm playing favorites."

He wandered toward a group of men. Meg stood there, delighted that she had Mr. Wilberforce to herself. Hildegarde and Ruth had gone to fill their cups with punch.

"You must have experience with giving parties, Miss Brooks."

"Actually, this is my first big event."

"I like the decorations." He casually slid one hand into his trouser pocket, standing in a relaxed manner that would be considered discourteous to a real lady. Meg didn't mind at all. In fact, she wished she could stand in such a way. She'd been on her toes about keeping her posture ramrod stiff, shoulders squared, bosom out, and taking delicate steps as she walked.

"I'm glad you like the decorations, Mr. Wilberforce" she said, feeling painfully self-conscious of her stiff words. This whole notion of pretending. Talking, standing, thinking. It was so hard to keep it up.

When they'd been alone, she hadn't found it difficult to keep a subject afloat. Now she didn't know what to say without it sounding forced. "I got the decoration ideas from a book on party planning."

"Indeed?"

Ridiculous. He didn't care how she came up with the ideas.

To Meg's dismay, Ruth and Hildegarde left the refreshment table and came to join them. Meg watched as Ruth stood beside Mr. Wilberforce—not close enough to be forward. But close enough to make Meg notice.

"Oh, Margaret, you've done a wonderful job," Ruth said, holding her punch cup. "I think parties are such fun. Don't you, Mr. Wilberforce?"

"Depends on the company."

"I agree," Hildegarde added. "My mother says—"

"We don't need to talk about mothers, Hildegarde," Ruth interjected. "Are you enjoying your stay in our fair town, Mr. Wilberforce?"

"Yes, as a matter of fact, I am," he replied, looking right at Meg. She dared hope he was enjoying his time because of her.

Hildegarde's cheeks blushed pink when she asked, "Mr. Wilberforce, do you think you have a chance of winning that prize money?"

"There's always a chance for anything to happen, Miss Plunkett."

The girl grinned.

Meg frowned.

"Pardon me, ladies," Meg broke in and continued

right along on so they couldn't protest, "I need Mr. Wilberforce's services. I see we're nearly out of ice in the bowl of blackberry nectar. There's a block out in front that I could use help chipping."

She turned and retrieved a clean water bucket from beneath the table. "It's this way, Mr. Wilberforce." As if he couldn't find the front of the hotel. She hoped he didn't think she was the henpecking type of woman. Far from it. But for some reason, the thought of Hildegarde and Ruth ogling the man she'd pinned her hopes on brought out a streak of possessiveness in Meg.

Thankfully, Mr. Wilberforce followed her as she went outside, closing off the noise from the lobby as she took in the evening.

Dusk settled over the westward sky, streaking it with ribbons of orange and pink. Houseplants in painted cans and tin pails stood along the edge of the hotel's porch floor. Suspended from the awnings were scalloped canvas sunshades. Ferns in wire hanging baskets had been interspersed between the posts. Beside the large picture window to the hotel's lobby sat two white hickory rockers, tilted at an angle so as to face each other for intimate conversation.

Meg had done that. Another one of her special touches.

She went toward the wraparound corner to a galvanized washtub with a gutta-percha liner holding a large, jagged block of ice. An ice chipper laid on top of it.

"Let me do that, Miss Brooks," he gallantly offered.

"Thank you, Mr. Wilberforce."

He grasped the sharp pick and began to chip away the solid, cold chunk. "I don't mean to bring up a touchy subject, Miss Brooks," he began as he worked, "but what Mr. Gushurst said about a dispute . . . I couldn't help be interested since it was about the fly-fishing contest. Could such a problem happen again this year?"

Inhaling and holding her breath a moment, Meg let it out. Reluctant, but knowing she had to speak. "I suppose you'll find out anyway," she said, leaning against the railing. "As you know, my brother won the contest but there was speculation surrounding his entitlement to the one thousand dollars. But he caught those fish with all honesty and Mr. Gushurst has been a dear to stick by his official ruling that Wayne won fair and square. Others have pressed Mr. Gushurst to have Wayne forfeit his prize and give it over to Oliver Stratton, the boy who came in second. But Mr. Gushurst has remained adamant that Wayne keep his standing in first place."

"Then he must have thought your brother won legally."

"My brother *did* legally win." She didn't want to talk about this. Not when the evening was so soft and pretty. "Do you have any brothers or sisters, Mr. Wilberforce?"

He grew pensive a long while. She didn't think he was going to answer her. Then his voice wrapped quietly around the night. "I had a sister . . . Virginia. She died."

Meg knelt beside him and put her hand on his arm. "Oh, I'm so sorry to hear that. Was she young?"

"Nineteen."

Since he didn't turn away, she went on. "What happened?"

Mr. Wilberforce set the ice pick down, slid along

the wall and sat down on the whitewashed floorboards of the porch. Meg did likewise. The pair of them rested beside each other, backs up against the hotel wall, legs out in front of them. Quite unrespectable. Quite pleasant.

"She married when she was eighteen and her husband took her to England with him on an extended honeymoon. She conceived a child while abroad and had been in too delicate a condition to travel home to California."

"But I thought you said you were from North Dakota?"

Mr. Wilberforce furrowed his brows, then rephrased, "She was living in California with her husband while I was living in Battlefield." He stared ahead at the sunset. "As the month of her delivery neared, my parents boarded an ocean liner to be with her when the baby came. The *Presidio* was lost at sea near the Isles of Scilly. Two weeks later, Virginia gave birth to a stillborn son and then died of the birthing complications. I think she died of grief over the loss of our parents."

Meg wanted to cry. How horrible. "Mr. Wilberforce, how you must have suffered, too."

He brought one knee up and rested his hand on his thigh. "I didn't mean to tell you this."

"But I'm glad you did." She gently put her hand on his. "I have two parents who I often take for granted. How terribly hard for you to have lost not only your sister, but your parents as well."

Turning toward her, she saw the sorrow in his eyes. Genuine. True. He was a man with feelings. His hurt ran deep. She wished she could do something to make him aware that he didn't have to be alone.

Quite softly, with barely a conscious thought, she sat taller and leaned toward his cheek, giving him a comforting kiss. Bold. She knew it. But she couldn't help herself. She felt his sadness deep in her heart.

"Mr. Wilberforce," she whispered, but she was unable to speak further. Every sense within her was new, untried. She wasn't experienced at this, at deep emotions that gave her warmth, longing.

He didn't say anything either. He caught her chin with his fingers and tilted her head to his. And kissed her. Quite unlike the kiss they had shared before, this one was filled with tenderness and words that didn't need to be spoken. Compassion and the blend of heartbeats.

Meg wanted the kiss to never end.

Gage shouldn't have kissed her. He knew it would lead nowhere. And yet, he was so drawn to her . . . so compelled by her, he couldn't help himself. She was pretty. More than pretty. Innocent. Not that he went for innocent women. But Meg was different. Something about her. A freshness, vitality and eagerness that he had once known long ago in himself.

As he slanted his mouth over hers, taking simple pleasure in the taste and texture of her lips, he damned himself. Damned for getting involved. Damned for telling her about his sister. His parents. Those were memories he never shared. Too painful. Reflection on them was rare. He had moved on with his life.

Yet the life he had now was not his own. Too much deception.

Even so, he allowed the quiet but potent kiss to hang between them. Grazing the tender skin of her mouth, he closed his eyes and resisted the urge to feel something more than the physical moment. Too many cities, too many names. They kept Gage apart from the rest of the world. He'd closed himself off years ago.

But this moment in time . . . it hovered, it took hold in the deepest part of his heart. Touching him. Almost making him feel worthy.

Somebody laughed inside the hotel, their voice tumbling outside onto the porch. Gage was brought back to reality with a thud. He broke their kiss and looked into Meg's eyes. They glimmered with emotions he didn't dare define.

He didn't want her to say anything about what had just happened. So he got to his knees and then stood, helping Meg to rise. "I think this should be enough ice, Miss Brooks."

"Oh . . . yes, it should be." Her voice was low and barely composed.

He knew she was disappointed. He hadn't meant to make her feel that. *He* hadn't meant to feel anything.

She acted as if she wasn't affected. She was able to revert back to her hostess of the party demeanor. Dignified and on her best behavior. In that moment, he wondered just who she was. There were too many facets to her personality that didn't fit together. Gazing at him, she must have sensed his speculation and was uncertain what to do about it.

They began to walk toward the front doors when he noticed that Meg stopped and gazed with a meditative eye at the bellman's cart.

"Is there something wrong, Miss Brooks?"

She mutely shook her head, still staring at that cart as if she longed to jump right on top of its platform. Gage pondered her actions, sizing up the rickety base with its cast iron wheels and the velvet flatbed—the nap of the burgundy fabric having been crushed and worn out long ago. There were two side poles that made an upside-down U-shape on which to hang bags and valises.

Giving him a questioning raise of her brows, she opened her mouth as if to ask him something, then snapped it closed.

"What is it, Miss Brooks?" he inquired, unable to contain his curiosity.

"I don't suppose you could have feelings for a woman who makes a spectacle of herself."

The question threw him and he couldn't readily answer.

"I figured as much." Meg gave the tired luggage cart one last glance.

Her disheartened expression got Gage right in the gut. "Do you have some kind of attachment to this bellman's cart?"

She sighed. "I used to ride it. All the way down to the train depot. But my mother said I made a spectacle of myself."

It was hard to keep a straight face as he replied to Meg, who was eyeing that cart like a kid who just lost her favorite piece of candy. Yet even so, she maintained an air of superiority—as if it were beneath her. She was a heady mix of propriety and suppressed wildness.

"Why, Miss Brooks, is this what you were talking about?" Gage remarked. "I wouldn't object to a little girl who liked to ride the bellman's cart. I'll bet your pigtails got to flying pretty high past your ears."

"Yes . . . well." But that's all she'd say on the subject, giving Gage the distinct impression there was more to it than she let on.

In his mind's eye, Gage could see Meg Brooks riding the bellman's cart, eyes dancing and laughter lighting her mouth. In that moment, he had a glimpse of the Meg that had been eluding him. The Meg he would have liked to know.

"We should go in now," she said, putting on her reserved face.

Gage followed her, thinking.

It would appear they were both playing roles.

He knew his part.

What was hers?

Chapter

7

Meg sat at the kitchen table with her grandmother while Mr. Finch did the dinner dishes. Grandma Nettie worked on her latest batch of flyers and Meg read the April issue of *Women's Journal*.

She'd taken the advice on petticoats, but after stepping on hers twice, she concluded that she obviously wasn't cut out for longer petticoats. She would have shortened them back to their original length if she thought she could without doing more harm than good.

Turning the magazine pages, Meg looked for fashionable words of wisdom that would set her apart from other women . . . and gain the undying attentions of Mr. Wilberforce.

She was so smitten by him, she could barely eat, sleep, or breathe without her thoughts continuously wandering to him. To his kisses.

She hadn't seen Mr. Wilberforce since the night of the April Fool's party three days ago. Each morning he'd left the hotel early and returned late, fishing gear in tow. That was why he'd come to Harmony, after all, and she couldn't expect him to while away his time courting her. He had prize money to win.

And she did have her pride. She wouldn't throw herself at him.

Although yesterday she'd been waiting hours for him in the lobby, pretending she needed to fix things up. When he finally returned, he tipped his hat to her, said he was tired, and went upstairs to his room.

A bold-titled article in the magazine caught Meg's attention and made her brows shoot upward.

The State of the Bosom in 1901

Gentle readers, it used to be a woman with a bust size of 34 was considered lilliputian. As fashion dictates our changing society, corset covers are now being sold in sizes as high as 48 inch. To this modern creature with her generous endowments and wasp waist, we address the following: Men turn naturally to robust women, so beware! The man who calls on a woman of this figure may not have the best of intentions. He could be without scruples. He could be after a kiss! Remember, real beauty depends upon good health, good manners, and a pure mind. Not one's bust size.

Meg gazed at her bosom with a grimace. Not much there. And at her age, she wasn't going to get any more either.

Maybe this was the something she lacked for a man to be head over heels about her. Then again, in the dimmed shadows on the hotel porch, Mr. Wilberforce had kissed her. Passionately. And he'd told her personal things about himself. He *had* to have *some* feelings for her.

Mr. Finch pulled one of the dish bars from the wall and hung his damp cloth over the wooden dowel. Then he pulled out a chair and sat. Meg stared at him a moment, taking in his well-groomed features.

He was an attractive man who appeared to be in his mid-sixties. She'd never seen him without his bowler and suspected he was bald. But it surely was a cruelty of nature if he was—because he sported the thickest, finest beard and mustache she had ever seen. Black as pitch and not a whisker out of place. He didn't use wax on the wiry hair; it looked smooth and soft.

"Would you like some help, Mrs. Rothman?"

Meg wouldn't have picked up on the admiring gleam in Mr. Finch's smoke-colored eyes if she hadn't been studying him. But it was there, plain as day.

Mr. Finch was sweet on Grandma Nettie.

Did Grandma Nettie know? Did she want to be alone with him? The potential for a grand romance made Meg smile. Imagine, a woman grandmother's age—at least five years older than Mr. Finch—being the object of an infatuation. It was too wonderful for words.

"Yes, Mr. Finch, you can sort through these pamphlets and make sure I haven't forgotten anything. They should all look like this one." She slid an original toward him and their fingers kissed like a pair of butterfly wings; a gentle whisper of skin to skin.

"If this town had a newspaper," her grandmother decreed, "we could spread the word in half the time."

"Speaking of word, have you had any from Mrs. Gundy?" Mr. Finch asked.

"Yes, as a matter of fact, I got a letter from her this very morning. She was arrested in a tambourine campaign last week. She wouldn't leave peacefully with the others and hit a copper on the back of his head with her pocketbook." Grandma Nettie's hands stilled and she gazed at Mr. Finch. "You don't suppose honey is more effective than vinegar as a medium for catching flies?"

"I prefer vinegar myself," Mr. Finch replied. "It gets more notice when no notice has been given in the strongest of efforts."

Her grandmother nodded. "I quite agree. We must take drastic measures. It reminds me of Sarah Edmonds." She smacked a rubber stamp wet with red ink in the middle of the flyer she was working on. "She was a nurse and spy in the Union Army. She used the name Frank Thompson to enlist. In 1884, she fought Congress and got her pension."

Meg asked, "How could a woman get Congress to give her a pension for impersonating a man?"

"Because it was the right thing to do," Grandma Nettie said with conviction. "Her nickname was the Beardless Boy and she double-disguised as a rheumy-eyed crone to get secrets from the Confederates."

"Really?" Meg murmured. "A woman dressing like a man only to pose as a woman to get information."

"Sarah Edmonds was forced into serving her country the only way it would let her," Mr. Finch answered, licking his forefinger to examine another pamphlet. "By dressing in man's attire."

Meg stood, taking her magazine with her. She poked a finger into her high bun, trying to wiggle the pins loose. The weight of her hair gave her a headache. "Margaret would disagree with me," Meg said, "but I think it would be fun to dress like a man to help my country."

"I agree," Grandma Nettie seconded. "So tell Margaret she's being too delicate." Her grandmother gave her a smile.

Meg returned it. "Yes, I'll do that."

She left the kitchen and climbed the stairs to her room. When all was said and done, playfully discussing Margaret as if she weren't Meg was not all that humorous. Meg had to decide who she wanted to be. Herself or a likeness of herself bound by rules and conformity. Men noticed Margaret . . . not Meg.

Heaving a sigh, she resolved to give Margaret every opportunity to prove herself.

Meg went into her bedroom and sat on the coverlet of her bed, flipping through the magazine once more and stopping at the article on bosoms. She then gazed down at hers while biting her lower lip. Could she go through with it?

Actually, if she borrowed some nerve from Meg, she could.

Gage opened the door to Wolcott's Sporting Goods store and entered.

The place was a man's man place, with a few exceptions. Gage noted the giant stuffed grizzly bear in the corner held a bouquet of wildflowers in its paw. Blue ribbons tied back the old window curtains. The light hint of a woman's floral perfume and the lunch box on the counter.

Customers milled around the tackle section. Bamboo rods stood in straight rows against the green felt of their wall rack. Fly reels had been strategically placed like checkers in an open case. But the center of attention was the glass-topped teakwood case that held thousands of flies.

One of those in the discussion was Ham Beauregarde who, upon Gage's entrance, looked up. Gage gave him a forced, friendly wave. Granted, Ham had been an asset. He'd told Gage what type of fish Wayne Brooks had caught. But beyond that, Ham Beauregarde could prove to be a nuisance. He liked to talk too much.

"Can I help you find anything?"

Gage turned toward the welcoming voice, apparently the owner. He sat on a stool by the cash box snacking on a tin of candied walnuts. His hair needed a cut, yet it didn't look all that bad on him; he was wide enough in the shoulders to have played college football and clobbered quite a few opposing team members.

"I need a new rod." Gage glanced at the broken pole in his hand.

A good fly-fisherman wouldn't have busted the most important piece of his tackle, not to mention his leader and tippet. The *New American Fly-Fishing Manifesto* chapter on casting said to anticipate the fish's behavior on the end of your line before you even threw it out. Easier said than done.

He didn't think like a stinking trout.

The damn fish had taken the hook and run with it. Hard and fast into the brush. The weight of it put a snap into his rod as he pulled.

"Spring weeds can do that to you," the man said as he set his walnut tin on the counter.

Gage appreciated the lack of censure. Though his

lightened spirits were short-lived as Ham ambled over with an all-knowing look on his puss.

"A smart fisherman never holds his rod high on a hard run," Ham spouted as if he were a first-class expert on the subject. "He aims it low and to the side, even points the tip underwater to keep his leader underneath the bush."

"That doesn't always work in heavy weeds," the owner offered.

"Well, Wolcott, I suppose you've got a small point."

Wolcott stood, took the rod from Gage, and laid the broken lengths on the counter as if he were going to assemble it. "Here's your problem. Whoever sold you this rod sold you the wrong one. You're not getting the right balance. This rod was meant for a shorter man than you."

In his mind's eye, Gage saw Wilberforce standing in the jail cell next to his—Gage being a good head taller.

Bringing his fingers to his chin, Ham stroked his clean-shaven jaw. He may have come across as a blowhard suitcase man, but he wasn't stupid. "It seems implausible to me that you'd be lame enough to buy the wrong rod."

Wolcott broke in. "Some salesmen will sell you anything just to make a sale."

"Speaking of salesmen." Ham stared at Gage. "You never did tell me about your territory. The other night you distracted me with fly-fishing politics. We're not at the party anymore so there's no reason not to talk business. Just how big is your territory?"

"Small," Gage offered, then to Wolcott he went on, "As to the fishing, what kind of a rod do you recommend, sir? By thunder," he slapped his palm on the countertop, "I fear I've been the victim of unfair selling practices."

The owner paused, sized up Gage, then explained, "It depends on how a rod feels to you. The same one will feel different to me. So you have to be comfortable with its length and balance providing its right for you. I'll help you find the right rod. You want split bamboo, lancewood, or jointed steel?"

"Split bamboo."

"Good choice."

Leaving Ham behind, it took Gage and Wolcott a solid half hour to outfit him with the right equipment. Gage had had to try out a half a dozen Genesse rods by imitating the action of casting and forcing the point forward. Unlike Wilberforce's broken pole, the Genesse Gage selected sprang rapidly back to a straight line, and without a vibration.

Back at the cash box, Ham still hovered around like a pesky mayfly as Gage reached for his billfold. He moved in so close, Gage could have ground his heel in the man's scuffed shoe toe.

"So, just how small is small, Vernon?"

Ham evidently judged a salesman's selling prowess by the size of his territory. Gage didn't want to deflate Ham's ego and agitate him into a verbal debate. He had no idea if salesmen could check up on each other's areas. "Just Montana and the western side of North Dakota."

Ham laughed, with a snort that sounded like water gurgling down a drain. "Well, Vernon, then you've got it easy. My territory runs east of the Missouri and west of the Cascades."

Paying for his rod and stowing it in the new case

he'd bought, Gage grasped the handle and said his thanks to Wolcott. Then to Ham, "Been a pleasure to see you again, Ham. The best of luck to you in the contest."

"Oh, I don't need any luck. I've got pure skill. And that prize money nearly spent."

"It isn't over until it's over," Gage said, unable to help himself.

On that, he left the sporting goods store glad to be out in the fresh air.

Beauregarde had turned out to be a flea weevil— an annoying itch just out of Gage's reach. Now Gage wanted to win that damn contest just to rub Ham's face in his loss. But at the rate Gage was learning how to whip a line, he'd be dead last.

There was a whole lot more to fly-fishing than could be learned from a book. It was one thing to read about it; another entirely to actually do it. A lot depended on a sixth sense. An inner clock of timing and speculation and cunning, kind of like chess. You had to read your opponent before, during, and after he made his move. Your countermove depended on what he did and what he would now do.

Trout were sharp strategists—they'd encountered flies before and they knew when to bite and when not to. Gage didn't know when they were on the end of his line and when they weren't. It was solely trial and error. More error and cursing than anything else.

The simple truth was, he wasn't going to learn how to fish out of a book, not in two weeks anyway, and he had a broken rod to prove it.

He'd gone over to Waverly the morning after Meg's April Fool's party and had spoken with the hatchery owner, Leroy Doolin, under the guise of starting up his own trout farm in Oregon.

Gage had taken notes on everything but the most important piece of information he'd gleaned was that nobody using the name of Wayne Brooks had bought brown trout last year.

He hadn't expected Wayne to use his real name. And asking after him had had to be done in a roundabout way. Gage had said he'd been thinking about going partners with a man named Brooks, but Brooks had decided to go it on his own. Doolin swore he didn't know Wayne Brooks.

Going a step farther, Gage had inquired after Doolin's larger orders last year. Doolin said he rarely did big order business with the public. His dealings were with private sectors and the government, most of the time.

Gage had nodded his thanks, then mounted the horse he'd gotten from Hess's livery and rode off. No wiser than he'd been when he'd arrived.

As he walked up Birch Avenue, Gage allowed himself the small luxury of thinking about Meg Brooks and himself.

She chased daydreams.

He chased rats.

Would there ever come a time he could look at the world and see things without them being woven between possible investigations? If ever there was a woman who could make a believer out of Matthew Gage, it was Meg Brooks.

While walking back to the hotel, Gage imagined what might have been if he'd met her under different circumstances.

*　　*　　*

Meg practically ran down Sugar Maple, the town's main street. It wasn't the proper thing to do—bound across a sidewalk with one's petticoat ruffles kicking up an awful fuss with one's hasty steps. There was a time and place for exceptions and this was one of them: She had to get home without anybody seeing her. Or worse yet, without anyone stopping her.

She pressed her newly purchased parcel so tightly against her breasts that what little she had in the bosom could very well be concave by the time she secreted her way to her bedroom.

The corner of Birch Avenue was steps away and she breathed a sigh of relief. But her optimistic cloud rained right through its silver lining the second she slammed shoulder-to-shoulder with Mr. Wilberforce.

"Miss Brooks!"

He held out his arms to steady her and the package slipped from her grasp. She made a grab for it and missed.

The brown-wrapped item landed next to Mr. Wilberforce's right shoe. He could step on it and break the jar. Then what would she do? She couldn't buy another one for a whole week. Mr. Plunkett only left the store for ten minutes every Friday to go to the bank and make the weekly deposit. During that time, Hildegarde was in charge. Meg could *never* buy what she'd just bought from Mr. Plunkett. Thank heavens Hildegarde had double-wrapped the jar.

Meg's chin shot up. "I . . . ah, Mr. Wilberforce. I didn't see you."

"Apparently not. Where are you off to in such a hurry?"

"Home." Her voice sounded squeaky to her, high-pitched and tinged with so much worry, she felt like she could just keel over and die.

"Is there a problem, Miss Brooks?"

If she scooted forward and bent her knees a little, her skirt hem could cover the package.

"No. There's no problem." She crept her way toward him, and in turn, steered him backward.

Mr. Wilberforce's dark brows slanted down. "Miss Brooks, are you feeling all right?"

"I'm fit as a fiddle," she replied, stepping closer.

However, her plan came to a standstill as she gazed into his face, thoughts of the jar momentarily forgotten. Her murmur of "Hello" sounded shallow even to her.

"Hello," he replied back in a monotone, his eyes glinting like shards of green stones.

Crowding him wasn't working. Physical force was her only option. She laid the palm of her hand on his suit shoulder and gave the hard slab of muscle a slight nudge. He didn't budge an inch. A frown marred her lips.

Having no other choice, with a pull of breath and the strength of sheer will, she shoved him with one hand. Fairly hard.

If he moved even a hair, she didn't see it.

A blanket of impending doom fell heavily on her spirits as her eyes fell to the dreaded parcel, which was right out in the open. The wrapping paper might as well have been as red as the Fire Department's No. 1 engine. The only thing left to do was to bend down and get the dreaded thing and . . . and lie like a rug if he asked her what was in it.

But before she could snatch it, Mr. Wilberforce leaned over and picked the package up.

"Is this what you're after?"

Meg's mouth went dry as burned toast as he examined the string-tied, brown paper–wrapped parcel by turning it over in his large hand. He certainly couldn't tell what was in there. It was pure fear of discovery making her so sensitive about . . . *it.*

Mr. Wilberforce lifted his gaze to hers. "Did I step on this?"

"No," she shot back quickly and thrust her hand out so fast she'd robbed him blind in the blink of an eye. This was, after all, her package and she couldn't keep a clear thought in her head with him touching it.

Meg felt perspiration bead on her upper lip and the afternoon wasn't even a hot one, mild at best. A lady must never lose her composure. But she was failing quite miserably.

The package now safely in her custody and clutched with a possessive grip by her gloved hands, Meg tried to regain her dignity. That is until she noticed a small tear in the paper. Could Mr. Wilberforce see anything?

"I'm glad I ran into you, Miss Brooks." Then he chuckled. "Not figuratively speaking. I know you like Rosemarie's Tearoom, but would you consider an ice cream at Durbin's with me?"

An ice cream? She'd thought her ice cream parlor days were over. Even though she sometimes longed for a vanilla fizz, she'd forsaken them to be respectable and drink dishwater-tasting tea.

He was asking her to join him. How could she say no? How could she say yes? She had *the package* with her.

"I'd be delighted, Mr. Wilberforce. Just let me drop off something at the hotel, then I can—" She'd barely taken a step toward the hotel's porch when she heard her name called out as if she were a street vendor.

"Hello, Margaret!" came Harold Adams holler from the opposite side of the street. To her dismay, he crossed and headed directly for them.

"Never mind about the hotel," Meg said, linking her arm through Mr. Wilberforce's and steering him in the opposite direction. "Let's go right now."

Unfortunately, Harold Adam's Apple caught up to them. "Margaret, didn't you hear me?"

"Hmm, no," she replied, keeping her steps swift.

"How are your headaches, Margaret?"

She wasn't enthusiastic to answer in front of Mr. Wilberforce; he would think she was sickly. "They're fine now."

Mr. Wilberforce turned toward her. "You've been having headaches, Miss Brooks?"

"Nothing to worry about."

"But you've had a sick headache every night for nearly a week," Harold said. "Your butler told me so."

"Yes, he's such a dear. I'll sorely miss him when he goes back to Des Moines with my grandmother. He's been in her employ for years."

Little did Harold know, Mr. Finch had been staying in the hotel looking for work when Grandma Nettie asked him if he'd like employment at their house.

Suddenly, Mr. Wilberforce stopped walking, Meg coming to a halt with him. "Is there something else, Mr. Adams, or are you going to keep making a nuisance of yourself?"

Meg's eyes widened.

Harold Adam's apple bobbed, and he wasn't even saying anything.

"Good. Since you have nothing else to discuss with Miss Brooks, good-bye." Mr. Wilberforce propelled them along with a brisk stride. She with her secret package tucked in her arm; he with a fishing pole case in his hand and her elbow looped through his.

Meg thought it the most romantic thing to ever happen to her.

Not once did she look over her shoulder to see if Harold was following them. From Mr. Wilberforce's tone, he wouldn't be.

Her Bissell salesman had really taken command of the situation and was now ushering her through the door of Durbin's Ice Cream Parlor as if it were an everyday occurrence for him. She wished it was, would be.

Once inside, Mr. Wilberforce showed her to a red-and-white striped oilcloth–covered table. He pulled out a white lacquered wrought-iron chair for her. She sat, but she didn't let go of her package.

"I can take that for you, Miss Brooks, and set it on the floor next to my fishing pole."

"No thank you."

With an uneven smile, he teased, "You're guarding it as if it were the crown jewels."

Meg felt her cheeks heat up hotter than the tin roof on the feed and seed on an August afternoon. Her knees went a little weak. It was a good thing she was sitting down.

"Your cheeks are flushed, Miss Brooks. Are you going to faint?" His voice was low and deep, suggesting something wicked.

Unbidden, Meg raised one hand to her cheek. "That's an excellent idea. But unfortunately, I don't think I am."

"Well, that's good to hear. Because if you did, you wouldn't be able to have an ice cream."

Mr. Durbin approached the table and Mr. Wilberforce looked directly at Meg. "What would you like, Miss Brooks?"

Staring at his mouth, she thought: *I'd like for you to kiss me again.* Instead, she said, "I'll have a vanilla fizz."

"Make that two," Mr. Wilberforce said, relaxing into his seat.

Meg tucked her feet together at the ankles, held her back straight, and rested her package in her lap—both hands on it for safekeeping. She glanced at Mr. Wilberforce, who occupied a chair more deliciously than any man she knew. His shoulders filled out the back while his elbows rested on the arms. He'd removed his hat and it rested on the tabletop.

Gazing at the soft turn of his mouth, Meg wished she were alone with him instead of in an ice cream parlor. Mr. Wilberforce's attentiveness flattered her, yet perplexed her. Here she hadn't seen him for several days, then he runs into her on the street and asks to be in her company. If she didn't think it was an act of fate . . . she'd think he'd planned it.

"Miss Brooks, you're looking especially nice today."

Meg looked down at her attire. Just a plain white shirtwaist and a somber black skirt. She'd wanted to be inconspicuous when she went into Plunkett's mercantile and talked to Hildegarde. "I am?"

"Yes, you are."

Mr. Wilberforce leveled his eyes on her. Why was he looking at her that way? She saw light smoldering in the flecks of his golden green eyes. Was it a gleam of pleasure? Of passion and yearning? Yet, she de-

126

tected sadness and regret. Regret over what? The unknown confused her.

The potency of it all, the prolonged anticipation of what he really thought of her, was almost too much for her to bear.

Their ice cream sodas arrived and Meg was forced to place her package on the table so she could daintily grasp the tall glass and straw without being gauche. After all, she couldn't exactly slurp through the straw with no hands.

Mr. Wilberforce hadn't yet touched his ice cream. He let the glass rest in front of him. "I was admiring your handiwork in the lobby, Miss Brooks. I even took one of your Pilsens to smoke."

"You did?"

"Yes. I'd never tried one before. An excellent choice."

"Thank you."

"Do you have other ideas in mind?" He finally brought the straw to his lips and sucked in the fizzy soda. Meg watched, mesmerized, not thinking at all about his question. Only after he stared at her, did she blink out of her light entrancement.

"Ideas?"

"For the lobby."

"Of course." Meg stirred her soda with her straw, collecting herself. "If I had the time and funds, I'd refurbish the entire area, giving way to brighter carpets and bolder window curtains. I think it's a little too dark in the lobby. Almost gloomy. Do you find it that way, Mr. Wilberforce?"

"Now that you mention it, yes." He leaned back in his chair. "Your expertise never ceases to amaze me. You know furnishings, cigars, and fishing."

Fishing. Meg held on to a frown. She didn't want to classify fishing with imaginative experience on decorating and knowing how to pick out a fine cigar. "Fishing is the least of my talents." Then she bit her lip. She didn't want him to think she preferred casting to drinking tea in a tearoom. Surely if he figured that out, he would be put off.

"But a talent nonetheless," he said with a smile.

Then again, since he'd brought it up . . . he must think it an asset. She had better continue the subject, only slant it toward him. "I noticed you've been out fishing the past several days. How has your luck been?"

"The rainbows are rising to caddis. I've yet to see a brown trout."

"They like cover," Meg said, trying to put him at ease for not having hooked a brown. "The large ones typically run to a brush pile or undercut bank so you have to be careful or your leader is apt to tangle."

"Yes, I found that out."

Dragging her fingertip over the glass's dewy surface, Meg watched as water droplets rolled downward. "And what about you, Mr. Wilberforce? What are your talents?"

He looked nonplused for a moment, then said, "I'm a good salesman."

"Truly? It must be difficult."

"Not if you believe in what you sell."

"Have you been selling Bissells for a long time?"

"Since I was twenty-one." Then his expression darkened—as if he'd said something wrong.

"From the age of twenty-one is a long time. You must have a strong knack for selling things." She sipped on the fizzy soda with its creamy taste of melting vanilla ice cream. "Do you mind . . . that is to say, would you be offended . . . and you don't have to answer—but," she looked into his eyes, "how old are you, Mr. Wilberforce?"

When he replied, his tone sounded as if he felt older than he was. "I'm thirty-one. And you, Miss Brooks?"

Heavens, she wasn't keen on speaking her age aloud—knowing that she might as well put "old-maid" after the number. But how could she deny him when he'd told her his?

"I'm twenty."

He merely smiled as if it didn't mean a thing to him. Relief flooded her; she'd feared he might find her less than desirable if he knew she was an overripe apple on the tree.

They drank their sodas in companionable quiet for a while, Meg barely tasting hers. Her gaze kept drifting to Mr. Wilberforce, taking in the way he sat, the way he drank his soda, the way he looked with the sunlight shining on his black hair. On his shoulder. The way he effortlessly filled the parlor with his strong and masculine presence.

She thought she was the luckiest woman in the world.

"Miss Brooks," Mr. Wilberforce said at length, "forgive my asking at such a late date, but I was wondering if you have an escort to tomorrow's Fish Festival."

She had been hoping, wondering if, he'd ask her. She had no plans to go with anyone. Well, that wasn't exactly true. Nobody of the opposite sex—she'd told Ruth and Hildegarde she'd go with them.

"Why, no, Mr. Wilberforce, I don't." She made the words sound casual as a Sunday afternoon, but in reality, her heartbeat was thumping double-time.

"Then would you be able to accompany me?"

Her breath hitched, but she kept her euphoria dignified when replying. "I'd be delighted to go with you."

"Splendid. You pack a picnic lunch and I'll bring my fishing pole." He gave her a disarming grin. "I want to see you cast a line, Miss Brooks."

"Really?" She could barely give him a return smile, thinking it odd he would want to watch her fish. Then again, some men didn't mind a woman who was the outdoors type. Mr. Wilberforce might very well be one of them. At that thought, she grew anxious. It had been some time since she'd waded out into the water. She enjoyed the sport. "Well . . . all right, then. I'll look forward to it."

As Mr. Wilberforce walked her home, Meg thought she was the most fortunate woman in Harmony.

Standing at the gate of her house, Mr. Wilberforce tipped his hat to her and said he'd see her in the morning at eleven o'clock. When he was gone, Meg hugged her package and hurried up the walkway and into the house.

Once upstairs in her room, she set the parcel on her desk and sat in the chair. Glancing at her diary, she smiled. Maybe, just maybe, *soon* she'd be picking out wedding invitations like Johannah Treber.

In class, some months ago, Mrs. Wolcott said that a lady almost always found her heart's soulmate when she wasn't looking. That was how she'd found Mr. Wolcott. They were a perfect couple in Meg's eye. He was as handsome a man as they came; and she was awfully pretty and gay.

Meg hadn't been looking for Mr. Wilberforce. She accidentally found him in his room. She wondered if she needed what was in the jar after all. Because Mr.

Wilberforce had asked to escort her to the festival tomorrow. That meant a whole lot. On the other hand, one should never take anything for granted.

Pulling the string on the package, Meg peeled back the wrapping. Inside a nest of brown paper laid a jar of Princess Bust Cream. Guaranteed to make plump, full, rounded a bosom that was before scrawny, flat, or flabby.

Meg unscrewed the lid and put her love life into the hands of the Seroco Chemical Laboratory.

Chapter

8

Gage and Meg strolled side-by-side and took in the festivities of the annual Fish Festival—the official kick off to the fly-fishing contest.

A band, its members wearing white uniforms with sharp creases, played from the gazebo in the town square while accompanied by a full brass section. Barrels of beer and soda fountain–size freezers of ice cream were disbursed in lines where men jovially patted each other on the back and children ran circles around their parents. A group of boys played leapfrog while a foursome of young girls laughed behind their hands at them.

With Gage carrying the picnic hamper and his fishing pole and tackle, he didn't have a free arm to offer Meg. But maybe that wasn't such a bad thing after all.

He was a reporter and his job was to get information. In this case, any leads from Meg about her brother. Gage had to find out what he could about a rigged contest. That's why he'd asked her to come

with him. The part he was playing was that of a staid
Bissell salesman, Vernon Wilberforce.

Why then, was Gage thinking of today as more than
an assignment?

Maybe because the woman by his side was more
than just any woman. She was the most refreshingly
different woman he'd ever met. From one moment to
the next, she kept him guessing. What would be her
thoughts? Her gestures? How would her laughter
sound? Her smile look?

Tried and true and quite ladylike?

Or whimsical and without restrain?

He preferred the latter. He suspected she did, too.
Why she felt the need for pretense, he couldn't
fathom.

"Oh, look," Meg said, pointing. "How very clever
of them. I like that."

Gage followed her gaze to the hardware store.

The local businesses competed against one another
for the best fish display in their town square
storefronts.

Kennison's hardware store suspended a seven foot
long, crepe rainbow trout in the display case using
fishing line. The farm implement store touted a papier-
mâché fish of drab brown. The notary was decorated
with paper chains in fish shapes. And the secondhand
shop sported a giant speckled cutthroat in their roof.

"If our hotel was in the town square," Meg thoughtfully said, "I would have put up something really out-
standing. Like a fish totem pole. There's a
woodworker—Alex Cordova—who lives on the edge
of town and he not only makes furniture, he carves
totem poles."

Gage respectfully nodded. A fish totem pole would

have caught his attention. Such a woodcarving may have sounded odd, but Gage thought Meg was damn ingenious with her ideas. Given the competition she would have had this year had she been able enter, Gage would have voted for a totem pole over a papier-mâché fish.

"We shouldn't have any trouble finding a good picnic spot by the water. Most everyone is staying here." Meg shaded her gaze with the flat of her hand as she scanned the area. The profile she presented him was quite soft and feminine. The brim of a plain straw hat extended far over her forehead; it was unadorned except for a dark apricot-colored ribbon band that encircled the crown. He wondered why the hat contrasted so with the others she had worn. The statement this one gave off was simplicity and self-assuredness. It was completely unlike those gargantuan hats she'd worn previously with their blossoming flowers and bird wings and rosettes.

"I was supposed to meet my friends, Ruth and Hildegarde," she went on. "You remember them from the tearoom? Anyway, I wish I'd run into them so I could tell them there's been a change in plans."

"I wasn't aware you were supposed to meet up."

"Oh," she blurted, "well, nothing was *really* set . . . I mean, they won't mind my not being with them. Once I tell them I'm with you."

Gage could have sworn he caught her blushing. Normally, he would have liked knowing he could make a woman's cheeks color. Right now, he felt like a lowdown dog. He couldn't afford to let her get to him.

Kissing her once had been to charm her.

Kissing her twice had been because he'd wanted to.

Kissing her a third time would be tempting fate.

So Gage vowed he wasn't going to kiss Meg today.

"Miss Brooks, where is it your brother fished last year when he won the contest? Let's try that spot," Gage suggested as they continued to walk through the crowd.

"That would be where Evergreen Creek meets Fish Lake."

"Splendid."

As they walked past Durbin's Ice Cream Parlor, the Harmony Fire Department was giving a demonstration, "from the frying pan to the fire"—a pantomime of what went on in the station house dormitory seconds after the alarm was sounded. Since they didn't have brass poles to slide down, that part was improvised as the men swung on the ice cream shop's awning posts. Parked in front of the store stood their draft horse teams, the hook and ladder and polished hose carriage with a Button & Blake steamer gleamed beneath the spring sun. The firemen harnessed the horses in record time. Then safety net crew asked for a volunteer from the audience.

Guffaws and laughter followed when Harold Adams took the challenge as soon as he saw Meg approaching. He heartily waved while being escorted up to the boardwalk, his baggy pants and big white canvas cloth coat appearing too large for him.

"Hello, Margaret! I'm going to jump. Watch this."

Gage observed Meg cringing, and he hoped Adams would miss the net.

"Let's keep on going," Meg said, looking down at the tips of her shoes as if pretending she hadn't noticed the young man.

She wove her way through those lined up for turns at a fishing-for-treasure booth where a player dropped their line over the five-foot curtain and then reeled in their line, the hook having landed a penny prize.

Ahead of them, people cleared a narrow path and Gage wasn't sure why until the culprit bore down upon them. Somebody's bloodhound ran through the throng with a string of hotdogs in his chops.

Meg swayed to the right to let the dog pass—as if it were an everyday occurrence. Swerving to his left, Gage glanced over his shoulder to watch the bloodhound lumber off, hotdogs trailing in the grass behind his haunches.

"That was Barkly," Meg offered without Gage asking. "He belongs to Mr. Wolcott. Barkly does this kind of thing a lot—stealing, that is. Mostly food."

"I'll remember that," Gage remarked.

A group of five ladies, properly gloved and hatted and with parasols on their shoulders, came toward them. Gage recognized the pair from the tearoom. The other three he hadn't seen before.

Meg stopped, as did Gage, and they waited for the women to approach.

"Margaret, there you are," Ruth chimed.

"And Mr. Wilberforce," added Hildegarde. She grinned at him like a cat did at its cream.

Gage shifted his weight from one foot to the other. He stood under the shade of a maple, its young leaves not quite unfurled and translucent. He would have removed his hat—had he a free hand. "Ladies," he greeted.

Meg made introductions. "You know Miss Elward and Miss Plunkett. And that's Miss Johannah Treber, Miss Lucy Calhoon and Miss Camille Kennison."

"Ladies," he replied once more.

"We're on our way to have a picnic," Meg supplied.

The two women who appeared to be her closest friends glanced at each other, then nodded. As if there were some ritual secret passing between them. Gage wondered if any of them had ever been proposed to or had men interested in them. Although he knew he wouldn't have put any weight into a woman of their age not being married, many did.

Christ almighty, he hoped to God they didn't think that *he* was some kind of prospective . . . somebody for Meg.

"A picnic is so nice and wonderful." Ruth Elward gazed at him, giving him a wide smile.

Hildegarde added, "I do like a picnic. My mother says that eating with nature around brings out the best in a person."

"I agree," the young woman named Lucy concurred. Then she turned to Meg. "Margaret, you have to see Johannah's engagement ring. It's simply stunning."

Johannah held her hand out for Meg to examine the diamond on her fourth finger. "Yes, it's very lovely."

To Gage's discomfort, Johannah showed him her ring as well.

"That's some shiner," he mumbled, readjusting his hold on the handle to the picnic hamper. "Ah, Miss Brooks, I think we should be on our way."

"Oh, of course." Meg said her good-byes and they walked on.

Gage noted Meg smiled to herself as she kept in stride with him.

"What are you thinking, Miss Brooks?" he asked.

She gave him a turn of her face, lips parted, teeth barely showing. "I just happen to like spring, Mr. Wilberforce. It smells nice."

Raising his brows, Gage pondered her words. Then he inhaled. Spring did have a certain quality to it. He'd never noticed.

The day had the warm mellowness of freshly mown hay and smelled like warm bread just out of the oven. Field grasses sprouted in the nearby vacant lots, as did dandelions, lamb's quarters, and wild mustard. They all perfumed the air with uniqueness. Something he wouldn't have noticed if it weren't for Meg.

It was a startling thought to Gage. He thought he noticed everything. Rarely a detail slipped past him. And yet, he'd never smelled a season until today.

Together they headed for the outskirts of the town square and onward toward Evergreen Creek. The small tributary ran parallel to Dogwood Place and beyond the lumber mill. Walking to Fish Lake wasn't much of a jaunt. A fifteen minute span of time, if that.

Soon, the rush of water came to Gage's ears. Meg walked up the high bank and just beyond a stand of cottonwoods. Wild yellow daisies grew in scattered patches along a blanket of low grass. The sky soared in shades of cobalt with tufts of airy clouds. White sunlight glimmered off the rippling surface of the lake, while the rush of reeds and cattails framed its far sides.

"This is the spot," Meg declared, going so far as to twirl in a light circle; the gesture seemed relaxed—as if she felt at home. "Here, let me take that from you." She reached for the picnic hamper with its blue-on-blue checked pattern. "You've been awfully nice to carry that. I could have."

"I wouldn't allow you, Miss Brooks."

She looked at him as if he were a chivalrous knight with some tarnish on his armor. "But I could have. I'm not breakable."

At that, he smiled. No, she most certainly was not. Although the color of her attire was a soft peach with folds and tucks and white piping on the long sleeves, she wore the shirtwaist and ruffled skirt with a fluidity and confidence he didn't normally associate with such blatant feminine garb. To him, she would have been at ease in a pair of trousers with suspenders, a white shirt, and a bowler hat.

The image intrigued him. More than it should have.

He set down the fishing pole and tackle, then removed his hat and ran his fingers through his hair. After Gage settled his short-brimmed hat back on his head, he folded his arms across his chest.

Meg took the checked cloth and snapped it open. The pale blues and darker checks muted as they floated down to the carpet of grass.

"There. You must be hungry," she said and went for the hamper.

Gage was hungry . . . very much so.

"I made tomato and pimento sandwiches and brought some bottles of Dr. Pepper." She knelt down and took out the food items, each wrapped in pieces of waxed paper. "I hope you like cherry cake with powdered frosting. I spread it an inch thick. That's the way my father likes it."

"Sounds good." And it did. But Gage's stomach usually regretted when he indulged in fare like this.

She spread everything out, even going so far as serving him. He took the plate and sat down.

A bee hummed through the air. Overhead a songster chirped. The boughs of trees seemed to whisper to one another. Not another human was in sight. It was just him and Meg.

If Gage didn't know any better, he'd swear this was

as good as it gets on the other side—that other side of the paper that people took for granted. Where a person only had to sit and read the words. Never think about how they got in the newsprint. Never wonder what would have happened if the story had never been penned.

Sometimes, Gage wished he could go back to those long ago days of not knowing, not dissecting and perfecting. Always wanting the facts. Trying to make things right.

"Mr. Wilberforce, did your father encourage you to sell Bissells? Was he in the carpet sweeper business like you?" Meg asked.

Slowly, Gage replied, "No."

"What then, if you don't mind my asking, did he do for a living?"

As the sun warmed his shoulders and legs, while he held a plate of food prepared for him by a woman who didn't know what a truth-seeker he was, he momentarily lost himself in thought.

His childhood came back to him, serving to remind Gage why he did what he did.

He'd grown up the only son of a respected Taylor Street family. His sister, Virginia, had been born six years after Matthew. By then, Matthew Gage Sr. had a solid foothold in the San Francisco stock market due to his gold mining speculation. It had been a rude awakening for Gage when he found out about the shrewdness of his father's business dealings.

When the Comstock went bust in 1880, his father's financial holdings hadn't been damaged. The thousands of small investors whose blind faith had bloated the value of certificates and whose endowments had been sucked away throughout the years, were the ones who'd suffered. For years, the little man had supplied the money for exploratory tunneling, for rising milling costs, for new equipment—while those in control raked everything off the top.

The knowledge had humiliated Gage.

"My father wasn't a nice man," Gage said aloud, realizing after the fact how personal a statement he'd just made about himself. Nobody but David West, his editor, knew the truth about what Gage had done after his parents' deaths. Many readers in San Francisco thought Matthew Gage was just a rich snob writing for a newspaper because he'd bought his way into the job. They didn't know the whole story. The real story. Because Gage would never write it.

"I'm so sorry for you." Meg's voice drifted to him. He grew vaguely aware of her hand on his, warm and comforting.

"Don't be, Miss Brooks. We all make choices. His choices hurt people." Gage damned himself for revealing so much. He never talked about himself, his family.

"But it must have been hard for you. What did he do that was so bad?"

Gage set his plate aside. Meg's hand softly left the top of his. "He took advantage of people." As he said it, Gage's gut tensed. That's exactly what he was doing with Meg.

But he wasn't—not really. Not for any monetary gain. He was fooling her so he could get his story. So he could expose a cheater, a liar. Serve the readers of *The Chronicle* a no-good person: her brother, if that turned out to be the case. And by yet again revealing another criminal, he silently said he was sorry for what his father had done.

The fact that he had loved his father, made it all the more painful for Gage to accept his father had been wrong.

He'd loved his father. Loved his mother. Loved the life he'd grown up in. But it had all been based on the misfortune of others. And he'd had no idea. Not until a week after their deaths; those who had been wronged began to speak out because Matthew Gage Sr. could no longer stop them from doing so.

Gage recalled the first time a shopkeeper had spit on his shoes and called him a swindler, just like his father. Several incidents followed. He'd been disliked by barkeeps, shoemakers, domestic workers, and the miners themselves.

"Last year, my father wanted to increase the room rates at the hotel and my mother asked him why," Meg remarked while opening one of the Dr. Peppers and handing the bottle to Gage. He took a slow sip of the drink as she continued.

"My father said he wanted to make more money so that he could build her a better house. She said that the one she lived in was just fine. But he wanted her to have a modern one with every newfangled amenity. She flat out told him she wouldn't feel right living in a house that was paid for by hard-earned money of others. He never did raise the room rates, but if he had, that wouldn't necessarily have been taking advantage of people, Mr. Wilberforce. Guests would have had the option not to stay at the Brooks House Hotel if they didn't want to pay an extra fifty cents a night."

The bottle of dark soda pop glimmered in the sunlight as she raised the neck to her lips. "Is that the kind of thing your father did?" Then she took a sip and waited for his reply.

What Meg had just said, was the nicest thing anyone had ever done for him. She'd offered Gage a way out. A kind of sweet and sentimental excuse. Too bad Gage couldn't tell her she'd gotten things right.

His father had known exactly what he was doing.

When his father's lawyer had read the will, Gage had been shocked to learn how much his father was worth. Close to a million dollars. But Gage didn't touch it. It was dirty money in his eyes.

Instead, he'd donated it to various charities and the miners' funds, all anonymously, as a way of restitution. If those who despised his father knew where the money had come from to fill their coffers, pride most likely would have prevented them from accepting the contributions. He'd given away his inheritance in the hope of finding closure for his father's ill-gained monopoly. What money Gage now had was hard-earned.

He sought redemption with each story.

This was why Gage took on the corrupt and dishonest and brought them to the public's attention, why he tried to expose them before they ruined others.

If he had been thinking clearly and smartly, Gage would have stopped his and Meg's conversation cold. Right now. Bring up her brother. Ask her about him. Find out what he could. Instead, he said, "Charging more for a hotel room and outright taking people's money are two different things. If I had known what he did, I would have told him it wasn't right. Just like your mother told your father."

"You sound as if it's your fault," Meg quietly spoke.

Shrugging with a half-breath, Gage looked at the lake's glimmering water. "In a way, maybe it was. My father wanted things for his family. I was his son. He wanted me to have the best. If I hadn't expected that, then maybe he wouldn't have done some of the things he did. I don't know. You can't change a person like that, I suppose."

Meg propped her Dr. Pepper next to the picnic hamper. "People can change if they want to. But I think it all depends on why they're changing. If it's to better themselves, then I think that's good. If it's to please others, then . . . that's not so good." She bent her knees and hugged them with her arms. "I'm afraid I have a confession to make, Mr. Wilberforce."

A confession? He didn't know if he wanted to hear it. He had so damn many of his own. The foremost: His name was not Wilberforce. And each time she said it, it became harder to hear.

"I hope you won't think any less of me, but I feel I must get this off my chest."

Gage arched a brow, waiting for her to drop the anvil.

Her words barely registered when she spoke them. "It's about the bellman's cart at the hotel."

"The bellman's cart?" he repeated.

"Yes, I'm afraid so." She looked directly at him from beneath the plain brim of her hat. "You see, I wasn't honest with you. I led you to believe that I was a little girl when I rode it. Well, that's not the truth. I only gave up riding on that luggage cart three months ago." She swatted at a dragonfly, then frowned. "I can see it in your eyes you're shocked. No more so than my very own mother. I promised her I would give it up and I did. I have to also say that I do have bouts of wanting to hop right on it again when I hear the afternoon whistle as the train pulls into the depot.

"You just don't know the thrill it is to have the

wind blowing in your face, knocking off your hat, and letting your hair down while speeding over the cobblestones. But I was told afterward that my behavior was vulgar. I suppose I could take hearing the term *vulgar* from my mother. But when my friends agreed . . . well . . ." She sighed.

"It shouldn't have mattered that I stopped because it was getting me nowhere riding the darn thing where men—I mean," she hastily rephrased, "nowhere where respectability—was concerned. So I gave it up. That and a few other things I used to do."

Gage was so caught up in her story, all he wanted to do was look at her. The light in her eyes, the way loose tendrils of copper hair fell around her temple.

She barely took a breath. "You're disappointed. I knew it. I shouldn't have confessed. But I'm not sorry I did. If you want to go back to town, we can."

She must have really thought riding a bellman's cart unforgivable in a man's eyes, because she went as far as moving to stand. He caught her by her slender wrist and said almost too loudly, "No."

"Mr. Wilberforce?"

"No, Miss Brooks. Don't go. I'm glad you told me. I don't think you're a," he grinned in an effort to make her smile, "vulgar person for riding on a luggage cart. In fact, I think that you should do it if you want to."

Her eyes filled with relief. "Really?"

"Yes." He let her go and she put her hands over her heart.

"You honestly don't mind? I can't believe it."

"Believe it."

"Well . . ." She giggled—as if by accident because she quickly changed the tone of her laughter to a more sophisticated sound. "I'm happy I told you about it, Mr. Wilberforce. You just don't know *how* happy. I feel so much better."

Gage's smile weakened as a knot of conscience twisted in his gut. If he confessed vulgarities of his own, she wouldn't be happy. She would tell him to go to hell faster than he could explain. And then *she* would leave.

Deception came with a bitter taste.

But the truth would cloud over the only ray of sunshine he'd seen in a long, long time.

What woman needed bust cream when the man of her dreams didn't care if she rode a luggage cart?

Meg couldn't believe she'd paid cold hard cash for a jar of something so frivolous. Well, she wasn't going to use it anymore. She'd slathered some on last night—twice the recommended amount, and this morning she measured exactly the same. Not a single fraction of a fraction bigger.

But why did she care?

Mr. Wilberforce wasn't put off by her former behavior. That meant she wouldn't have to be so careful to do and say the right things anymore. The very idea was so *freeing*. However, she should still be cautious and not just outright go back to her old ways. She'd hate to go back to square one.

For the moment, keeping on an even keel was best. Stay with things she knew he approved of. And right now, that was her showing him how she cast a fishing line.

They'd finished their lunch and Meg had put the plates away while Mr. Wilberforce assembled his fishing pole by the edge of the water.

He called to her over his shoulder. "Miss Brooks, I've just about got this ready for you."

"I'll be right there, Mr. Wilberforce."

With the picnic basket in order, Meg went to rise from the checkered cloth. Her shoe tip caught on her petticoat hem and she grimaced when the rip of elastic at her waist snapped free.

"Hells bells," she murmured beneath her breath, using one of Wayne's favorite expletives before she caught herself. More annoyed than flustered, Meg managed to stand and clutch the slipping petticoat before it fell to her ankles. Looking left and right, then keeping an eye on Mr. Wilberforce, she went to a thicket of willows. Once concealed behind them, she kicked off her petticoat and left it there—promising herself to buy new ones so this would never happen again.

"Miss Brooks, where are you?"

"I'm right here, Mr. Wilberforce," she replied and came out to meet him at the creek. Surely he wouldn't notice she was without her undergarment. She didn't think men noticed much about women's clothing. Not like women. Because she'd noticed every single detail of Mr. Wilberforce's attire.

Never had a coat and trousers looked finer on a man. He wore his with such ease and masculinity, he took her breath away.

After lunch, he'd removed his coat and had rolled up the sleeves of his fine white shirt. The sleeves had tiny pleats at the shoulder seams that gave the impression of broadness—not that he needed any superficial help. His vest was scarlet—a startling color; its back panel silk. When he'd first removed his coat, she'd been tempted to touch the shimmering fabric with her fingertips to see if it felt as cool and sleek as it appeared.

The pockets of his deep navy trousers had front buttons in the slashes. She'd noticed them when he'd casually slipped his hand inside to bring out a type of mint or something like that. She wasn't sure. She had an uncle who used to chew on soda tablets after every meal. But of course a man like Mr. Wilberforce wouldn't need such a remedy. With his rock-hard physique, his stomach would be made out of cast iron.

Once at the bank, she examined the fly rod Mr. Wilberforce held. He'd strung the line nicely and knotted a fine hook where he'd attached a Prince Nymph that hadn't been stripped.

"If you'd like, Mr. Wilberforce," she began, not wanting to sound superior to him—after all, he was a fishing expert since he was entered in the tournament, "I could strip a Prince Nymph for you."

"You could what?" He looked down at her, his black hair falling over his temples, the chiseled outline of his chin not so set.

"The fly. It's too fuzzy. I'd like to tone it down."

The hook dangled, practically brushing over the wet embankment, and he pulled up the silk line and grabbed the fly. "Sure."

She looked in his tackle box, picked up what she needed, then trimmed down the lure. "There. That ought to do."

Glancing at the water's sluggish current, she pondered her next move. Since she didn't have her waders, she decided to fish from the pebbled bank. She preferred wading out to fish, but that would mean hiking up her skirt.

"All right," she said while taking the fishing pole

from him, "I'm ready. Is there any type of cast you like to see?"

Mr. Wilberforce walked alongside of her as she assessed the best point in which to cast her line. His voice came across clearly and self-assured. "I like all casts."

Meg laughed. "But not all casts are right for all situations." Then she bit the inside of her lip, fearing he'd think she was trying to impress him so she quickly added, "But you already knew that."

"Of course."

Without further conversation, Meg began to move the rod as if it were a magical wand. She became a musical conductor and the water became her orchestra. Some people connected with a fly rod the first time they held one. Meg was one of those rare people. She didn't understand why or how it had happened. It just had.

She'd been eight when she first tried. Her father and Wayne said the way she moved the silk line—it all just looked right from the beginning. If she thought about it, she couldn't cast. But if she watched the water, then her silhouette on the bank, she could get everything to flow.

The warmth of the midday sun raised the water temperature enough to awaken the trout. They nipped at the water's surface, leaving little rings and the occasional *plop* of a splash. Caddis flies danced here and there over the water; a wren dipped down to catch a quick drink before flying off.

After a half dozen casts, a rainbow struck the fly and she reeled it into the bank. Flapping and flopping, the fish's scales shimmered dark speckles. Contrary to its name, rainbows weren't all that colorful. Brook trouts were a sight better to look at.

"Isn't that beautiful?" Mr. Wilberforce declared.

"Not as pretty as a brook trout," Meg remarked, enjoying the way they shared a camaraderie about fish.

"I wasn't talking about the fish, Miss Brooks. I was talking about you."

Meg lifted her chin, then straightened to stand fully. Her pulse raced with an unnatural swiftness. When she spoke, her voice betrayed her by sounding faintly breathless. "Me?"

"Never have I seen such an exhibit of . . ." His green eyes darkened, as if he were grappling to come to a conclusion—and was annoyed with himself because he couldn't. "I can't believe I can't think of the right words. Me. I'm never at a loss for them. It's my j—"

He cut himself off with a scowl.

With every nerve-ending focused on the man beside her, Meg waited for him to complete his thoughts. "Yes, Mr. Wilberforce? It's your what?"

Shoving both hands in his pockets, he looked out at the water. "It's not anything about me, Miss Brooks. Watching you cast that line is like seeing something done for the first time and realizing that all the other ways are insignificant because they are too mechanical. I'm amazed. Truly." Then turning toward her, he urged, "Show me some more."

Chapter

❦ 9 ❧

"If your brother is half as good as you at casting, Miss Brooks, there is strong probability that he fairly won the contest last year," Mr. Wilberforce commented as Meg flicked the fishing line over the water.

"No doubt about it, Mr. Wilberforce," she replied without missing her stride.

"*But*—if people wonder," he went on, "if they talk, then don't you think there is a chance he *did* cheat?"

"No I do not." Meg's elbow tensed with Mr. Wilberforce's last words and she missed her mark.

Not having been snapped back by a flick of her wrist, the fly floated on the downstream current. Meg barely looked at the fuzzy lure as she lowered her lashes to hide the hurt in her eyes. Suddenly, all the pleasure left her.

They'd been having a wonderful time. Why did he have to bring up Wayne? And in a manner that was defaming.

Yes, people talked about her brother winning that prize money as if he hadn't honestly earned it. But he

151

had. And he'd done so with spectators in plain view. A person couldn't cheat when he had an audience, much less do anything to rig the contest. Meg had stood on the bank herself and watched him. She'd seen with her own eyes the number of brown trout he'd caught.

"Miss Brooks, I'm sorry if I said anything—"

"I'm sorry, too," she broke in, unable to bear any attempt at an apology that would be feeble at best. Clearly he had his doubts about her brother's integrity, like so many others in town.

A fish struck her bait and fought to get away. Having been distracted, her hand wasn't properly connected with the simple click reel. Rather than the line letting out, Meg was pulled forward by a small jerk. Just enough to put her off balance, causing her to take a few steps, and end up in the softly lapping creek.

Gaining control of the reel, she looked down. She stood in three inches of water that soaked her skirt hem. Cold seeped into the leather soles of her shoes and her stockings quickly grew wet.

"Give me the fishing pole," Mr. Wilberforce directed.

Meg did so and walked out of the creek. Her footsteps felt soggy as she made her way to the picnic blanket and sat down. The laces to her shoes lay in a wet knot and she began to work them free. She removed both, then in a discreet turn of her legs, she rolled down her stockings and slipped them off.

Sitting in a man's company with bare feet was a strong breach of etiquette, but Meg remembered the last time she'd sat too long with wet feet. Her toes had numbed and when she got home, she'd had to soak her feet in a warm foot bath to keep from sneezing. Ironically, she had also been with Mr. Wilberforce . . .

With a heavy sigh, she removed her straw hat and tossed it beside her. She was half-tempted to pull the pins from her hair. Her head ached at the scalp where the weight of her bun pulled. Disappointment wrapped around her as she settled back to observe Mr. Wilberforce reel in the line.

He managed to do a fair job, unhooking the fish, then coming toward her. Once at the blanket, he set the pole down.

Sincerity framed his mouth. "Miss Brooks, I wish you'd let me apologize."

"There's no need."

"Yes, there is." He paused, glanced behind her, then: "Wait here."

As if she were going anywhere.

Meg brought her knees to her chin and fanned the edge of her skirt up her calves a bit. Indecent. But right now, she didn't really care. She gazed down at her toes, watching an ant crawl on the edge of the cloth. Then her vision was filled with yellow. A floral explosion of yellow. A bouquet.

Yellow daisies.

"Allow me to apologize properly." Mr. Wilberforce bent to one knee. "For you."

Stunned, Meg barely moved. Then, hesitantly, she reached out for the flowers. "Thank you."

"They should have been roses."

Lifting her chin, she shook her head. "No. The daisies are perfect. I forgive you, Mr. Wilberforce."

The bouquet was a sweet endearment. Meg brought the flowers to her nose and smelled. Light, barely a scent, but wonderful.

As she lowered her hand, one of the daisies fell from the bunch and Mr. Wilberforce picked it up by

the stem. He leaned toward her; she leaned back a
little. The bouquet in her hand dropped softly beside
her hat.

"I could give you a hundred roses, and none would
be as pretty as you are today, Miss Brooks."

Then he raised the yellow daisy to her jaw and caressed her with the buttery petals. Meg's neck relaxed;
her eyes closed. The weight of her hair pulled and
then she felt Mr. Wilberforce's fingers sliding the
pins free.

She shouldn't let him.

But his fingertips massaged as they slipped hairpins
loose; the nape of her neck tingled and she sighed.
Her hair tumbled down her shoulders and her back,
in what was probably a wave of copper—made more
coppery by the high sunshine.

"I've wanted to see your hair like this again. Ever
since that first time in my room," he drawled close to
her ear.

Meg's eyes opened slowly. His face was mere inches
from hers, the daisy still in his hand, only now sliding
over the side of her neck. A question came to mind;
though she didn't want to know the answer if it was
contrary, she asked anyway. "You don't find the color
too . . . too red?"

"No. I like it." His breath tickled her cheek. "And
I like you."

He cupped her face in his wide hand, and touched
his mouth to hers. The kiss ebbed through her, stirring
her response. Shyly, her hand rose to his shoulder and
rested on the softness of his shirt. Beneath her palm,
the hard cords of muscle flexed beneath her touch.

The kiss changed, growing deeper. As if he were urg-
ing her to explore him. Meg moved up the tendons of

his neck and buried her hand in his thick jet hair. Silkiness teased her fingers. He smelled like coconut soap and spicy aftershave of exotic fragrance. The combination was heady; an intoxicating mix that made her want to lay back and kiss Vernon Wilberforce forever.

As he sifted his fingers through her hair, she held on to a shiver of pleasure when he stroked the nape of her neck. Then he traced the fullness of her lips with his tongue. She grew still. Startled. This was going beyond a simple kiss. A flirting kiss. A divine kiss.

This was sinful.

But Meg Brooks didn't really care. Not with the way he made her feel. This was too heavenly to describe.

Whether it was her idea or his, Meg found herself laying on the picnic cloth with her skirt caught on her knees and her legs bare. Mr. Wilberforce laid beside her, kissing her softly on the mouth. He ran his hand along the side of her waist, then downward across her hip where the gathers of her skirt bunched together. Then farther to her knee and bare leg. Gently, he grazed his fingertips over her skin; the light skim of his hand brought out gooseflesh.

Much to her regret, he broke their kiss to gaze into her face.

With a crooked smile, he teased, "Miss Brooks, I believe you've lost something again."

He'd found her out. She supposed there wasn't much chance of fooling him. After all, the thin layer of skirt didn't do much to disguise the fact she was missing something beneath it.

"I haven't *actually lost* my petticoat. It . . ." Words failed her. Even though he'd already seen her in this very predicament before, it didn't make things any more easy to explain.

A woman whose underwear habitually fell off wasn't a woman to be admired—not to mention, that being without it once was perhaps acceptable, twice, she looked like a floozy. "You see, I had a bit of an—"

"Accident," he finished for her, capping her words with a delightful kiss to her mouth.

She sighed against him. *He didn't care.* How could he when he kissed her like this?

They kissed for an endless entity in time. Meg grew overwhelmed. This was the single most passionate moment of her life and she was poised on the edge of something undefinable.

It was a mad moment.

A moment that would have been her undoing if Mr. Wilberforce hadn't suddenly stopped.

Staring into his scowling face, she asked, "What is it, Mr. Wilberforce?"

Exhaling, he closed his eyes, as if burdened. "I wish you wouldn't call me that."

"Your name?"

"Mr. Wilberforce."

Meg's breath hitched in her throat and caught on her lips as she said in a quiet voice, "Would you rather I call you Vernon?"

"I'd rather we . . . but we can't, so I think we should go back to town, Miss Brooks."

Then he sat up and raked his fingers through his hair, leaving his palms at his temple and his head in his hands.

"Do you have a headache, Mr. Wil—" She cut the name short.

"No, Miss Brooks. Just a pang of conscience in more ways than one."

Conscience? He meant scruples, surely.

Meg blushed, suddenly embarrassed. She shouldn't have let him kiss her for as long as she had. Or kiss her the *way* that he had. He'd had to be the one to put a stop to things and now it *did* look like she was a . . .

"Yes, it's been a long afternoon, a lovely afternoon," Meg said, "but I have to get to home and I'm sure you have to . . . do something, too."

Sitting up as well, Meg stood. Without a word, she went to the thicket of willows to retrieve her petticoat with the plan of discreetly tucking in her skirt folds while Mr. Wilberforce took his fishing pole apart. When his back was turned, she would put the underwear in the picnic hamper. No point in waving it like a flag—even though he already knew she wasn't wearing it.

When she went behind the trees, she looked at the ground. The green grass and stalks of columbine. The orbs of cottonwood seeds that had floated and landed here and there in white, spiky puffs. It was a wooded scene. An undisturbed one.

Because the petticoat of pristine white with the ruffled and ribboned hem was *gone.*

Looking around the area, she told herself she must not have left it where she thought. But after circling around the thicket twice, she had to accept the conclusion it had vanished.

Seemingly into thin air.

Distressed, Meg went back to the blue-checked cloth and sat down.

"What's the matter?" Mr. Wilberforce asked while putting his fishing pole into its case.

"Nothing." She wouldn't dare tell him.

Her gaze on his broad back as he turned to put his tackle box in order, she *wanted* to tell him. Tell him everything that was in her heart. How she felt about him. How he made her feel. Petticoats were such an insignificant thing when compared to the gamut of emotions rocketing within her.

But she couldn't speak. She feared his response. This was happening too quickly. Not even she understood it.

Meg reached for her stockings without bothering to ring them out. The clammy wet wool stuck to her skin as she rolled each stocking up her leg.

Maybe she'd catch a cold.

Because the ailment that was threatening her right at this instant was far worse. She could be love sick.

And if Mr. Wilberforce didn't catch it, too, Meg would have to put the bedcovers over her head and wish for pneumonia.

"Mr. Wilberforce," Mrs. Rothman greeted from behind the hotel's check desk. "Did you have any luck today?"

Gage fought back a smile. *Luck?* He'd been lucky enough to kiss Meg, but he'd been unlucky at keeping his emotions below the surface. Dangerous turf to be on. Ground he rarely walked. The harder he tried to ignore what was happening, the more he realized how much trouble he could be in.

He cared about Meg Brooks.

She wasn't just the sister of a man who could be a liar and a cheat, and he didn't like deceiving her. She was a woman with a range of emotions and feelings. She'd shown him many during the time they spent together. But if he let that get in the way, then he might as well quit writing. Because plain facts were: Sentimentality didn't have a place in journalism.

At least not the kinds of stories Gage wrote.

He had to keep up the ruse. He had to remain focused on why he was in town and what he had to do. If he didn't, Gage might as well tell his editor he was through.

With his fishing pole in one hand and his tackle box in the other, he strode toward the older woman and replied, "Indeed I did, Mrs. Rothman," in his false and lilting tone. "I was lucky to watch your grand-daughter cast and reel in fish. She's quite the champion."

"I could have told you that."

"I'm sure you could have," he responded. "I enjoyed her company today. She is a pleasure."

Mrs. Rothman looked at him, her eyes studying. "Do you really find her a pleasure?"

Gage stopped, puzzled. "What exactly do you mean?"

"Her speech, her actions, her manners. She's not really herself."

"I believe she is with me, Mrs. Rothman." Gage leaned his elbow on the counter and relaxed a moment. "She told me about the luggage cart."

"Really?" One gray brow lifted. "I'm delighted to hear that. I do like the unpredictable Meg better. She certainly didn't get that trait from Iris."

"I take it Iris is your daughter-in-law."

With a merry twinkle in her eyes, she laughed. "How did you know Iris was my daughter-in-law, Mr. Wilberforce?"

"I remember how my own grandmother referred to my mother. It was her tone of voice."

Mrs. Rothman's smile softened. "Is your grandmother still with us?"

"Sadly, no."

Gage traveled down a rocky road all of a sudden. Talking about his personal life opened him to discovery. Yet, he was reluctant to let the subject go. He'd been endeared to his grandmother. They'd often corresponded with one another until she'd passed away when he was in college. He'd taken her for granted until now when Mrs. Rothman reminded him of her. How much he missed sparring with his grandmother and reading the wizened wit in her letters.

"How old are you, Mr. Wilberforce?"

Pulled from his memories, Gage didn't flinch when he answered, although he suspected Mrs. Rothman wanted him to. "Thirty-one." He wondered how old Wilberforce really was.

"And still a bachelor."

"Afraid so." The truth rolled off his tongue easily enough, but it left him cold. The truth, lies—they were mingling. There seemed to be no beginning or end to either. He hated leading this kind old woman down a fictitious path.

"My husband and I married when we were both twenty—Margaret's age. I was a late bloomer. I suspect she will be, too. She needs to come into her own and not worry so much what other people think. Why," she said, removing a pair of spectacles from her face, "if I cared about propriety and all its silly rules as much as Iris did, I never would be able to be a fighter for the Cause, now would I? The time has come for women to make their own way in this world. What is your view on the suffrage movement, Mr. Wilberforce?"

A suffocating feeling closed in over Gage. The question was a hard one for him to answer. As himself, he could easily say he had no objection to women having certain rights in public life. But would Mrs. Rothman believe Wilberforce? She already suspected he wasn't everything he appeared to be.

Gage met her expectant gaze, then gave her an answer he hoped would be satisfying. "There's nothing stronger than the human voice when its spoken en masse."

Mrs. Rothman's blue eyes darkened with emotion. "That was very well said, Mr. Wilberforce. Have you ever considered writing?"

The foundation of confidence he'd built in his ability to fool people was just cracked; albeit a hairline fault, it was a fault nonetheless. If he wasn't careful . . .

"A time or two," Gage replied while pushing away from the desk. He headed up the stairs, feeling her watchful eyes on him as he departed.

Fully clothed, Gage reclined on his bed, an unlit cigar at the corner of his mouth, and his hands folded over his chest. He had half a mind to lift open the window and light the smoke. But he suspected Mrs. Rothman made inquiries, asking the help if any rooms smelled like burnt tobacco. He didn't want her snooping in his. It was hard enough to keep things hidden on maid service days.

The day had been over hours ago. He should have gone to sleep. But he wasn't tired. He kept thinking about Meg. About being with her today on their picnic. Then he thought about her grandmother.

Then he thought about himself. Where he saw his life headed.

Gage didn't devote time to who or what he would be in ten more years. He'd always assumed: a journalist, a muckraker. One and the same. It was all he knew. All he desired to do with himself.

His thoughts meandered as he laid quietly in his near dark room. The only bit of light coming in through the window was that of the moon. Sprawled in disarray around him were his fishing books and notes. After watching Meg cast a fly rod, Gage knew he was a goner. He'd be found out as soon as the contest got underway. He was no fisherman.

And he was fast becoming a lousy liar.

He never should have said what he had about considering writing to Mrs. Rothman. Too personal. A damn dead giveaway if ever there was one. But he liked the spunk and all-out confidence Meg's grandmother projected. She made him aware of things he didn't think about.

Her views were rarely portrayed in the papers— no help from Gage either. She'd make a good story. Especially since the newspaper he wrote for seemed to be undergoing a change in direction in this first year of the new century.

The Chronicle's style of yellow journalism had slowly been made over since its extensive coverage of the Spanish-American War. After an armistice had been signed two years ago, the front page had been progressively dropping the more objectionable features. Fewer and fewer were the scare headlines with excessively large type in black. Photos without significance and fake interviews were also fewer in number. Gage's style had survived simply because he wrote the truth, no matter how hard it was to swallow.

But Gage was beginning to wonder . . . was the

stark truth really what readers wanted? Gage had stripped many people bare, revealing their illicit dealings; the stench was starting to stick with him long after the fact.

His first editor had wanted him to write about ordinary everyday life: white picket fences, rose bushes and gardens, homey houses, ladies who bought Bissell carpet sweepers, men who worked for their community, ministers, dogs, cats up trees—all the little idiosyncracies that were the daily slice of apple pie in Americana.

All those things he'd told himself were insignificant.

Well, maybe they weren't. Stories like that could make a person feel good. He could have used one right now. He wasn't feeling all that great about himself.

If Gage learned one thing today, it was that he could no longer pretend this fly-fishing article was just another story to be written. He had to either get on with his investigation or get out of it. If the accusations about Wayne Brooks proved to be false, Gage would drop the whole thing. If they were true . . . It was time to talk with Oliver Stratton. Gage didn't want to unnecessarily hurt Meg.

She made him feel worthy of her company. And she didn't even know who he was. She liked him for him— or the *him* he showed her. What would she think of the real Matthew Gage?

The answer was one Gage didn't want to speculate. He'd had the door closed on his face too many times before.

Chapter
❧ 10 ❧

Meg woke up Sunday morning feeling awful. Her heartbeat fluttered as if she were soaring high on a swing, and her pulse tripped whenever she looked at the standing vase of yellow daisies on her night bureau. She laid in bed with her chintz coverlet up to her chin. A sneeze tickled her nose. At least she thought it would be a sneeze. Nothing happened. She was coming down with a bad case of something. She just knew it.

But what she was getting couldn't be cured by Dr. Porter.

She was in love.

Honest to goodness real love.

And she was . . . *miserable*.

Meg dragged herself out of bed. Maybe she was wrong. Being in love was supposed to feel wonderful. Maybe she really was getting pneumonia.

As Meg sat on the edge of the bed, she put her hand on the bottom of her foot—Warm, not cold. No pneumonia. Then again, she felt feverish. For good measure, she made herself shiver. Yes, definitely feverish. She rose, went into the bathroom and snatched the thermometer.

Trudging back to her room in her nightgown, she pursed her lips over the thermometer and sat back down on her bed.

What was wrong with her?

She'd wanted to find a man and get married. Well, she'd *found* a man. Vernon Wilberforce. She never expected to feel something for him. In all her fantasies of romance, love hadn't really been a part of the picture. The frame had been surrounded by a doting husband, a house, and children. The very essence of domesticity. That love would play into the scheme of things . . . well, she just hadn't prepared herself.

Removing the thermometer, she read the mercury. Normal.

But it could rise at any second.

Meg set the thermometer by the daisies, her fingers absently brushing the yellow petals. She smiled. Then she frowned as soon as her stomach flip-flopped. She pressed her hand to her ribs where it felt like the wings of a thousand butterflies danced.

Yesterday, those daisies had done her in.

She had to find out for sure if there was any cure for this love sickness of hers. She'd go see Mr. Wilberforce this morning and take a long, hard study of him. Maybe he wouldn't look so appealing. He had to have faults. Things she didn't particularly care for about him so if he didn't return her affection, she wouldn't be crushed.

Character weaknesses. She didn't like when he used words like "By gum" and "I'll be jiggered." At times, he seemed to be forcing them. Like he would forget, then remember to say them. In any case, they didn't fit with the sound of his deep voice.

And another thing, he really did have a weak stomach. She suspected as much yesterday, but had discounted the fact because he was just too virile looking. However, confirmation came when on their way home from the Fish Festival, they passed a variety of food booths that her uncle would have avoided. Mr. Wilberforce was just like him. He couldn't tolerate "sinful" food because he suffered from dyspepsia. Unappealing.

Then again . . . she didn't really care about any faults he had. She had hers, too. Nobody was perfect. She wasn't. Far from it.

The picnic had been heaven and perhaps she was putting too much into it. The day had kind of passed in a haze. And after he'd kissed her, she hadn't fully come back to reality.

He'd said he liked her. Well, just *who* did he like? Margaret or Meg? Even she was getting them mixed up these days. What if she showed him Meg's true colors? Would he still say the things he did to her?

After dressing in the first shirtwaist and skirt that her hand touched in the clothes wardrobe, Meg hastily put herself in order. Which, now that she thought about it as she walked the boardwalk to the hotel, wasn't her very best effort. Definitely a Meg influence—*she* didn't overly worry about appearances.

Gazing at her reflection in the window glass of Treber's men's store, Margaret was dutifully horrified that her hat sat crooked on her head and finger curls had come lose from pins; gossamer spirals of copper bounced on her shoulders. She had forgotten her gloves and parasol; also her handbag. Not that she had any need for calling cards. Mr. Wilberforce already knew who she was . . . Or did he?

Meg took the porch steps to the hotel just as Mr. Wilberforce exited the front doors. Standing back, she looked up into his face. Cleanly shaven, his jaw was set and determined; an unlit cigar rested between his lips. He wore a suit coat and tie, the vest beneath a shade of blue. In his hand, he grasped a black case.

Her Mr. Wilberforce appeared to be going out on a call. Off to sell some Bissells. She wanted to sigh with pride. In the face of the contest and all the readiness it took to prepare, he wasn't going to shirk his job responsibilities. Such devotion overwhelmed Meg.

"Mr. Wilberforce," she said with a soft exhale. She brought her hand to her cheek. Her skin felt overly warm. Hot—but not from any fever.

She really was in love.

"Miss Brooks." His eyes narrowed as he passed his gaze across her. Of course he was staring at her hat and lack of essentials. "You look awful."

He needn't tell her that.

And if he was in love with her in return, then he'd have signs. But he didn't. That disappointed her. "If you felt the way I feel, then you would at least have misbuttoned your shirt or have your hair out of place."

"What's the matter with you?" he asked, taking a step down. He talked around the cigar in his mouth; it gave him a drawl she found fascinating.

Her reply was riddled with a hopeful tone. "Nothing that you couldn't cure."

He looked up the street a moment, appearing to be in deep thought. The outline of his profile intrigued her. The smooth and strong plane of his forehead beneath the brim of his hat. The way his nose was kind of crooked. The silhouette of his lips. Lips that she had felt against hers.

Gage grew aware of her stare on him. He turned to search her face. It was hard to forget about her. Hard to tell himself not to care.

Despite every reason he knew to steer clear, Gage brought his hand to hers and squeezed her slender fingers. Her skin was warm and felt as soft as sunshine.

A startled sigh caught on her lips. He wanted to kiss her. He wanted to forget Wilberforce and fishing tournaments and all the garbage that went with his job. For just one moment, he wanted to be Matthew Gage again. A man without any kind of occupational attachments. Just Matthew—who felt deeper emotions than those he let show on the surface.

He let her hand go and took the cigar from his mouth. "I don't know what cure you're talking about. So this will have to do." He leaned forward and kissed her. A slight and brushing kiss. Just enough to make him ache for more. That first warm taste made him desire her. He wanted to kiss her breathless. Give her passion and fire. But this was all he could let her have of Matthew right now. All he dared give.

Breaking apart, he looked into her face. He saw her in a way that he had never seen her before: vulnerable.

Christ. He didn't want to hurt her. Didn't ever want to see her cry because of him.

With a forced smile, he placed his cigar on her lips. She bit down, her pearly white teeth revealed. "You need this more than I do, Miss Brooks. I won't tell anyone."

He strode down the rest of the porch steps giving

the impression of a confident man. But inside, he was more torn than he had ever been in his life.

Gage led his horse to the dilapidated log house the clerk at Schutter Wagons told him belonged to Oliver Stratton and his mother. From the looks of the place, a prayer was holding the framing together. The roof sagged and the attached lean-to was barely wide enough to hold a clothes-washing basin and stock firewood. Only one window, two six-over-six panes, greeted visitors beside a door that didn't seem strong enough to hold back a breeze.

Tethering his horse to the branch of an apple tree and unhitching his writing case, Gage made his way toward the front door. He didn't have to wait to announce himself; a yellow dog came from behind the house. A scrawny looking thing, but with a nice wag to its tail and without a gruff bite to its bark.

The dog's noise brought a young man out of the barn. He wiped his hands on a red bandanna, then stuffed it into the back pocket of his faded overalls.

"Help you, sir?" he asked.

Gage gave him a quick study. Tall, thin, and with a light brown mustache on his upper lip that looked like a down feather. His humbling eyes, though, expressed a maturity his mustache did not. Deep-set and soft in their brown color, they looked at Gage straight on with no prejudgment, even though Gage wore a suit and shoes whose combined value could have bought this man a month of supplies. In that moment of sizing each other up, Gage made a decision unlike any he'd ever made before in his career as a reporter.

Gage backed his hat off his brow with his thumb. "Are you Oliver Stratton?"

The youth nodded. "Yes, sir."

"Are you a man of integrity?"

His brows lifted with slight confusion.

Gage clarified, knowing that Stratton could never comprehend how much of a concession it was for Matthew Gage—who trusted very few, to take a man on his assurance. "You just tell me if you live by an ethical code, and I'll take you at your word."

"Yes, sir." His head bobbed. "I pride myself on it."

Nodding, Gage said, "Good enough for me." Then he shifted his case from his right hand to his left and lifted his arm as an offering. "I'm Matthew Gage of *The San Francisco Chronicle.*"

Ollie took Gage's hand and shook it. "You're a long way from home."

"Yes I am."

Stepping back, Ollie asked, "What can I do for you, Mr. Gage?"

"The reason I asked if you were a man of your word, is because I've got to ask you for yours."

Ollie slowly tucked his arms over his chest. "You've got it."

"I'm staying in Harmony under the name of Vernon Wilberforce—an entrant in the fishing contest, but my true business is to expose any wrongdoing in last year's competition."

"Can't help you there, Mr. Gage. I didn't do anything wrong."

"Didn't figure you did. But I've heard you were expected to win. And when you didn't, quite a few people were outraged."

"None more so than myself." He motioned to the house. "Why don't you come on inside and I'll get you a cup of coffee."

170

"All right."

Gage followed Ollie; the dog followed Gage. Once at the door, Ollie opened it and called out in a loud voice, "Mother, there's a gentleman come calling."

"Who's that?" came a weary and aged voice from the corner of the room; Gage became aware of the fact the woman was hard of hearing.

The whole of the house was in one space. A kitchen area, sitting area, and sleeping area. Two beds, neatly made with threadbare quilts, occupied the far right corner.

Gage looked at the woman with silver hair and a face that sagged from years of exposure to the sun. Gage deduced she'd plowed a field a couple thousand times in her lifetime. She sat in a rocker by the pot-belly stove.

"This here is Mr. Wilberforce." Ollie enunciated the words clearly and within an inch of the woman's ear.

Gage appreciated the man's confidence. Ollie could have easily said he was Matthew Gage and he doubted the old woman would have remembered.

"I don't know any Wilberforce."

Her son patted her hand. "You just sit and we're going to talk a spell."

Ollie gathered two cups and filled them with coffee from a dented enamel pot that had been resting on a back burner of the stove. Then he motioned for Gage to have a seat on one of the beds.

"Sorry. It's nothing fancy. But we make due." Ollie sat across from Gage, cupping his coffee mug in his hands. "I don't know what all I can help you with."

After setting his cup on the floor, Gage opened his case and took out a pencil and notepad. "Just start by telling me about that day. What happened first."

Ollie proceeded to give him his account of last year's contest in which nothing out of the ordinary happened. "I never saw him fish, but I was told his cast only had one fly attached. Some people speculate there was more than one fly on his leader. It's a possibility, but doubtful. Caddis are small flies, but anyone with a trained eye can see if more than one is on the gut. Not to mention, it's only obvious when you snare two fish on the same line. You've got two hooks. That's against the rules and would have instantly disqualified him."

"Is there a way he could have stocked that lake? I spoke with Leroy Doolin at the Waverly hatchery and he claims he never sold Wayne Brooks any fish."

With a smile of conspiracy, Ollie said, "I went and saw Leroy myself. Got the same story as you. But one thing is for certain: Leroy Doolin has a tailwater trout fishery that lets him unload browns into Evergreen Creek."

"You think that's what happened? Wayne got him to let fish go?"

"Yes, but I've got no way to prove it." Ollie took a sip of coffee. "This is for true: Rainbows spawn so close to high river flows that their eggs are often washed away in comparison to brown trout in the local streams. But the contest takes place in early spring. Wayne Brooks didn't catch any fry—he caught adult browns, which don't even spawn until fall. Brown trout have only been around since eighty-three, so it surely does leave the mind open for speculation on how that big of population got into the creek during the contest."

Gage reached for his coffee. "Is there a chance there could be a bunch of them in one spot?"

"It's more than possible." Ollie's mouth fell to a grim line. "They like to hide in deep, slow water under overhead cover—usually in a logjam. So if Doolin did let all those fish go, they'd settle into one spot. And if you're fishing that spot, you've just hit the mother lode."

They talked some more on the subject; Ollie even brought out his pride and joy—a split-cane Leonard rod and Wheatley fly boxes with individual lids on each inner compartment. He'd organized his flies by what they were supposed to imitate rather than by color or size. Ollie proudly declared he'd been saving for three years to buy it all, then practiced another year before entering the contest.

"Is there anything else you can remember?" Gage questioned, rubbing his jaw with his fingers. "Like what happened the day of the lottery? How did Wayne get picked to have first choice of spots?"

"That I don't know. But I was witness to Gus Gushurst pulling his name. He won that spot on the square. I can only guess if he had a plan to begin with or not. But winning the lottery gave him the most advantageous place around that lake. I don't know if you've been out there, but it's right at the top of the creek. I did my practice casts there."

"What about the day of the competition? Anything out of the ordinary?"

Ollie grinned. "Ham Beauregarde had a case of barrel ache. He drank too much beer the night before. I limited myself to one. But some of them had quite a few."

"Some of them?"

"The other entrants."

Gage arched his brows in silent question.

"The night before the contest, all the entrants get together at the Blue Flame Saloon to talk bull." He shot a glance at his mother, obviously to detect if she'd heard him swear.

Mrs. Stratton rocked in her chair, smiling at her son when he looked at her. She plainly was unable to hear a word he said.

Folding over his sheet of paper, Gage asked, "Was Wayne Brooks at this get together?"

Ollie inhaled while pondering the question. "Come to think of it, I can't see him in that saloon. I don't recall him being there. Don't know why it never crossed my mind until now."

"Where do you suppose he was? At home?"

"Couldn't say. He might have been any place."

"Up at Waverly talking with Leroy Doolin?"

"Possibility."

Gage put his things away in his writing case. "I appreciate you taking the time to talk with me." He rose to his feet. "I'll let you know what I find out."

"I'd be grateful."

"Why aren't you entering this year?"

"My heart isn't in it, Mr. Gage. I worked for four years to get there. I had my chance and lost. I won't go back to be beaten again. If they play foul once, they can do it twice."

Gage didn't like to hear the defeat in his tone. Before he went to the door, he hesitated. "What would you have done with the money?"

Oliver Stratton got a wide grin on his mouth. "Live a lot better than I do now that's for true. I'd buy a new house—nothing highfalutin. Then I'd get some help around here and hire a nurse to watch over my ma while I'm off at work. I wouldn't quit digging for the gasworks. A man's got to pride himself on his labors. Those who sit back and do nothing but count their cash, I don't abide by." He scratched his head. "I'm the youngest of nine boys and Ma's my responsibility. Everybody else has scattered."

Gage nodded, understanding Ollie Stratton was committed to his mother for as long as she was living. He liked the boy, liked his outlook. "I wish you would have won."

"Me too. But it's water under the bridge."

"Not until I say it is." Gage set his coffee cup on the counter.

Opening the door for Gage, Ollie offered, "I wish you the best of luck in the contest, Mr. Gage."

"Thanks. I don't expect to win. But I do expect to find out what happened."

Gage left the house, untethered his horse, mounted and rode out of the yard. The yellow dog followed him to the road, then stayed behind.

A lot of thinking. That's what Gage had to do before he went off half-cocked. He believed every word of what Ollie Stratton told him. Gage was now fully convinced that Wayne Brooks had used illegal tactics to win. And Leroy Doolin played a part in the duplicity.

But the burning question was still: How to prove it?

And how to prove it without bringing grief to Meg?

She was connected to all this. He wanted to believe she didn't have anything to do with her brother's win. From appearances, she seemed innocent, yet she only reluctantly discussed Wayne's win. Perhaps she didn't want to dredge up the ill-will that had no doubt plagued her family last year. In any case, even with her not knowing how her brother had won, whatever he uncovered would cause her pain.

But if Wayne Brooks had rigged the contest, then Gage owed it to his readers to expose him. They expected him to air dirty laundry in his column.

Gage didn't like this assignment. Wished he hadn't told David about it. But David knew and told Gage to run with the story. Said it would show that not even small-town America was free of corruption.

Corruption? Or was it plain greed that made Wayne Brooks do what he did?

One thing Gage did know was, he could no longer deceive Meg. His feelings for her had begun to cloud his judgment. He'd have to come clean with her. Maybe she'd admit to being a part in it. Gage wouldn't write the article if she had been. But he didn't know how to fix the wrong without going to the authorities. Perhaps he could get the police to stay quiet and deal with the matter without going public.

If it weren't a thousand dollars at stake, and a hard-working man and his old mother going without, Gage would have walked away. But dammit all to hell. He had principle. And principle didn't let him go without fighting for the cause.

Harmony came into view and Gage rode across Sugar Maple Street to Hess's livery to return his rented horse.

Gage was tired. Not only physically. But tired of trying to right the wrongs in the world. Maybe he ought to retire. Maybe he ought to write those slice of life stories now. Let somebody else who had an iron stomach for dishonesty take over.

With his conscience weighing down his stride, Gage

rounded the corner and took Dogwood. He climbed the steps to the hotel and let himself inside.

Just what *exactly* had Mr. Wilberforce meant by giving her his cigar?

That thought had been with Meg all day as she rearranged the bric-a-brac on the hotel mantel around a new floral centerpiece. While she moved, her new petticoat crisply brushed her ankles. She hoped the petticoat from yesterday's picnic didn't end up any place embarrassing. Once, Mrs. Wolcott had had her petticoat and skirt stolen from her clothesline and the police had found them at the disposal bin of Nannie's Home-Style Restaurant and in the alley behind Dutch's poolroom.

But petticoats were neither here nor there. Cigars were the issue at hand.

Mr. Wilberforce's suggestion that she smoke his, even if he had been joshing, came with an implication on his part: He wasn't the pure gentleman he appeared. Because a true gentleman would *never* offer a woman a cigar.

Was it possible he could tell Meg wasn't a genuine lady? She never had admitted to having actually smoked a cigar, even though she had. Wayne had given her one. She'd lit up just to see what it was like, but she hadn't done very well with the Havana. The smoke in her lungs made her cough. But for the sake of being like the other college girls, she'd tried a few more puffs. And a few more. Until she'd been able to smoke half of the cigar. By the time she'd gotten the manner of puffing and rolling it in between her fingers down, she thought she was a regular spotted dog on a red wagon. A real in-the-know girl.

Of course she could never tell Mr. Wilberforce she'd enjoyed her cigar.

Turning around and placing her hands on her hips, she surveyed the lobby with a critical eye, then frowned and slumped into a plush velvet chair. The room was empty so there was no need to sit properly.

She checked the time on her chatelaine watch. A mere five minutes had passed since the last time she'd looked at the dial.

Sundays were slow.

Where had Mr. Wilberforce gone and why hadn't he returned yet? Meg vowed to wait for him to come back and ask him just exactly what he meant by giving her a cigar.

Absently, she put her fingertips on her lips.

She should have been angry he'd kissed her in plain view on a Sunday morning. But she wasn't. She'd wanted him to kiss her on a public boardwalk for anyone to see. She'd wanted him to tell her how he felt about her.

Heaven help her, she wanted him to be a part of her life.

Gage entered the lobby. Meg stood beside the check counter, as if she had been waiting for him. A worried smile curved her mouth, then fell into a fretful frown.

"Mr. Wilberforce," she said in a rush, leaving the station behind as well as the weekend desk clerk, who watched them with interest. Meg navigated them toward the fireplace in the sitting area. "I was beginning to think you'd fallen by the roadside. I was just about to visit the police department and tell them to send out a search party for you."

Nobody had ever worried about Gage before. In

fact, nobody had ever been waiting for him when he'd come home. God, it felt . . . nice.

Meg brushed the traveling dust from his coat arms with a quick swish of her fingertips. Genuine concern filled her eyes when she looked up at him, as well as a mixture of emotion Gage didn't care to define at the moment.

"My goodness, where have you been to sell those Bissells of yours?"

There was no reason to lie. Anyone could have seen him taking the road to Alder. "Alder."

"All the way over there? I think some of the local ladies in town would have been receptive to a new carpet sweeper."

"Sometimes a salesman has to stretch himself," Gage remarked, noting the soft color of her hair beneath the room's overhead light. The orbs of glass sputtered quietly; the hiss of wicks whispered.

"Well, I'm glad you came back unscathed." She stood taller. "It makes what I have to say easier. I couldn't exactly question you if you'd been hit over the head by a thug."

What was she talking about?

Placing her hands on her hips, she asked, "Why did you give me your cigar?"

Gage caught his laugh before it left his mouth, but he was unable to stop his smile. "Did you smoke it?"

Her eyebrows shot up in surprise. "That's not the issue."

"Did you?"

A long pause separated them. She softly bit her lower lip, wrinkled her nose and exhaled. Then finally: "Yes. What of it?"

This time Gage did laugh. "I knew it."

"You knew no such thing. I never told you I smoked cigars."

"You didn't have to."

"I suppose there are things," she shot back, turning the tables, "that you haven't told me about *you.*"

Gage stiffened. How could he tell her the truth when she didn't know what she was asking? She figured he was a slouch who gave women cigars because he liked to trifle with them. She had no idea who he really was. If he told her now—right here—she'd slap him for sure.

He had to return to his room, go over his notes, and figure out the best way to approach things with her. Do things slow and easy, without painful words.

"I would like to tell you about myself, Miss Brooks, but I'm tired. I've been gone all day with . . . no luck."

At that, her eyes softened. "You didn't sell any Bissells?"

"Ah, no."

"Not a one?"

"No."

"Well, that's too bad." Sincerity marked her voice and she lowered her hands from her hips. "But don't you worry. You'll do better. Selling things is very hard work. Not everyone has the talent for it. I know I don't. But you're very likable and you're honest, so you won't have trouble."

Honest? Gage bit back a grim curve of his lips.

"If you don't mind, Miss Brooks, I've had a long day. I'm going to retire to my room."

"Yes, I know you've had a long day." A sparkle glimmered in her eyes; her expression stilled and grew serious. She stood back, knitted her fingers together.

and rested them in front of her skirt gathers. "Have you eaten any supper, Mr. Wilberforce?"

"I was going to have an apple that's in my room."

"An apple? That won't fill you up. You're invited to my house. Come and have Sunday supper with us."

"Miss Brooks, the invitation is very thoughtful, but I have to decline." He searched his mind for an excuse she could accept. "I can't come because I have to . . . map out some new territory. My supervisor won't be pleased that I haven't sold any carpet sweepers. I must do my work first. You understand, of course. Business."

She solemnly nodded. "I do understand. Very much so, Mr. Wilberforce. But not to worry. I have an idea. You be at my house in one hour and everything will work out. You'll see."

"Miss Brooks—"

"See you in one hour."

One hour. That would give him enough time to pour through his notes, see if there were any holes that would give Wayne an alibi. For Meg's sake, Gage wanted to vindicate him. But he couldn't see how.

"One hour," she repeated. Her smile went straight to his heart. "And bring your traveling case."

"My traveling case?"

"Yes. This one." She pointed to the bag in his hand. "I want to look at all your Bissell catalogues. Pictures of carpet sweepers are so fascinating."

He had no opportunity to deny her. She'd already rushed out the hotel doors.

Mr. Wilberforce sat in the Brookses' parlor with teacup and saucer resting on his bent knee. His large hands dwarfed the delicate china. With all her mother's ferns and violets, and the soft furnishings, he seemed out of place. Yet she couldn't take her eyes off him.

He'd come.

She'd been able to plan everything in one hour, returning home just minutes before he'd turned the front bell. Barely enough time to go upstairs and freshen up.

Dinner had gone well. Grandma Nettie had joined them. Talk ranged from Grandma's hurrah and tambourine campaigns, to the upcoming fly fishing tournament. Mr. Finch sat at the table like he normally did; Meg wondered if Mr. Wilberforce would be put out by the "butler" eating with them. But he didn't appear uncomfortable, which made Meg love him all the more.

After dessert, they'd retired to the parlor. Grandma Nettie took her place in the sitting chair and worked on her needlepoint. Meg sat primly on the organ seat. Mr. Wilberforce occupied her father's chair, his case at his side. She'd taken it from him when he'd come through the door and put it in the parlor where the literature could be readily removed.

The tick-tock of the mantel clock with its fancy shaped case beat through the room—the only conversation. Meg nervously glanced at the hour. Nearly 7:00. The hands were never off; striking hours and half-hours on a cathedral gong. Her father oiled the mechanisms once a month with a chicken feather.

The crank of the doorbell startled Meg, even though she was expecting it to ring. All seven of them had agreed to come.

"Who could that be on a Sunday night?" Grandma Nettie inquired, lowering her stitchery.

"I'll get it," Meg exclaimed, bolting from her seat.

Meg swept the door inward.

The ladies had arrived. Right on time.

Mrs. Grayce Kennison. Mrs. Olive Treber. Mrs. Lulu Calhoon. Mrs. Fanny Elward. Mrs. Prudence Plunkett. Mrs. Crescencia Dufresne. Mrs. Edwina Wolcott.

"Do come in," Meg offered in her best hostess voice. "I'm charmed you could pay a call on us this evening."

Mr. Finch took the appropriate hats and coats, then Meg paraded the ladies into the parlor.

On their entrance, Mr. Wilberforce rose from his chair, passing his gaze from her to the ladies. His eyes landed speculatively, and with puzzlement on her; she reassured him with a soft smile. She took great delight in formally introducing him to the mothers of her school friends, her former schoolmate who was married now, as well as her teacher. The women in turn, gave her Mr. Wilberforce their courteous nods of approval.

"Ladies, please sit down and we can begin right away."

The seven of them took seats throughout the room. Meg remained standing, as did Mr. Wilberforce, the muscles in his jaw having tensed as if the ladies had stuck him with their hat pins.

"Mr. Wilberforce," she said with excitement, "you have these ladies' undivided attention. They've come to hear your presentation on marvelous carpet sweepers and, by the end of the evening, I'll bet you'll have sold eight of your top of the line models."

Chapter

❧ 11 ❧

Sweet Christ. She wanted him to sell carpet sweepers.

His gaze followed Meg's bright one, which was on his leather bag.

The case. The only reason he'd brought it was because he believed Meg really wanted to look at the pictures in the Bissell catalogue. Didn't women like to do that sort of thing? Pour over photographs and make out their wish lists?

Hell and damnation. He could see now that she'd cooked this evening up to save his hide—*Wilberforce's* hide. His earlier words came back to haunt him. Meg had asked if he'd sold any carpet sweepers. For simplicity's sake, he'd said no. Never dreaming she'd go to such extremes to help him.

She thought he needed help.

If she only knew how badly. But for all the wrong reasons.

The gamut of emotions running through him went from leashed misery to a muted stirring deep inside his heart. Meg Brooks had found him worthy of help-

184

ing. Never mind she thought him Wilberforce. It was Gage who had shown defeat this afternoon. Gage who'd walked into the hotel feeling the pull of those loose threads in his investigation tightening around him.

She didn't know the real reason for his disquiet. That didn't matter. All she had seen was a man down in his spirits and she'd taken the initiative to try and put him back to rights.

The tenderness welling in his chest was so profound, Gage had the strongest urge to take her into his arms and kiss her with gratitude. But he couldn't. Not now. Nine pairs of eyes were leveled on him. Waiting.

Meg resumed her seat on the organ bench, folded her hands in her lap, and said, "We're ready, Mr. Wilberforce."

With no choice but to go through with the ridiculous sales pitch—of which he knew squat—Gage withdrew the Bissell catalogue from his journal case. Absently, he flipped through the worn-edged pages as if he could draw inspiration from them.

One thing was on his side—he knew the company's history. He'd read the introduction in the bathtub. Four days ago he'd gone over his notes so many times he hadn't been able to think clearly. In an effort to sharpen his mind and rid it of fishing facts and notations about Wayne, he'd brought the Bissell catalogue into the bath and read all about Melville Bissell and how he had developed his sweepers.

Clearing his throat and sticking his forefinger into his collar in a manner he assumed Wilberforce must do when confronting nine observant women, Gage closed the catalogue and put it behind his back.

"Thank you for coming, ladies," he began, words

circulating inside his head like an old newspaper, dry and dusty. "The Bissell carpet sweeper company was founded in eighteen seventy-six by Melville Bissell, and is headquartered in Grand Rapids, Michigan."

The reddish-orange haired woman he believed was Mrs. Dufresne stared at him through wire bow spectacles perched on her thin nose. Without blinking. She appeared hinged on his every word.

Gage forgot where he was, then had to recover. "Uh, Mr. Bissell's wife, Anna, grew frustrated with the sawdust that embedded itself in their carpet. You see, Mr. Bissell used to be a crockery salesman and their store connected to their home so he had to walk back and forth and he tracked in sawdust . . . obviously from the store." He swallowed, not liking the way that Plunkett woman was eyeing him as if he'd exposed a hole in his trousers.

"I don't abide sawdust," Mrs. Plunkett remarked with the sourness of a lemon candy—minus every drop of sugar. "My Hy tracks sawdust footprints on my carpets all the time when he comes in from our mercantile. He has no consideration for the trials we women have to go through to keep our homes in shipshape order."

"That's why you need a new sweeper, Mrs. Plunkett," Meg warmly interceded with a glance at Gage. "So you can collect those hard to pick up shavings."

Meg's smile wrapped Gage in an invisible warmth—and filled him with a sense of obligation. He felt he owed her his best shot. When all the bull from the evening was over, and the ladies marched out armed with their hats and coats, he was going to tell her the real reason he was in Harmony.

Mrs. Plunkett made a noncommittal *humph* in the

back of her throat over Meg's comment about a new sweeper.

Gage proceeded, walking in front of the center-table. "Mr. Bissell's ingenious design was a success and word quickly spread about his invention. People began to ask him where they could purchase such a sweeper for themselves. And the rest, as they say"— he tried to interject an iota of melodrama—"is history."

The Elward woman laughed. *He hadn't been funny.* She wore so many beads and jeweled ribbons, she made a jangling noise when she dabbed her nostrils with her pink handkerchief.

Undaunted, Gage said, "Mrs. Rothman, you may find it interesting to know that in eighteen eighty-nine, following Mr. Bissell's untimely death, Mrs. Bissell stepped in and took control of the company."

"Yes, Mr. Wilberforce, I was aware of that," Mrs. Rothman replied without a missed stitch in her needlepoint.

Damn. He'd hoped to draw the conversation out. Now what? He had to look in the catalogue and actually try and make a carpet sweeper sound enticing. He'd rather face a nest of hornets. And from the unhurried study Mrs. Plunkett gave him, she'd be more than willing to stir up the hive.

Removing the booklet from behind his back, he opened the cover to the table of contents and skimmed the list of models. Randomly, he picked the Grand Rapids to showcase first.

His discomfort was like a steel weight. He held the book up so they could see. And he could see over the top to read the description because he didn't know diddly.

"Bissell's Grand Rapids is the most famous of the Bissell's, generally accepted as the standard of the line. It contains the patented Bissell Broomaction—the only device invented which makes a sweeper self-adjusting to every kind of carpet—"

"How does it perform on hardwood floors?" came the question from a skeptic.

Gage cringed. *Mrs. Plunkett.* He would have liked to plunk her out the window. She had an attitude worse than an editorialist with a case of writer's envy.

"Just ducky," he replied, trying not to grit his teeth.

Fortunately, the trio on the divan appeared to have some faith in him. Mrs. Treber. Mrs. Kennison. Mrs. Calhoon. None of them looked at him as if he didn't know spit from shoe polish.

"This particular model," he woodenly went on, "has our automatic reversible bail, which holds the sweeper always firmly on the carpet."

"Bails are the bane of my existence," Mrs. Plunkett announced. "The bail on our Prize model Bissell is broken."

It took all Gage could muster not to lunge at the woman and knock the wind out of her. She was fast spoiling his pitch. "Madam," he enunciated in a voice so stiff with pleasantness, he could have rung the starch out of his words, "you should report your malfunction to your salesman."

"The salesman was my husband, the nincompoop. He exchanged the carpet sweeper for credit. It was already two years old. I told Hy he had gotten the short end of the stick with his deal, but what was done was done. And I'm made to suffer for it."

Mrs. Wolcott spoke up. "Prudence, perhaps my husband can fix the sweeper for you. He's very mechanically inclined. He made the clock that hangs over our parlor fireplace."

Mrs. Plunkett wrinkled her nose. "The clock that's a zebra's backside with the wagging tail that ticks the minutes?"

Her chin lifting, Mrs. Wolcott wouldn't buckle under to the barbed remark. "It's quite accurate. It was one of his wedding gifts to me, and I'll cherish it always."

"My Johannah received a bridal gift from my aunt on my mother's side," Mrs. Treber chimed in. "A tea service entitled Spring Butterfly. The handles on the cups are the most delicate china butterfly wings you'd ever see. The saucers are ashes of roses, alabaster, and teal. With gold around the edges. They're simply divine."

That's all it took. One mention of a tea service and the room hummed with excitement like a beehive that had been invaded by a bear.

Pitchers, platters, dishes, servers, cruets, vases, trays, tureens, celery holders, finger bowls, jelly dishes, pickle jars; figurines in silver, porcelain and cut glass; art glass; embroidered pillows; memory books and paintings.

The women rattled them off so fast, their voices were like those of auctioneers. Each trying to out-do the other; each new item bringing "oohs" "aahs" and a fast change into the next thing to be gushed over. Even the pragmatic Mrs. Rothman succumbed to the fever.

The collar on Gage's white Oxford shirt moistened with sweat; he had to clamp his jaw tight to keep it from ticking. He was trapped in feminine bedlam with no escape.

Some minutes later, Meg stood and called the parlor to order. "Ladies, as much as I'm enjoying our discussion, we owe it to Mr. Wilberforce to give him our full consideration." To Gage, her cheeks flushed from the animated talk of women's paraphernalia, she said, "Please proceed." Then she sat back down.

Their amusement having died from their eyes, the ladies stared at him once more. Gage's mind floundered. Maybe he ought to mention flatware and duck out of the house as soon as they were preoccupied with what patterns it came in.

Instead, he fingered the catalogue pages and stabbed his forefinger between two sheets of the paper. He chose the carpet sweeper on the left-hand side of the page to continue with. "Thank you, ladies. Next is our . . ."

Over the next half hour, he went through every single model. He talked up rubber frictions, rubber furniture protectors, pure boar bristle everlasting brushes, cases of popular wood and wood veneer, the advantage of cyco bearings—*whatever the hell they were*—and no noise or oiling, pans that opened at once by an easy pressure of the finger, trimmings that were nickeled, and spring dumping.

When he was finished, his underarms were damp and he could have used a stiff shot of bourbon. But he had a new respect for salesmen. It was a horror of a job. And from the looks on their faces, he hadn't impressed a single woman. Not even the sympathetic ones.

Closing the catalogue, he nodded his thanks. "If you don't mind, ladies, all this talking has made me thirsty."

Gage quit the parlor, went through the dining room

and into the kitchen for a much needed glass of water. The butler, Finch, looked up on Gage's intrusion. He sat at the table reading a newspaper spread between the salt and pepper shakers.

"Did they get too much for you, Mr. Wilberforce?" Finch queried with a grin. "You're looking a little soggy."

"I could use some water."

"I'll do you one better." The butler stood and disappeared into the pantry; he came back with a bottle of brandy. "For cooking purposes," he amended after Gage lifted his brows.

Finch took two glasses from the cupboard and poured a splash of the amber liquid in each one.

With a nod of thanks, Gage took the glass and knocked back the brandy in one swallow.

"Tough job. Selling things for a living, that is," Finch commented, taking Gage's empty glass and setting it in the sink.

Gage thought about what he really sold: printed words. He had always been tough on people to get at the truth. Maybe he'd been going at it wrong all these years. Just make them sit through a Bissell sales presentation and they'd be spilling their guts before he ever got halfway through, just to get him to shut up. But he didn't say that. Instead, he simply said, "Somebody has to do it."

"I suppose." Finch leisurely sipped his brandy and sat back down to glance at his newspaper.

Folding his arms across his chest, Gage asked, "What rag are you reading?"

"*Montana Herald.* I believe it's printed up near Helena." The butler wet his fingertip with a quick press against his tongue, then turned the long sheet to the next page. "The only newspaper in town. It doesn't have any local interest pieces. Kennison's baseball team is without a star pitcher this year after Will White ran off with Pearl Chaussee—that stage actress who was in town early March playing Cleopatra in *Antony and Cleopatra*. The show only ran two nights because the Women's League of Harmony voted it was unconstitutional for a woman to display her legs in a pair of tights in public. I find that newsworthy."

"You do?"

"Don't you?"

Gage shrugged. "Women in tights have never bothered me."

"I wasn't referring to Pearl Chaussee. The newsworthy part is Kennison's Keystones needs a pitcher who can burn up the catcher's glove. Opening day is only two and a half weeks away." Finch took a sip of brandy. "I think a newspaper should advertise for a man who can throw strikes."

As Finch's simplistic ideas rolled around in Gage's mind, Meg came into the kitchen. She appeared somber and with almost an imperceptible note of apology on her lips.

She quietly spoke. "Mr. Wilberforce, you may return to the parlor now."

With a rake of his left hand to brush the hair from his temple, Gage followed her.

The parlor was empty except for Mrs. Rothman who'd remained seated in the same chair she had occupied during his presentation. On his arrival, she stilled her hands and said, "I'm sorry, Mr. Wilberforce."

Sorry for what?

The room had cleared. He didn't have to write up

192

any orders. Although, he was somewhat slighted that his efforts hadn't produced at least one sale of a carpet sweeper—he'd done a reasonable job, if reading catalogue text counted for something—he could also walk away thankful his livelihood didn't depend on Melville Bissell's modern apparatus.

From the look on Meg's and Mrs. Rothman's faces, they pitied him his failure.

"Ladies, I assure you it's all right that the others have left." To console them in some small way and make them believe he was disappointed, he added, "I wasn't at my best this evening. My fault things didn't go better."

"But you tried so hard," Meg said, her tone sympathetic. "If it's any comfort, the ladies thought you very charming."

Mrs. Rothman laid down her needlework. "I heard them say so myself, Mr. Wilberforce."

"They've never said that about King Merkle or Orvis Schmidt when they've delivered their pitches," Meg reflected with optimism. Then with a frown added, "but they've always bought something from them. Why is that?"

"Probably because they make the product sound invaluable," Mrs. Rothman pointed out. "They could talk a duck out of its feathers—not that that's a trait to be admired."

"No, it's not," Meg agreed. "I'd rather have a salesman who's unassuming instead of self-glorifying."

"There's always next time, Miss Brooks." Gage put the Bissell catalogue back into his case, wanting to forget about the sweepers.

"But you did make one sale this evening," Meg said

with promise. "I have decided to purchase the Grand Rapids model."

Gage stilled. "You needn't do that."

"Oh, but I want to. Grandma and I are going in half-and-half on the cost. Neither one of us are very fond of housework—" She cut herself short as if what she said was taboo. "That is to say, housework would be made faster if one had a top of the line model carpet sweeper helping them whisk over the rugs."

"Miss Brooks, I don't want you spending your money because you feel like you need to help me with my sales."

"But I want to."

"I'd rather you didn't."

He had to talk privately with Meg before he left her house. Words of explanation were few in his head. How could she understand the why of things? That she couldn't buy a carpet sweeper from him because he didn't really sell them. That he thought Wayne Brooks didn't measure up. All she would hear was he thought her brother was dishonest, and that he was using her to discredit him.

Whichever way Gage chose, it would be hard for Meg. But he sensed she was the type of woman who wanted the truth, no matter how raw. Her emotions would be just as ragged. He hoped he was prepared to soothe her. He didn't handle hysterics well, or tears. He was better with swearing and damning his soul to eternal hell.

Gage needed to get Meg alone, but asking Mrs. Rothman to leave the room would be inconsiderate. And Wilberforce had been anything but thus far.

"Miss Brooks," Gage began while grasping the handle to his case, "would you accompany me to the verandah?"

Her cheeks blossomed a floral pink as she nodded. She apparently thought he wanted to get her alone for amorous reasons. His throat went dry and the muscles in his legs tensed. He felt like scum. Right at this moment, Gage wished he really was a Bissell salesman.

Meg went ahead of him and led the way to the door. As they stepped outside, darkness enveloped them. They walked on the verandah and to the railing. The night air was unseasonably warm for April.

Gage disregarded the chirp of crickets, whose songs were an invitation for lovers to cuddle on a porch swing. Instead, he set his case down and turned to face Meg.

"Miss Brooks . . . Meg," he amended, having wanted to call her that a dozen times. Wilberforce wouldn't have, but Gage would. And right now she would find out he was Gage.

"Yes?" Her face tilted up toward his. The lights from inside the parlor sifted through the lace curtains and bathed their shadows in soft yellow. He could make out her face, her features. The heaviness of her eyelids and the length of her thick lashes. Glistening eyes, their color muted by night. The way her full mouth had no bow to the upper lip, its shape still soft and inviting.

If he were the despicable wretch he'd been accused of being many times, he would have kissed her. Maybe there was something redeeming about his character after all.

Meg smiled at him.

Then again, maybe not.

He took her face in his hands, tilting her chin toward his mouth. Then he lowered his lips over hers and kissed her. Her breath mingled with his . . . sweet and tasting slightly of apples and spices from dessert.

Gage slanted his mouth fully over hers, deepening the kiss and pulling her close to his chest. She lightly laid her hands on his shoulders. Slipping his hands to hers, he captured their delicate softness and brought them around his middle. She complied, holding on to him as he held her while he explored her mouth with his.

How slight she was. Shirt buttons and a woolen suit coat against near-sheer linen and lace. Body against body.

Splaying his fingers, he ran his palms down her waist and to her hips. The fabric of her skirt felt like satin next to his fingertips. Everything about her was feminine. Her touch; her smell. She wore no store perfume that he could decipher. The light scent that touched the air was pure Meg; sunshine, wildflowers, and a trace of rebellion.

What would she be like if she let herself go? Gage wondered.

If she were to put the proper Margaret in her hope chest for good and let the radiance of Meg shine through?

The snippets of true personality she'd showed him, he honestly adored. The Meg he wanted smoked cigars, cast a fishing line, rode on luggage carts. She was like a summer rainbow in his stale world of dark clouds.

Cupping her face once more, his thumbs traced a path across her jawbone as he lifted his mouth from hers and stared into her face. His fingertips grazed her skin, then downward on either side of her neck. Her skin was warm; the pulse at her throat beat as unevenly as her breathing. Moist lips remained parted, waiting for him to kiss her again.

The innocence of her expression sobered him. Christ, what was he doing?

Not what he should have been doing.

Talking. Explaining. Confessing.

Although the night was warm, Gage felt chilled as soon as he put an arm's length between himself and Meg. Puzzlement filled her eyes, tearing into Gage's heart. He would have liked nothing more than to be her Mr. Wilberforce at that moment, but he could not.

Instead, he forced himself to say, "Meg, there's something I want to discuss with you."

"I already know." Her whisper was throaty.

Gage couldn't fathom how; much less why she would have allowed him in her house tonight if she'd known. "You do?"

"Yes." Compassion etched across her face. "The way you kissed me told me everything." She looked down a moment, then at him. Her eyes glistened. "It's hard for me to come right out with it, but you gave me courage after you faced those ladies the way you did and tried your best. So I have to tell you now because I might never be feeling this brave again."

Brave? Brave for what?

"Meg, you don't have to tell me anything."

"Yes I do. Right now. Or I might never be able to." Licking her lips, then snagging the lower one with her teeth, she blurted, "I love you, Vernon."

Before Gage knew it, she'd raised herself on tiptoe, kissed his cheek and had twirled to head for the door.

Precious seconds passed where Gage stood, stunned. Then: "Meg, wait."

But she'd closed him out. The door had slipped into place and he'd heard the latch lock.

Gage remained rooted in the darkness. Alone. Meanings and consequences sinking into him.

She uttered words to him that he'd never heard from a woman. Never mind they were spoken to a man whose name was not his. It was still Gage who she felt this way about.

I love you, Vernon.

She'd given him her heart, and he'd give her grief. How could he tell her now?

Gage rode to Waverly the following morning rather than practice his casting. The competition was set to begin a week from today; he only had seven days left to learn how to fish. Maybe he wouldn't have to get to know Evergreen Creek and its surface tension, what insects hatched when, which fly to use—wet or dry depending on the temperature, and how to anticipate the fish's behavior by studying water.

There was an outside chance he could prove once and for all whether or not Wayne Brooks had come to the hatchery.

The idea hit him last night around three in the morning. He hadn't been able to sleep. His mind had been full of Meg: her feel, her touch, her body, her mouth, her words.

"I love you, Vernon."

He had to remind himself over and over, she hadn't meant them for him. Not for Matthew Gage. If she knew who Gage was, she never would have declared such a sentiment.

Even knowing this, he couldn't help wanting her to mean it. For him.

But how could he ask her to feel anything at all for him but contempt? Once she knew who he really was, she'd hate him. No more so than Gage hated himself for lying to her. The bitter battle of telling the truth weighed him down. Bogged his thoughts. Kept him from focusing.

When he'd come to town, he never had expected any of this. Never had expected a woman to fill his heart. Now he was going to make her miserable. He wished he could take all the hurt from her.

Unable to sleep, he'd spread his notes around him, going over them dozens of times and trying to put them all together. Nothing made sense. There was nothing concrete, just a lot of hearsay. Yet Gage felt the guilt.

At one o'clock, he'd turned down the light and laid in bed fully dressed. Resting his back against the bed frame, he'd stared into the darkness and reflected how he came to be the man he was. He was thirty-one and not fit to live with. He obsessed over details. He couldn't leave anything to fate. He had to know the why of wrongs.

For ten years, he'd chased whispers in whirlwinds never knowing what he'd find out or where he'd end up or who he'd have to pretend to be. He was growing old with no memories that he could call fond. Love for a woman had never lived in his heart.

Christ almighty, what a sad commentary on his life.

He'd never had a sweetheart; he'd had fancy women.

He'd never taken a girl to a dance; he'd taken her to bed.

He'd never done the things a woman like Meg Brooks wanted from a man. Courting and cooing. Love words. Expressions of desires. Talk of building a life together. Settling down.

Maybe he didn't have it in him.

Maybe he didn't want to find out.

By three o'clock, he knew what he had to do.

Chasing thoughts from the night away, Gage exhaled and reined into the yard of the hatchery. Leroy Doolin stepped out of the shack he worked in; beyond the grounds surrounding the outbuildings lay dozens of pools. Evergreen Creek wound its way from Harmony to here, then up and beyond into the mountains.

"Vernon Wilberforce," Doolin greeted with more than a hint of irritability. "Didn't expect to see you again."

Not bothering to dismount, Gage rested his forearms on the pommel of his saddle. "Mr. Doolin, I asked you once before if you'd sold brown trout to a man named Brooks."

"And I told you no, I did not." Doolin wasn't a very large man, and when he spoke his denial, he straightened as tall as he could with a puff of indignance filling out his chest. Something was there that Gage didn't quite believe. In the eyes, in the coloring. The way the irises widened into the gray color.

"Let me describe him for you anyway, Mr. Doolin. Perhaps it will jog your memory." Gage proceeded to describe the man in the photograph he'd seen on the center-table in Meg's parlor last night. He was a gutter dog for using the image to further his investigation, but he was doing this for Meg. He wanted to be proved wrong.

Gage was sure the man in the studio portrait was Wayne Brooks. He looked like Meg in many ways; same skin tone, jawbone, nose and forehead. In the gallery setting, Meg sat on a chair and her brother stood behind her with one hand on her shoulder. When Gage had gone to her house, he'd never intended to use her invitation to his gain. But the photograph had been there, and he couldn't ignore it.

When Gage was finished with his description, Doolin shrugged. "No, sir, I have never seen such a man. Wayne Brooks or anyone else with his description and another name. I wish you would let this go, Mr. Wilberforce. I conduct delicate work here and interruptions from you fishing contest men are getting on my nerves."

"Fishing contest men?" Gage returned. "Has somebody else from Harmony been up here?"

"Just this morning." Doolin turned on his tall rubber boots and waved Gage off.

"Who was it?" Gage shouted at Doolin's retreating back.

The hatchery owner paused and looked over his shoulder at Gage. "Said his name was Ham Beauregarde."

Chapter

❧ 12 ❧

Never in her life had Meg told a man she loved him. She didn't know what possessed her to tell Vernon.

Meg had been presumptuous.

Margaret had been fainthearted.

So it was Meg who had done the talking, but Margaret did the running away. As soon as she'd spoken the words of love aloud, she'd had to flee and catch her breath. Thank goodness he hadn't rung the bell. She didn't know what she would have said to him.

Actually, she should have waited for him to say what he was going to say to her while they'd been on the porch. He hadn't been specific and she had jumped to conclusions. All he'd announced was he wanted to discuss something with her. Looking back, Meg realized telling a woman you loved her wasn't a discussion.

Maybe he didn't feel the same way about her as she did him.

But if that were true . . . Why did he take her into his arms the way he had?

The day was sunny and bright, but cool enough for Meg to wear her blue coat trimmed with gold braid and buttons. The mandolin sleeves set with double box-plaits from the shoulders gave the impression her shoulders were set and squared. When in reality, she really wanted to hunch over with regret.

Being in love wasn't easy.

Being deceptive was even worse.

Meg had decided this morning that she must tell Vernon just exactly who she was. Wasn't.

Margaret Brooks was a fraud.

Meg Brooks was the real her. But with that realism came undesirable traits. Or so she'd been told. Frankly, none of that mattered to her anymore. She had to be who she was or she would suffocate from trying to fit in. She just couldn't anymore.

She didn't like gloves or overdecorated hats or parasols. Or petticoats that showed a flirt of lace. Or tea and tearooms. Or polite, witty and oh-so-strained conversation. Or pretending like she was the epitome of perfect etiquette. She preferred swinging on the tire swing by Fish Lake and going for a refreshing dip, or drinking a glass of lemonade in her bare feet or reading the next chapter in her romantic book.

In the light of day, Meg couldn't believe she'd actually gone through with speaking words aloud that she had only recently dared to pen in her diary.

She didn't know what she'd say to Vernon the next time she saw him.

Well, that wasn't true. She would tell him that she wasn't sorry for being so bold by making her feelings clear and that if he returned those same feelings— which he must, surely *had* to by the way he kissed her—he needed to get to know who she really was. If he was receptive, she'd be the happiest woman in the world. If he was not . . .

Vernon had already left his room by the time she'd arrived at the hotel this morning. Putting the lobby in order had been easier with his absence. She hadn't had to look over her shoulder at the stairs and wonder when he'd come down and see her.

But she had wondered where he'd gone.

Surely not back to Alder. He'd tried his luck at selling there. Perhaps to Waverly.

Thank goodness Meg had an errand to do or she would have gone crazy waiting for Vernon to return to the hotel. Grandma Nettie had asked Meg to collect the hotel's mail and to see if she'd had any word from Mrs. Gundy. Final plans had to be made; they were going full steam ahead and chaining themselves to the White House.

As Meg walked to the post office, she felt a thousand different things at once: joy, fear, elation, nervousness. Everything looked new, seemed new. She was different. She was back to her old self.

Sunshine filtered through her transparent hat brim, casting her gaze in a pearly white. The whole world looked wonderful today. The trees seemed bigger; their leaves seemed greener. The sky seemed bluer; the clouds higher. Flowers that had begun to bud seemed more colorful; tulips and iris more plentiful than she'd recalled from last year.

Meg was in love with a man who made her insides flutter. The way Vernon made her feel, put Harold Adam's Apple to shame. How could she ever have considered a man like Harold as her beau? Considered marrying him and living with him the rest of her life? Thank heavens he hadn't come to call lately.

The post office came into view, a whitewashed building, located right on Sugar Maple Street, or as it was more commonly known, Main Street. Awning canvases of forest green added some character to an otherwise modest clapboard structure.

Meg let herself inside and went toward the postal grate to see Mr. Calhoon.

Mr. Treber stood at the counter engaged in a heated political conversation with Mr. Calhoon. Mr. Calhoon talked politics with anyone and everyone. Meg's own father could spend hours ranting and raving about the trust's and how they were ruining everything and how President McKinley was a schlemiel. On and on about how Bryan would have saved them all if he'd been elected president.

Waiting patiently for her turn, Meg couldn't help overhearing the two men with their raised voices.

"How can the trusts sell anything when they've got all the money to buy the property in this country?" Mr. Calhoon lamented. "There'll be a war between the trusts and the Socialists, let me tell you."

Mr. Treber, who dressed fashionably from head to toe—he did own the men's store in town—made a fist and aimed it skyward. "What really gets my goat is the latest talk from Washington. They're stirring up a pot of trouble. All this drivel of taxing incomes again."

Pointing his forefinger, he declared with a growl, "Any man who says he's from the Bureau of Internal Revenue, I'll avoid like the plague. It's pure folderol, that's what it is!"

"I thought we got rid of income tax in ninety-four. Only lasted one year, so that tells you it isn't worth salt. The very idea of the government taking our hard-earned money is absurd."

"This nation wasn't founded for religious freedom or freedom of the press or speech," Mr. Calhoon avowed. "No sir. What chipped off our ancestors to the point of going to war was taxes. The Stamp Act. Boston Tea Party."

He drew up to the metal postal grating and glared. "Taxation without representation."

"Scoundrels, every last one of those bureau men. Everything that the poor man consumes, we tax, and yet why aren't the rich taxed? I ask you that."

"I'd spit on an Internal Revenue man. Scallywags, all of them."

Meg gave an impatient sigh which got their attention.

"Oh . . . Miss Brooks," Mr. Calhoon said apologetically. "I didn't hear you come in."

Mr. Treber turned around. "Didn't see you come in, Miss Brooks."

"Yes, well, that's quite all right. Just so long as you'll allow me to interrupt for a moment so I can get the hotel's mail. And our residence mail, too, please."

"Certainly." Mr. Calhoon adjusted his visor and licked his fingertips as he began to sort through letters on the counter before him, then check the pigeonholes labeled: Brooks House Hotel and 215 Elm Street.

A moment later, he handed her several envelopes and one postcard from New York—her mother had written from the Clifton Hotel at Niagara Falls. A reproduction of the sprawling four-story hotel with its covered piazzas was on the front.

"Miss Brooks," Mr. Calhoon slid two more envelopes beneath the grill, "might I ask you to bring these

letters to Mr. Wilberforce? He came by twice yesterday but the mail he was waiting for hadn't arrived.
Mr. Seymour from Waverly just came not fifteen minutes ago. I can see why Mr. Wilberforce was so anxious. One is marked 'urgent' and I was meaning to
get to the hotel myself to deliver them but I haven't
had a chance yet and as long as you're here—"

"I'd be happy to do that for you, Mr. Calhoon."
Meg grew relieved, glad to have the excuse to seek
Vernon on an official capacity. This way it wouldn't
look like she was hovering. She took the envelopes as
if they were gold in her hands. "Good day."

"Miss Brooks," Mr. Calhoon and Mr. Treber said
together, then the two men continued their lively ora-
tion on the evils of the Bureau of Internal Revenue.

Meg walked away from the post office, the letters
for the hotel stowed without regard into her pocketbook. The two letters for Vernon remained in her
hand. She didn't dare look at them. Not yet. She
wasn't a snoop, really. It wasn't as if she were going
to open them or anything. She just wanted to see who
had written to him.

Urgent. Impressive. Nobody had ever written her a
letter marked "urgent."

Meg had to cross the street by Storman's feed and
seed, then traversed the alley behind the Blue Flame
Saloon. Without conscious thought, she stopped.
Standing close to the building's wall, she lowered her
gaze and looked at the letters.

The one marked "urgent" was from David West
and the postmark was, of all places, San Francisco.

She slid the top letter behind the bottom letter and
gazed at the return address which was penned in a

very flowery, feminine-looking script. Meg grew very still.

Mrs. Vernon Wilberforce
Flickertail Street
Battlefield, North Dakota

Mrs. Vernon Wilberforce.
Mrs. Vernon Wilberforce!
Mrs. Vernon Wilberforce!
Her eyes began to burn and she blinked rapidly in an effort to focus on the writing. The letters slipped from Meg's hand and fell in a slow, airy swirl like leaves onto the ground.
Mrs. Vernon Wilberforce.
The man she loved was already married.
Meg bit back a sob. There had to be an explanation. There had to. He would not have gone stepping out with her if he'd already been married.
Tears fell down Meg's cheeks, and she brushed them away with a trembling fist. Not her Vernon. He wasn't a liar. But then . . . he was a traveling man.
And those traveling men were so good at what they did. Travel from town to town and call women "girlie" and "bright eyes" and other things of an illicit nature. To a traveling man, each city was a new conquest. Her mother had warned her about them, her words came back to haunt Meg.
"Those men are a bold and bad breed, Margaret. If you ever look really hard at one, you'll see little wrinkles of knowingness at the corners of their eyes. And they smile all too readily. Too flexibly."
Meg tried to think if Vernon had wrinkles at the

corners of his eyes. She couldn't remember any. But
he was considerably younger than Ham Beauregarde
who definitely had them, the swine. And Hamilton
also wore one of those dastardly pinkie rings. Vernon
did not.

Sniffing and trying not to fall into a complete crying
spell, Meg didn't want to believe it.

Mrs. *Vernon* Wilberforce.

There was that chance. Oh, a very good possibility.
Of course. That explained it. Vernon was named after
his father—although he'd never told her that—but
she'd never asked, and so Mrs. Vernon Wilberforce
had to be *his mother.*

His mother. Yes. That's who she was. Wasn't
she . . . ?

Meg looked at the two letters that had fallen in
front of her feet. Precisely, in a puddle of the Blue
Flame's cast off dishwashing water. Crouching down,
she went to pick them up. They were wet so she shook
them. In the process, the glue seal on the back of the
one from his *mother,* loosened and the flap opened.

She hadn't done that on purpose. She never would
have opened the letter. No matter how curious.

Never.

But since it had been an . . . accident.

Meg guiltily gazed left and right, then stuck the letter from David West into her coat pocket. She sucked
in her breath and slipped the stationery from its bed.
The faint fragrance of apple blossom came to her
nose. Mothers didn't perfume the stationary they used.
Grimacing, Meg swallowed her unsteadiness.

She unfolded the single-folded letter to read the
words meant for Mr. Vernon Wilberforce, Bissell
salesman.

Coward. Liar. Vagabond. Womanizer.

The syrupy salutation broke down any reserve she had left. She gulped hard, hot tears slipping down her cheeks. The fat drops of her heart-wrenching sorrow plopped on the letter that began:

> *My Dearest Sweetums:*
> *I miss you more than you'll ever know.*
> *I wish you were with me now, my darling.*
> *Hurry up and catch all those fish so that we*
> *can be together soon.*

Meg couldn't read anymore. She could barely breathe. As distraught as she was though, a quiet and calm type of anger overtook the bitterness and feelings of deceit.

Vernon had some explaining to do.

With her heart pounding in her chest, Meg slipped the door to room thirty-two closed behind her. Her gaze traveled the contents of the room that she had been in once before. On that fateful day when she'd met Vernon and had gotten stuck beneath his bed.

Today the room wasn't neat and tidy the way it had been on his check in. The furnishings were still the same, but everything else was in a shambles. Paper everywhere. There was barely a single vacant spot for another sheaf. What in the world was he up to?

It was amazing how simple it had been to break into Vernon's room. Grandma Nettie had been conversing with a guest in the lobby—her letter not having arrived from Mrs. Gundy, and Delbert had gone to the train depot to see if there were arrivals for the hotel. Meg had purposefully waited until she'd heard the No. 4 blare its afternoon whistle. Then she'd snuck behind the registry counter, snagged the key to Vernon's room, and rushed up the stairs without anyone noticing.

Closing the door behind her, Meg walked through the cleared path that had been left on the rug. She now understood why Vernon had forgone having the housekeeper come to his room on a daily basis. Agnes only came once a week on Friday morning. He must tidy up before she comes, Meg thought. He neatens up all this mess because Agnes hadn't said a word about it. Meg had, very innocently of course, inquired once after the state of Vernon's personal effects.

Like what sorts of things he kept in his room, or what quirks it looked like he had from outward appearances. But the maid never said anything out of the ordinary was in view. Aside from his room being cleaned once a week, Mr. Wilberforce asked for fresh linens from Delbert on an every-other-day basis.

At least he liked clean towels.

Now Meg knew why he never asked for housekeeping like the other guests. Vernon was slovenly.

She continued through the clutter and gazed at this and that. The typewriter at the writing desk held a sheet of paper on the roller. Meg furrowed her brows in thought. Where on earth had he gotten a typewriter? And what for? He wasn't writing up hundreds of orders.

There were books on the bed. At a glance, they were all on fishing. Fly-fishing to be exact. One with a worn cover and numerous bookmarks sticking out from it caught her eye.

The *New American Fly-Fishing Manifesto* by Arliss Bascomb.

What was all this?

Her intention had been to pull up a chair and be waiting for the bounder when he returned to his room. She didn't have the nerve to make a scene in the lobby so she felt he deserved a surprise attack. After all, that's what that letter from Mrs. Wilberforce had been to her.

Meg inadvertently stepped on a copy of the *Montana Herald*. There were several issues, their pages sloppy and not even folded. And another newspaper, *The San Francisco Chronicle*. Why did he have that? David West was from San Francisco. Who was he?

Beneath the desk sat a traveling case with his initials emblazoned on the worn leather: *V.W.* The bag was half-open and she saw the Bissell catalogue with order pads inside. This was *not* the traveling case he'd brought to her house last night. It was there, in the corner, *that* was the correct case. Why were there two?

If she hadn't been so distressed about the letter from Mrs. Wilberforce, Meg would have turned tail and ran. Foreboding came from the room. That and . . . *wait a minute.*

Meg walked slowly to the desk. There, laying curled on a handkerchief, was her hair. Several strands of it. She knew it was hers, plain as day. Copper. Such a coppery hue that was unmistakable. Why did he have her hair? Gooseflesh rose on her arms. Any other circumstance and she would have thought the find was utterly romantic. Vernon Wilberforce had saved her hair. But now, she was fearful of his motives.

Inasmuch as she felt she had the right to be here, she felt like a lowly peeper. She didn't like it, not one little bit. Seeing his private things didn't give her the satisfaction she thought it would. Instead, she felt ashamed that she was looking at them without his knowledge.

She might very well have left and confronted him elsewhere had she not seen the stack of notations—and a name, a name that was very familiar to her.

Lowering herself onto the bed, she picked up the notepad with its numerous pages written on and folded over. The top sheet, not yet wrinkled but with doodles on the headline, had several fragments and sentences. But the two words written on it jumped out at her as if they'd been penned in red. Both were underlined.

Wayne Brooks.

She skimmed the page.

Motives. Objectives. Probability for stocking the lake. Money spent. Waverly hatchery. Talk to fish farmer again. Monday. Read about speciality casts. How to control loop shape and speed to get different results.

Then once more below the notations:

Wayne Brooks.

She couldn't get her heartbeat to cease its fear-filled thumping. Why would Mr. Wilberforce have her brother's name written down? Those horrible and untrue words: stocking the lake.

Wayne had never been found guilty of cheating in the contest last year. Yet there had been many men who had believed otherwise because he'd won. And yes, it was suspect that he'd only caught brown trout in a lake that supported mostly rainbows. But Wayne wouldn't do anything deceptive. As much as she and Wayne had their spats, she knew his character was above low-down tactics.

Mr. Wilberforce was trying to dredge up trouble against her brother. This was almost a worse slap in the face than the letter from Battlefield. He was now trying to ruin her family's respectable name. Wayne might be a bit starchy, but he was the only brother she had.

With renewed offense, Meg flipped through the other tablet pages and found endless notations on how to fish and what different parts of the tackle did what—as if Mr. Wilberforce hadn't a clue. In between the third and fourth sheets of paper, a letter had been stored. She looked at the return address.

David West. San Francisco.

Having no qualms now at all about rifling through Mr. Wilberforce's things, she easily slipped the letter from the envelope and read:

> *Matthew—*
>
> *I've looked over the preliminary notes of your article on the fishing tournament in Harmony and I think an angle on how it was rigged will go over well with our readers. Who says modern cities are the roots of all evil? Hanky panky goes on in even the smallest of towns.*

Rigged!

The word shot from the page. So did the name "Matthew." Matthew Who? Not Matthew Wilberforce . . . or was it Matthew Somebody and Wilberforce was a nobody?

Meg turned and looked at the other items on the

bed. There was a writing box with initials on it as well. Only these were not V.W. They were M.G.

M.G.

Matthew G.

Oh my goodness. What horrible thing had she stumbled onto? Or worse . . . what had happened to . . .

A key fit into the door. Meg's chin shot up. Alarm knifed through her. But she had no time to escape as the panel swung inward.

Gage stopped just shy of entering his room as soon as he saw Meg sitting on the bed with David's letter in her hands. Her complexion was as pale as alabaster paint and her fingers quivered as she dropped the piece of paper and stood.

She knows.

He expected as much. He'd just come from the post office. Calhoon told him that he'd given Meg his letters. Two of them. Gage didn't have to guess who they were from.

Closing the door behind him, he set his journal case on the floor beside the jamb.

"Meg." He took a step toward her.

She ran to the fireplace and pressed her back up to the mantel. "Don't you come near me, you . . . you—whoever you are!"

Gage remained where he was, not wanting to agitate her further by going closer. He thought through how much she knew about him from the return addresses on those letters she'd just picked up. He didn't think she'd read them. But obviously she'd read David's letter addressed to Matthew Gage.

From the frightened look on her face, she was wondering who Matthew was. Dammit, he should have told her last night.

"Why do you have my brother's name written in your tablet?" she lashed out.

Rubbing the roughness of his chin, then removing his hat and tossing it onto the bed, Gage folded his arms across his chest.

"I'm investigating him."

"Investigating him! For what?"

"Illegal activities."

Her neck grew flushed and she put a hand to her throat. "My brother hasn't done anything illegal."

Gage calmly replied, "I'm trying to find hard facts to prove that."

Meg's voice was quiet, but held an undertone of icy fear. "Who's Matthew?"

Gage moved to the bed, bent down, and picked up David's letter, then began to straighten the papers that littered the coverlet.

Sinking onto the edge of the bed, he rested his elbows on his knees. "I am."

Her body stiffened, less from shock and more from indignance. "Why did you lie?" Then without warning and with pure terror in her eyes, she gazed at Wilberforce's traveling case. "What did you do with Mr. Wilberforce? Did you shoot him with your gun?"

"I left him in a Bozeman jail cell. Very much alive."

"I don't understand." Her whisper sounded petrified. "Who are you?"

He couldn't blame her for being scared. He'd put fear in bigger fish than her. Men in high places; women with shady pasts.

"My real name is Matthew Gage. I work as a stunt reporter for *The San Francisco Chronicle*."

Chapter

❧ 13 ❧

"Stunt reporter!" she exclaimed. Then added in a distasteful tone, as if she needed a harsher noun, "A flimflammer."

Gage didn't care to think of himself as such.

"You write all that nasty trash about people and then people have to go around apologizing for it or admitting it was the truth. Either way, they're ruined."

"I wouldn't put it like that."

Meg buried her face in her hands. Her fingers trembled She gasped for breath, as if she were fighting back tears. Humiliation. That's what he'd given her, and it cut Gage to the quick. "You're not Mr. Wilberforce." The words were muffled with acute pain and a wavering sense of loss.

Right at that moment, Gage wished he was Mr. Wilberforce.

"No, I'm not."

"You l-lied to me." Her voice broke. Then she shot her chin up. "Why did you put Mr. Wilberforce in jail?"

"I didn't put him there. He was able enough to get himself arrested."

"On what charge? As if it matters," she went on, tears pooling in her eyes. They were a mixture of grief and anger and Gage could do nothing to comfort her.

"Theft."

"Why are you pretending to be him? No wonder you couldn't sell a carpet sweeper. You aren't a salesman. You've never pushed a Bissell in your life."

"You're right."

"Of course I'm right," she all but shouted. "You may think me stupid, but right now I'm seeing things very clearly. You lied to me. You lied to everybody. And to think I told you . . . things." She colored, fiercely and emotionally. Her body shuddered. Remorsefully. Her eyes lowered, then lifted. She rapidly blinked.

"I wanted to tell you last night, Meg. But you wouldn't let me."

She aimed her finger at him. "You let me make a fool of myself. You let me tell you what I told you and you did nothing to stop me. You kissed me."

"You kissed me back."

"How dare you point that out."

Meg's shoulders trembled. Gage wanted to reach out to her, but he knew she wouldn't have anything to do with his empathy. He had wronged her. He admitted that to himself; he should have admitted it to her. He'd wanted to right that wrong last night. She hadn't given him the chance. This wasn't how she was supposed to find out.

"Meg, I'm sorry."

"Sorry doesn't begin to make up for what you've done. What you're doing." She laid her palm across her forehead and knocked a wisp of fiery bang from her eyes. "Why are you trying to ruin Wayne? How did you even know about my brother?"

Gage straightened, tucking his arms at his side. "Sit down and I'll tell you. Everything."

Meg's hand fell on the back of the chair. She slid the feet away from the desk and lowered herself onto the cushion. "Go ahead. And don't spare me."

Gage told her everything from the Ladies Cultured Artists Society to meeting up with Wilberforce by accident two weeks ago in Bozeman. He went on to tell Meg about Wilberforce being entered in the contest. How Gage hadn't been interested in Harmony until after Wilberforce mentioned somebody had won a thousand dollars in last year's fishing competition, somebody who was an unlikely winner. Gage told her how he and Wilberforce concocted a story that would keep Wilberforce's wife from finding out he'd been incarcerated, and Gage in disguise.

"Wayne caught those fish honestly," Meg interrupted. "People saw him bring them in on his line, for heaven's sake. How could he fake that?"

"By paying Leroy Doolin to release brown trout into Evergreen Creek the night before the competition."

"He wouldn't have."

"He could have." Gage rose and paced the room. "I've seen Doolin twice. Even described your brother to him."

"How?" came her soft question.

Gage stopped and faced her. A heaviness settled in his stomach. "I saw his photograph at your house last night."

Meg abruptly stood. "You came to my house to see

if you could find a picture of my brother?" she squeaked. "You're lower than I thought."

"That wasn't why I came, Meg. I came because you asked me to. Remember? It wasn't my idea."

She sputtered, "Well, you made me feel sorry for you. Silly me."

"Meg, don't."

Slowly she sat back down. She worried her lower lip. "Did Mr. Doolin ever do business with my brother?"

"Not that he will admit."

"There." Her eyes brightened. "You see. Wayne isn't guilty."

"I want to believe he's innocent, Meg. More than you know. But something isn't right." Gage omitted the fact that Hamilton Beauregarde had been out to see Doolin. Uncertain of Ham's motives, Gage didn't want to bring his name into this.

"You're not right," Meg returned. "You've been . . . teasing me. Making me think you were somebody you're not. You . . ."

Hurt me. Used me . . .

The words were left unspoken in the room, hovering there between them.

"I never meant to get involved with you."

"How could you not?" She dashed a tear from her cheek with the back of her hand. "Wayne's my brother. Let's see what his sister knows about him, shall we? Well, now you know the truth. He did nothing wrong. And you'll have to live with yourself you . . . you . . ." Gathering her momentum, she taunted, "You scallywag."

Gage lifted a brow. "Scallywag?"

"I was desperate," she said, shoulders slumping in

that Meg-like way that made him want to smile in spite of the tension charging the room. "The word was fresh in my mind. I just heard Mr. Calhoon use it. I wouldn't have picked such an archaic insult, but I was at a loss for a good punch."

She fiddled with a fold in her skirt.

He smiled; he liked her way too much for his own good.

She straightened and ran her fingers across the nape of her neck as if her head ached. Pointing at him with accusation, she spouted, "You're worse than a scallywag, *Mr. Gage.*"

Mr. Gage.

He didn't care for the way it sounded when she said it. As if he were a piece of dirt.

"Meg, my intentions—although you may not see this, are good. They always are when I take on a project. I'm a purveyor of the truth. Like it or not. It's an ugly job at times. But the truth has to be told." He splayed his fingers and ran them through his hair. "I admit that when I came to town, I thought about writing a sarcastic story about how ludicrous Harmony was for being up in arm's over a silly fishing contest. Then I met Oliver Stratton."

"You saw Ollie?"

"I did."

Astonishment dulled her voice. "Does he say Wayne cheated him?"

"He believes he did."

"And I'm telling you Wayne did not."

Her defense of her brother was nothing shy of admirable.

"Maybe you don't think a fishing contest is important," Meg continued, her curt voice lashing out, "but it was to Wayne. He wanted that money so that he could go to a good college. And he was willing to practice hard to win it."

"I want you to be right."

"I *am* right." She lowered her hand, only to put it to her right temple and massage. "Wayne has his faults but he isn't a liar. Unlike somebody else I know. Or thought I knew." Then unexpectedly she blurted, "You got a letter from your wife. Rather, the woman who thinks you're her husband but her real husband is in jail. I'm very confused, and I'm getting a nasty headache."

Mrs. Vernon Wilberforce had struck him down. He'd known that the moment Calhoon told him he'd given Meg his mail. Gage had been very careful to get to the post office when the express man was coming in from Waverly with his delivery.

"She's not my wife. I wouldn't have even opened that letter. It's for Wilberforce."

"You think you're Mr. Wilberforce," she admonished. "For a newspaper man, you're not very inventive. You could have at least come up with something that you knew how to be. A horse swindler or some other such occupation that would fit your dark character."

Collecting herself she stared him in the eyes. "And when were you planning on giving Mr. Wilberforce this letter from Mrs. Wilberforce?"

"When I met up with him as soon as he's released from jail."

"So you've got it all figured out." Meg opened her arms as if setting a stage. "You come to Harmony, you say you're Vernon Wilberforce, you get the sister of the man you think is a crook to tell you intimate things about herself, then you write an article about it all for the big city paper and everyone has a good laugh." Knocking her hair from her brow once more she added, "But you forgot one important thing. Actually, two."

Placing her hands on her hips, she knowingly declared, "You don't know how to sell Bissells and you couldn't hook a fish if you were starving to death. All these books prove that fact, Mr. Gage. See, I'm not as stupid as you thought."

"I never thought you were stupid, Meg."

"Well, you didn't think very much of me, that's for sure."

An electrified current stung the air. "You're wrong. I think quite a lot about you. I . . ." He'd felt himself falling in love with her. But she wouldn't believe him now. And any confession he could offer would sound cheap and insulting.

"You're right about the fishing," was all he could concede. "I can't cast worth a damn. For the life of me, I don't understand why a dry or wet fly is chosen. And I've read that *Manifesto* from one end to the other. Twice."

She gazed at him as if he were as dim as an automobile headlamp.

Then her hand came down on the book; she grabbed it, and in a swift move, threw the beat-up volume at him. He dodged the manifesto. Behind him, the hard cover and pages smacked against the wall.

"You only asked me on a rowboat ride so you could find out about Fish Lake. And you only asked me on a picnic so you could watch me fish," she said in a voice heavy with accusation and nicked pride. "I ought to put a hook through you. My only consolation is that even after you watched me, you couldn't cast. I ignored the fact because I didn't want to hurt your feelings. But now that I just found out you don't have any, I can say this: You will never be a fly-fisherman."

Arguing his cause would be futile. Gage thought fishing was a hell of a thing. If he had learned anything, it was that you didn't learn fishing from a book. You had to experience it with somebody who knew, breathe it with them.

Trouble was, Gage had no patience. No tolerance for incompetence. And he was one sorry incompetent when it came to trying to get that fly hook on his silk worm gut leader.

He had large hands, clumsy hands. His fingers could wield a pencil and pen and pluck at a typewriter. But those big fingers weren't meant for skills that required him to attach a fly no bigger than a speck to a hook just about as small. He could doggedly pursue a man for weeks, months. But he could not beat a fly hook. Damn things.

"I could be a fisherman if somebody showed me how it's done." Gage's voice cut the quiet in the room.

She disregarded his comment.

"One more question," Meg returned.

Gage lifted his chin and met her in the eyes. "What?"

"Are you—that is, Matthew Gage—are you married?"

"I'm not married," Gage replied. "And that's the God's truth."

Meg gazed at him with clear and conflicting emotions.

"That's why you're so upset, isn't it? You thought I was married either way."

It took her a moment before she nodded. "I don't know what makes me more mad. The idea that you were really the married Mr. Wilberforce or that you're Mr. Matthew Gage, busybody reporter. I think I dislike both notions the same."

He could accept that.

A long pause filled the room. He saw that she was digesting what he'd said. It still didn't put to rights what he'd done to her. He could apologize all he wanted but he could see she was hurt. Very much.

"Whatever you think, Wayne didn't do it," Meg reiterated. "He's good and trustworthy. He would *never* cheat."

The way Meg insisted on her brother's innocence with such conviction and passion had Gage doubting his instincts.

Weaving his fingers through the hair that rested on his temple, Gage nodded. "Okay, then help me prove it. You know a lot about fly-fishing these waters," he said, making his words as gentle and unaffecting as possible.

Her eyes narrowed with suspicion.

"You can show me how it's done," he continued. "Then I can be in the contest and look like I belong. If somebody else cheated and made Wayne look bad, the best way to ferret them out is to enter their world and become one of them. Chances are, that if somebody cheated last year, they'll cheat again this year. I could expose him and the truth would come out, Meg."

She sighed. Heavily, somewhat resentfully. "You already think you know who did the cheating."

"I never said I had concrete proof your brother cheated."

"But you want to prove he did." Contempt electrified her tone.

"You think he's innocent. And if you're right, you can help me prove he didn't and once and for all put this matter to rest. Keep my identity a secret and help me."

Meg stood and went to the window. Her back to him, she remained stiff, unyielding. Quite angry by the way she held herself. He didn't blame her. Not one bit. But anger would get them nowhere.

For a while, she stared out the glass in thought. Her fingers lifted to her hair and she dug them into the bun and rubbed, knocking the pinned up style askew. "I can't say yes," she said to the panes where her reflection caught. On another breath, she said, "And I can't say no."

Turning to face him, she frowned. "I'll have to think about it."

Then walking toward the door, she slipped her hands into a hidden pocket in her skirt and produced his letters.

He'd risen as well and came to stand behind her.

"These are yours." She lowered her head and stared at the patterned rug, unable to meet his gaze. "And just so you'll know, I didn't intentionally open the one from Mrs. Wilberforce. It was an . . ."

"Accident," he finished for her, rather fondly.

"Yes, it was. Very much so." Her voice became heated again. "I have to go now."

He let her leave, closing the door in her wake.

For the first time in his life, Gage didn't know what to do next.

Meg was supposed to meet Ruth and Hildegarde at 2:30 at Rosemarie's Tearoom. She hadn't intended on going when she left the hotel, but she began to walk, mindlessly. No, not mindlessly. Her mind was full, spinning. She just needed to walk. Get some fresh air. Where she ended up really wasn't a concern of hers right now.

She was in a state of shock.

Stunned disbelief.

She'd been tricked. Fooled. Bamboozled. Made fun of.

Fury almost choked her. Resentment tore through what remained of her dignity at this moment. She wanted to throw something. Hit something. Scream, stamp her foot, yell. Anything to make her feel better. But she knew nothing would.

Matthew Gage.

Here she'd told him she loved him—and really meant it. He must have had himself a good laugh over that one. Fresh tears rolled down Meg's cheeks and she wiped them away with the cuff of her jacket.

Mr. Wilberforce—no, *not* Mr. Wilberforce—Mr. Gage, had treated her as if she were a laughingstock. She'd fall for kind words and kisses. Pretend to be sweet on her and ask her about her brother.

Oh, how she hated Wayne at this moment.

How she hated herself for being such a dimwit.

She was furious over her vulnerability.

All this la-de-da lady pretending to find a man. And look at the man she'd found. He was a fraud. Just as much of a fraud as Meg was.

As Margaret was she more popular? No. Was she happier? No. More admired? Perhaps. But she didn't want to be admired for chatting about the social topics of the day.

Dismally, she came upon the tearoom. She was sure

her face was a mask of rage, but it was too late to turn around. The pair of school friends saw her and waved her in from the window.

Clenching her teeth, she opened the door.

"Margaret, we've been waiting," Ruth said and pulled out the chair next to her.

Hildegarde called for Rosemarie. "Margaret's here. She'll have a cup of the same tea we're drinking."

Meg woodenly sat down and stared at the lace tablecloth.

English tea.

Yes, of course. Have a cup because her friends were having some. Well, she didn't like it. All that cream and sugar she had to doctor it with left a bad taste in her mouth.

From the corner of her eye, she saw Rosemarie moving toward the teapot.

Meg abruptly turned and spoke up. "Wait. Don't pour me any." She went to her feet. "I'm going across the street to Durbin's for a glass of sarsparilla."

The girls stared at her, mouths agape. It was Ruth who finally spoke up. "Margaret, what's gotten into you?"

Already feeling as if her burden were lightened, she declared, "Not what. Rather, who. *Meg* is back."

After dinner that night, Meg sat on Wayne's bed and looked around the room. Heaving a sigh, she noted everything was as he'd left it when he went to college last fall. The belongings were a mix of items he'd collected through the years.

A Hohner harmonica collected dust on his bureau beside a tin drum bank and a baseball. The wall was a patchwork of various posters; the White Squadron

ship and World's Columbian Exposition, the fearless
Rough Rider Theodore Roosevelt on horseback, and
an advertisement bill for Old Republic Whiskey—
which Mother frowned on.

On pegs, a boy's soldier cap and a pair of suspenders remained hooked next to a worn-out man's pine-
ridge scout hat—favorite of the cowboys. The desk by
the dormer window remained cluttered with a wooden
box of assorted villages, farms and animals, a jumping
jack, box of matches, and a shaving mug that was used
as a stationery cup for pens and pencils.

In the days and months that followed Wayne's departure, Meg hadn't been in his room. There had been
no need, and frankly, she and Wayne didn't get on all
that well and she hadn't wanted to nose around in his
things because she had no interest in them whatsoever.

But now she felt a connection to Wayne. A sort of
bond that had enveloped her when she'd entered the
room. The air even smelled vaguely of his cologne.

Meg sighed once more.

What was she doing here? Really?

She didn't want to think about the real reasons. The
ones that had been in her head since the moment
she'd left Vern—Matthew Gage.

Matthew Gage.

The name suited him. He was more Matthew than
he was Vernon.

Why hadn't she seen this?

Love was blind.

Well, she didn't love him anymore. And she didn't
want to help him unearth any of Wayne's supposed
misdeeds—as if he'd done anything wrong. Which
Meg knew, was not true.

She recalled last year and how proud she'd been to

be his sister when he'd won. Even though a cloud of speculation had surrounded his win, nobody had proved an iota of wrongdoing. Her mother and father had been pleased as punch and bragged for weeks afterward. Wayne was elated to have the money for school.

He was older than her and had wanted to go back East to college for years. But the Brookses simply couldn't afford Cornell. So his win had been a godsend for him.

Nobody had ever asked Meg if she wanted to go to college. In truth, she hadn't thought about it. She'd always wanted to be a part of the hotel and when that hadn't worked out, she'd accepted she wouldn't become a businesswoman. She'd become a wife and mother and have a house of her own to keep and a husband to please.

Only those plans were nothing more than a dream now.

Meg laid back on the bed and stared at the ceiling.

Matthew Gage. She wanted to hit him. Sock him in the arm. Take him for a few rounds like she and Wayne used to do when they were little.

She'd blackened her brother's eye once. An accident, of course. He'd never lived it down with his chums. And Meg's girlfriends had been mortified she'd used physical force on a boy. Well, she hadn't done so on purpose—at least not that first time. Wayne had just put a slimy toad down the back of her best pinafore and she merely reacted: She took a swing at him. She couldn't help it if his eye got in the way.

Looking back, growing up with Wayne hadn't been all bad. He had come to her rescue the time Petey Chalkley told her he loved her and trapped her by the kissing tree and tried to plant his mouth on hers. She'd been seven at the time and boys were about as appealing as spiders in her washbasin. Wayne had grabbed Petey by the shirt collar and told him never to try and kiss his sister again.

Wayne had been her champion.

She should be his now.

But how?

The last thing she wanted was to be trapped fishing with Matthew Gage. It wasn't enough that he'd humiliated her. Tricked her. Used her emotions as if they were a dishcloth to be slopped in a bucket of scrub water and tossed aside.

Meg still hadn't cried. Not hard anyway. She was saving her big cry for the shower bath tonight where the tears could go right down the drain. She refused to sully one of her good handkerchiefs on Mr. Gage.

Even if she did take him up on his idea to help him fish, she couldn't possibly go traipsing off to Evergreen Creek with a . . . married man.

While she knew he wasn't, Mr. Calhoon, the postmaster, could very easily put the letters and Mr. Wilberforce's marital status together. The possibility he would eventually notice the return address, even if he wasn't looking, was inevitable.

In the blink of an eye, he could read that the mail coming in for Mr. Vernon Wilberforce was from Mrs. Vernon Wilberforce. There was no way Meg was going to lose her reputation for Wayne. With a soft sigh, she realized it might even be too late as it was. She would rather die than become a sneer and a by-word for the sake of helping Matthew Gage expose a criminal.

If she did this one thing, she'd have to do so in disguise. Take no chances.

Grandma Nettie's words came back to Meg. *"Sarah Edmonds was forced into serving her country the only way it would let her. By dressing in man's attire."*

Meg pondered wearing mens clothing.

Turning her head a little, Meg gazed at Wayne's wardrobe, which was cracked open; she'd looked inside before she'd sat on the bed. The dowel wasn't empty. He'd left some suits, town clothes, trousers and shirts, along with linen collars and cuffs that needed starching, several hideous neck scarfs, and an old pair of high-cut storm shoes.

With a groan, Meg brought her arm over her forehead and closed her eyes in an effort to dull the throb of her headache. If she didn't have to be in Matthew's company while wearing her brother's clothes, she would have been excited to do such a thing. It was so . . .

Scandalous. Shocking. Improper.

The new Margaret would never consider such an unladylike thing.

The old Meg would jump at the opportunity.

The prospects were so very . . . intriguing.

Later that night, Meg left the house without Grandma Nettie knowing. Her steps were crisp and concise as she walked to the hotel. She'd made her decision.

She now had a mission.

And that mission had little to do with getting married. Her new objective was to clear her brother's name once and for all.

As she passed the dark interior of Treber's men's

store, she thought over how great marriage might have been. Though in truth, deep down even she had known that marriage wouldn't have been all that rosy if she married a man who didn't really know her. She'd clearly met the wrong man in Mr. Gage. "I dos" might not be for her after all.

She'd never really know, as now she had no desire whatsoever to take part in that institution. Love was too painful. She was going to wash her hands of it. And she would wash her hands of Mr. Gage just as soon as Wayne was vindicated. For now, however, she'd have to spend time with him in order to get to the truth of what exactly had happened during last year's fishing contest.

Stepping inside the hotel, she marched through the vacant lobby and right up to the registration desk where Mr. Beasley sat with wire spectacles perched on the tip of his nose.

"Miss Margaret, is there something wrong?" he called after her, sitting up straighter.

"Not a thing, thank you," she responded without missing a step.

She headed for the stairs that lead to the guest quarters. Only that once did she make eye contact with the startled night manager. Not another sentence passed between them. Her determined gaze dared him to say one word about her late-hour visit.

She obviously filled him with apprehension as she lifted her chin and put on a no-nonsense air. He didn't utter the slightest squeak of protest when she laid her hand on the rail and took the risers upward. Even so, her heartbeat pounded at a reckless rate. She'd defied convention—right in front of Mr. Beasley.

And it felt great.

Meg walked purposefully to Mr. Gage's door and knocked once.

And waited.

For the longest time.

Just when she stared to knock again, the door opened.

Mr. Gage pulled the door inward only a marginal degree but she saw through the slit that he wore no shirt or trousers. Just a towel. She'd caught him right out of the shower bath.

Again.

The lump in her throat increased and she had a difficult time forming words in any kind of coherent capacity.

Water dripped from the ends of his hair, a lock in front resting over his damp brow; brows that she had always thought were his best features. He hadn't yet shaved, the stubble on his strong jaw making him appear forbidden. Like a hero in one of her romantic novels; swarthy and reckless.

Although she could only see through a slash in the opening, her gaze had a mind of its own and fell to his chest—broad and taut with muscles. A light covering of hair swirled around his navel and disappeared into the band his towel made around his middle.

The manliness exuding from his half-naked body should have made her bolt, but it was the very outrageousness of her conduct that appealed to her and gave her the mettle to go forward.

If he was surprised to see her, he didn't show it. Neither did he speak up and ask her what she was doing knocking on his door at this time of night.

At length, she said, "Mr. Gage." That seemed the logical salutation. It was, after all, his name. His *real* name. But speaking it put him on the defensive right off; she saw the color in his eyes darken as he shot a glance down the hall.

A second later, before she could think much less scream, he reached out, grabbed her hand, pulled her inside, and slammed the door shut.

"I asked you to still think of me as Wilberforce," he said in a ludicrously polite tone given he was all but naked, "it would keep things from getting *messy*."

"Messy?" she parroted, her eyes locked on the swirls of dark hair that dusted his chest. "I believe things have already gone beyond messy."

Then, realizing she stood in a hotel room conversing with a man in a towel, Meg steadied her voice and quickly proceeded with what she came here to do.

"I won't keep you. I merely wanted to say that I accept your proposition. I'll help you learn how to fish." Holding herself taller and determinedly avoiding everything beneath his chin, she added with conviction, "Not because I'm sympathetic with your plight, but because I want to prove to you my brother is innocent of any crime. If my helping you can better put this matter to rest, then I'll do it."

Matthew Gage leaned into the door jamb, his bare shoulder glistening with bath water. The maneuver distracted her. She wondered if he did it intentionally. "I appreciate your offer."

"As I said, I'm not doing it for you."

"I understood that." His stare practically charred her bloomers the way his eyes burned into hers.

"Yes, well . . ." She felt the need to fix her hair or do something to herself to make her appearance more presentable. As if she cared.

"We should get started right away," she continued,

refusing to let him make her ill at ease. "Meet me tomorrow in front of the hotel at precisely nine o'clock. And be fully prepared to spend the day at the lake."

"I'll be there."

"All right."

"Good."

Nothing else needed to be said.

Meg let herself out then and walked proudly down the hallway, listening for him to close the door so she could relax the tension from her spine. But she heard no sound of hinges. He had to be watching her. She felt the fine hairs on the back of her neck rise. Not with repulsion of any kind. On the contrary, with a delicious tingle she cared not to examine.

After all, she was through with love.

She rounded the corner and stepped down the stairs, dismally aware of the traitorous tingles that still teased her spine. She might not be in love with Mr. Wilberforce any more but she wasn't immune to Mr. Gage's broad chest. Those marble-hard pectorals of his put the sketched pictures of muscle men in Wayne's *Whitley's* exerciser magazine to shame.

And here she'd gone and committed herself to spending the next four days with Matthew Gage in close company out in the middle of near-nowhere.

If she had been any other woman—one who didn't possess her staunch willpower—she would have said the woman was doomed.

Chapter

❧ 14 ❧

First thing the next morning, Meg entered Plunkett's mercantile with a dollar and change in hand. There was no help for sneaking her way into the store. She needed Hildegarde to buy her something and she didn't want to be seen making the purchase.

After gliding into the store unnoticed behind a customer, Meg hid in back of a coal oil can display.

"Pst," she whispered from the dark corner.

Hildegarde stood at the counter sampling a saltwater taffy from one of the jars.

At Meg's call, Hildegarde lifted her chin and stopped chewing.

Meg dared to lean forward and wave her hand for Hildegarde to come over.

Once in front of her, Hildegarde said in a too loud voice, "What are you doing hiding?"

"Shh!" Meg dragged the girl into the dim slash of gray created by the cans. "I need your help."

Hildegarde instantly adjusted her smile. "Did you finish that jar of breast cream already?" Then she lowered her gaze to Meg's bosom. "It sure isn't fast acting."

Meg frowned. "Never mind about the bust cream. I need you to buy me a theatrical beard. Not the kind you glue on, but the kind that hooks over your ears. A really full and bushy one. In auburn."

"What do you need that for?"

Not wanting to go into an explanation, Meg simply said, "Just buy it for me, and whatever you do, don't let your father see you taking it from the case. He's busy helping Mr. Addison so he won't notice if you do it now. Hurry up."

Prodded into action, Hildegarde moved with sneaky purpose behind the item counter.

Moments later, Meg departed the mercantile, package beneath her arm. She retrieved her suitcase, which she'd hidden in the dense growth of alder brush at the corner-post of the store.

She now had everything she needed to check herself into the hotel.

Gage stood on the quaint porch of the Brooks House Hotel, arms folded over his chest, with his fishing tackle at his feet. He scanned the length of Birch Avenue and looked for Meg. Not a sign of her. The hour was exactly nine o'clock.

He'd thought about Meg most of the night. It had taken nerve for her to come to his room and talk with him. He had assumed she'd either turn him down flat or, if she did agree to help him, she'd tell him in a public place like the lobby or passing him by on the street.

She must have been one hundred percent sure her brother was innocent or else she wouldn't have agreed to help him. Gage hoped for her sake that she was right.

And now there was Ham Beauregarde, who could figure into this. Gage didn't want to bring up Ham's name to Meg. Not until he knew more about the traveling man. There were only four days before the contest. Precious time was ticking by.

But on the other hand, Gage wanted the clock to slow down.

Four days.

Alone with Meg.

Last night when he'd laid restlessly on his bed after she'd gone, he'd thought about the times he'd kissed her and held her. He hadn't been able to pull her image from his head as he stayed awake until nearly dawn.

When he'd opened the door after stepping out of the shower bath, he never expected to find her there. She'd stood in the hallway with confidence and pluck. She looked different, acted different. Although subtle, the changes were evident. But the Meg that showed up last night was a risk taker. A woman of her own mind, a free-spirit.

The new Meg appealed to him more than ever.

But she would rather roast him over hot coals than give him her smile. He could tell that she wasn't going to like having to help him; she said as much by the way the corners of her mouth turned down. She was sacrificing many unpleasant hours with Matthew Gage to help Wayne Brooks.

Gage didn't like how her obvious reasoning made him feel.

Behind him, one of the hotel doors opened. He gave the gentleman stepping out a brief glance, then returned to looking up the street wondering when Meg was going to show up.

"Are you ready?" came Meg's voice beside him.

Turning, Gage lifted his brows as he tried to make sense of the sight before him. Dressed from head to toe in man's attire, Meg sported a pine-ridge scout hat, her hair tucked in the crown—which must have been quite a feat because she had thick hair—a linen shirt and ill-fitting coat with a badly tied neck scarf; and on her feet were a pair of rubber storm shoes that came to her knees.

But what surprised him the most was her beard. A bushy reddish-brown thing with a mustache to boot that came down to her collar.

"What's the matter?" she asked casually beneath his stare—as if it were every day she met him rigged in men's clothing.

"I wasn't expecting this."

"You didn't think I'd go off with a married man, did you? Mr. Calhoon has to know Mr. Wilberforce is married. Or if he hasn't put two and two together from the real Mr. Wilberforce's letters, he will soon."

He barely followed her logic. More because his gaze had automatically fallen to her mouth, which was enveloped by a fringe of theatrical hair, than because of the words she spoke. Those soft lips that he had kissed were covered with a wiry artificialness that looked real at a distance, but obvious up close. The fakery of it made him want to laugh, but he held himself in check.

"I'm not married," Gage said, feeling cheated by not being able to enjoy her face.

"So you told me. But Mr. Wilberforce is. Right now, Mr. Calhoon isn't aware of that. However," she added with a serious note, drawing Gage from his perusal of her outlandish get up, "if he were to find out, my reputation would be ruined. I know it's a very marginal chance that he'd ever really know who Mrs. Vernon Wilberforce is, but I can't risk it."

"But we've been off alone together before."

"You needn't remind me," she returned with a sourness to her tone. "That was different. I didn't know who you were. And everybody thought you were somebody else. In a small town, things have a way of coming to the surface. If anyone ever asks you who Mrs. Vernon Wilberforce is, say she's your mother."

Gage scowled. "It seems like a hell of a lot to go through when nobody is ever going to find out."

"I beg to differ." She held her shoulders erect. "*I* found out who *you* were."

Inasmuch as Gage could understand Meg's desire to disguise herself, he had a hard time looking at her without frowning his disappointment.

Now he wouldn't be able to watch how she fussed with her hair, adjusting the pins all the time and poking the knot of burnished apricot tendrils on her head this way and that to get the coif just so. All that luscious red hair was hidden beneath a man's hat. So was her figure. Behind ridiculous clothes.

He wondered where she got the outfit. Then assumed the clothing belonged to her brother.

Meg lowered her eyes. "I see you have all your things, so we might as well go and get this over with."

She made it sound as painful and about as pleasant as a visit to the dentist to get a tooth pulled.

His male ego became slightly bruised and his tone showed as much through his cool tone. "I know the way."

He bent and picked up his gear.

They walked the fifteen minutes to the creek in silence. Fine with Gage. He didn't feel like talking with a woman whose shapely backside was hidden in a pair of pants a size too large.

Meg made every effort to keep the lead for most of the walk, but Gage had longer legs than her and overtook her every time she trudged in front of him.

They reached a section of Evergreen Creek that was farther to the north of the town than the spot they'd rowed to on the lake. Here, a dainty copse of Rocky Mountain ash grew in abundance with willows and berry thickets.

The shore at the water's edge came up to them in a sandy slope. From above, warblers sang; a marsh bird of some kind swooped down, dragged its feet over the bubbling water's surface, then soared upward, disappearing into the boughs.

Depositing her fishing tackle around her, Meg drew up to the water's edge and seemed to size the area. Gage followed, looking into the clear stream and moss-covered rocks, then beyond to the muddy-looking pool.

He saw nothing. His gaze slipped to Meg.

She saw something.

Beneath the brim of her soldier hat, her eyes narrowed. He watched, fascinated, as she studied; she observed.

After a moment, she shook her head. "Wrong sound. I don't like it." She backed away and snatched her things. "We have to go that way. Downstream just a bit more."

Gage fell in line behind her, letting her lead the way as he had no idea where to go. A short minute later, they came upon another section of the stream. She stopped and listened, this time nodding.

"This is where we'll start."

Dropping his gear to the ground, Gage shrugged. "What was wrong with that other spot?"

"The water flowed too wide. It had a hiss to it. Too powerful for your first lesson. This is better. Here the water gurgles and there's an alder tunnel." She pointed to the dense foliage that plunged part of the stream into deep shadows.

Gage didn't see the significance of an alder tunnel, but he took her word for it.

Meg went to the water's edge and stood very still. She positioned herself in a way so that her reflection didn't hit the surface. Gage kept back and watched her. In the slash of shade her hat brim made, he observed her gaze skimming the water. From where he remained, he didn't see a thing.

"Water pennies have hatched. There's one."

Drawing closer, Gage looked. Barely discernable was a bug that looked like a spider gliding across the water's surface.

To his right, came a plop. A fish had just surfaced and snagged something for its meal. Gage folded his arms across his chest, feeling pretty damn smart. "We'll use water penny flies."

"No."

Her reply stabbed Gage's self-esteem. "Why not? That's the kind of bug that's on the water. I read you use what insect is hatching."

"If the fish are biting that particular insect. But they aren't." Meg turned and walked to where she'd put her tackle.

Gage felt like knocking her hat off. "Well that fish didn't just jump out and take a bite of air."

"It was a cutthroat and it ate an ant that dropped off one of those alder leaves."

"How in the hell did you see that?"

"I was watching."

"So was I. I didn't see a thing."

"You weren't looking right." She lowered herself onto the ground and sat in a crossed-leg fashion—a mannish position made possible only because she wore trousers. He sensed she preferred sitting like this to a more ladylike pose.

Rifling through her tackle, she took out a fly box much like Ollie Stratton's. "We'll use terrestrials. Not exactly a fly. A terrestrial is an insect that falls, drops, jumps, hops, or is windblown from shore onto the water where they can be eaten by trout."

She poked around and came up with a small fussy thing no bigger than the head of a fourpenny nail. Lifting it for him to see, she said, "Black fur ant." She tilted the ant so he could look at the underside. "There's the hook."

"Christ, how did that lure get so small?"

"I made it."

"You did?"

"A long time ago with my brother."

Her brother.

The reminder served to sober him.

"Sit down and see if Mr. Wilberforce has anything in his tackle that looks like this ant."

As he did so, she talked while she arranged her line and pole. "There's more to fly-fishing than baiting a hook and swinging it over the water. A lot of what you do is felt inside your gut. For a lack of better description, I'll use the one my father told me about fly-fishing."

Gage caught a glance of her; her slender fingers as they poked around in her tackle and sorted flies and threads. That god-awful beard drove him crazy. Its full bushiness obscured most of her face. The man's facial hair seemed a ridiculous companion to her feminine voice as she spoke. "Starting to fly-fish for trout is like falling in love. Keep in mind that my opinion of this emotion is no longer important because I'm no longer of the opinion that this emotion is worth its trouble."

Her analogy caught him by surprise. "Is that so?"

Her hands stilled. "I was expecting you to say 'Indeed' or some such word."

"I don't talk like that. That was Wilberforce. Or rather, Louis Platt."

"Who's Louis Platt?"

"An editor I once had. He was as stuffy as an old moth-eaten shirt."

They exchanged a lengthy and silent stare.

Meg broke the silence, her voice quiet. "I don't know who you are."

"No, you don't."

Studying him, she asked, "Did you make up stories about your parents? Your sister? Or was that real?"

Gage held her gaze. "It was the truth."

Their eyes held a long while.

Then Meg went back to the trappings that lay littered around her, adjusting this and that, and continued her explanation as if nothing had passed between them. "In the early stages of fly fishing, your feelings are heady and decidedly unscientific. They exist of the moment and for the moment. And that's enough." She blew a puff of air between her lips, the mustache hair fluttering. She must have been hot beneath the bushy hair covering half her face.

"Take it off," Gage heard himself say without thought.

She glowered at him. "I beg your pardon?"

"Take that damn beard off. No one is around for miles. Who's going to see you? And if somebody comes, you can put it back on."

She laid both hands on her knees in contemplation. A few taps of her fingers on her inseams said she was thinking it over.

Should she or shouldn't she?

To his immense pleasure, she unhitched the beard from behind her ears. "I can't breathe very well in this. The mustache whiskers are too long." With a toss, she discarded the theatrical piece onto the top of her tackle basket. "That's the *only* reason I'm taking it off. Not because you suggested that I do so."

"Of course not." Gage cracked a half-smile at her, then forgot what he was supposed to be doing. All he could do was look at the woman who sat across from him.

She may have been dressed in a lumpy jacket and trousers, and sitting in the fashion of a longshoreman, but he found her utterly captivating. The way the sunlight cast its golden glow over her, the way a butterfly flickered close to her shoulder, the way she went through the process of readying a line for casting. Then she brought out a length of superfine silk line and cut a piece to her specifications with the sharp edge of a blade.

Mesmerized, Gage didn't readily follow her next words.

"But sooner or later," she went on with her fly-fishing philosophy without missing a beat in her method of preparation, "things calm down a little, and as the infatuation continues, you want to know more about the sport. In the end, you become hooked. Just like love can hook a person without them least expecting it." A melancholy frown flitted across her features. "Or so my father told me."

Gage felt a foreign trip in his heart. Then he scoffed himself. He doubted he would ever be hooked by the inclination to fly-fish, much less fall in love without his being aware of it.

Standing, Meg held her pole and looked at his. He'd attempted to tie a leader on his tippet and run the silk gut through the loops and make a decent knot for the fly and hook. He had a few tangles in places, but other than that, not half bad.

"You know all that material you read in that book?" she asked, one hand on her hip.

"What about it?"

"Forget every word. You've botched your line in the worst way I've ever seen."

Gage hated to admit failure; a part of him wondered if she was just saying that to make him feel like an ass. "Have I really?"

"Quite."

Rising to his feet, Gage didn't bother to bring his rod with him. "You could at least smile when you tell me I've made a blundering idiot of myself."

"I'm saving my smiles for when I get to watch you cast," she quipped, her tone making it clear that those smiles wouldn't be of encouragement; they'd be blatant guffaws.

They spent the next quarter hour revamping Gage's

line and Meg instructing him on how to hold his arm when he aimed the pole over the water.

Once they stood on the water's edge, she gave him some last-minute hints. "The object in casting is to extend the fly line, leader, and the fly in a straight path from you to the fish." She pointed to the rod in his hand. "That fly rod can multiply the motion of your arm, so be ready for it to travel a lot farther than you think. I'll show you what I mean."

Gracefully, she drew her arm back and released the line. It floated like a thread of gossamer over the still water in a distant pool, then snapped right off the surface just about as quick as she reeled in the line.

"See? Now you do that."

Gage tried. And bungled it.

His line ended up tangled in the brush because he'd overshot his mark.

Meg reprimanded him. "I told you not to flick your wrist so hard. That line is going to move way out there."

Gritting his teeth, Gage talked between his clenched jaw. "I know that. Do you think I did it on purpose?"

She disregarded his quip. "Beginners need to relax. Mr. Gage, you're more wound up than a watch coil. I can see tension written over every inch of you. It's in the way you stand and the way you frown at me— like I'm enjoying this."

"Aren't you?"

She said nothing for a long moment. When she spoke, she ignored his question. "You need to slow your casting stroke timing and let the rod do the work. It can't make a cast by itself any more than a baseball bat can hit a home run. Try it again."

Gage disguised his frustration and tried again.

And again.

And again.

After a couple of hours, Gage got the wrist motion right to where he could cast without having to think through every move he made.

At noon, Meg sat down and opened the lid on a small lunch tin. Without so much as an offer to him, she began to eat.

Gage hadn't thought to bring a meal. He'd been too anxious packing his tackle and anticipating spending the day with Meg to think about food. But now that he saw her nibbling on a sandwich, his stomach grumbled.

But he'd be damned if he'd ask her to share.

Setting down his fly rod, Gage sat next to Meg and took a load off his feet.

"Why do you think Wayne cheated?" Meg asked out of the blue. "What are your hard facts?"

They'd spent hours together and she hadn't mentioned his story once. Now he could read the purpose in her eyes and knew that she wanted details. Some of his opinions she would think were unfair. Others, she would dismiss as unfounded. Perhaps she might agree with him on a few points, although he doubted it. In any case, he didn't feel like arguing with her.

"A newspaper reporter doesn't always have to have hard facts," Gage finally said. "Sometimes there's an aroma about a story that stinks. If something smells, it's usually corrupt."

"You didn't answer my question. Why, exactly, does Wayne's win—as you put it—stink?"

He gave her every theory he had, going down the list of the people he'd talked to and what he'd found out. He omitted Ham Beauregarde. "It doesn't add up that your brother draws the best spot, doesn't show up at the kick off party at the saloon, and catches nearly all brown trout when that creek supports mostly rainbows."

"Coincidence," she stated firmly, "all of it. Luck was on his side when he drew the lottery and won the best spot—he couldn't possibly have trifled with that, and he's never been an overindulger of liquor so that's probably why he didn't go to the saloon, and lastly, there is no evidence to prove that those brown trout didn't have an established school in that creek. They are known to be in these waters. If he'd pulled out lobsters, I'd say you had a good point. But he didn't and you don't. All your theories are just speculation, Mr. Gage."

Gage felt a muscle twitch at his jaw.

Dammit, but she sounded convincing. Gage trusted his own instincts for truth but also recognized that those instincts had to be borne out in the facts of a story. Her facts and his differed on every level. Maybe this was the first time Gage was wrong. Blinded by worn-out inclination.

"I don't care for big city newspapers and their lies." Meg crumpled the waxed paper her sandwich had been wrapped in, and selected an apple from her tin. "It's awfully shabby of them to slander people in their scorched headlines on the front page. I don't know how you can live with yourself."

Tension worked through Gage until his joints felt like cement, hard and tight and unyielding. She didn't know a thing about his job and the demands that came with it. If she did, she'd know that he was always on the side of fairness. "I can live with myself because I know that what I write is the truth."

"Where's your compassion? I've yet to read a stunt column with compassion."

"There's no room for compassion in my columns. My words are buttressed by a disarming bluntness that makes reading me appealing. I produce colorful, compelling copy."

"My Grandma Nettie could write a more compelling argument on one of her flyers than you could in your column." She took a bite out of her apple; a slice of ruby red skin disappeared between her white teeth. He couldn't help watching as she delicately chewed, swallowed, then hammered him into the ground once more.

"And do you know why?" she asked.

He had no comment, so she answered for him.

"Because she cares about people. About rights and fairness. She's not out to hurt anyone. She's out to help women. To make them open their eyes to the Cause."

"I could write a column and sway women to take up the Cause, and I'll bet you I'd get at least two dozen recruits."

"Not very likely." She took another bite of apple, thought a moment while the sweet smell of fruit caught the current and wafted to him, then she remarked, "You analyze things too much. I've noticed that about you."

Narrowing his eyes with immediate censure, Gage opened his mouth to denounce her assumption, then closed it.

Christ almighty, but she was a loaded pistol today.

He would have given himself over to a wry laugh if she hadn't been so close to the truth. Conceding his opponent was right had never been one of his traits, but he found himself muttering, "I've been this way too long to change."

"You could try." She turned the apple, which was now little more than a core. "Pretend you really are a Bissell salesman. You have the perfect opportunity."

Meg went to her feet, then hesitated. She looked from the apple core to Gage. "Oh my, did you want some? Oops." Then she tossed the apple into the tin, and picked up her rod once more with a satisfied smack.

She moved to the shore and began to cast. She'd caught and released a half a dozen trout this morning. He'd caught none.

Hell and damnation.

Stretching his legs out in front of him, Gage leaned back on his elbows to discredit her suggestion about acting like a real Bissell man. A legitimate carpet sweeper salesman wouldn't know a hawk from a hand-saw. The world of traveling men revolved around sales and people. Talking up their products—not putting their customers under a magnifying glass to find out what made them tick. Gage usually had somebody's number within five minutes of observing their body language. A Bissell man would merely write up his order and be on his way.

In Gage's mind, he was ruined. He could never enter a room and not size the whole of it up.

Exhaling, he rose and picked up his bamboo rod. Positioning himself next to Meg, he cast and promptly overshot his aim and landed in a clump of weeds. He swore. Giving her a sidelong glance, he yanked the silk line until it broke.

"Trouble?" she queried sweetly.

He ground out, "Looks like it."

"Hmm. It sure does. Weren't you listening when I told you to conserve your arm motion?"

"I was listening. But in fly-fishing, listening doesn't have a whole lot to do with things, now does it?"

"I suppose not."

Gage sat and rifled through his tackle box to get another tippet for the end of his line. Meg stood in place, staring out at the water. Then furrowed her brow. "I want you to know," she began not meeting his gaze, "that what I said the other night—I didn't really mean it."

It took him a moment to comprehend what she was getting at. *I love you, Vernon.*

Pausing with the spindle of silk gut in his grasp, Gage couldn't help saying, "What if that's what I had wanted to say to *you?* You never let me finish."

She grew still, startled. Flustered. A flicker of hopefulness contouring her profile . . . then disbelief. It shouldn't have mattered what she thought of him, but it did.

"I wouldn't have cared what it was as long as you'd been honest. And as long as you'd meant whatever it was." Lifting her chin and giving him a stern frown over her shoulder, she added, "Which we now know you never meant anything sentimental you ever said to me so we can just go right on and forget about past history, *Mr. Gage.*"

Staring ahead once more, she murmured, "I told you, I don't believe in love anymore."

Chapter

❧ 15 ❧

Meg and Matthew walked back to the hotel together, barely trading enough words to keep a telephone operator busy. She had nothing to say to him. Well, she had a lot to say to him. But that wasn't the point. The point was, he disrupted her sense of balance more than any man she'd ever met.

But the fact of the matter was she had to be with him in order to clear her brother. And rather than being polite, she'd almost been downright rude when she'd told him her opinions of newspaper reporters. She'd never dared to voice such uncensored words in her life, especially in a high-handed way. What in the world had gotten into her?

She wasn't today's Meg any more than she was yesterday's Margaret. She felt caught in the middle. Still hurt. Still reeling from her discovery and those two letters. What if she hadn't taken them from Mr. Calhoon? How long would Matthew have tricked her? She could just weep at the thought because she knew the answer.

As Meg reached for the door handle of the hotel, Matthew's hand went out a fraction before hers—as if he were trying to be chivalrous and open the door for her, of all things. Their fingertips met. The contact sizzled through her, and she quickly moved out of the way.

She gave him a hard stare, then let him open the door.

Crossing the lobby in a mannish gait, Meg slowed her steps when she saw Grandma Nettie sitting at the registration counter.

Keeping her head low so that the brim of her hat hid her face, she trudged along and would have managed to get right by her grandmother with a simple nod of her head if Matthew hadn't short-stepped her on the heel of her left boot. She stumbled and caught herself from falling by taking a long and noisy step. Her tackle box and gear made an awful rattling sound.

She shot him a stern warning, which he probably couldn't see because of her beard. So she made sure her eyebrows came down in disapproval.

He merely smiled at her.

"Are you all right, sir?" Grandma Nettie asked, giving her a concerned lift of her brows that turned to curiosity. She swept her gaze over Meg's costume ending at her face with a suspicious twist to her mouth. Then a narrowing of her wise eyes.

Meg planned on telling her grandmother who she was, only not right now. She nodded and fumbled her way up the stairs, switching her fishing rod to her tackle holding hand so she could grip the bannister and not slip-slide her way up the stairs. Wayne's boots were too big, even though she'd stuffed the toes with socks; her stockinged feet slid around in the shoes making walking difficult.

Matthew followed right behind her. Directly behind her, without so much as an inch of breathing room.

Once they rounded the corner on the second floor, she hissed beneath her breath, "What's the matter with you? Are you trying to get me to fall down?"

"I think you can do that on your own."

Meg stopped in front of her room, took out the key from her trouser pocket and gave Matthew one last parting glance. Unfortunately, room thirty-three was the only vacant one in the hotel when she'd checked herself in. Her room was directly across from Matthew's. He stood at his own door, shoulder leaning against the jamb, making no move to turn the knob and let himself inside. He just stared at her. Watched her.

She felt itchy and hot. Sweaty and bothered. Needing to shiver, but unable to do so with his eyes pinned on her.

"Tomorrow. Same time," was all she managed before letting herself into the room and closing the door behind her.

Meg dropped her tackle and all but slid down the door, melting. That's what she was doing. Melting. Right beneath his nose. He had to be aware of what he was doing to her by simply *looking*. Making her feel like a chip of ice in a warm mouth. Slowly melting no matter how much she wanted the coolness to stay on her tongue.

She just couldn't let him do that to her.

Meg left the door, flung her beard onto the bed and began to unbutton her shirt. She was hot. Stifling hot. The room was stuffy and warm.

She went to the window and stuck her hands into the part in the sheer curtains. She flung the sash up, allowing a breeze to trickle through the opening.

Sitting on the bed, she took her boots off, then slipped out of her shirt. She rose to her feet and undid the fly to her trousers. Standing in bloomers and corset, she dressed in her petticoat and shimmy.

As she tied the ribbon on the top of her corset cover, she took in a deep breath of satisfaction. From this day forward, no more of those newfangled straight-fronted corsets for her. She'd gone back to her old short hip corset. It might be plain and not give her meager bosom a lift, but it was a lot more comfortable.

Once she was put together, she left her room and went downstairs into the lobby.

Grandma Nettie had been at the front doors recommending the Home-Style Restaurant as a nice supper place to a newly arrived couple. They left just as Meg approached.

"Come with me to the registry book, Margaret," Grandma Nettie said. "I have a question for you."

"Grandma, you don't have to call me Margaret anymore," Meg said while walking. "I've decided to go back to Meg."

"Oh—well, that's good news. Meg suits you much better." She nodded her head once with gladness. Then, "Now, about the registry book . . ."

Meg knew precisely what her grandmother wanted to question her about. That entry she'd made earlier when her grandmother had been busy with Delbert.

"Meg, you wouldn't happen to know who this is, would you?" Grandma Nettie pointed to the line in the registry book where Meg had signed a name. Her grandmother squinted behind her spectacles and tried to read the sloppy slants in black ink.

"Suppose I do?"

"I'm quite certain you do. Who is it?"

At the time, Meg hadn't come up with a name for her character. She'd merely signed the book in her sloppiest penmanship. "Let's see . . . I would say that's . . . Arliss Bascomb." She remembered the author's name on Matthew's fishing book and decided to use it for her character.

"Arliss Bascomb," Grandma Nettie repeated.

"Uh-huh."

"With red hair?"

"Uh-huh."

"About your color?"

"Yes."

Grandma's knowing eyes leveled on her. "You could have at least told me ahead of time what you were going to do."

Meg lifted her brows. Although it had been obvious her grandmother had recognized her, Meg really didn't think the disguise was all *that* telling. From a distance. "How did you know he was me? I had a beard on."

"It's a thin disguise, Meg. I recognized your brother's clothing."

Sliding the heavy bicycle chain aside, Meg plopped her elbows on the registry counter and frowned. "Do you think anybody else will figure it out?"

"It all depends." Her grandmother closed the fat book. "Why are you dressing like a man? Does Mr. Wilberforce know who you really are?"

At the mention of that, Meg huffed. "There's a lot to tell you. But I'm not supposed to divulge a certain identity. His *real* one. Suffice to say—the guest in our hotel isn't Vernon Wilberforce. He's someone else. And that's the part I can't say because I sort of promised I wouldn't."

Eyes filling with wonder, her grandmother asked, "What are you going on about?"

Meg clued her grandmother in to what she could. Mostly, the simple facts. Vernon Wilberforce was a Bissell salesman, all right. Only the man checked into room thirty-two wasn't really him. He was a newspaper reporter.

"A *reporter*," Grandma hissed. "I suspected he wasn't who he seemed but I cast a blind eye to him because . . . well, the man has charm. And you were taken by him. I never should have let my guard down." Her tone mirrored her disgust. "What's he doing in town?"

"The long and short of it is," Meg said in a flat tone, "this man who we know as Vernon Wilberforce, wants to reveal Wayne as a cheater in last year's fishing tournament." Then she went into the details of what Matthew told her about his suspicions and how he wanted to expose her brother in the newsprint.

Grandma Nettie slammed her palm down on the countertop with a dry bang. "I'm so angry with myself. I can't believe I didn't do anything about my hunch. All that marble-mouth language of his when it suited him. I even asked him about writing and he said he'd thought about it. The bounder. He's done more than think about it. He *does* it. And to think we nearly bought a Bissell from him."

"No wonder he said we didn't have to. He doesn't really sell them."

"I'm turning him out right now. How dare he come

into my George's hotel under false pretenses. And to think I allowed him into my son's house, too. And had Mr. Finch feed him."

"I know," Meg commiserated. "But throwing him out won't solve anything. In fact, we have to stay in his good graces or he may very well write a slanderous article about Wayne without any proof whatsoever."

"If he does that, I'll call my sisters. We know how to put men in their places. And I can physically incapacitate him, too. Would you like me to, Meg? Or have you already?"

"I haven't touched him." *At least not in that way.* "I have another idea. And it doesn't require physical force." She braced her hands on the edge of the counter. "I'm going to help him learn how to fly-fish so he can enter the contest and find out what really happened—nothing illegal. But I can't exactly go gadding about town with a married man—should that information become public.

"So I came up with the plan that the safest, and most respectable, way would be to dress up like a man. I picked the name Arliss Bascomb and I've given him an occupation, too." Meg came in closer to put her head together with Grandma Nettie's.

Her grandmother's dour expression was exchanged by a smile of secret partnership for Meg to continue.

"Well," she went on, "I heard Mr. Calhoon and Mr. Treber at the post office yesterday talking politics. If ever there was an occupation to make a person be avoided, it's to say they're from the Bureau of Internal Revenue."

Sucking in a breathe, Grandma Nettie declared with a low whistle, "A Bureau man. That's a good cover, Margaret. Nobody likes them. I know I don't. The government can't tax our income. It's unconstitutional. People will avoid him like the plague."

"Those were my thoughts exactly." Meg bussed her grandma's cheek. "So will you keep my secret?"

"Yes, of course I will, dear. Although it's going to be awfully hard seeing that man come and go. I'm liable to give him a good piece of my mind."

"I trust you can control yourself."

"Hmm. Yes. There is one thing, however." With a broad smile, her grandmother asked, "What man do I get to dress up as?"

Gage concealed himself in the entranceway to Gale's butcher shop, keeping watch on Ham Beauregarde across the street. The salesman had left the hotel over an hour ago, stopped at the Blue Flame Saloon for twenty minutes, then moved on to the restaurant. From Gage's vantage point, he could see the man sitting at one of the front tables. Just the top of his head. The rest of him was hidden by the half-window gingham curtains.

Leaning back and folding his arms across his chest, Gage waited.

Waited for Beauregarde to make a move.

Anything remotely suspicious. They had two days until the contestants drew the lottery spots for the contest. Then two days until the contest itself. If Ham had plans about cheating, he'd have to do something from now until then to put the odds in his favor. Just his going out to Doolin's hatchery was suspect—even if Doolin hadn't told Gage what Beauregarde had wanted. Not that he would have.

Doolin was a tight-lipped man. Loyal to those he did business with. Gage hadn't been convinced Doolin hadn't done business with Wayne Brooks, or Ham Beauregarde.

Cool evening air sluiced over Gage, and he decided to walk a moment to get the circulation back in his legs. There was no fear in being discovered. The time must have been going on nine. There was no one on Hackberry Way at this hour.

As Gage strolled up the road, he paused at a building that had a large sign in the window with bold lettering: FOR RENT OR SALE.

Cupping his hands together, Gage brought his face up to the glass and peered inside. Though the interior was dim, he could see the space was an adequate size. Whatever had been here before had a front counter, then a cleared space behind, as if there had been a lot of shelving. The lighting was nothing modern. He could see by the fasteners that were strung from the ceiling, the lamps weren't hooked up to gas. They were oil. Simple shop lamps. But they could throw off a lot of light at night.

Gage stood back to read the former establishment's sign, but it had been removed. Taking another step forward, he continued to study the place. The broker offering the building was Otto Healy of Granite Home and Farm Realty.

Behind Gage, came the good evening call of a patron as Ham left the restaurant.

Quietly, Gage disappeared into the dark night ready to go wherever Ham Beauregarde would take him.

The next morning, the soft April afternoon had a drowsiness to it that made Meg want to lay back, fling off her brother's hat, and bask in the sunshine. Watching clouds go by. Watching patterns in the leafy

branches overhead. Skimming her bare feet in the
water as she gently kicked them from the boulder she
laid on.

But she wouldn't. Because she wasn't alone.

She sat with her lunch bucket beside her, yards
away from Matthew, who reclined on his jacket, which
he'd spread out on the short meadow grass. Today he
hadn't forgotten to bring a meal. Rather than having
a sense of retribution, she didn't feel all that great
about not offering to share some of hers yesterday.

Meg nibbled on her cheese sandwich, barely tasting
it. She had none of the vigorous appetite she'd had
the other day. After the smoke had settled from their
initial battle of wills, she realized this was not a game.
This was real. There could be no more tiny moments
of emotional triumph in which she convinced herself
she had no feelings for him, or of speaking her mind
and not worrying about the consequences. Everything
she did and said to Matthew Gage came with
consequences.

She had to quit taking the situation lightly.

Wayne was in trouble.

She had to help him.

That meant being with Matthew. She had had to
get over her hurt in one night. Not easy, but she had
done it—or she thought she had.

She dared to slant her gaze toward him. He stared
right at her. With those intoxicating eyes of his. Green,
like a carpet of grass, just hazy and lazy enough to
make a woman want to lie down in the lush lawn and
put her hands over her head and murmur, "Kiss me."

That's exactly what his lips were saying.

That's exactly why her eyes were now averted
from his.

Meg's stomach knotted as if she'd swallowed a peach pit. She'd never been one for indigestion, but she felt a bad case of it coming on. With a soft groan, she gave up trying to eat another bite of her meal and dropped her half-eaten sandwich into her pail.

"Are you all right, Meg?" Matthew drawled. That voice of his could be like tempting candy—sweet and slick and slippery.

"I'm fine, Mr. Gage," she all but snapped. "The afternoon is too hot, is all."

"Feels fine to me." He rolled onto his side and stretched his legs out in front of him. "Why don't you call me Matthew? There's a distinct distaste to the way you say 'Mr. Gage.' I'm hoping you won't have that problem with my Christian name."

Meg made no reply. *Matthew.* How could she call him Matthew? Matthew was a name a woman said when she felt something intimate for a man. She called him mister when she either respected him or was too enamored by him to dare call him something more personal. And since she was now feeling neither about Mr. Gage, she supposed that calling him Mr. Gage was a moot point.

Matthew.

Could she? Dare she?

Of course she could. She could say Matthew and make the name sound just as bothersome as Mr. Gage.

"You told your grandmother about me, didn't you?" His tone wasn't grating, but nor was it honey-smooth.

"Why would you think that?" she replied, neither admitting or denying the question.

"When I went into the lobby this morning, she aimed her fountain pen at me and gave me a look."

Meg laughed at the image of Grandma Nettie pointing an ink pen in a threatening direction. "Did she squirt you?"

"No." He gave her a half smile. "Disappointed?"

She made no comment.

After a moment, he resumed their conversation. "When are you going to tell me what all those flies are in Wilberforce's tackle box?" he asked in a tone as unhurried as a Sunday afternoon.

Meg wrinkled her nose. She'd been meaning to go through the flies and tell him which one to use for which situation. He'd have to know that for the contest.

From where she sat, she couldn't clearly view the variety of flies Matthew had spilled onto a cloth napkin by his elbow. Getting to her feet, she walked to him and crouched down. There was something to be said about wearing trousers. She didn't have to worry about stepping on petticoats.

With her forefinger extended, she shuffled through the colorful lures. "This is a bumblepuppy, that's a rooster's regret, black ghost, golden darter, black-nosed dace bucktail, black woolly bugger, zonker, yuk bug, and those are your nymphs."

Matthew made no comment. He merely gaped at the multitude of lures she'd rattled off.

One fly in particular looked out of place. She picked it up and then with an inward smile declared, "This is a screech owl."

"A screech owl?" he asked with a bit of dubiousness.

Turning the fly over in her hand for him to look at it, she said, "It's made out of screech owl feathers. Quite a clever invention."

"Let me see." Matthew took it from her, the warmth of his fingers a whisper across her palm, and held it to the sunlight for a closer inspection.

"I'll bet Mr. Wilberforce made it." Meg was careful not to look at Matthew's hair and the way the sun played on the glossy strands. He was without his hat. He'd hung it on a tree branch and it swayed gently in the breeze when the air ruffled the branch. She still had Wayne's hat on. She didn't care for it. All her hair stuffed in there was a nuisance.

Meg became aware of Mr. Gage perusing her once more. She frowned and said, "That fly doesn't have a distinct look, so it could pass for a variety of bugs. I wonder if it works?"

"You can use it if you want," Matthew said, his gaze slowly skimming over her neck and shoulders. Then higher. "You've got a dragonfly on your hat." When he whispered, she shivered.

She could have easily said—no bother, it would fly away. Instead she caught herself murmuring, "Can you brush it off?"

"I can." But he moved slow. So slow. Her every nerve ending focused on him. His hand as it lifted upward. With a quiet *swish* the bug was gone. If indeed there had been a bug at all.

Meg didn't want to think about why he would make up such a thing. It would be like he was . . . flirting with her. Wanting to touch her. This out of the way brush of his hand had to be a lie. Just like everything else.

And yet . . .

After she'd foolishly blurted out that she hadn't meant a word of what she'd said Sunday night, he could still hold her captive. And it was as if he knew just how much hold he had over her with a mere glance. Like he still wanted her to be in love with him.

She was being silly. It had been Vernon Wilberforce she'd fallen in love with. The fact that Matthew Gage was in his body—so to speak—had been an unfortunate circumstance.

She had to stop thinking this way about Matthew. It would serve no purpose at all. *Keep reminding yourself you're on a mission, Meg, and you'll be all right. Be strong enough to ignore him.*

"Yes, I wouldn't mind giving the screech owl a try," Meg replied in a tone that was all business as she reached out to take the wispy lure.

Matthew closed his fingers around it. "You have to call me Matthew if you want to use it."

Meg would have liked to tell him to sit on his request. Then again, if she did, he'd think she was afraid to say his name. Which was a bald-faced lie. She could say it. She'd say it with pleasure.

"Matthew." Her mouth hummed the "m" longer than necessary.

"You could have said it without making it sound like a dead fish."

"That wasn't part of the deal," she responded with a shrug, taking the fly then standing.

"Hell," he muttered.

She was used to him using Veron Wilberforce's archaic expletives. These little "hells" and "damns" that slipped past his lips were surprising. He didn't talk with Mr. Wilberforce's old fossil language anymore. She didn't know if she was happy about that or not.

What she wasn't happy about was the longing he could put in her heart just from the way he looked at her. How could she get him to stop it? She had to get him to ignore her. Plenty of men had ignored Meg. In fact, she was used to being passed by for dances and parties.

As she walked to the shoreline, she pondered the way of things. Under other circumstances, she would have welcomed the attentiveness. Meg had never received this much consideration from a man. As soon as she turned into Margaret, she'd had Harold Adams calling. Who, thankfully, had stopped calling as of late.

Matthew had told her that he cared about her. Inasmuch as she felt certain he'd fibbed about that, there was an underlying denial that held on to her heartstrings and wouldn't let go. She couldn't forget the times Matthew had kissed her. Embraced her. Looked at her as if she were . . . special. Maybe he had had *some* genuine feelings for her.

At that, she almost laughed. The feelings he'd had for her were for Margaret. Not Meg. And they'd been faked just so he could get his story.

She had never shown him the real her. At least, not all of her. He would be disappointed. He wouldn't want to brush dragonflies off her hat anymore. Nor quietly watch her.

Yes . . . all she had to do to put him off was be herself.

Her *real* self.

That's what she wanted. Wasn't it? Of course it was.

Dropping the screech owl fly and her fishing rod with hardly a glance at them, she strolled up the stream side, not too far, to where she knew there was something so indecent for a woman to do, that she'd never done it in front of any man—not even Wayne.

Hildegarde, Ruth, and Meg used to sneak over on hot evenings, strip down to their underwear, and indulge in pure frolic. Nobody had ever caught them. Their mothers would have a fit of the vapors if they ever knew what their daughters had done.

As Meg spied the stately cottonwood beside the stream, she bit back on a smile of mischief. She wouldn't go as far a disrobing to her underwear in front of Matthew Gage—even she had her limits. But she could still have the same scandalous affect with a plunge in her clothes.

Hanging from a thick rope on one of the high branches, was an old tire from the one and only automobile that had ever managed to drive into Harmony. On all four rims. Mr. Hollyhock, of the Mammoth Garden and Flower Seed Company, had had four flat tires. He'd had to sit and wait in their hotel for three weeks for four spanking new tires and tubes to arrive so he could drive out. Those four flat tires of his had scattered and ended up in various places.

One as a back scratcher for the Addison's plow mule. Another as a makeshift set of hobbles for Max Hess's livery. Another as a picture frame at the Blue Flame Saloon—or so she'd been told; she'd never seen it firsthand.

And the last tire, the local hooligans had made off with to use as a swing over Evergreen Creek. As luck would have it, in the tree not ten yards away from where Meg and Matthew had been fishing.

Meg saw it and put a light stride in her steps.

Intending to call Matthew over so he could watch her make a spectacle out of herself, she stopped and turned. Practically right into him.

"Oh!" she cried as he nearly slammed into her.

With his mouth so precariously close to her ear she literally gasped, he wickedly mused, "That's twice now you've stopped cold in front of me, Meg. I'm beginning to wonder if you have an underlying desire for me to bring my body next to yours."

After seconds of speechlessness, Meg managed to say, "If I wanted you to touch me, I'd tell you."

"Would you?" She didn't like the way he arched his brow. "That's not the Meg I know."

"Well, just like I don't know the real Matthew Gage, you don't know the real Meg Brooks."

At that, Meg removed her boots and walked to the tire. She tested the rope for strength by giving it a few firm tugs, then brought one leg through the center. She used her right leg to push off and give herself some momentum. Holding on to the rope and swinging over the pool of water, she thrust her weight forward and back until she had a darn good sway going.

With a quick glance at Matthew to make sure he was watching, she arced high once more. So high her hat flew off and went sailing the same time she did.

She landed with a grand splash in the frigid water and scissored her legs to bring her to the surface. The brace of water was like a douse in ice.

But she had to prove a point.

And prove it she had.

The telling was glorious. Swimming to shore with strong, sure strokes, she climbed out of the water. She didn't care that her teeth were chattering, or that her long hair drooped around her face, or that her man's socks were so heavy she could barely walk.

"W-well," she stated boldly, her teeth clicking together, "W-what d-did you th-think of that, M-Matthew?"

Fire danced in her velvety brown eyes, giving Gage quite the show of defiance. Her expression grew spicy and reckless with her taunt. Lips, red and blushing from where she pressed them together, became quite enticing. In that moment, he saw passion in her.

He'd wanted her before—yes. He had tangled with physical attraction, enjoying their kisses and the times she'd been in his arms. Gage thought he was the type of man who wanted nothing more.

Now a multitude of untried emotions took hold of him. He saw before him a woman emerging from a Victorian stuffiness who had been reposed and safe. This new enchantress got to him in his gut, his groin. The urge to kiss her senseless drew him in. To sink his fingers into the fiery curls that matched the fire in her eyes.

His body ached. His insides burned. With her forbidden plunge into the water, she had ignited within him a desire the likes of which he'd never felt. She, on the other hand, was oblivious to her power—which made him want her all the more.

At length, and in a voice deceptively hoarse, he conceded, "I think you are the most captivating woman I know."

Then he walked away.

Shaken, he dared to admit the truth to himself. It was as if it had been staring him in the face the moment he'd discovered her in his hotel room. He just hadn't been able to accept the fact that he wasn't immune.

Realizing this, he nearly smiled with irony at the twist of fate. The tables had turned. Most anyone would tell him it was hopeless. But Gage wasn't a quitter—although he should be because, chances were, nothing could ever come of what he felt.

Even so, as he walked back to his spot in the shade,

his hands almost trembled from the potency of his discovery.

He'd fallen in love.

No doubts.

The real thing.

God help him. He'd been hooked.

Chapter

❧ 16 ❧

Gage stood amid the small crowd of fishermen waiting his turn at the lottery to see which spot he'd land for the contest. Quite a few people were at the town square to view the drawing of numbers.

Slipping his hands in his trouser pockets and putting his weight on one foot, Gage looked for Meg beneath the domes of parasols. They hadn't made plans to meet, but he was fairly sure she'd show up.

He'd be disappointed if she didn't.

He wanted to see her in a dress. Gaze at the soft curves of her figure. Follow the dappling shade from her parasol over her hat. Watch the fluid way she walked without a man's forced gait. Follow the smile in her brown eyes and the tilt of her mouth as she laughed.

The picture would have been a pretty one. But there was more to the canvas than beauty. More than the obvious. It was who she was inside that made him want to see her.

Made him want more than an image of a dress and smiles.

But complications stood in the way of simple pleasures.

He lived in San Francisco. She lived in Harmony.

His occupation was his life. She hated his occupation.

He'd lied to her. She couldn't forgive him.

He thought her brother was dishonest. She thought his investigation was unfounded.

Big obstacles to overcome.

Gage had never been one to compromise—not himself or his ideals or his ways. Even if he was, he wasn't the type of man to settle down anyway. In the past, he'd avoided falling in love. He had nothing to offer a woman but a one room apartment with lackluster furnishings. He rarely used that address in the city. While he traveled the country for stories, what would Meg do? What kind of woman would accept a man who was never around?

"Next!" called Gus Gushurst as Gage came to the front of the line.

Seeing Gage he said a polite hello, then, "Mr. Wilberforce, reach in and pick a card. On it you'll find a number."

Gage did so and drew a six. Not bad.

Gushurst prompted Gage to fall back into the crowd. "Wait for the last few gentlemen to take their numbers and we can proceed in the staking of the stream spots."

Walking through the fishermen, who compared cards and numbers, Gage saw Ham Beauregarde with a sour look on his face. Spying Gage, Ham lifted his card for Gage to read the number. Seventeen.

"I suppose I've got my work cut out for me. I've drawn dead last," Ham remarked. "By the time I get to pick my spot, all the good ones will be taken. What number is it that you've got there, Wilberforce?"

Gage showed him.

Ham's eyes gleamed with envy.

In Gage's nightly following of Beauregarde, the man hadn't made an illicit move yet. He never left the town. He had a clear routine: Go to the Blue Flame for a beer, then the Home-Style restaurant for dinner, then back to the hotel. In the mornings, he took his fishing gear and left for the day. Gage couldn't tail him all the time, but he suspected Beauregarde really was fishing because he talked up his prowess every chance he got in the lobby while smoking cigars.

If Gage confronted him and asked him why he'd gone to Doolin's, getting an honest answer from the Gurney man would be like waiting for snow to hit San Francisco.

Beauregarde put his arm over his shoulder as if they were friendly old chums. Gage's gut tensed as he let himself be led away from the crowd. Away from prying eyes and listening ears.

"Tell you what I'm going to do, Wilberforce," Ham said, his breath smelling of strong peppermint drops. The Gurney salesman was an in-your-face pitchman, and at least he had the foresight not to have bad breath. "Here's my offer of the day, okay, Wilberforce?"

They stood off to the side from the others at the base of the gazebo.

Ham's weighty arm began to feel oppressive on Gage so he slipped out from under it.

"Here's the deal, Wilberforce," Ham began, "I will

pay you twenty-five dollars to trade cards with me."
Before Gage could get in a word, the salesman went
on, a lift to his hands as if he had to show he wasn't
hiding anything sneaky on the palms. "I propose we
make a trade—not a sale or anything so vulgar as that.
A trade. That's all it would be. Just a little payolah
from me to you. And the beauty of it is, nobody has
to know. What's a quiet trade between friends?"

Ham reached into his breast coat pocket and discreetly pulled out his billfold and fingered several bills.
"Twenty-five dollars is a lot of money. That's—what?
A Bissell or two for you? Surely two sales. And this
is all on the side. Nobody has to know."

Gage remained quiet, watching the way Ham's mind
worked through the linear expressions on his face. The
wrinkles in his forehead; the crinkles at the corners of
his eyes; the furrows on either side of his mouth.

Beauregarde was slick. A real smooth operator.

If something smells, it usually stinks. Only: Where
was the proof?

Gage made himself indignant and put out by placing
a hand on each of his hips. "Great Scott, Beauregarde,
now why would I want to go and give up my good
number for a bad number?"

"Because, we both know you can't fish worth a
damn," Beauregarde explained as if his words were
nothing at all offensive—merely a statement of facts.
"You wouldn't have broken your rod if you knew
what you were doing. Anyone can see that this isn't
a big deal to you. Why, I haven't seen you practicing
along any of the banks the rest of us have been. You
clearly aren't in this for the glory like we are. So you
must be needing the money. Well, Wilberforce, I have
money. Twenty-five dollars. Right now. It's yours."

He slipped the money into Gage's right hand and tried to slip the card out of Gage's left. Gage held firm. If he hadn't been playing Wilberforce, he would have propelled his elbow into the man's ribs.

"No trade." The words may have been Wilberforce's, but the voice was pure Gage: deep, unaffected, threatening. He neatly stuffed the money into Ham's pocket.

Beauregarde backed up a few steps and glowered at Gage as if looking at him for the first time. As if he were really thinking hard about something and trying to put together a puzzle.

Wilberforce might have gone too far.

But for Gage, it hadn't been nearly far enough.

"Meg," Ruth said, "is that a new hat you're wearing?"

Meg, Ruth, and Hildegarde strolled toward the town square. Meg's two friends, decked out in big hats and trimmings, kid gloves and sheer parasols, flanked her. She looked like a plain candle in comparison to their showy attire.

"Yes, as a matter of fact, it is," Meg replied. She wore an originally styled creation that she'd made last night. The straw was simple java braid, closely woven, with a very wide brim. She'd accented the low crown with her favorite green taffeta scarf. There were no birds, no veiling, and no fruit to be had. Just like the apricot-ribboned hat she'd dared to wear on her picnic . . .

Ruth nodded sincerely. "I like it."

"I like it as well," Hildegarde added, looking intently at the crowd. "I used to have one similar to it."

"We all used to have hats similar to it," Ruth sighed.

"Then why don't we wear them again?" Meg proposed.

Hildegarde and Ruth gazed at her as if she'd suggested they go out in public in hair curlers.

"We used to wear simple hats," Ruth clarified, "but that was before we were looking for men to marry."

"Give me a man over a plain hat any day," Hildegarde wistfully stated, then practically stood on tiptoe to peer over the hats of men in the distance.

To a point, Meg understood their desire to put away simple hats and outgoing manners. But she no longer agreed with their thinking that by doing so, they'd land the perfect husbands. "Well, I never did get used to those fancy five-dollar hats. So I'm going back to my old ones."

"You're more daring than me," Hildegarde remarked, looking left and right.

"And me," Ruth added. Then with a pucker to her brows: "Hildegarde, just *who* are you looking for?" Ruth gazed around herself as if she were missing anything.

"I'm looking for that new man who came to town. Mr. Bascomb. Mr. Arliss Bascomb."

Meg stopped in her tracks and exclaimed, "Mr. Bascomb? What do you want with him?"

"My mother said he registered at the hotel and she saw him yesterday and thought he might make a fine catch for me."

"I didn't see him," Ruth claimed, "but I did hear that he came back to the hotel all wet."

Meg wanted to cover her face with her hands. She didn't dare confess *she* was Mr. Bascomb. Then she'd have to explain all about Mr. Wilberforce. And she didn't have the heart to tell them that Mr. Wilberforce had lied to her. *And,* after all his lying, she was *still* attracted to him.

"My mother did mention he was wet," Hildegarde replied thoughtfully. "Soaked through."

Ruth nodded. "I heard Mr. Hess threw him in a horse trough when he held his hand out and said to pay up his taxes."

"That's not what I heard," Hildegarde piped in. "My mother said that he was a victim of circumstance and happened to be right in the pathway of Mrs. Kirby's scrub water as she emptied the bucket from her porch."

Not convinced, Ruth said, "I can't believe your mother would want you to snag a Bureau man."

Hildegarde twirled her parasol, her chin held high. "Well, my mother said that a new man in town should never be discounted until he's proven himself unsuitable and that I should always give a newcomer, regardless of his occupation, the benefit of the doubt. Granted I've never even seen him so I don't know if he'd be appealing to me or not. Then again, beggars can't be choosers."

"Oh, Hildegarde," Meg chided. "Stop selling yourself so short."

"Have you seen Mr. Bascomb, Meg?"

Meg frowned, wishing she could just blurt out the truth. "Yes I have. And he isn't very attractive. As a matter of fact, he's positively ghastly. Red hair. I dislike red hair on a man. And he has a full beard. It hides his entire face. So he must have a pretty awful one beneath all that hair. I wouldn't go too close to him if I were you."

Tilting her head at an angle, Hildegarde's announcement sounded airy and full of anticipation. "My mother is going to invite him over for Sunday supper. She thinks he could be just the husband for me, but first she has to talk to him and make sure he's not a ruffian. You know."

Meg wanted to scream her frustration.

"Since you've seen Mr. Bascomb, Meg," Hildegarde stated, "point him out to me right away."

"Yes, certainly." Meg all but sighed her exasperation. "I'll point him out the minute I lay eyes on him."

Which won't be any time soon.

"I'll bet Mr. Bascomb isn't going to be here." Hildegarde added extra shade to the brim of her ostentatious hat with her gloved fingers. "I'll bet he's gone to try and tax somebody. My mother says taxing people's money should be illegal."

"Then why does your mother want you to marry a Bureau man if she thinks taxing is illegal?" Ruth asked, eyes wide.

"Because she said if I married him, he'd be good assurance that he wouldn't tax my father's mercantile. Morally, how could he tax his father-in-law?"

"Oh, I hadn't thought of that." Ruth searched the crowd once more. "I'll have to see this Mr. Bascomb for myself. I might want him, too."

"Honestly," Meg said, all but putting her hands on her hips. "You're carrying on as if you are the only women in the world who aren't married. Really, it's beneath you to even talk such a way. Like you're miserable old maids."

"But we are," Ruth said.

"Yes, we are," Hildegarde seconded. "And so are you."

Meg shifted a pin in her hair while proclaiming, "Not anymore."

Ruth and Hildegarde's eyes went wide as Meg continued, "I prefer to think of myself as a gay and carefree woman. I don't need a husband to make me happy."

Ruth wrinkled her nose. "That's not what you said last week."

"Never mind about last week." Meg jammed the pin into her hair, knocking her hat askew.

"Have you and Mr. Wilberforce had a misunderstanding?"

A misunderstanding. Meg wanted to laugh. That wasn't the half of it.

"He doesn't appeal to me anymore." Meg attempted to straighten her hat, but her efforts were futile and she just left it alone. "I find that I'm no longer fond of him."

"You aren't?" came their dismayed cry.

Ruth said, "You were mooning over him awfully bad."

"Well, I'm fickle," Meg replied defensively. "My feelings for him were nothing more than a silly schoolgirl infatuation. The real thing is serious. Love, that is."

Hildegarde sighed. "You sound so certain."

"You're only twenty once in your life and you should make the most of it," she declared. "I don't need Mr. Wilberforce to make me feel younger."

"Well," Ruth whispered, "don't look now, but here comes the man you don't need."

In spite of herself, Meg locked her gaze on Matthew as he approached them. A strange tickle caught her ribs. On the inside, next to her heart. Light and fluttering. Unwelcome, the image of Matthew in the door-way of his hotel wearing nothing but a towel and water droplets came to mind. The hard and naked planes of his chest, muscles everywhere. The way he'd looked at her. The sound of his voice all deep and husky.

She blinked out of the thought with a pang.

Matthew came upon them with a casual walk, a smile on his mouth and his coat flung over his shoulder.

"Meg," Ruth said beneath her breath. "Since you don't want him, I'm going after him."

"What?" she gasped before she could stop herself. She had no opportunity to say another word because suddenly he was there. Tall and handsome. An intelligent humor flickering in his eyes.

"Ladies," Matthew addressed, while doffing his hat. "It's turning into a nice day now that the sun has come out. I'd say it's a good afternoon for fishing."

"Yes, it is," Ruth remarked in a cultured voice.

"Quite nice," Hildegarde agreed.

"What number did you draw in the lottery?" Meg asked, trying to keep the immediacy from her tone. It wouldn't help to have Hildegarde and Ruth wonder why she cared so much. But she was concerned. Matthew had to get a five or better to draw one of the best spots.

Putting his hat back on, he held up his hand for her to read his card, his eyes meeting hers.

"Six," Ruth verbally supplied. Then with a coquettish smile, added, "Six is my lucky number."

Meg ignored Ruth and asked, "What spot did you pick?"

"Marker twenty-two." He looked at her in silent question.

A fair spot from which to fish. Not the greatest, but it could have been worse.

She gave a quick nod of her head. He nodded in return. They looked at each other without speaking. Emotions she didn't understand skimmed across his face.

"Six is my lucky number," Ruth repeated, interrupting the moment.

"Is it now, Miss Elward?" he responded in that way of his that was deep and dusty at the same time. "By thunder, I hope it brings me luck."

That was all the encouragement Ruth needed. She went on in a blushing rush, "I could bring you a picnic lunch today while you're fishing and keep you company."

Meg stiffened, waiting for his answer. She stared at his mouth long enough for him to be aware of what she was staring at. And if the truth be told, she wasn't staring in wait for his answer. She was staring because he had the nicest lips she'd ever had the fortune of kissing. And that skunk knew it. Because he cracked a slight smile. Just enough to get her heartbeat skipping.

"Miss Elward, that's a gracious offer. And a very tempting one." Matthew tucked the number card into his trouser pocket. "But I'm afraid I have to decline. You see, I'm meeting Mr. Bascomb and we'll be discussing business while we're fishing."

Meg flinched involuntarily.

"Mr. Bascomb," Hildegarde blurted, forgetting herself. "You're fishing with Mr. Bascomb?"

"Yes I am." Matthew's snowy white shirt sleeves ruffled a little as he better aligned his coat on his shoulder. The move caused a tautness over his chest, shirt buttons pulling tight and defining the contours of his rock solid physique. "As a matter of fact, I've got to be getting back to the hotel."

"He's at the hotel? Right now?" Hildegarde's cheeks grew as red as apples.

Matthew looked at Meg when replying, amusement sparkling in his eyes. "No, I don't suppose he's there yet." After his answer, his gaze lifted to her hat. Whatever his opinion, she couldn't tell what it was.

Hildegarde breathlessly rambled, "My mother is going to introduce Mr. Bascomb to me."

Matthew seemed to force his attention back to Hildegarde and replied, "Is that so?"

"Yes. She's inviting him over for supper."

"Really?" he asked, his lips quirking as he turned back to Meg. "I'm sure he'd be delighted."

Meg would have kicked Matthew in the shin if she thought she could get away with it. The very idea. He knew good and well Arliss Bascomb couldn't go to the Plunketts' for dinner.

"You honestly think he would be delighted?" Hildegarde nervously asked.

"Quite." With a nod to Ruth and Hildegarde, then to Meg, he offered, "Miss Brooks, I believe your grandmother is expecting you back at the hotel right about now. I can walk you back."

Ruth had the bad taste to invite herself. "I can come, too."

Meg began walking without so much as a word. She was cross as two sticks. The nerve of her dearest friend thinking she could waltz into Matthew's affections as if he welcomed them.

Did he?

She took a quick glance over her shoulder to catch a glimpse of the pair side-by-side behind her. A passionate yearning was slathered on Ruth's expression like jam on a baby's cheeks. All gooey and revolting.

Yes, revolting!

The very idea of the two of them together was ridiculous. Ruth didn't know a thing about Matthew Gage. But Meg did. And she didn't like him. Not at all.

Why then, did her heart swell every time she looked at him?

"What's the matter with you?" Meg fired at Gage as soon as they were out of town, she in her Bascomb get-up and he toting their poles and gear to the creek. "Saying that I—*Mr. Bascomb*—would be delighted to go to Hildegarde's for dinner. It's as if you want me to be found out."

"The thought never crossed my mind," he replied with an innocence she clearly didn't buy. He couldn't quite hide his smile as she frowned.

On one hand, he wanted her to be found out because then they could quit this game and start being honest with one another. And honest with the whole town. But on the other hand, if she was found out, how could he clear her brother without her help?

Did her brother really need redeeming?

Gage didn't know.

Ham Beauregarde complicated things. First Ham's trip to Doolin's, then today's attempt at buying Gage's lottery card. Two strikes against him. But did two strikes mean guilt?

So as much as Gage didn't want to admit, he was back to Wayne Brooks being his prime suspect.

"I'll just have to avoid Mrs. Plunkett," Meg announced, drawing Gage from his thoughts. "That should be easy enough."

Meg knocked a branch out of her path and Gage ducked beneath it as they went to the northern side of Evergreen Creek—a spot they'd yet to fish. Today she was going to show him how to use a hare's ear nymph while fishing upstream.

Once Meg reached the location, she set her lunch tin down. "Right here will do."

Gage deposited their things and began to put his rod together. He'd gotten a lot better in the assembly, actually being able to string his line and be ready to go not all that long after Meg.

Removing that farcical red beard of hers, Meg brought out her own tackle and readied her line. After several minutes passing without a word between them, her question threw him off.

"What is it you like about your writing?"

His hands stilled and Gage looked up at her. The set of her mouth and the wonder in her brown eyes said she was deadly serious. Nobody had ever asked him what pleased him about his articles. Managing editors usually pointed out the parts that needed to be redone because they lacked luster or definition. Rarely, if ever, was praise given—it would be an invitation for him to ask for a raise in his salary—or so the newspapers thought.

Gage would write for free. He enjoyed it that much. It was his passion, his life. He could communicate to thousands and impress upon them his views and make them see things differently. The good; the bad. Mostly the bad. Which had been nagging at Gage more and more lately.

"Well?" she queried. "Do you have an opinion?"

"The best thing anyone ever said about my writing was it wasn't breezy."

"You viewed that as a compliment?"

"I did."

Her brows knit together. "I think that if I were a writer, I'd want people to be moved by my words. Inspired or motivated to do something different about their lives."

"I believe I do that."

"Do you really?" Her tone clearly implied the opposite.

"I do."

"Hmm." Meg went back to arranging her four-weight line and tying on a longer tippet with many fine knots.

"You've never read anything I've written," Gage responded, his ego out of joint, "so how can you form an opinion on what I do and don't do for my readers?"

"I'm going by what I've seen in the newspapers. No stunt reporter has ever written a piece that isn't slanderous to somebody or something. And, clearly, you anger people. Why else would you carry a gun? Has anybody ever tried to shoot you?"

Gage laughed. "No."

"Then why do you have to arm yourself?" She brought the line to her mouth. Gage watched straight white teeth bite the fragile thread, his whole consciousness focused on what she was doing. "I never figured reporters as needing to defend themselves. But I guess it all depends on the type."

Gage gazed down into Meg's upturned face, her lashes shadowing her cheeks like lace fringe as she worked on her line. It would have been easy to lie, but he couldn't.

"I've kept men at bay with it on a few occasions."

"How come?"

He thought through all the times he'd palmed the grip to his revolver.

"I once drew it on a guy in the Golden Gate Park for getting a policeman drunk so that his cohort could ride around and pick up girls new to the city and lure them into prostitution."

Her hands stilled, and she lifted her eyes to his. "Really?"

"Yes. My exposé busted the story wide open."

"Well . . . I guess that was one time you did a good thing."

Gage's nostrils flared. *One time?* Hell, he'd done a lot of good things. "I held a senator at bay while he was served a warrant. They charged him with skimming city funds. He was as corrupt as a dice joint. He got out of jail after only serving five days. I might have been tempted to shoot him if I hadn't nailed him in print. Front page news. He was voted out of office last election."

She stared at him a long while. "You don't think you're ever wrong, do you?"

"I am wrong. But not often." He rested his fishing rod on his shoulder. "There was that one time when I posed as a private detective to trail a man, only it turned out my informant's wife really did have herself a lover and my story on fidelity went flat. The informant had the nerve to wave at me from his apartment window while he was—" Gage didn't finish the explanation. "Anyway, I figured out the couple liked an audience and I fell for it."

Riding the trolley home that night, he'd thought about going back and drawing his gun on the man just to scare him. Instead, he'd gone to his fourth floor loft on Long Wharf. Drinking a bottle of beer, he'd sat in the open window frame until well after midnight, pondering the angle of his next article while vowing not to be taken in again.

Meg's soft laugh pulled him from his thoughts. "I'm glad to hear that you are as gullible as the rest of us." Then as if the implication of her words sunk in, her cheeks flushed.

He held her with his eyes.

Even while wearing a man's shirt and trousers, a lumpy hat that hid her hair, and knowing her way around a fishing box, he was more attracted to her than he ever had been to another woman. He admired her for going to such lengths to prove to him that her brother was innocent.

She tamped down her blush and said, "Since I seem not to understand the function of your type of reporting, enlighten me."

"A stunt reporter is hired to increase newspaper circulation." He didn't get into the fact that *The Chronicle* combined a taste for the lurid and grisly sensations, and crusaded after scandals of the day to capture in its provocative headlines. Hell, that sounded low-down even to him. In lieu of the reality, he said, "We can't do that with articles on tea parties and who's who columns."

"So instead you'll slander my brother's good name."

His jaw went tight. "I have never slandered anyone's *good* name. Only people who are dishonest. As to your brother, that remains to be seen. And *only then* will I know if there is an article to be written."

She frowned with obvious displeasure. "But you intend to if you think you have enough evidence against him."

"Meg, you're trying me without jury and judge."

She stood, breath hitching in her throat and a hand at her temple. "I am not. But Ruth Elward would if she knew the real you."

Gage sat stunned a long moment, then gave a low laugh. "You're jealous."

"I am not."

Standing as well, Gage said in a low voice, "Sure you are, darling."

Meg's eyes widened. "Don't you dare to call me *darling.*"

Gage took a step closer to her, the light hint of her hair soap teasing his senses, fresh and sweet. "I can dare to call you whatever endearment I want."

A mere whisper now separated them. He took the fishing pole from her hand and tossed it on the ground. He could hear her suck in her breath as he lifted his fingertip to her face and slipped it down the curve of her cheek. Catching her chin in his fingers and tilting her mouth up to his, he lowered his head toward hers. "Darling, I've been wanting to kiss you again for the longest time."

Then he brought her mouth to his in a kiss that wasn't demanding or trying to prove a point. Just a slow and lazy, lingering kiss that coaxed her out of her anger and had her leaning into him with a moan.

Gage liked knowing he could melt her resolve. That he could make her feel woozy, wanted, cherished—desired.

He ached to feel her hair, sift it between his fingers. Its silkiness the day he'd untangled her from his bed was a lucid memory he couldn't shake. Sliding one arm around her to pull her close, he knocked her hat off with his right hand.

Her protest caught on his lips.

"Right now, you're going to be a woman," he said against the cry that tore from her mouth.

With a few tugs on hairpins, that satiny hair of hers fell down in the softest cloud he'd ever had the pleasure of delving his fingers into. Her hair came to her waist, thick and coiled with soft curls.

Closing his eyes, he deepened the kiss, breathing her in and feeling the softness of her hair and her body as he ran his hand up the nape of her neck. Gage put his hands around her shoulders and pulled her to him, pressing her breasts into his chest. He stroked the column of her neck with his thumb, then the base of her ear with gentle swirls.

"I don't even like you," she murmured as she surrendered.

Gage smiled into the kiss as Meg kissed him back with gentle pressure of her mouth against his. "Let me change your mind."

The tip of Gage's tongue coaxed the seam of her lips to part and she gave him intimate entrance. A low grown flowed from her throat, dissolving against him. He brushed her mouth with his tongue as his fingers bunched up her hair into his large fists.

The kiss seemed timeless.

Heartbeats keeping tempo together raged in Gage's ears as he held her face in his hands and kissed her, enjoyed her velvet sweetness. She was soft and pliant, yielding to his mouth. He'd caught fire, wanting more than a kiss. Wanting . . .

He didn't think about what he was doing when he

skimmed his hands over her; he caressed the side of her breast until she gave a light gasp against his mouth. He merely stroked and lightly traced the subtle fullness of her. He could feel the erratic beating of her heart next to his. She kissed him, as if to say he could do more.

But could he?

He wanted to. However, Meg wasn't a woman a man tangled with and left. He didn't want to leave. But how could he stay?

"Why do you do this to me?" she moaned against him. "I don't want you to make me feel like this." Her gentle plea brought a rush to his already burning body and his heart wrenched.

He held her close. "Why do we do this to each other?"

Their breath fused together in a hot, moist cloud that surrounded them.

He forgot where he was. Who he was. Who she was pretending to be.

His entire focus was on Meg. Holding her. Touching her. Kissing her. Being intimate with her. Wanting to be closer. Feel her flesh to flesh next to him. Be inside her. Make her a part of him.

Gage wanted her more than he had ever wanted a woman and his need for her was tearing him in two. He was nearly beyond the power to stop. He might not have if he hadn't felt the warmth of something wet against his cheek.

He broke away and lifted his head to gaze into her eyes. Moisture pooled in them, as if she were warring against her feelings and emotions. "I don't want to feel this way about you."

292

His thumb caught a droplet before it fell down her jaw. "Meg, don't cry."

"Then don't make me . . . make me forget I don't like you."

Softly, Gage smiled at her. "I could make you forget a lot of things, darling."

They stood there a moment, holding each other, a fragile truce between them—when no truce should have been necessary if they'd been willing to admit how they really felt. Gage thought it somewhat ironic. And somewhat sad. For all his touting about his honesty in his stories, he couldn't be honest with Meg and tell her he loved her. Not yet, anyway. He didn't have the words. He didn't have anything settled in his mind. Like what he would do after he spoke his heart.

Gage wouldn't have moved if a voice hadn't suddenly cut the air behind them.

"Yo ho, yo ho, a pirate's life for me!" came a boy's call from the river. "The sea has a fair wind today with good weather. Aye, mateys! Let's look alive! Look alive, you salty dogs."

Meg jumped out of Gage's arms and brought her hands to her cheeks. "Where's my beard?"

A rush of air cooled Gage's skin like a winter gust, sobering him in a scant second. He had been caught in compromising situations with women before, but never had one cried, "Where's my beard?"

"There." Gage pointed. "Where you left it."

Meg swooped down on the hairy piece, and with quaking fingers, hooked the beard in place. Spying her hat, she grabbed it, and tucked her hair in the crown just as the boy whose calls had torn them apart came into view.

A towheaded lad wearing overalls rode on a raft

he'd constructed. Unmistakable from the material used to tie the logs together: men's neckcloths, a variety of hemp ropes in differing thicknesses, and bridle reins. But it was the frothy white piece of fabric that comprised the sail that caused Meg to gasp.

"Yo ho, yo ho!" he screeched, a buccaneer hat angled over his scruffy hair.

He commandeered the raft with a rowboat oar that he plunged from side-to-side.

As he drew nearer, Meg took a step forward, eyes narrowing on the raft's ruffled sail. Her bearded mouth fell open as she declared, "That's my petticoat."

Chapter

❦ 17 ❦

Clovis Lester used Meg's petticoat as a boat sail—
the very petticoat that had disappeared during her and
Matthew's picnic.

The starch in the fabric had lost its stiffness, and
the petticoat was billowing like a soggy hanky from
the mast. Several grass stains marred the once snowy
white cloth. The ruffled and ribboned hem was run
through with what appeared to be hammock fringe in
order to keep it attached to the pole. It was ruined,
utterly useless.

But it was hers.

If she hadn't been so emotional from Matthew's
kisses, she probably would have been laughing. Instead, she felt vulnerable. Meg wanted to yell at Clovis
to return her underwear that instant. But Mr. Bascomb wouldn't demand a lady's petticoat.

How had the precocious eight-year-old gotten it?
Didn't he realize his sail was a woman's undergarment? He probably didn't care. Not by the looks of
what else he'd procured to rig his pirate ship.

Clovis spotted them and coasted toward the shore. "Ho there, you lily-livered land lovers."

His piratical attire was comprised of bib overalls with rolled cuffs and a faded red shirt underneath. A black patch covered one of his blue eyes, and he'd outfitted himself with wooden swords slashed through a thick black belt. A closed chest that looked more like his father's tool box rather than a booty, laid on the deck at his feet.

"Matthew," she whispered into the fringe of her mustache. "Do something."

He turned to look at her. "Like what?"

"Like get my petticoat back for me."

In a low voice, he asked, "How's anyone going to know it's yours?"

With her knuckle, Meg knocked back a tear that had remained on her cheek. "My initials are embroidered on it."

Docking, Clovis hopped off his vessel, his Little Gent Dongola oxfords sinking in the muddy bank. Indifferent to the brown goo he'd splattered on his pants legs, he instantly withdrew his makeshift sword and aimed it at Meg with a sneer. "The infamous Red Beard, I presume. I'll have to mince you into giblets."

"I most certainly am not," Meg returned in a man sounding voice that was fraught with a gruffness and bristle that sounded menacing, even to her. "And it's Black Beard, you chicken gizzard."

Clovis scrunched up his round face. "You're Black Beard?"

"No." Meg collected her frazzled nerves, put her hands on her hips and leaned forward. "I'm Mr. Arliss Bascomb of the Bureau of Internal Revenue."

Clovis's sunshine washed cheeks burned red as he uttered, "Huh?"

Meg felt Matthew's strong presence beside her.

"My name is Mr. Wilberforce," Matthew began, "and you are?"

"Clovis."

"Well, Clovis, that's a fancy sailing ship you've got there." Matthew walked to the boat with an impressed smile on his mouth. "Did you make her?"

Following after Matthew, the boy wrinkled his nose. "Her?"

"All ships are her."

"Oh."

"What's her name?"

"I don't know."

"Well, she should have a name. Let's think of one."

Meg stayed back, a quiet tide of awe sneaking past her outrage and flooding her. This was a side of Matthew Gage she hadn't expected—patience, tolerance, generosity.

A way with children.

Unbidden, there went her heart swelling in her throat again.

"Who's your best gal?" Matthew asked, the tip of his shoe bouncing the front of the raft to test its buoyancy.

"My best gal?" Clovis wandered to Matthew's side and brought his shoe on the raft's edge as well and gave the logs a few bounces.

"Sure. The woman in your life. The one you love."

He made a grimace. "I don't love any girls."

"You have to love one."

"I do?"

"Sure. Sure. Who keeps your clothes laundered?

Cooks your supper? Makes sure your room is cleaned?" Matthew casually ran his hand up the mast, tugging a little on Meg's petticoat. She wondered if he was testing it for soundness. Maybe he had a plan to rip it from the rafters and run.

No . . . that didn't seem his style.

Matthew went on, "Who combs your hair? Who buys your shoes?"

When Clovis skewed his lips, the freckles on his nose crinkling, and made no comment, Matthew supplied: "Whoever it is, she's your best gal. She makes your birthday cakes and tucks you in at night."

"Oh!"

Matthew grinned.

"That'd be Gerty."

Brows arched, Matthew questioned, "You call your mother Gerty?"

Clovis's eyes clouded with confusion. "No. My mother's name is Ada."

"Who's Gerty?"

"She's our housemaid. She bakes good cookies."

Shoving his hat back with his thumb, Matthew lifted his forehead. "I guess you would have to be partial to a woman who bakes." Then he went back to the matter at hand. "All right, then you should call your ship Gerty."

"I should?"

"Absolutely."

"How will people know?"

"You paint her name on your hull."

"I don't have a hull." Then he smiled slyly. "But I have a heinie."

"Good Christ," Matthew muttered beneath his breath. "No, boy, you don't paint the ship's name on your bottom. You paint the name on the side of the ship."

"I don't know if Gerty will like that."

"Sure she will."

Not fully convinced, Clovis said, "I don't got any paint."

"Well," Matthew slipped his hand into his trouser pocket, "I happen to have fifty cents that you could use to buy the paint. I saw Kennison's hardware sells a quart of black paint for thirty cents."

"Gee! You'd just give me fifty cents?"

"No. I didn't say I'd give it to you. But I'll make you a trade."

He shoved his hand into the bib pocket of his overalls, produced the cast-off tail of a lizard and thrust his arm out. "I got this!"

Matthew examined the lizard's tail and shook his head. "Nope. I don't need one of those." He strolled to the boat and made an inspection of its ragtag sail. "How about I trade you for this?"

Clovis drew up behind him. "But how can I sail my boat without a sail?"

"Buy a few yards of canvas with the leftover twenty cents." Matthew laid a hand on the boy's shoulder. "In fact, you'd have enough paint to draw a Jolly Roger on your new sail."

"Gee whillikins! That's a swell idea." Clovis began to disassemble his sail, which served no purpose other than every ship needed a sail. Except Clovis Lester manned his with an oar so what difference did it make?

None to Meg.

She was getting her petticoat back. With any luck, nobody had seen the two satin-stitched lavender ini-

tials she'd embroidered on the first tier of ruffles—
that is, on what was left of the first tier of ruffles.

Clovis removed the ruined undergarment, stuffed it
into a wad, and shoved it at Matthew. "There you go,
Mr. Wilberforce. And now for my fifty cents." He held
his hand out, palm up, fingers twitching.

Dropping the two silver coins into Clovis's grasp,
Matthew said, "Nice doing business with you,
Captain."

After testing each coin between his teeth—one of
the top front ones missing, Clovis replied, "Nice doing
business with you, too, Mr. Wilberforce."

The boy hopped onto his ship, picked up his oar and
shoved off. To Meg, he hailed, "Yo ho, Mr. *Infernal*
Revenue man."

She waved him off, much like she'd do a fly buzzing
too close to her face, as Matthew drew up to her side.
They watched Clovis Lester sail down Evergreen
Creek, beyond the willows that bordered the bank
until he couldn't be seen any longer.

"I believe this is yours." Matthew gently handed
the petticoat to her, his fingers resting on top of hers.

"Thank you."

She was touched. Truly. In a way that she had never
been before.

She was supposed to be giving Matthew lessons. Instead, she'd had one of her own.

Not all stunt reporters stirred up trouble and angst.

In fact, this one had stirred up nothing more than
her passion.

Beyond that, he could talk to children as if he remembered what it was like to be one. Meg suspected
Matthew would make a fine father if he ever married
and wanted to have a family.

Suddenly it occurred to Meg that by not marrying, not having a husband, she would never have the chance to be a mother. No children. No boys or girls. No toys to clutter her house.

The thought brought a tear to her eye and she quickly blinked it away before Matthew could see. "Now," she said, her voice cracking with an emotion deeper than she'd ever experienced, "about fishing upstream. This is what you'll need to know . . ."

She was speaking, but she couldn't hear the words. The uneven beat of her pulse had taken over the rhythm of her thoughts.

Sighing heavily, Meg sat at the kitchen table resting her chin on her fists, one fist stacked on top of the other. An unladylike position if there ever was one.

In two hours, she was supposed to be at Johannah Treber's bridal shower. A party she didn't want to attend. Even though she'd decided *she* wouldn't be getting married, she feared the excitement surrounding the shower would carry her away and get her thinking things she ought not to.

She had to accept marriage wasn't for her. In twenty years, she'd had two prospects.

Harold Adams and Vernon Wilberforce.

A namby-pamby and an impostor.

Meg sighed once more and fingered the newsprint edges of Grandma Nettie's *Sisters in the Suffragette* gazette.

She sat watching Mr. Finch prepare supper. He moved with efficient energy, never wasting a minute. Bowler hat on and apron in place, he was a veritable treasure. She wondered if Grandma Nettie knew he fancied her.

"Mr. Finch, do you and my grandmother talk about things?"

"And what things would those be, Miss Margaret?" The carrots he'd sliced on a wooden board were shifted into a pot.

"Oh, I don't know. Just things. Anything."

"We discuss a wide variety of topics. Your grandmother is quite worldly."

Meg dared to say, "You're in love with her, aren't you?"

Mr. Finch faced Meg, the knife in his grasp pausing in thin air. She could swear he blushed, his dapper cheeks softening to pink. "I . . . Miss Margaret, where would you get such an idea?"

"I watched you once when you were watching my grandma."

After a moment, Mr. Finch conceded, "Yes. I am fond of your grandmother. Does that bother you?"

Meg sat up, laying her hands palm down on the table and scooting forward. "Oh, no! In fact, I think it's the most romantic thing given yours and Grandma Nettie's ages. You should tell her that you love her."

Mr. Finch gave her a wistful smile as he set the knife down and folded his arms over his chest. He uncharacteristically leaned his backside into the counter and stood in a relaxed manner she'd never seen from him before. He really was a dear-looking man, so polished and refined. Why, any woman would be glad to have him as her husband.

"Miss Margaret, your grandmother has so many important things she wants to do," Mr. Finch began in his perfect British voice. "I don't believe she'd be anxious to add me to her busy life."

"But how do you know unless you ask her?" Meg

insisted. Then an idea came upon her, sparkling with hope and optimism. "Ask her to Durbin's for an ice cream. Right after supper tonight. I know that she adores chocolate."

"I couldn't. I'm merely the butler."

"Of course you could. And you aren't a real butler. Besides, Grandma doesn't base her friendships on social ranks and all that. She isn't stuck up at all."

"What if she turns me down?"

"Well then," Meg said thoughtfully, grazing the tip of her fingernail with her teeth, "if she does decline, at least you'll know. If you never ask her, you'll always wonder if she would have said yes."

Mr. Finch broadly smiled, bringing his hand to his neat beard and drawing several strokes down the manicured black hair. "I'll do it."

Meg brought her hands together. "Wonderful."

Even if she wasn't getting married, there was no sense in Grandma Nettie missing the boat—so to speak.

Missing the boat.

That's what Meg was destined for in her carefree, independent, do-as-she please and untamed—yet solitary—life. When she got old, she'd be left in dry dock. The only one not sailing on a sea of matrimony.

On that thought, she slumped back in her chair and brought her hand to her temple. *Don't feel sorry for yourself. You stop it right now.*

Absently, she began to flip through the pages of her grandmother's rebel-rousing gazette. The inside was filled with the accounts of fearless exploits. Sketches of militant women—none that Mr. Gibson would have drawn—appeared beside some of the articles. Meg gazed at several ladies who wore britches and carried brooms.

The print blurred; she blinked her eyes and tried to refocus. A headache nagged at the base of her head. She'd been getting them more frequently the past three days. She knew the cause. All that stuffing her hair into Mr. Bascomb's hat and pinning the thick weight onto the crown of her head for long periods of time. It was such a nuisance to manage.

Mr. Finch slapped the lid on the pot, a smile still pinned on his mouth, and then he wiped the countertop. Meg looked at his beard once more. So tidy. So very in order—spit-spot, clipped, cut short.

Clipped. Cut short.

Once more, she glimpsed at the page she'd been staring at. A woman posed with her arms folded across her breasts. She wore her hair short. To her shoulders. Curls swept softly next to her cheeks. Quite shocking.

Meg raised her brows. Dare she even think it? Surely not. A woman who did such a thing—why, it was beyond scandalous to even consider cutting her hair. Then again, why keep it if it made her head hurt?

Who would she consult? A barber would be the logical choice to get the job done. The mere thought of Moses Zipp slicing away her hair with his razor-sharp scissors caused Meg to shiver. His reputation wasn't all that grand—more times than not, he was too preoccupied with discussing his hunting abilities than his hair cutting abilities. Not to mention, his shop was practically across from the hotel. She couldn't sit in one of his chairs with people walking by and looking in. Not even the newfound Meg had that much nerve.

"Mr. Finch," she said, her brows turned down in thought, "who trims your beard for you?"

"I do it myself."

Meg slanted her head, eyeing his thoroughly symmetrical beard once more. "It looks very respectable."

"Thank you, Miss Margaret."

With an inward sigh, Meg thought through her decision, giving herself ample opportunity to talk herself out of it. But she realized she'd kept her hair long all these years to please her mother and to be pleasing to society. She'd never thought about what she liked about keeping her hair long. Frankly, she was sick and tired of all the pulling on her scalp when she pinned the long lengths up.

Meg stood. "Mr. Finch, I'd like for you to cut my hair," she firmly said.

He smiled at her as if he thought she was teasing.

"I'm deadly serious, Mr. Finch. I want my hair short." She raised the gazette for him to view. "Cut it like this." Looking down at her shoulder, she brought her hand to rest at the base of her neck. "Right about here should do the trick. As short as the woman's in the picture."

Understanding she wasn't making light of her request, he stammered, "Miss Margaret, I don't think you really want me to do that."

"I do. I must have been thinking about it for months because it came as no surprise to me that I want it cut. I think it will be quite invigorating to shake my head without the weight of a twist on top of it."

"What will your mother say?"

"Don't worry about my mother," Meg replied, reaching for Grandma Nettie's sewing basket that she'd left in the kitchen this morning. Pulling out the sharp scissors, Meg gave them to Mr. Finch. "I trust you."

Then Meg began to slide the pins from her hair. The curly copper strands shivered down past her shoulders and to her waist. "Shall I sit or shall I stand?"

"Sitting would be better," Mr. Finch remarked. "Really, Miss Margaret, I don't want you to do anything hasty."

"I'm not."

Meg dragged a chair from the table and sat. Conviction fueled the tick of her pulse as it beat at her wrists. She waited, barely conscious of breathing in and out. She had come to a decision. An important one. And yet . . .

Mr. Finch stood behind her. "Are you quite sure, Miss Margaret?"

She had a moment of uncertainty. She thought of all the times that she'd looked at her curly hair in the mirror, waiting for the iron to heat in the lamp chimney and testing it with a moistened finger. There would be no more high pompadours for her. No more finger curls.

No more headaches.

"I'm quite sure. Cut my hair."

A raspberry dusk had long since descended behind the trees growing on Main Street and the day had broken up with people setting off for home. Lamplight filled parlor windows. Fireplaces had been stoked, curls of smoke rising from chimneys to tinge the air with a homey, cozy scent.

Gage ground out his cigar into a butt can, stuffed

his hands into his coat pocket, and began to walk to the hotel. Ham Beauregarde had left the restaurant minutes ago and from where he stood, Gage watched the salesman make a straight path to the hotel's porch, up the stairs, and right inside.

Nice and smooth.

Nothing out of the ordinary.

Gage had stayed behind. No sense in chasing Ham; Ham wasn't running anyplace sneaky. If the Gurney salesman had been planning something devious, he was doing so in secret. Because his actions hadn't disclosed a thing. Gage had all but decided the man was innocent.

So he'd wanted to buy Gage's lottery number. He hadn't.

So he'd gone to see Doolin at the hatchery. What good would it do him? Ham hadn't garnered one of the best fishing stakes so how could he stock a place at the end of the creek? Impossible.

So . . . ? Gage was back to where he started.

Though he still couldn't figure out how in the hell Wayne Brooks had done it. But he couldn't yet put it from his mind, no matter how badly he wanted to.

David West had sent another letter several days ago asking for a rough draft on the contest article. Gage had yet to write one. He couldn't. His usual zest for describing events as he saw them, just wasn't with him these past few days. He couldn't do a hack job on this piece. So he'd let David's letter go without a response. For all Gage knew, he could be on the road to getting himself fired.

He had to grasp the tail of what seemed to be a nasty local rat and expose it for the crooked-minded rodent it was. *Wayne Brooks.*

Only Gage couldn't think through the fiery piece. Couldn't think through the angle without seeing Meg's face on the page of his blank typewriter paper.

As Gage passed the Harmony bank, he knew the hour had to be near eight. That's the time Beauregarde went back to the hotel for the night. So Gage might as well, too. Only one more day to practice before the contest.

Only one more day alone with Meg. The thought of going back to San Francisco left him aching.

Crossing the street, he paused in the middle of it hearing the laughter and voices of women coming from up Sycamore Drive. A group of ladies gathered on a house porch, talking in an animated way—much as those at his Bissell sales pitch had done. The near-darkened street was lit by the many lights beaming from the house's front windows. Otherwise he wouldn't have been able to make out Meg.

He knew her form well. The way she held her head. The tilt of her chin. The way she kept her shoulders erect.

Gage slowly walked across the street and changed his course. He took Sycamore even though it wasn't the direction he needed to go. Although he made no conscious effort to do so, he stayed close to the shadows created by picket fences and shrubs that lined the sidewalk.

The group of women began to scatter, some coming toward him, others taking the north route up the street. As a pair of ladies passed him, he put his hand to his hat and murmured, "Good evening."

He watched Meg as she walked with those two friends of hers, Hildegarde and Ruth. Then the pair broke off around the corner and disappeared into one house together, leaving Meg alone.

Gage held back, liking the way Meg strolled—as if she were in deep thought. She reached her arm out and brushed the picket fence boards in front of her house, then she stopped at the gate and stared at the sky.

He looked as well. A high ceiling of elms marred his view. But he heard what she had to hear. The tree toad's chanting barreled up from the elm branches in an unchanging rhythm. A sliver of moon shown. Stars scattered high, some dim, others brighter.

Meg stood there a long moment. Listening. Gage heard and saw it, too. There came the song of the trees, of the moon, of the night.

She gave a sigh with a wistfulness that pained him. He felt it from where he stood and could no longer remain.

As he approached, he said her name. "Meg."

With a start, she turned to see him walking toward her.

"Matthew."

He liked the way she said his name in return.

"I was out," he offered, feeling suddenly foolish. As if he'd been spying on her and lurking like a youthful boy.

"I was out, too."

In the pale light, he noticed she wore her hat. The same one she'd worn today at the lottery drawing. He liked it. Very simple. No bows or garish ornaments. Simple straw braid with a scarf tied on the crown. Gage deepened his stare. Something else was different besides her hat. Her hair. That thick coppery mass he always longed to sink his fingers into. She'd styled it differently or done something else with the curls. Because they framed her face, teasing her cheeks and forehead in a way they hadn't done before.

"Well, I should be getting in," Meg said, clicking the latch and letting herself into the yard.

Gage didn't want to leave her yet. "I'll see you to the door."

"That's not necessary."

But Gage was already beside her, offering the crook of his arm to guide her up the porch steps.

Once at the top, Gage heard soft laughter, then a masculine chuckle. He felt Meg stiffen at his side, then yank him back down the stairs and around to the back of the house in a dash over the lawn.

At the stoop off of the kitchen, she sat down on one of the steps and plopped her elbows on her knees. "I can't believe it."

Gage lowered himself beside her. "Believe what?"

"That was my Grandma Nettie and Mr. Finch on the porch swing."

"Really?"

"Yes." She faced him, eyes wide. Gage wished he could see their warm brown color as she spoke. "It was my idea. She must have said yes. Mr. Finch asked her for an ice cream. He's in love with her."

Saying nothing, Gage smiled. He supposed that love knew no bounds. Age or otherwise.

Meg sighed and fanned her skirt over the tops of her shiny shoes. "I can't go in until they're done spooning on the swing. The kitchen door is always locked after Mr. Finch is done throwing out the dishwater. The only way inside is through that front door and I don't want to interrupt them."

"I'll stay with you." Gage removed his hat and let it dangle in his fingertips.

"You don't have to."

"I want to."

In truth, Gage didn't want to ever leave her. He wanted to stay. To flirt with her. Flirting wasn't something Gage cared to examine about himself. He either liked a woman enough to invite her to his room, or he didn't. There had never been any "flirting" involved. He was a cut to the chase type of man.

But Meg was complex and flirting and cutting to the chase weren't simple options. She needed to be held, kissed, loved.

Meg cradled her chin on both her hands and stared into the yard. Gage saw her profile, the short curls that hugged her cheek and brushed against the line of her jaw. Without thought, he reached for the brim of her hat and lifted it from her head.

It was then that he knew what was different.

"Christ, Meg . . . what happened to your hair?"

Chapter

❦ 18 ❧

He didn't like her hair.

Neither had the ladies at Johannah's bridal party. Except for Mrs. Wolcott and Cressie. They thought she looked vogue—or at least that's what they said. Ruth and Hildegarde had been surprised, as had been their mothers. At least her two friends hadn't voiced their opinions out loud. But their mothers had. And their words had stung.

Even so, Meg refused to change her mind about her hair. It felt light and free and even a little sassy as it bobbed on her shoulders and tickled her neck. She liked to shake her head and let the springy curls fall where they wanted. Even Mr. Finch thought she looked becoming. He'd said so.

"I had it cut," Meg eventually replied in a guarded tone.

The back of Matthew's hand brushed her cheek as he straightened a curl that fell to her jaw line. She felt his knuckles across her skin as he skimmed her ear and then higher to her cheek where he caressed her.

She wasn't prepared for the avalanche of sensations that ran through her. The mere casualness of his touch sent her spiraling, like she was flying off the tire swing and into the sky—sailing, swooning, almost dizzy.

"What did you do with the hair you cut off?" he asked, throwing her off balance.

She'd saved it. Heaven help her, for all her talk of wanting to be her own self and have her own style and mannerisms and not caring about attitudes or things of sentimental value, she hadn't been able to part with her hair. It had taken twenty years to grow that long. She couldn't throw it away. So she'd put the long lengths in a pillow slip and tied a ribbon around the top and stored it in her . . . hope chest.

Not that she'd ever be using her hope chest.

But that's where she put all her treasures. All those things that made her Meg. Everything she'd experienced, thought, or felt in her life thus far. Her old diaries, magazine clippings, coins her grandfather had given her for her birthday, her first corset, her baby blanket, a picture of her mother's grandparents, a tooth of Wayne's that he'd given her when it had fallen out . . . personal things.

Hair was awfully personal.

"I saved it," Meg managed to reply, trying—with no success—to disregard the warmth of Matthew's fingers against her skin.

"Why did you cut it?"

"Because I wanted to." She looked into his face, her gaze determined despite the hammering of her heart. His hand lowered to her shoulder. "I suppose you wouldn't like it. But my Grandma Nettie loves it. When she saw me before supper, she couldn't believe her eyes. She thinks it makes me look . . ." She didn't want to say *"like a fireball ready to take up the charge for womankind"*—that sounded a little *too* renegade. So Meg redefined her grandmother's reaction. "She said it makes me look sophisticated. I'm glad I cut it. It's only hair. After all, if I decide I want it long again, I can grow it back." She suddenly stopped talking. She was babbling and trying to defend her actions— two things she promised herself she wouldn't do.

"I didn't say I didn't like it." His thumb caressed the column of her neck.

Against her will, Meg found herself asking, "What do you think of it?"

His smile brought a rush of warmth across her skin. "I think it suits you."

Suits you. What did that mean?

All of a sudden, Meg wanted to cry.

Did it mean that she was more suited to short hair than long? That she was too different to be like everybody else so it was all right to have hair that bounced on her shoulders when she walked?

Meg managed to say, "Thank you." But she didn't mean it.

Why should she care if he liked her hair or not? It didn't matter. And yet . . . Her thoughts trailed off to a whispered gasp when his lips touched her cheek.

He must have seen the hurt on her face because he said in a low voice, "I'd be proud to show you off. I'd be the envy of every man in town with you walking at my arm."

She could hear him breathe against her as he grazed her skin and sought her mouth with his. *Proud to show you off. Envy of every man.* Sweet words like that were fatal to a woman who was in love. Who was trying not to be in love. But just couldn't help it.

Refusing to think, Meg's arms came around his shoulders and he drew her in close and snug next to him. She had never held a man this way before—like she thought she'd die if she couldn't.

They had shared kisses before. She'd felt like an innocent. All dreamy and wanting. Now she knew that she wanted more than kisses. She wanted him to touch her intimately again. She wanted more than caresses. She wanted him in that way a woman wanted a man. But she didn't know how.

Matthew felt cool and warm at the same time. The back of his coat held the chill in the night air, yet the collar of his shirt had captured his body heat. She dared feel his cheek while he kissed her. Rough at the jaw, yet smooth as marble the higher she teased her fingers up his cheek.

She snuggled against him and let him kiss her the way he wanted to. She relaxed into the feel of his lips over hers, letting him rouse in her those passions he'd ignited in her this afternoon.

His tongue swept across her lips, testing, seeking, then inside her mouth in an erotic way that made her toes curl in her shoes. Nobody had ever talked about this. At least none of the girls she knew.

Meg lost herself in the heated kiss, letting his fingers explore her curves. A shoulder, her collarbone, chin, the length of her neck. Then lower. To her breast. When he'd done this earlier, she tensed, shocked at first and feeling very self-conscious about what she lacked in the bosom department.

But Matthew hadn't minded. Or at least he hadn't said anything. And it had felt so good, she hadn't wanted him to stop. And yet, she got that odd feeling again . . . like she was lacking. And he knew it.

She loathed herself for saying against his lips, "I'm not a big woman."

To her horror, he laughed. Soft and low, then kissed her hard and said, "I think you're perfect."

How could he think she was perfect? She was tall and thin. Not curvaceous and well-rounded like her friends. Even if she did have the right figure, she was a mix of so many things on the inside. Unconventional. Conventional to a degree.

Meg held on to a soft sigh as his hand leisurely explored her. Her nipple tightened beneath his touch. In spite of the corset and shimmy she wore, she was sure he could feel her. He deepened the kiss and she clung to him.

Dear heaven, she'd let him unbutton her shirtwaist. If he wanted to, she would let him. What was she thinking? She was poised to tell him to do it. To pull at the ribbons on her chemise. Just so he could touch her without the hindrance of clothing. But she was unable to speak.

Yet she was bold enough to take his fingers and guide them to the top tiny pearly button. His hand lingered a moment. Then he rested his palm over the tattoo of her heart beating beneath his fingers.

"Meg . . . you know I want to. But not this way. Not on a porch."

She swallowed, suddenly feeling chilled to the bone. Feeling like a floozy. She sat up, away from him, and pulled at the collar of her blouse to right the crooked fabric. "Of course," she managed. "You're right. I . . . I wasn't myself. I don't know what happened . . ."

"When I kiss you," he murmured, "I'm not myself either."

On a sigh, Meg pointed out, "Even when we aren't kissing, we aren't ourselves. You're Vernon Wilberforce and I'm Arliss Bascomb. I think we need to remind ourselves or else . . ." She couldn't finish. *Or else we'll do something we'd regret.*

From the front of the house came the squeak of the door as it closed. Grandma Nettie had gone inside.

Meg stood. "I have to go in now."

Matthew followed her around the house. She climbed the steps to the porch and disappeared into the darkness. She didn't want him to see her; see the affect he had on her. She tingled and shivered. She wanted to be with him. But Wayne stood between them. Wayne, and her emotions that went crazy when Matthew kissed her. Was she so in love with the idea of love that she forgot about how things really were?

She'd struggled for independence. Had let it go. Gotten it back. She hadn't come half-close to discovering what her life could be like without love. Here she had the opportunity, and she was cheating herself.

How could she have allowed what happened on the porch? It seemed everything and more told them not to be involved. Why couldn't she listen to reason?

Behind her, she heard Matthew call out.

"I'll see you tomorrow. It's our last lesson."

She couldn't make herself reply. Her voice was too unsteady. She didn't want him to hear the quiver.

And she didn't even know if she could be in his company anymore. It was getting so hard to remain indifferent, uncaring. The pretending was wearing her down to a nub.

Without a word, Meg gripped the door knob and closed the door behind her.

She stood in the foyer and leaned her back against the door, fighting back a sob that threatened to engulf her.

"Meg," came her grandmother's voice from the parlor. "I just got in myself. How was Johannah's party?"

Meg didn't feel like talking about it, but she went to greet Grandma Nettie. "It was fine."

Grandma Nettie sat on the organ bench. "I feel like playing. It's been so long. Come join me, dear." She patted the seat. "What did they think of your hair?"

Not wanting to put a damper on Grandma Nettie's high spirits, Meg sat down beside her. "I shocked most of them."

"They'll come around. I think your hair looks wonderful. I've decided to cut mine, too. Do you suppose that Mr. Finch would mind doing the honors?"

"I don't think so." Meg pressed down on the middle C key with her index finger. "How was your outing with Mr. Finch?"

Her grandmother laughed. "Griffon is a very interesting man. I've been too involved in my campaigns to see it." She gave Meg's shoulder a squeeze. "Thank you for suggesting Durbin's, Meg. I felt like I was a young girl again."

Meg smiled. She was happy for her grandma.

"And how are things coming along on the Arliss Bascomb front?" her grandmother asked.

"I don't know." Meg removed her hat and set it on top of the organ's mantel. "Everything is going to depend on the contest this Saturday."

"I haven't been very nice to *that reporter* ever since you told me he was a fraud," Grandma confessed. "He only gets a nod from me these days."

"You can do more than nod to him, Grandma. He doesn't bite."

"His words do."

But he hadn't written any thus far—not any that Meg knew about.

"Well, after Saturday it will be all over and he'll know that our Wayne is innocent. Then your newspaper man will be gone from Harmony for good."

Gone. Forever.

As Grandma Nettie played "Love's Old Sweet Song," Meg wanted to cry. Her vision blurred on the sheet music, and she lowered her chin.

The tune's notes filled the parlor. Sweet and melodic. Meg knew the words. They flowed inside her head.

So till the end, when life's dim shadows fall, love will be found the sweetest song of all.

Why did loving a person have to hurt so much?

The following morning, Meg stood in the backyard of her house, struck a match to the side of a matchbox and tossed the flame onto the refuse pile. Her current diary sat on top. Mr. Finch had yet to burn the week's trash so Meg was doing it for him. And burning the book that was filled with all her personal thoughts.

She was through with writing down sentimental overtures.

Smoke curled and red sparks spit from the mound of leaves, twigs, kitchen waste, and rubbish.

Meg was burning Matthew Gage out of her life and getting on with her new one. In a way, the prospect of living as a spinster was exciting. Look at all the things she could do or say. Because old maids had a way about them. They never had to conform much—they were usually thought of as eccentric, anyway.

Perhaps Meg was meant for eccentricity. She'd find out if she was—now that she had no future with men. At that thought, her excitement faltered. So much for a brave front.

Ever since she'd fallen in love with Matthew, she'd been forlorn. All those silly words she'd written about Mr. Wilberforce, they embarrassed her now. Half of the things she'd said were made up anyway.

But mixed inside were her true feelings. The way she really did feel about Matthew. And that was the part that wouldn't go away. She'd pulled out all the stops when writing down her fantasies about him. Now that she'd come to her senses and realized they didn't have a chance, the entries were just too painful to read.

Meg watched as the corners of the blue leather book smoked and the air grew tinged with the smell of her lost dreams and . . . bacon.

Bacon?

"Miss Margaret!" came Mr. Finch's alarmed call of distress as he stood on the back stoop wearing his apron. "What are you doing?"

She thought it was obvious. "Burning the trash."

"You'll torch us all to the ground." On that, he hurried down the steps after grabbing a bucket and quickly pumping water into it from the pump.

Before she could blink, he'd doused the fire to a smoldering gray cloud of air that puffed skyward and choked her.

On a cough, she asked, "Why did you do that?"

"Because this isn't the burn pile, Miss Margaret."

Mr. Finch pointed to the other pile in a bricked border. "That is the burn pile. This is the compost pile."

"It is?" One pile of trash all looked the same to her.

"Yes." Mr. Finch adjusted the slope of his bowler which had gone askew as he dashed to put the flames out. "I just poured this morning's bacon grease onto the pile, Miss Margaret, and if the flames were allowed to continue, we might have had an inferno on our hands."

"Oh . . ." Meg bit her bottom lip. Yes, the yard did smell like an Easter ham.

Mr. Finch took a stick and stirred the singed mess, knocking her diary from the pile. It rolled, edges charred and still smoking, to her feet.

"What's that?" Mr. Finch inquired, bending toward her diary.

"An old schoolbook of mine with a ruined binding. Nothing important." She tried to step on her diary, but was afraid she'd burn the sole of her shoe. She was about to kick the journal out of the way, and out of Mr. Finch's view, when she grew distracted by the bay of a hound. Mr. Wolcott's dog, Barkly, to be precise.

The bloodhound loped upon them, no doubt attracted by the smell. He was a troublesome creature, but even Meg had to admit he was cute in an ear flopping, slobbering, kind of way. But when he started heading for her diary, all thoughts of cute ran dry.

"Barkly!" Meg shouted. "Get away from there."

But quicker than she could react, the bloodhound had her book of made-up stories and all-too-real emotions in his chops and was bounding toward Main Street in a stride too fast to catch. He'd absconded with her most private and intimate thoughts as if they were a ham hock.

Discovery in the wrong hands would make her the scandal of the century.

She wasn't coming.

Gage had waited for Mr. Bascomb at nine o'clock. By fifteen after nine, Meg hadn't showed. So Gage had gone to the fishing spot by himself.

Assembling his rod and tackle, he'd whipped silk braid over the stream for a good half hour, his arm stiff and his concentration waning. He couldn't unroll the line loop in a smooth motion and it kept getting tangled. Meg's instructions swam through his head, but he couldn't focus on any of them.

Early this morning, he'd stopped by the vacant building on Hackberry Way. He'd looked inside once more.

The space was ideal for a newspaper office, easily large enough to house a printer's press and a copy desk. The lighting was good. A location that was central to town. The place had a lot to offer, but could Gage make an offer on it?

Relocating was a hell of a thing for a man his age. Settled in a way of life that he had known for three decades. Change—to a pessimist, it was an optimistic word. Yet he found the prospect inspiring in a way that he hadn't felt in a long while.

Change. Could he?

For Meg, he thought he could do almost anything. But would that mean giving up who he really was? Stunt reporter. Muckraker.

The words were now sounding dirty, even to him.

He used to love the stories he'd penned. Now he

was starting to hate the thought of doing one more. Because this new one put a wall between him and Meg. She made him see that he wasn't doing the world a favor. That he was sometimes as low in his tactics to get a story as those he exposed.

Before Meg he'd been content.

Now he was questioning himself.

"Damn her," he said, tipping his rod in a forward cast. The fragile line flew in a wide arc that floated downward into a stand of willows and caught.

"You didn't release the slack on time," came a voice behind him.

Gage turned and a surge of emotion swept through him despite the sight of the red theatrical beard and stiff clothes of Meg as Mr. Bascomb. She stood at the top of the shoreline, rod and tackle box in hand.

"I know that," Gage replied. "I wasn't concentrating."

"That was obvious."

Reeling in what he could of the silk thread, Gage said, "You didn't show up. I left."

"I was indisposed." Meg made her way toward him, her gear rattling against the full leg of her trousers. "Hildegarde's mother waylaid me."

Gage found that interesting. He'd been waiting on the porch and he hadn't seen Mrs. Plunkett enter the hotel. "Where? In the lobby?"

"No. Upstairs. The nerve of that woman. She was waiting in the hallway trying to get her daughter a suitor. Me."

Meg made her way to Gage and set her things down with a thump. She removed her beard, took off her hat, and shook out her short hair. Sunlight captured the copper strands, suffusing them with fiery color.

Shimmering and bright, the curls reminded him of fall leaves in a variety of sunset hues.

Gage loved her hair. Very much.

"She got a good eyeful of me and still wasn't deterred from asking me over for Sunday supper. Honestly, this disguise is pretty thin—she must be desperate to find Hildegarde a husband if she's willing to settle for someone as ratty as Arliss Bascomb," she scoffed. "I told her no, of course. I'm glad today is the last day I'll have to be Mr. Bascomb."

Quietly Gage said, "After last night, I didn't think you'd come."

"My brother's neck is on the line. I had to come," she replied. "Are you happy?"

"I'm not happy that you don't really want to be here." Gage dug into his pants pocket for his Beeman's peppermint gum after dropping his fishing rod with disgust. He unwrapped a stick and chewed. Then he caught Meg staring at him.

"You have a bad stomach, don't you?"

He lifted his brow. "No worse than usual."

"You know what your problem is?" she stated, not in a tone that was holier than thou—but, rather, more matter of fact. "Your stomach acts up because of all the stress you put on yourself. Have you ever thought about another profession?"

Gage choked on a wry laugh. "No, but I've thought of altering the one I'm in."

"Really? How so?"

"You wouldn't believe me."

"You could try me."

"I don't think so. I'm not ready to convince myself yet."

Thankfully, Meg let the subject drop.

Gage bent and began to untangle his line so he could practice some more. Although, right at this moment, he really didn't give a damn about fishing or the contest or Wayne Brooks.

It wasn't until he was well ensconced with his line that all of a sudden he heard the clatter of a jar lid and Meg's soft oath of: "Hells bells." He'd never heard her swear before. So it was that fact that had him looking over his shoulder at her.

She held on to a jar of white lotion, the label half-hidden in her grasp. Some of the concoction had oozed onto her fingers. All he could make out of the writing on the jar was *Princess Bus—* and *—largement of the Bu—*.

"What are you doing?" Gage asked.

"Nothing."

She looked helplessly around, as if she wanted to ditch the cream and thwack the goo off her hand.

Gage straightened and walked toward her. "What is that?"

"Nothing that would interest you," she returned, plopping the jar into her tackle box and attempting to close the lid but unable to.

"I've learned the hard way that when you say 'nothing' there's usually 'something.' " Gage stood over her and looked down into her upturned face.

"Well, if you must know, this is . . . camphor. For itching. Just in case we come upon some poison ivy."

She apparently had no handkerchief on her, so she wiped her hand down the leg of her pants. Not all of the camphor came off, and she disregarded the rest that smeared her fingers. He watched her as she set up her line and affixed a badger spider on the hook. Some of the white gunk got on the fuzzy dry fly.

She stood and faced him. "What?"

"Do you think that camphor will attract any fish?"

"It doesn't work."

"You've tried it?"

"Yes. A liberal amount for one whole day—" She clamped her mouth closed. "I mean, I haven't personally tried it. I've had it in my tackle box for a day." Then she trudged off toward the shore without giving him the opportunity to say more.

Gage followed and cast his line, unfurling the silk gut from his simple click reel over the water in fast repetitions. Not a bite.

Meg, on the other hand, released hers in a graceful unrolling of airborne line before the fly settled to the river's current, a small spot of color barely visible as it floated for a few feet through the riverbank's green reflections. Then the badger spider was gulped in. Swallowed—hook, line, and camphor.

She reeled the line in, let the trout go, and examined her hook with a puzzled shake of her head. More of the white camphor from her hand got onto the badger spider again. She mumbled something beneath her breath, shrugged, and recast.

Again. Another trout.

Five more casts. Five more trout.

While Gage stood there without a nibble.

"I can't believe it," she murmured, going back to her tackle box, getting some more of the white preparation and liberally loading her fly with it.

As she returned toward him, he said, "Let me see the jar of that camphor. I want to try it."

"You most certainly may not. It's an . . . an old family recipe and I'm sworn to secrecy."

He held her gaze with his for a prolonged moment. "You're lying to me."

She stared at length at him. Then without spite: "It's awful, isn't it?"

She turned away from him and went back to the shore.

Hours later, as Meg walked through the hotel lobby once again dressed as herself, she should have felt relieved that she no longer would have to be alone with Matthew.

But the mere thought left her feeling lonely. And more than a bit sad.

She shook her head. Forget about him. Think about something else.

The bust cream.

Now there was a topic. That bust cream had caught her more fish than it had men. She wondered what was in it that made the trout go crazy and bite.

If she hadn't brought it to the creek to dump, she wouldn't have found out about its luring abilities. After the bonfire fiasco, she wasn't about to have Mr. Finch discover her bust cream. So she'd planned to get rid of it at the bottom of the lake. Only the jar lid had come lose when she'd been sneaking it out of her tackle box and Matthew had caught her. She hadn't been about to tell him that she'd been gullible enough to buy that kind of feminine product.

She'd rather curl up and die.

Matthew. She sighed.

Pushing open one of the double front doors, Meg paused on the hotel's porch when she saw Grandma Nettie at the boardwalk with Mrs. Treber, Mrs. Calhoon, Mrs. Elward, and Mrs. Plunkett around her.

Several of her schoolmates were there as well: Camille Kennison—the prettiest girl in class. Ruth and Hildegarde.

Voices drifted to Meg.

"Her behavior is not to be tolerated, Mrs. Rothman," quipped Mrs. Elward. "She and my Ruthy have been friends ever since they were babies. I always knew Margaret was on the flighty side, but I never minded because she was so innocent. Only now she's gone too far. Cutting her hair and breezing about on Main Street without the slightest bit of embarrassment."

"I quite agree," chimed Mrs. Plunkett. "Hildegarde, don't you dare take it into your head to cut your hair. It just isn't done."

"Yes, Mother," Hildegarde replied. "I mean, no, Mother, I won't cut my hair."

Mrs. Treber forged right in with, "I'm so glad my Johannah has found a good man. That's what Margaret is lacking. A husband would tame her. Teach her not to be so forward."

Mrs. Calhoon added, "A husband would solve everything."

"She's run amuck," Mrs. Plunkett voiced. "First she shows her petticoat hem in public, then she cuts her hair. What's next?"

Grandma Nettie had quietly listened to them, then straightened to her full height and made a hissing sound of disapprobation. "You don't know a thing about being women. And you don't know a thing about my Meg. Cutting one's hair does not a hussy make. It speaks of individuality. Of confidence."

Tension bristled the air.

Meg breathed in and out in a soft rise and fall of

her breasts. She lifted her hand to the doorjamb to steady herself. Her head swirled with doubts. Had she gone so far in the opposite direction of Margaret, she'd turned Meg into a public disgrace? That hadn't been her intention.

Her mind awhirl, Meg could barely comprehend what she was hearing.

"I like her hair," Camille said, slicing through the electrified quiet. "I think it looks darling on her and I admire her for having the courage to cut it. I wish I could be more like her. She never worries about what people think and she looks like she has an awful lot of fun with life."

Tears filled Meg's eyes. She'd never known Camille Kennison to have doubts about herself. She was so pretty and sought after. Why, she could have any man in all of Harmony . . . and yet, she didn't. Why was that? She wasn't engaged and she never talked about getting engaged either.

"Your mother would have a fit if she heard you talking that way, Camille," Mrs. Treber ostracized.

"My mother wouldn't mind at all," Camille defended. "She's modern."

"Amen," Grandma Nettie seconded. "Meg can be whoever she wants to be."

"Yes, like a luggage cart–riding hoyden," Mrs. Treber spouted.

Meg felt her whole life falling apart right then and there. She'd wanted to be herself. And she'd wanted to be accepted. She realized now that she couldn't have both. It seemed so unfair. She felt her temper rise in response to their unkind words.

A cry escaped her mouth as she pushed off from the doorway and approached them.

Lifting her chin and boldly meeting their eyes in turn, she said, "My, my, it does look like a nice day for a ride on Delbert's bellman's cart."

"Miss Brooks, really," tsked Mrs. Treber, "do be serious."

Serious?

Just then, the three o'clock train whistle blared its impending arrival at the depot.

Meg's thoughts dangerously raced.

The luggage cart–riding hoyden.

Her rebellious emotions got the better of her as she laid a hand on the cart's brass rail, let its wheels smack across the porch, down the steps, and onto the brick street.

Mrs. Plunkett cried, "You wouldn't."

"Wouldn't I?" Meg stepped her left foot onto the velvet platform, leaving her right foot on the ground to shove off with.

"When you're finished, dear, you bring it back," Grandma Nettie said, then excused herself from the ladies and went into the hotel as if nothing was amiss.

The whistle blew steam once more and Meg set off in motion.

Triumph flooded through her as the luggage cart gained speed on its rickety wheels toward the depot. Rattling and careening down Birch Avenue, she felt the wind at her cheeks, with her skirts flying and her hair blowing. And her tears flowing.

The bristle of their words could not be ignored. But she would be damned if she let them know how they'd hurt her.

As the depot came into view, she let go with one hand to dash away her tears and she even dared to smile at the engineer as he waved to her. Old Moe, a familiar soul who never once made an ill reference to her outlandish ways.

Coming to a stop in the gravel beside the depot, Meg hopped off the cart wondering what she would do now.

But she didn't wonder for long when a voice called her. One she knew. One she hadn't heard in months.

"Hey, sweet pea! Still up to no good, I see."

Meg turned, shouting the name on her lips. "Wayne!"

Chapter

❧ **19** ❧

"Gee it's good to see you, sweet pea."

The night swathed Meg and her brother in tones of grays as they sat on the front porch swing after supper. Wayne was in Harmony only overnight. He was on his way to Denver to meet with some friends for the spring semester break.

"I'm so glad you're home. I just wish you could stay longer."

"I know. I know."

They swung gently, quiet all round them.

"Did Camille Kennison get married while I was away?" Wayne asked, breaking the silence in a nonchalant manner. His question and consecutive blow of five cigar smoke rings were delivered at the same time.

Throughout the meal, Wayne had told Meg and Grandma Nettie—and Mr. Finch, too—all about Cornell University. Wayne had been elected to the student government and was even a member of an old and respected fraternity. His days were filled with classes and important meetings, while his evenings were filled with a myriad of social events and too many friends to count. From the sounds of it, Wayne was a big man on the New York State campus.

His clothing were sure ultra. He must have gone to a high class metropolitan tailor. The cutaway coat that encased his broad shoulders was of the most extreme style. Fancy worsted had been used on his horizontal striped vest, while the coat was of cheviot. The coat also had five buttons, but Wayne opted for the current fashionable way of fastening the front with only four. *And,* he'd even taken to using a gold-trimmed Congo walking stick. He'd also pomaded his hair. He'd never done that before.

When Meg had turned and seen him at the train station, she could hardly believe the gentleman before her was her very own brother. He'd changed so much.

"Camille?" Meg asked, after a length of time. "No, she hasn't gotten married. Why?"

"Just wondering, sis. She's awfully pretty."

"Yes, very." Meg normally would have voiced her words in a pining note. But since Camille had stood up for her this afternoon, Meg couldn't think or say anything but flattery about Camille Kennison.

Knitting her fingers together and bracing them on her lap, Meg changed the subject. "So tell me about school."

Wayne slowly puffed on his cigar. "I already did at dinner."

"I mean tell me the things that aren't fit for table conversation."

Winking at her, Wayne laughed.

Meg settled into the swing's wooden-slotted back-rest and listened to Wayne's exploits of riding an elevator for the first time, and in electric street cars, and seeing a Pierce motorette, which had been a gleaming black color, to shenanigans with his college chums. Of drinking beer in public gardens and going to burlesque shows.

"Do they really dance down to their shimmies?" Meg asked.

With a brush of his fingertip over the end of Meg's nose, Wayne said, "Never you mind about what happens after they get to their shimmies."

They sat quietly for a while, swaying back and forth, the rusty squeak of the swing chains keeping them company.

"So where are all your beaux, sis?"

Wayne's inquiry caused Meg to tense. "I don't have any beaux."

"I can't believe that." He playfully tugged on a lock of her hair. "And if I do say so, you look cute with this short hair."

Meg felt self-conscious about her hair all of a sudden and tried to play down the fact that she didn't have any men callers and never would again. "I've decided not to marry so why waste my time with suitors?"

"That's a change from the sister I knew. You've been fond of the idea of getting married."

"I've changed my mind."

"Maybe you'll unchange it." Wayne pitched his cigar over the porch railing and into the dewy lawn that stretched out before them. "Finch told me that a man named Vernon Wilberforce has called on you."

"Not lately," Meg corrected. "And he wasn't for me. Not to mention he's only in town for the fishing contest. He'll be leaving Sunday, I'm sure."

"The ol' contest," Wayne chuckled. "Wonder who'll win this year?"

"Certainly not Mr. Wilberforce," Meg said, "he can't fish worth a darn."

"You've seen him practicing, have you?"

Some confidences couldn't be shared with her brother. "I've heard."

"Who got the number-one lottery spot?"

"Orvis Schmidt."

"He's a decent fellow," Wayne commented while resting his arm on the back of the swing. "He has a chance at winning."

"I don't care who wins just so long as we can move on." In a softer voice, unable to meet his eyes, she said, "I've heard a few people talking about your win last year."

"Have you now?"

"Yes. And I don't like it. But I've stuck up for you, Wayne. I have."

"That's sweet, sis."

"You couldn't help it if you pulled the number-one spot," she stated, turning to him. "And you won because you were the best."

Wayne's leashed rumble of laughter unexplainably brought out gooseflesh on Meg's arms. There was coldness in the way he found humor in her words— as if he knew a secret.

"I was the best, Maggie, best at being the smartest."

For several driving heartbeats, Meg let the comment pass. Then she couldn't ignore the chill that swept over her.

"What do you mean?"

"Never you mind about what I mean, sweet pea."

Never mind? Why "never mind?" What did that

mean? Meg leaned forward on the swing and tried to see her brother's face clearly. "Are you telling me that you did something . . . dishonest?"

"Let it go, sis."

Although the lighting was poor, Meg could see his eyes narrow with unexpected anger.

Clearly, Meg had stumbled onto something Wayne wanted to let rest. But she couldn't; even if it meant an agonizing discovery. So she spoke words aloud that had only once flickered inside her heart—the day Matthew first said them himself. The day she'd adamantly denied Wayne would have done anything underhanded. "Did you have an arrangement with Leroy Doolin at the hatchery?"

He didn't answer right away. "Yeah, I paid him. So what of it? Doolin was happy to unload those fish." He spoke defensively, causing Meg to gasp. "I won that lottery spot fair and square. I never planned on doing anything before the drawing. But it was my luck that I got the best place. I'm a thinker and going to Doolin was the smartest thing I've ever done. Nobody can point a finger at me because everybody saw me pull up those brown trout. It was a clean win. Everybody got what they wanted."

In a chilling tone, Meg directed, "Oliver Stratton didn't."

Her brother stood and shoved his hands in his pockets. "I did what any man in my position would have done. This town doesn't have squat, Maggie. I won the best place in that lottery." The gold fob dangling from his vest pocket glimmered in the moonlight. "I got the best so I wanted the best. Not a single soul can prove what happened. Doolin's been paid to stay quiet. And that's the way of it. I won. I got the money and I'm enjoying the hell out of spending it. Because it's brought me respect."

At that moment, Meg lost her respect for Wayne.

He'd cheated.

He admitted it. The details. The way of things. And the why was very apparent: He wanted a lifestyle that their father simply couldn't afford: a notable college, smart clothes, and privilege.

The sobering truth hurt worse than anything Meg could ever have imagined. All this time she'd defended Wayne to Matthew. All this time she'd been waiting for the day when she could say to Matthew: "I told you so."

Instead, it would be Matthew saying those words.

Meg rose from the swing. "You were good enough to win fair and square, Wayne."

"No. Oliver Stratton was good enough to win fair and square," Wayne returned.

The hum of night songs blanketed them. Meg grew colder by the minute. Though she didn't know if it was from the night air or her breaking heart.

Rubbing her hands across her arms, Meg said, "Tell Grandma I'm going for a walk."

Wayne caught her shoulders and turned her to face him; she couldn't meet his eyes, not even in the dark. "Let it go, Maggie."

Meg lifted her chin and looked into his face. "What's in the past is in the past and you can't change it."

He all but patted her hand when he released her. "That's right. Now, hey, sweet pea, you want me to come with you?" He winked once more. "A pretty girl like you shouldn't be walking alone at night."

"I'll stay on our street. It's perfectly respectable."

"All right. Well, you come in soon. I saw that Finch has made a pie for dessert. I'm going to find out what kind."

"You do that."

Meg woodenly went down the steps and let herself through the gate. When she began walking, she didn't have any idea where she'd go. It was only after she reached the end of her block that she knew she was going to see Matthew.

Gage tilted on the back legs of his chair. His stockinged feet were propped on the edge of the hotel room desk and his vest hung open as he studied the typewritten sheets he'd completed earlier in the evening. His article on last year's fly-fishing contest and Wayne Brooks's win was chock-full of details, browraising speculations, and worded in a way that was typical Gage. Three pages of flaming prose that would surely sell newspapers.

He'd reread the piece dozens of times. There was nothing wrong with the story itself. It was the kind Gage scooped. Yet each time he viewed his work, he drew the same conclusion.

Something was missing. And that something, he knew, was that one piece of information that proved that Wayne Brooks had rigged the contest.

Gage dropped the article and went for another. One he'd written much earlier in the evening. He skimmed the words. This piece had heart. It had warmth, a vibrancy.

The story made him smile, not with satisfaction, but with fondness.

As Gage began to reread the article once more, a knock sounded on his door. He gave the clock on the

338

mantel a quick glance, then rose and walked quietly across the rug to answer the door.

When he opened it, he paused, his heartbeat quickening as he drank in the sight of Meg, who stood in the hallway.

Without a word, she let herself in. Gage slowly closed the door after her.

She appeared distraught. Lips parted, then closed. Eyes looked down, then directly met his. Slender hands clasped together, then unclasped with a tremble. Sighing heavily, she sat on the end of his bed. She wore no cape or shawl, no gloves or hat, as if she hadn't given any thought to coming to see him. He watched her shiver, a tiny quake of her body and shudder of breath.

"You're cold." Gage went to the bed and picked up his coat and draped it over her shoulders. Their hands touched briefly as she lifted hers to the coat's collar.

"I . . . thank you," she said, then stared at the tips of her shoes.

Gage sat down beside her. "What happened?"

She was as quiet as a bench judge awaiting a jury's verdict.

Her voice was distant when she said, "My brother came home today."

Wayne. Gage waited for her to continue, his pulse surging.

"He talked about the university. He's quite the man around town. I almost didn't recognize him. He was dressed so uptown. All the go in his suit. He's in the student government and he's in a sought after fraternity. He really has done well. He's getting good grades, too." Her monotone recital of her brother's merits sounded hollow to Gage. She took in a shaky breath. "He's only here for tonight. He'll be leaving tomorrow."

Then silence. A shiver from Meg and a bite of her lower lip as if she were trying to keep from crying.

Gage put his arm around her and drew her close. "What's wrong, darling?"

She sighed into his shirt and let him hold her while she pressed her body next to his. A hunch washed through his conscious and somehow he knew what had distressed Meg.

The truth.

That one piece of unequivocal truth that would complete his article.

"He talked about last year's contest," Meg said, her words bringing an intimate warmth against the side of his neck. "He told me he paid Leroy Doolin to let those brown trout go upstream. That's how he won. He had fish coming right at him. Nobody had a chance against him." Her voice broke as she sucked air in her lungs; then with a strangled cry said, "You were right, Matthew. You were right from the start."

"Meg," Gage murmured into her hair, several strands catching on the beard stubble at his jaw. "Ah, Meg. I didn't want to be right." And he realized as he said the words, how true they were.

"But you were. You were able to see what I refused to believe. I never thought it possible. I . . . he's my brother. He isn't a . . ." She never finished the thought.

Gage caught her chin in his fingers and turned her face toward his. "Meg, don't do this to yourself. I know how it hurts. I let what my father did eat me up. It doesn't do any good."

Tears shimmered in her eyes.

Gage touched her hands with his and coaxed her to look at him. The anguish in her eyes wounded him to his soul. He pressed a soft kiss to her cheek.

The pools of moisture on her lower lashes spilled freely. He stopped a trail of tears with the pad of his thumb.

On a half-sob, Meg lifted her arms around his neck and hugged him tightly. Gage drew her next to his chest just as closely, breathing in the fragrance of her hair, her skin, her perfume.

They held each other for a long while. Then Meg lifted her head, her eyes glistening. She wet her dry lips, then a soft shudder escaped her—as if she were holding herself in check.

Her lips quivered. A brave front. So he consoled her with his touch. A caress of her temple, a tuck of hair behind her ear. A smoothing of his knuckles across the slight hollow of her cheek. A fingertip that traced the fullness of her mouth. Her breath stilled. And in that moment, Wayne was forgotten.

The mood changed. No longer gentle; comforting. An undeniable magnetism had built between them. Meg's eyelids lowered and she leaned toward him. He took her into his arms once more, happy to cradle the nape of her neck in his hand as he brought her snugly to him. Touching . . . body to body.

Gage enjoyed the feel of this woman in his arms. The delicate way she seemed at this moment. So dependent—on him. He liked how she made him feel. Like he was worth something. Like he meant something.

Taking her face in his hands, he lowered his head to claim her lips with his. The kiss was slow and gentle. The longer he kissed her, the softer her pliant mouth became—relaxing, inviting, opening. He slipped his tongue into the sweetness of her mouth—exploring, savoring.

Meg returned his kisses, her arms entwined around his neck, drawing him close. He could feel the small swells of her breasts pushing against his chest. Her size had never bothered him. Her figure wasn't that of a curvaceous temptress. He always thought he preferred women with larger breasts, flared hips, and narrow waists. With Meg, he liked her just the way she was.

He lowered them backward onto the bed, side by side. His coat fell from her shoulders, a blanket for them to lay on. Kissing. His hand at her hip, he slid it upward, grazing the bow of her waist. Then to her breast.

She gave him a hesitant kiss. Barely a brush on his mouth. As if uncertain. He could feel her pulse beat beneath his palm when he pressed his hand over her heart through the thin fabric of her shirtwaist. Their lips melded. Blending and warm. Growing fervent. Her breasts thrust against the stiff edge of her corset and he discovered the nipple; a tiny bud. A treasure.

He wanted to undress her. Make love to her.

As he broke away from her mouth, he looked into her expectant face and saw the trust written in her eyes. Her slow gaze caressed his face and she brought her hand up to cup the contour of his cheek.

Meg. Sweet Meg.

She would let him. He saw it in her eyes. She would let him make her his.

Christ almighty.

"Meg. Not this way," Gage whispered as she

mapped his jaw with a light rasp of her fingernails. She laid her sweet hand on his shoulder. This woman, with all her ways of Meg. The old Meg. The new Meg.

The Meg he loved.

He couldn't envision life without her.

He wanted to prove himself worthy of her. So he stopped. He had to show her something.

"I want more than anything to be with you," he said. "But I have to do things right. I want you to see this."

Gage went to his desk and picked up the first article he'd written. He handed it to Meg for her to read.

Meg sat up and lowered her head to follow the words. His words. His new voice. Would she like it? Scoff it? Tell him that he should tear it up?

Once, she glanced up at him. A mixture of confusion and disbelief in her brown eyes. The she tilted her head once more.

As she read, she absently ran her fingers through her loose curls. When she was finished, she let the sheafs of paper lay on her lap. Awe marked her tone. "You wrote about my Grandma Nettie."

Gage nodded, hopeful that she'd liked what he'd had to say.

"You wrote about her and her sisters going to Washington. You made it sound so . . . noble. You were on their side. I . . ." Her voice broke. "I'm touched by what you had to say. You told it like everything they planned to do meant something." Her lips curved softly. "Even her bicycle chain sounded important. I don't know what to say."

A tightening took hold of Gage's throat. To say he was overwhelmed was an understatement. "You said everything I wanted to hear."

"You're a great writer, Matthew. You have a lot of talent. I'm sorry I said you didn't do good things." She lifted the pages and returned them to him. "Will you send this to your editor?"

"I don't know." And he honestly didn't. This wasn't the kind of article *The Chronicle* published from him. If he wanted to see it in print, he'd most likely have to ink the pages himself.

Looking to the future, Gage didn't see the tarnish and distaste of sensational journalism sustaining him in his old age. He finally saw what he really wanted out of life and he had the chance to get it. He wanted Meg. Harmony. He wanted to start a local paper in the building on Hackberry Way. To report on everyday goings on without always having to prove a point. Like a group of elder suffragettes convening on the White House steps to fight for equality.

Gage's paper would be a cauldron of modern vision, steaming up a mist of larger purpose than to sensationalize. The little man or woman would get his or her turn to speak up. Gage would be doing something that would make Meg proud of him.

He wanted her for his wife.

He wanted marriage. A family. And all the responsibilities that went with being a husband.

Through the quiet and without preamble, Gage uttered words he never thought he'd hear himself say. "Marry me, Meg." He went to her and cupped her chin in his hand. "Be my wife. Marry me."

Her reaction was not what he would have predicted. Instead of blissful kisses and yeses, she began to weep. Quietly. Then in soft shudders that ripped pain through him to the core. God help him, what had he said wrong?

Meg shook her head. "How long have I waited to hear those words?" she asked, her voice as soft as velvet. "It seems like forever."

"Is your answer yes?"

She sighed. "I don't have an answer."

Then she stood and she faced the cold fireplace. After a moment, she looked toward the ceiling, and to his uneasiness, laughed without humor. "Am I crazy? I should be saying yes."

Turning to Matthew, she gave him a melancholy smile that went right to his heart. "You don't know how desperately I wanted to be asked. During my time in finishing school, that's what all of us talked about. You could say I was rather preoccupied with marriage. Until Mr. Wilberforce."

Gage frowned.

"No, it's not a bad thing. Not really. I fell in love with you as Mr. Wilberforce . . ."

I fell in love with you.

She loved him. Gage could hear his heart beating in his ears.

"I also fell in love with you as Matthew Gage. So between the two of you, I have been in love, truly, twice in my lifetime. But I've only just come to understand that both of you are the same man."

"Yet you won't marry me."

"Wanting a wedding and a husband is only part of the package. It's the loving somebody part that's everything. If I said yes right now, I think I'd always wonder if I said yes simply because I want to have a wedding like Johannah Treber's."

Gage stood and went to her. "But you said you loved me."

"And I do." She touched his lips with her fingers.

"I have for a while. I tried not to, but I can't help it. Even knowing what you do and why you do it. Maybe that's why I can't give you an answer. Believe me when I tell you my heart is screaming yes. But my mind is telling me to think about if we really know each other. Or if what we feel is passion with an abundance of hat trimmings." She attempted a feeble smile.

"What I feel for you is more than—" he attempted to smile along with her but he didn't do a good job of it, "hat trimmings."

He watched the different expressions playing on her face—confusion, uncertainty. Yet a determination that strengthened her appeal.

"I'll walk you home," Gage quietly offered.

"I'm not going directly home."

"Where are you going?"

Meg went toward the door, conviction in her stride. "I have to get one thousand dollars to give to Oliver Stratton." She laid her fingers on the knob of the door and was ready to walk out on him without any explanation.

He caught up to her, put his hand on her shoulder, and turned her to face him. "How are you going to do that?"

She didn't give him an answer. Instead, she asked a question. "Do you believe in what you write?"

His shoulders came back and he made no immediate reply. His mind was a maelstrom of charged emotions. Did he believe in what he wrote? He had never questioned himself before, but this little town of Harmony and a sweet woman named Meg had turned his thoughts upside down.

"Do you?" she repeated.

He was unable to give her a simple definition as to what his writing meant to him. In agonizing detail, the past six years of working for *The Chronicle* flashed through his mind. He'd made his living digging deep into sordid stories and sustaining himself through a great deal of criticism and controversy. Yes, dammit, he had always believed in what he wrote.

"Yes, I believe in my writing," Gage said at length into Meg's expectant face.

"I knew you'd say that. And I think you should. What you said about my grandma is very special to me."

"Writing is who I am."

"See—you know who are, but I'm still figuring out who I am." She moved from him, twisted the door-knob, and opened the door. "And I have to know I can be happy just by being Meg before I can be a wife."

Then she left.

Gage stared at the closed door as time ticked by on the mantel clock behind him. A quagmire of thoughts sludged through his head. The woman he loved loved him. But she wouldn't commit to marrying him until she figured out if she could be just as happy without him.

What if she could be happy without him?

Hell.

So what would he do if she turned him down? Either he finished the fly-fishing article with a flourish and became the success he'd come to Harmony to be, or he gave it all up.

The article and success. But those thoughts were quickly pushed aside by others. Meg. The idea of his

own newspaper. Small town ideals. A new start
Marriage.

He remembered that he had told Meg he believed
in his stories. But suddenly, he understood that the
world wasn't so clear cut. The world was not black
and white. Between the typeset lines were shades of
gray. Christ, you'd think with his journalism back-
ground he could convey this coherently. But he
couldn't. He believed that he was not able to go on
the way he had been without falling victim to severe
cynicism.

Gage sat down at his desk. He picked up the sheets
of the fly-fishing article he'd typed on the secondhand
Smith Premier. A quick scan of the words and he now
saw them clearly.

Meg had given him the information he'd needed.
He could hang her brother in print.

He knew what he had to do.

In spite of the inappropriate hour, Meg left the
hotel and went straight to Gus Gushurst's house on
Dogwood Place. Mustering her wits, which had been
faltering since leaving Matthew, Meg rapped on the
door. Thoughts swam in her head. She'd found out
about Wayne and received a marriage proposal all in
the course of one night. It was too much to think
about at once. She couldn't face the future until she
confronted the past.

Mr. Gushurst opened the door and exclaimed in
surprise, "Miss Brooks. Has something happened?"

Without thought, Meg blurted, "Yes, it has. I need
to speak with you right away."

He stood aside and let her into the parlor where
Mrs. Gushurst sat in an overstuffed chair with a book

in her lap and a look of alarm on her face. She wore a housecoat wrapper over her nightdress and had taken down her hair and plaited it for bed. It was then Meg noted Mr. Gushurst wore his smoking jacket and felt slippers.

What time was it anyway?

Never mind about the time. She had no time to waste.

"Miss Brooks," Mrs. Gushurst cried, "is your grandmother all right?"

"She's fine."

"Oh . . . are you fine?"

"Not really."

"Sit down, Miss Brooks," Mr. Gushurst offered, standing himself and more than a little self-conscious.

Meg declined. "I don't want to keep you. I just need to fill out an entry form for the contest tomorrow. I've got to fish in it."

Mr. Gushurst's eyes widened. "Why?"

"I just do, that's all."

Meg couldn't tell him the reason without involving Wayne and telling what he'd done. She wanted to avoid a scandal at all costs. It wasn't herself she was protecting. It was Grandma Nettie, her parents . . . and her brother. He'd committed a criminal act.

Meg froze. She realized in that second that she had given Matthew everything he needed to ruin her brother. Dear God, what had she done?

Oh, if only she hadn't gone to Matthew. But he'd been the only one she could turn to to unburden her heart. The only one who could . . .

She shook off the thought. Matthew could, and probably would, write the article. And if he did, how could she ever marry him? She pressed her eyes closed and laid her hand on the wall to support herself.

"Miss Brooks, are you all right?"

"Yes . . . yes. I just need an entry form." She shook the worry from her mind and concentrated on the task at hand. She had to enter the contest and win. To make amends, Meg had to give one thousand dollars to Oliver Stratton in lieu of the money that Wayne had taken away from him.

She knew of no way to come into such a sum other than entering the fishing contest.

"Miss Brooks, I can't just give you an entry form," Mr. Gushurst said, his uncomfortableness evident by the deep creases on his forehead. "The contest has been closed to entrants for nearly a month."

"But can't you make an exception in my case? It's an emergency."

He shook his head. "I can't."

"Well you should." Meg all but stamped her foot. "I am a member of the Woolly Bugger club, after all."

Wayne had been enrolled in the junior division, which was broken into Rainbows, Steelheads and Chinooks—depending on the boy's casting skills. Meg had desperately wanted to be a part of the Rainbows, but she couldn't because she was a girl—an inconsequential thing to her at the time. So Mr. Gushurst had made her an honorary Catfish. There was really no such title, but little did she know. She'd been nine at the time.

"But, Miss Brooks, that was years ago."

"So?"

"So, there really isn't a Catfish. I only gave you that title because you were Wayne's little sister."

Meg's cheeks heated as she insisted, "I'm still Wayne's little sister and I should be allowed to enter."

Mr. Gushurst flushed, his sagging jowls quivering as he shook his head denying her her request. "Miss Brooks, even if you had come to me before the deadline and I had an entry form, you cannot enter."

"Why not?"

Nostrils flared on his broad nose and he all but yelled, "Because you're a woman!"

Meg's mouth dropped open. Forgetting herself, she snapped, "Well!" with a fair amount of indignance. There was no disputing the fact—even if she was flat-chested. But why did that mean she couldn't enter? "What does my being a woman have to do with it?"

"Women don't enter sporting contests. And a fly-fishing tournament is a sporting contest."

"Who said women don't enter?"

"Women."

Frowning, Meg asked, "What women?"

"Any one of them in town, Miss Brooks."

"Not my Grandma Nettie."

"Beg your pardon," he remarked in a stuffy tone, "but she's not to be included."

Anger simmered in Meg. *Grandma Nettie not to be included.* Yes, the dear was an outspoken advocate for the movement. Yes, she could get too carried away with her flyers. Yes, she was a rebel who intended to fight for women's rights by locking herself onto the White House fence with a bicycle chain . . .

Her mind spun.

A bicycle chain.

"Now, Miss Brooks," Mr. Gushurst said, taking her arm and ushering her toward the door. "You run along home and get a good night's rest. You'll feel better in the morning. I'll bet you'll have forgotten all this nonsense and come back to your senses. Even bake up a batch of cookies like your mother. She's a fine baker. I make a habit of buying her confections at the fair every August."

He opened the door, gently guided Meg over the threshold, and closed the door after her.

She stood there a moment. Mad and frustrated. Her grandmother's words came to her: *Vinegar is a better medium for catching flies.*

Meg pressed her lips together and came to a decision.

She knew what she had to do.

Chapter

❦ 20 ❦

Early the next morning, Gage took the hotel stairs into the lobby and found Mrs. Rothman behind the registry desk. Puzzlement lit her eyes as she bent down to view the floor beneath the counter; then she straightened and put a hand on her cheek. She scanned the surrounding desk with its papers and envelopes, lifting sheets here and there.

"Is something wrong, Mrs. Rothman?" Gage asked, keeping his voice pleasant. Meg's grandmother had been about as friendly as a beehive since Meg had told her about him.

"Did you take my bicycle chain?" she returned with a smidgeon of accusation in her tone.

Gage noticed the two-foot length of metal links was no longer on the front of the counter by the registry book. It had been there every day since he came to Harmony.

"No," he replied, stepping closer.

"The lock is gone, too," she said, her lips thinning. "Who on earth would steal it?"

The front door to the hotel was pushed open with a *humph* and Mrs. Plunkett stepped inside, voluptuous skirts swishing as she came to an abrupt halt. "Mrs. Rothman. Do you know where your granddaughter is?"

Undaunted by the woman's outburst, Mrs. Rothman pulled a drawer open and rummaged through the contents—ink pots and a variety of other odds and ends. "I'm afraid I do not. She wasn't here this morning when I came in."

"I'll tell you where she is." She went right on with hardly a breath. "She's chained herself to Mr. Gushurst's fence."

"She's *what?*" Grandma Nettie blurted.

"She's chained herself to Mr. Gushurt's fence in protest of something. I'm on my way there now to find out what she's up in arms about. I suggest you come along and tell her to stop this nonsense."

With that, Mrs. Plunkett turned in a flurry of petticoats and black skirts, and slammed the door closed in her wake.

Gage traded glances with Mrs. Rothman as she anxiously called for Delbert Long. As soon as the bellman took charge behind the counter, Gage held the door open for Meg's grandmother.

"You lead the way," Gage said to Nettie.

"That's what I've been trying to do for years," she said as she converged on the boardwalk with a swift stride. "Apparently Meg has decided to do the same."

In the wee hours of the morning, Meg had snuck across the back alleyway to Mr. Gushurst's house, a thrum of exhilaration beating in her heart. Mischief.

It wasn't her speciality, but like she always said: A woman had to do what a woman had to do.

With each careful step she'd taken over the pavers, she'd tried to keep Grandma Nettie's bicycle chain from clinking together. She'd put the chain in her apron and folded the hem up to make a big pocket. Once at the front of the house, she'd bitten her lower lip in trepidation.

This was a big to-do. Really big. Even for her—chaining herself to a fence wasn't even close to riding a luggage cart. This was trespassing and a violation of Harmony's city law—public nuisance. If she did this, she'd be on the tongues of everyone in this town—and not in a flattering way. There might never be any going back. But she didn't let that stop her.

Meg had squared her shoulders with mettle. She'd had to do it. For Ollie Stratton. She couldn't live with herself if she didn't do anything about her brother's wrong. And since she would never turn her brother in, her only other option was to enter the contest. Then win.

So she had picked the solid iron post to the left of the gate, stood next to it and wrapped the length of heavy chain around her waist and several of the fence posts. Then she'd brought two links together and secured them with the lock. She hid the key in the front of her corset—she remembered that's where Grandma said she was going to hide hers.

The first to find her had been Gerty, Clovis Lester's housemaid. She'd been on her way to the Lester house when she'd seen Meg and questioned what she was doing. Meg told her. Then several more people came by.

They'd been gathering for nearly an hour.

Now a small crowd surrounded her, their voices apparently stirring the Gushurst house.

Mr. Gushurst came out and pitched an awful fit. He went on so that she didn't have the opportunity to tell him what she was protesting. He kept going on about how she needed to go home and quit all her tomfoolery and act like a woman.

Then, realizing he was still in his silk-tasseled nightcap and red flannel pajamas, he told her he'd be right back. He went inside and, at that precise moment, Harold Adams showed up.

"Margaret?" he croaked, his Adam's apple bobbing. "Margaret Brooks, what in God's green earth are you doing chained to Mr. Gushurst's fence?"

She lifted her chin and declared, "I'm protesting."

"Protesting what?"

"Unfair treatment of women."

"Good grief. Not that."

"Yes that."

He turned up his coat collar and slouched his hat over his eyes—as if he couldn't stand the sight of her. "Margaret, you're all boss and bluster. It looks like you're back to your old ways."

"Yes, it most certainly does. Doesn't it?"

"Well, then, I'm glad I stopped calling when I did. And to think, I was going to give you another chance." Harold all but snorted his disapproval as he stomped off.

He was barely gone, when Grandma Nettie and Matthew showed up. Grandma without her hat, her short gray hair soft around her cheeks and curled up a little at her collar. Meg smiled. She was just like her Grandma Nettie. And she felt a kindred spirit with her that she had never had with her mother.

Within seconds, Mr. Gushurst came barreling out his front door wearing a suit and a tie that had been knotted in a slapdash manner.

"Meg," Grandma Nettie declared, "What's this all about?"

"I'm fighting for equality," Meg replied to her grandmother, but her eyes were on Matthew when she spoke. Would he disapprove like Harold? Find her behavior intolerable? Her breath caught; she wasn't sure she wanted to know.

She couldn't read a thing on his face. For a newspaper man who made his living with words, he could certainly conceal his thoughts. Except for that bit of fire dancing in his eyes. That she saw. The green hue of his irises gleamed with a spark of emotion. What that emotion was, she couldn't tell. She didn't know if he was fighting mad *with* her or *at* her.

"You're not fighting for equality on my fence," barked Mr. Gushurst.

Dragging her gaze away from Matthew, she said, "Yes I am." Then to the crowd that had begun to press in on her, Meg added, "Mr. Gushurst won't let me enter the fly-fishing tournament today. He says I can't because I'm a woman."

"That's right," Mr. Gushurst fumed, putting his finger into his collar to loosen the chokehold of his tie. "Unchain yourself from my fence right now. I've already sent Mrs. Gushurst for the police. Chief Officer Conlin should be here any minute."

"Then let them take me away," she decreed, raising one fist . . . getting a little carried away. "I will not leave until you tell me I can fish in today's contest."

"Oh, my!" Grandma Nettie cried. "I do so wish we

had an extra chain. I'd lash myself right alongside of you, Meg."

Meg smiled. "Thank you, Grandma."

Mr. Gushurst's face reddened to the shade of overripe strawberries. Meg could swear she saw steam billowing from his ears. She'd always thought him such a dear, sweet man. She had just been proven wrong.

"I told you last night, Miss Brooks," Mr. Gushurst ground out, "that even if you had come to me before the deadline, you could not have entered. Even if I was inclined to disregard the fact that you are a woman, which I am not, you can't fish in today's contest because you don't have an official spot from the lottery."

A smug expression took over his face. He thought he won.

Meg froze. It was true. She didn't have a lottery spot. Even she knew the official rule was that every entrant needed to draw a designated fishing spot from the lottery. There were only seventeen, and all seventeen were spoken for. She had forgotten all about the lottery spots when she was attaching herself to the fence.

Meg's heart sank into the pit of her stomach. She had been so valiant. So hopeful, so determined. Now what? What was she going to do—

"She has a spot," came a resonant voice from the crowd.

Matthew.

She looked at him with all the love in her heart.

"She can have mine," he repeated. Loud and clear.

"Mr. Wilberforce," Mr. Gushurst bristled. "This is highly irregular."

"This is my choice." He slipped his hand inside his

coat pocket and withdrew his card. "Number six. It's hers."

"No it's not." Mr. Gushurst stood his ground like a guard dog. "She is a woman and she cannot enter."

Grandma Nettie stepped forward and buffeted Mr. Gushurst on the head with her pocketbook. "Where is that written in the rules? I want to see them."

Mr. Gushurst sputtered, "It's not written in the rules. It simply is the way things are done in the Woolly Buggers club."

"You are a narrow-minded man without an ounce of sensibility. It is from you and your kind, that we women must rebel. We must take control of our destinies!"

"Madam," he cried, "Control yourself."

"Gustave! I've brought the police." Mrs. Gushurst came rushing forward, her hair untidy and her flamboyant hat askew, stains of pink made two bright dots in the centers of her cheeks. She looked as if she'd dressed in the closet and had ran out before she'd been put in order.

Trailing close on her heels was Chief Officer Algie Conlin and Deputy Pike Faragher of the Harmony Police Department.

Meg's resolve lost a little of its bluster. *The police!* She didn't think things would go this far. She'd assumed that Mr. Gushurst would relent so as not to be embroiled in a public demonstration on his lawn.

Officer Conlin came toward her. "What's this all about?"

Then everyone was talking at once. The scene grew chaotic and voices shouted all around her. Matthew came in and out of her focus as people pressed in and were pushed back by the threat of Pike Faragher's billy club. She'd never seen him use it, and didn't think he would, but he got his message out.

When Mr. Gushurst demanded she be arrested, Meg refused to hand over the lock key. More chaos. Grandma Nettie sang a militant march over the shouting. Matthew tried to reach her, but was unable to get close.

Meg stood as stoic as a statue while the two policemen sliced through the thick chain with Mr. Gushurst's hacksaw.

Then handcuffs were slapped on her wrists and she knew she was in big trouble.

Matthew wasn't allowed into the jail cubical. Instead he had to wait in the front office while they brought Meg out. She wasn't wearing the fetters that had been locked on her wrists not more than an hour ago; she didn't seem any worse for the experience. In fact, she looked more beautiful to him than she ever had.

Her hair bobbed against her shoulders; her cheeks were still flushed with an attitude that said she meant business. And her chin was raised with iron determination.

Their gazes met across the room as Algie Conlin declared her free to go. Gage silently warned her not to ask any questions. He took her by the elbow and ushered her out the door.

To freedom.

"Where's my grandmother?" she asked as they cleared the police yard and took the boardwalk toward Sugar Maple.

"She's waiting at the hotel. She wanted to come, but I told her I'd bail you out."

"And she let you?"

"Yes. I told her I was on your side."

Gazing at her wrists, Meg rubbed them, then frowned. "I've got to get into that contest so I can get that thousand dollars for Ollie."

"You think you can win?"

She looked at him. "Do you?"

"You have a very good chance. I've watched you fish."

They continued walking. Several people peered out their windows at Meg when she passed by. Gage thought it damn admirable of her to face the issue head-on and not back down an inch. But how could she fish in the contest without getting thrown into jail again?

There had to be a way.

When Gage was on a train of thought, he rarely got off track. Yet as a man exited Miller's men's store just as he and Meg reached the door, Gage grew distracted. The man wore an Eastern-cut suit, a stick pin in his tie, and congress shoes polished to a bright black luster. He lifted his hat, then walked on past them.

It wasn't the man's snappy attire that had Gage staring. It was his facial hair. The biggest beard he'd ever seen, with a mustache waxed and curled at the ends like wood shavings.

Biggest beard . . .

Gage cracked a smile, then said to Meg, "You can still have my lottery spot."

"How can I?" She gave him a frustrated furrow of her brows. "I'm a woman. Women can't enter."

"That's right. But a man can."

She loudly sighed. "But I'm not a man."

"Aren't you?"

Meg slowed her steps and stopped, looking at Gage as if he were nutty as a pecan pie.

Gage produced the number six from his coat pocket and held it out to her. "I believe this is yours. *Mr. Bascomb.*"

For a stunned moment, she didn't move. Then her mouth broke into a wide smile and she laughed. The sound was sheer joy. It astonished Gage's senses by how much fulfillment he got from her melodic voice.

With a pang, Gage realized that if she wouldn't marry him, there would be an extraordinary void in his life that would never go away.

"Mr. Bascomb?" Mr. Gushurst queried, running his finger down the list of contestants in his grasp. "I have no Mr. Bascomb entered."

Meg stood off to the side—close enough to hear Mr. Gushurst talking with Matthew, but not too close for anyone to inspect her disguise.

"He's taking my number," Matthew stated.

Mr. Gushurst's mouth went sour. "Mr. Wilberforce, why is it you're so anxious to give up your lottery number?"

Ham Beauregarde called out, "Because he can't fish worth a damn and has probably taken cold hard cash from this Mr. Bascomb to get out of public humiliation."

Matthew ignored Ham, never flinching or turning, and continuing to stare directly at Mr. Gushurst. "Since there's nothing in the rules about forfeiting the lottery card, Mr. Bascomb will now be using spot six."

"Infernal hell—" Ham shot back, then cut himself off when a collective gasp of disapproval came from the ladies beside him, Mrs. Plunkett, Mrs. Treber and

Mrs. Elward. "Beg pardon," he apologized, then went on with just as much resentment as before, "Wilberforce is shining up to the Bureau of Internal Revenue man. Let's call a spade a spade, Wilberforce."

Eyes leveled on Meg, frosty glares. She inwardly cringed. When she'd made him up, she hadn't anticipated Arliss Bascomb having to face off with the town. How could she possibly pull this off? She didn't look like a man. She looked like a woman wearing Wayne Brooks's old clothes and a beard bought at Plunkett's mercantile.

Why, then, did Mrs. Plunkett smile at her?

And walk right toward her!

"Mr. Bascomb," she whispered once she reached Meg. "Do you see that lovely young girl standing by the elm tree?"

Slowly, Meg looked in the designated direction. Hildegarde stood with Ruth. Both girls gawked at her. Meg swallowed.

"The one in the pink organza with the rosy cheeks," Mrs. Plunkett clucked. "That's my Hildegarde. Isn't she pretty?"

Dumbstruck, Meg could only nod.

"Now, Mr. Bascomb, about that dinner invitation—"

But Mrs. Plunkett got no further. Mr. Gushurst interrupted in a voice that carried through the men gathered for the contest. "Mr. Bascomb, there is indeed nothing in the rules that says you can't have Mr. Wilberforce's spot. So to that end, gentlemen, we are ready to begin."

Meg mumbled her apologies, then left Mrs. Plunkett to join Matthew.

Ruth came up to them and gave Meg a long stare,

a wrinkle of her pert nose, then a shrug as she turned to Matthew. "I was going to wish you luck, Mr. Wilberforce, but now you're not fishing. So I suppose I should wish you good luck, Mr. Bascomb," she said to Meg.

Meg couldn't meet her eyes. This whole farce was going to come apart right in her face if she wasn't careful.

"We'd better be going," Matthew said.

Meg and Matthew started for spot number six. Meg hadn't told Grandma Nettie what she was going to do. She didn't want to involve anyone in her scheme—Matthew, of course, but no one else. If Meg was discovered, she wanted to take full responsibility for her actions. So she'd told her grandmother that the ordeal in the jail had worn her out and that she was going home to lay down.

Once at spot number six, Matthew came close to her, brushing arm to arm for a moment. In a voice low and quiet, he said, "I love you. I didn't say it before. I should have."

They broke apart and Matthew hung back with the spectators. She gave him a last glance; he mouthed the three words to her from a distance. She grew so conscious of him, she could barely think. The urge to be held by him, reassured, unnerved her. She was more connected to him than she ever thought possible. Then the realization hit her: Meg wasn't Meg without Matthew.

It was that thought that carried her through the events of the day.

The contest was run in a manner that anyone could, at any time, come upon a contestant and observe them. This made for a more fair tournament. It also—supposedly—detracted cheaters.

Nervously, Meg opened her tackle box and began assembling her rod and line. Her hands shook so that she had to take in a deep breath, still her body a moment, then continue.

There was nothing to fret about. She could win this on her own merit and with a little help. She had something that none of the other contestants had. And as far as she knew, there was nothing in the rules that stated she couldn't use her secret. A fisherman was allowed any manner of bait he chose—wet flies, dry flies, kernel corn, luring scents.

Meg chose a far different temptation. One she knew was foolproof.

Princess Bust Cream.

The day seemed to stretch on forever for Gage. A combination of nerves and excitement kept him on the edge of his seat on the ground beneath a shade tree as Meg reeled in one fish after another. Rainbows, cutthroats, and browns; also a variety of other fish. By noon, she'd had a small contingent of onlookers cheering her on. Their conversations centered on one topic: What was the white cream she used on her flies? Everyone wanted a jar of the seemingly magic concoction.

At three o'clock, Gushurst sounded a bell that signaled the competition was over and for the fishermen to gather their catches and their tackle and proceed to the official weigh in and counting area.

Meg had caught so many fish, she couldn't manage the four stringers she'd filled. Gage quietly went up to her and took three of them.

As the small group broke up, and Gage and Meg walked side by side, he felt her anxiousness. Looking at her, he saw the glint of hope lighting her eyes.

Unless somebody else had an exceptional day, she had to have won. He hoped she did. He wished she could unveil who she really was. He sensed she wanted to do just that by the way in which her steps were light and easy. No trace of a masculine walk—one which she'd used with him when they'd gone off to their practice sessions.

Once at the pavilion site where Gus Gushurst and the other members of the Woolly Bugger club had assembled, the counting of the fish began. People talked, joked, and chuckled.

But Meg remained quiet.

Gage wanted to reach out and hold her hand. But he couldn't.

"If you win, you've really won twice," Gage said in a low tone. "Once, for Ollie Stratton, and once for yourself."

She looked at him and nodded; her eyes glimmered with emotional tears. He would have kissed her softly on the mouth, beard and all, if he could have gotten away with it.

Moments later, Gushurst hushed the crowd, the long table before him strewn with baskets of fish, tally tablets, and three brass trophies. "Ladies and gents, we have our winners."

Voices hushed and the air went still.

"Third place goes to King Merkle."

The Rubifoam salesman, mouthful of teeth widening his grin, stepped up to the podium and took his trophy. Applause sounded as he nodded and went down the steps to join his fellow salesmen. Ham

Beauregarde stood among them and cast his glance at Gage.

Gage lifted his brow at him. Ham turned away.

"Second place goes to Orvis Schmidt."

Rather than King Merkle's gratuitous thanks and nods, Orvis dropped his chin on his chest and swore. He stood still a moment, heaved a sigh, and it seemed as if he wasn't going to collect his trophy. Then he lifted his head, his mouth set in a show of sour grapes, and took the steps to receive the second-place award.

Applause rang. Then Orvis retreated, slapping his hand on his thigh and glaring at Ham who was laughing. Beauregarde must have thought he had it in the bag, because he puffed out his chest like a pigeon and all but rubbed his hands together with glee.

"First place goes to . . ." Gushurst shook his head in wonder. "I don't know how he did it, but he broke the all-time record for catching the most fish in one day."

Gage glanced down and found Meg with her eyes squeezed closed and her lips pressed together.

"Winner of the grand prize trophy and a check for one thousand dollars is Arliss Bascomb."

Meg was silent, as if stunned; then she screamed with delight and jumped up and down a few seconds before she stilled and collected herself with a look at Gage. He would have given up his typewriter to take her into his arms and swing her in a wide circle.

Gathering her dignity as Bascomb, Meg made her way to the podium, her hand lightly on the railing as she climbed the steps.

"Mr. Bascomb," Mr. Gushurst said, "can you tell us how you did it? I've heard you used a special cream to attract the fish. Was it your own recipe?"

"Um, yes," she replied, stilting her voice in a low baritone that didn't do much to tamp out her feminine vocal chords, "it was my own recipe."

"What's in it?"

"A mixture of things. I can't say."

A grumble went through the crowd.

Gage caught the look of envy on Ham's face. He also saw the hatred and anger. "Can't say or won't say?" Ham shouted. "It must be something illegal if he won't talk. He should be disqualified."

Several contestants who had lost glanced thoughtfully at one another then shook their heads in agreement.

"It is not illegal," Meg said in her defense. Agitated, her voice sounded nothing like Arliss Bascomb's.

Beauregarde folded his arms over his chest and glared hard at Meg.

"It's at the discretion of Mr. Bascomb if he doesn't want to say what was in the jar," Gushurst announced. "As you all know, catching fish with any kind of bait is legal. Back in ninety-nine, Gabe Moody won by using flies made out of chicken feathers from his wife's best laying hen—so we can't go singling out any method as illegal when we let chickens in."

Ham shouted, "Feathers is feathers and white goo in a jar is something altogether different."

"Don't see how," King Merkle commented. "I believe you are just a sorry loser, Mr. Beauregarde."

Snorting, Ham unfolded his arms and held them straight at his sides. "I am not. Now if that Wayne Brooks had won again, I'd be a sorry loser. It is a known fact that he stocked the tributary off of Evergreen Creek last year."

Gage shot his gaze to Meg. Her body had gone tense; her brown eyes narrowed.

"Nobody proved anything," somebody said.

"Proved or not, speculation is speculation. Talk is talk," said another.

"Damn right," concurred a third.

Then Ham looked to Gage, suspicion written on his face like a column in the newspaper headlining the latest political shenanigans. "Wilberforce, where is Miss Brooks? Word has it you bailed her out of jail."

"I did."

"So where is she? I figured she'd want to be here to watch since she was so hot to enter herself. In fact, it's too bad Wayne isn't here to see how a real winner wins. But you know how cheaters are. They're chicken."

Gage watched Meg's fingers clutch tightly to the prize envelope as she bit her lower lip to keep from speaking out. He could tell she was just itching to give Beauregarde a piece of her mind. But if she broke her silence, she'd be setting herself up for accusations of cheating herself. After all, she wouldn't say what that white cream was and Gage doubted what was in the jar was camphor.

"Wayne Brooks," Beauregarde sneered. "You know, I went over to Leroy Doolin's place to ask about Brooks myself. Although Doolin didn't come out and tell me anything—he did imply that brown trout could be bought for a price. Dammit all if I didn't have the—" He sliced off his sentence like a butcher's cleaver did a cutthroat's head.

So that's what Beauregarde had been doing up at Doolin's. Trying to buy himself some browns just like Wayne Brooks had. Only Beauregarde hadn't had the cash. Not surprising. Doolin probably raised his price from last year.

"What's this about Leroy Doolin?" Gushurst wanted to know. "Are you saying that Wayne Brooks bought trout from Leroy last year? Ham, do you have proof of this?"

"No he doesn't," Meg interjected, her Bascomb voice no longer intact.

"What did you say?" Ham asked of Meg, clearly on to the fact that something was different.

Gage knew Meg was on the verge of unmasking herself. Hell, he didn't blame her. But she was only going to make things worse.

"Mr. Bascomb, I'd like to buy you a beer in congratulations," Gage said as he walked for the podium. "Come on down from there and let's go to the Blue Flame."

"Wait just a blame minute," Ham shouted. "You aren't going to take him anywhere." Then to Gage. "You're in on this, too. Infernal hell—you've been going off fishing with him all the time. You were there with him today. You know what's in that cream. And you know that he won illegally."

"I did not." Meg's voice rose indignantly.

"Oh yes you did," Ham said to Meg. "I don't know how, but you did. If this just isn't the frosting on the cake. This contest has gone to the dogs. Last year Wayne Brooks wins, and this year some citified Bureau man who has a secret cream wins. Who knows, next year the Woolly Buggers will be letting that no-good troublemaker girlie, Meg Brooks, enter. A woman. Fishing. Now that's a joke."

At that moment, Meg yanked off her hat and threw it at Beauregarde's head. He snapped his chin up, mouth falling open as her copper hair came tumbling down on her shoulders. Next went the beard—unhooked from her ears. She stood as straight as a rail and thrust out her bosom.

The crowd sent up a mighty den of voices rumbling like a bear.

"I am a woman, Mr. Beauregarde," Meg bit out. "And it's no joke that I won."

"Holy hell," Beauregarde blazed. Then to Gage with a pointed finger: "I hold you accountable."

A resentful sob moaned from beside Gage.

Mrs. Plunkett wailed into her handkerchief. "Margaret Brooks, you impostor! How could you do this to my Hildegarde?"

Hildegarde, eyes wide, said, "Meg . . . I was almost engaged to you."

Gus Gushurst whacked a trout on the table and attempted to rein the vocal group to order. "This is not to be tolerated! Miss Brooks, you are in violation of the rules that govern the Woolly Bugger club!"

"You gave me no choice," she said. "I would have entered as myself but you wouldn't let me. So Mr. Bascomb entered and won. Fairly."

"Not in my book." Gushurst tried to take the envelope way from Meg but she held onto it with a tight grip.

"You cannot take this prize money from me. It's mine."

"Oh yes I can. Not only are you a counterfeit entrant, but you won't tell what's in that cream."

Meg pulled the envelope away from Gushurst and pressed it next to her chest. "You said I didn't have to."

"I retract that statement on the grounds that suspicion surrounds you."

In a huff, Meg said, "If you must know—it's Princess Bust Cream. You can buy a jar of it at the mercantile. There. Are you satisfied?"

"No I am not," Beauregarde shot out. "What the hell is Princess Bust Cream?"

The crowd went silent as understanding came clear. And when it did, Ham Beauregarde turned a bright shade of red. "Well . . . well hell," he stammered. "I want to call the entire contest a sham and everyone should have to forfeit their prizes."

"That's not going to happen," Gage said, his tone low and lethal. "She won fair, and she isn't giving up her due."

Ham scoffed, "Shut your mouth, Vernon Wilberforce, or I'll shut it for you."

"Vernon Wilberforce? That is *not* my Vernon!" came a female voice from the crowd as she elbowed her way to the front of the onlookers.

Gage cringed. He had a sinking feeling he knew who the woman was.

Drawing up to him by mere inches, her hat feathers in a twitter and her lips pursed, she eyed him closely. "Who are you and why are you saying you're my husband?"

"I knew it!" Beauregarde spat, slapping his hat on his thigh. "He's no salesman. He didn't want to talk about his territory."

"So just who in the Sam Hill are you?" Gushurst asked, his tone about as friendly as a dog's bite.

All eyes leveled on Gage. He'd been backed into corners before. But rarely with the relief or sense of irony he was feeling now. Showing his true face couldn't have come at a better time. Because Vernon Wilberforce didn't have an ounce of weight to throw around.

But Matthew Gage did.

"I'm Matthew Gage, reporter for *The San Francisco Chronicle,* and if you take that one thousand dollars away from Meg Brooks, you'll be reading about it in the big city papers. In less than a month of Sundays, Harmony, Montana, will be known as a petty little town whose residents are a bunch of narrow-minded idiots."

His gaze traveled over the crowd. "You don't think I'll do it? Just try me."

Chapter

❦ 21 ❦

"Why are you impersonating my husband?"

"Mrs. Wilberforce, this is a discussion I think you need to have with Mr. Wilberforce," Gage said to Violet Wilberforce.

They stood in the lobby of the hotel where Nettie Rothman had been putting up whatever decorations she could find for a celebration party in honor of Meg's win at the tournament. Word had spread fast and Meg's grandmother beamed like a full moon over Meg's accomplishment. And she wanted the town to know it. Meg was upstairs in Arliss Bascomb's room changing clothes for the impromptu get-together.

Word had also spread fast about who Matthew really was. When he'd returned to the hotel with Meg, Nettie put him under tough scrutiny. Then simply said: *"I've read you before. All that talent wasted on fire and brimstone that doesn't do much but stir the pot. You should write about topics that will carry us into the new century."*

Corkscrew curls bobbing on either side of Mrs. Wilberforce's wide forehead and net-gloved hands raised to her cheeks, she tsked, "Vernon Wilberforce may be registered here, but my husband is nowhere to be found in this hotel. You may have signed in for him, but you are not my Vernon. What have you done with my husband?"

Gage put his hand lightly on her shoulder to assuage her distress. "Rest assured, Mrs. Wilberforce, he's alive and well." He hesitated, but knew there was no help for it. "You can find him in the Bozeman jail."

"Bozeman jail!" she shrieked, her cheeks becoming two stains of ire. "What's he doing in jail?"

"It's not my place to say."

"Bozeman jail," she repeated as if she couldn't quite assimilate the words. But then her eyes narrowed as the words finally took hold. "That man. Just wait until I get my hands on him."

The porter walked in carrying his violin for the party. "Delbert," Gage said, taking the fiddle and setting it on the registration counter. "I want you to escort Mrs. Wilberforce to the station and get her on the next train to Bozeman." Reaching into his coat pocket, Gage withdrew his wallet. "I'll pay for the ticket."

Mrs. Wilberforce sniffed, delicately pressing a handkerchief at her nostrils. "That's quite generous of you, Mr. Gage. Considering."

"It's the least I can do."

"Does my husband's 'unfortunate stay' have anything to do with one of those stunt articles you write?" She tucked the bills into her pocketbook and snapped the clasp closed with an efficient press of her fingers.

"No." Then to Delbert, Gage said, "There's the lady's bags."

Two suitcases sat on the porch of the hotel.

"I'm sorry you came all this way, Mrs. Wilberforce, only to be disappointed."

"Disappointed isn't the half of it. I wanted to surprise my Vernon."

"No doubt you'll surprise him in Bozeman."

With a sigh, Mrs. Wilberforce allowed Delbert to usher her out the doors; then Gage turned toward Mrs. Rothman, who was tacking a paper chain onto the registry counter.

"Such excitement, Mr. Wil—" She caught herself, then frowned a little. "Mr. Gage."

"Call me Matthew, please"

"I'd rather call you mud for holding out on us. Meg told me you were somebody from the newspapers but I had no idea which one." Her blue eyes narrowed, then grew soft. "Wait until I tell Mrs. Gundy and the ladies what goings on have taken place here today. This is such a milestone. Meg winning the fly-fishing contest. And being able to keep the money, too. I do have to admit I owe you some thanks, Matthew. If you hadn't given your spot to Meg, none of this would have been possible."

"Meg did the hard part, and the money is rightfully hers."

"Having a big city paper behind you made a difference. If you hadn't stepped in and told the locals that you'd print their ignorance in your column, they would have done Meg wrong." Her lips turned upward in a smile. "The power of the presses. May they always hold such influence."

"Unless the influence is the wrong kind," Gage said softly.

The admission came from a place within Gage that

he could freely acknowledge now. In the past, he'd felt that everything he'd ever done had been the selfless thing to do. But standing along the sidelines in Harmony's fishing contest after witnessing the truly selfless acts of Meg Brooks, he knew that he had rarely been in her league.

As if the thought of her made her appear, Meg came down the stairs, the animation in her eyes enchanting. She wore a figured chiffon silk dress with a narrow collar and sleeve. The navy and brown in the print brought out the red hues of her hair. Her eyes met his and she smiled.

"Matthew, I'm glad you're here. It wouldn't be the same without you to help celebrate."

He brought his hand to her cheek, not caring who observed him in the room filled with hotel guests and those who had been at the fishing competition. "I can't stay."

In a soft voice, she asked, "Why not?"

"I have to see somebody." *Somebody about changing our lives.*

"Who?"

Her smile was soft as he grazed her lips, heat simmering deep and low. She did that to him. The slightest touch. A mere glance. And his body yearned. Much as his heart yearned for her.

"I'll tell you tomorrow."

"Yes . . . tomorrow."

Right after the fishing contest, she'd asked him to ride out to Oliver Stratton's house with her. She'd said that her receiving the money was as much his doing as hers.

"I'll meet you on the hotel porch at nine."

"Yes, nine." She gave him a teasing smile. "But don't expect Mr. Bascomb. He truly is retired now."

"With what you can accomplish, Meg, you don't ever need him again." He took her hand, squeezed it, then left.

Meg had never been to Oliver Stratton's house before. Seeing it for the first time took her down a peg. She had things so much better than he did. Her brother should have been the one to come. But Wayne saw no wrong in what he'd done, and she doubted he ever would. Meg could never respect him the way she once had, but neither could she turn her back on him. He was family. And now it was her responsibility to fix things.

It hurt her to the quick when she thought about Wayne cheating a man who lived so . . . simply. Wayne had wanted to win so he could be a big man on a fancy campus. Oliver Stratton had wanted to win to put food on the table. Shame seared through her.

"Are you ready?" Matthew asked.

Nodding, Meg kept a firm hold on her purse. She'd never had so much money in one place in her whole life. This meant so much to her. To do right by her family. Hopefully no one would ever know what she had done. It would be disgraceful to the Brookses and she didn't want to look like she was trying to brush aside what Wayne had done. He'd been wrong. But telling everyone about it would serve no purpose. Other lives would be ruined, and one too many had already been hurt. She could make the wrong a right. This wasn't for glorification. Her reason for being here was to do good.

Matthew knocked on the door and it was opened

by a young man in overalls. His nails were marked by dirt, but his hair was clean. Freshly washed from the looks of the neatly combed wet strands.

When Oliver saw Matthew he smiled in recognition. But when he saw Meg, he stilled, the smile flattening into a hard line. It was evident he knew who she was.

The cheater's sister.

"Hello, Mr. Stratton," Meg said, adding what was obvious but feeling the need for a proper introduction, "I'm Meg Brooks."

"I know," Ollie replied.

Matthew put his arm around her shoulder. She didn't need to lean on him but she was glad that he was with her.

"May we come in?" Meg asked, trying to keep a waver of nervousness from her voice.

"The place isn't too fancy," he responded, evidently thinking she would be offended by the simplicity of the one-room dwelling.

Meg met Oliver's eyes. "I'm sure it's just fine."

Oliver looked to Matthew. As if he were asking him what this was all about and why Meg was here. If Matthew had an answer written in his eyes, Meg couldn't see.

They were shown inside and ushered to one of the beds—the only place to sit. Meg sat primly with her purse on her lap, her back stiff. She hadn't thought this would be so hard. But it was. She sensed Oliver Stratton was a very proud man. What if he didn't take the money?

Sleeping in a rocking chair by the sunlit window, sat an elderly woman wearing a worn thin house dress and mobcap.

"She's hard of hearing. She won't wake," Oliver said, following Meg's eyes.

Meg became embarrassed. She shouldn't have stared.

"Can I get you a cup of coffee?" Oliver offered, going toward the stove.

"That won't be necessary," Meg said, fingering the chain handle of her purse. "I don't want to keep you. I just wanted to . . ." But the words caught in her throat. How did she say she wanted to make amends for the shabby way her brother had behaved?

Oliver sat across from them. "I heard you won the fishing contest."

Matthew smiled. "She broke the record for most fish caught."

"I heard that, too." Oliver knitted his fingers together, put them in his lap, then looked at his shoes. Then up at Meg with a hesitant smile. "You'll have to tell me how you did it."

"Well, that's really not important," Meg said, anxious to disclose what had made her come to see him. "What is important is that I have something that belongs to you."

"Couldn't imagine what that would be." He scratched behind his ear and looked confused.

Meg opened her purse and withdrew the bills she'd gotten from the bank that morning after cashing the one thousand dollar check. "This is yours."

Oliver's eyes widened as he looked from the money to Matthew to Meg and back to the money. "That's not mine."

"It is." Meg extended her hand and held the currency out to him. "I want you to take it."

Stubborn pride laced his tone. "I can't do that."

"It's rightfully yours, Mr. Stratton. I wouldn't be giving it to you if I didn't know for a fact that last year you were the true winner of the contest."

His gaze lifted to Meg's. "What do you mean? Your brother won."

"Yes. But not fairly."

"How do you know?"

"I'd rather not go into the specifics and I would like this transaction to be kept between us." Meg pressed the money into his hands. "It is yours, make no mistake about it. But you will find no other proof than my word."

Oliver looked as if he wouldn't take the bills.

Meg glanced meaningfully at his mother. "If you won't do it for yourself, do it for her."

With a sigh, Oliver reluctantly accepted the stack of bills. "Gee . . ."

Matthew slipped his hand onto Meg's lap and reached for her hand. He held it, softly rubbing her knuckles with his thumb. A lump formed in her throat and moisture filled her eyes. This wasn't going to turn into something about her. It wasn't. She did what she had to do. There was no courage in doing the right thing. It was the honorable thing.

"You deserved this last year. I wish you could have gotten all the attention. But I can't fix that. All I could do was enter and hope I could win for you."

Oliver rubbed beneath his nose. "You mean you entered just to try and get me this money?"

"Yes."

"Well, gee . . . I don't know what to say."

"There is nothing to say," Meg replied softly. "I hope you'll accept my apologies on behalf of my fam-

ily. It was wrong of my brother to do what he did. I
hope you can forgive him."

"I did that some time ago, Miss Brooks. But I do
confess, I have been a mite angry with him at times."

"Understandably so."

Meg rose to her feet, not wanting to take up anymore of Oliver Stratton's time.

The two men in the room also stood. The moment
was awkward and defined by wary trust and the hesi-
tancy to say more than what had already been said.

Matthew opened the door, and Meg went outside.
The day seemed to be brighter. Her burden of rectify-
ing the situation lessened. Giving back the money
could never remove the sting of having lost to a cheat.
But it was the only thing she could do.

"I do appreciate your coming out here, Miss
Brooks," he said from the doorway. "You could have
kept the prize for yourself and I wouldn't have had
any call to ask you for it."

She gave him a parting smile. "Good-bye."

She began walking with her mouth still curved, un-
aware she'd been holding her breath since the moment
they'd gone inside. The ache in her shoulders from
tension began to slacken. And the fluttering in her
stomach, which had felt like a thousand butterfly
wings, started to still.

Matthew took her hand and helped her into the
rented buggy he'd rented from Max Hess's livery. Silently, he mounted the seat, clucked the reins, and
they rode from Oliver Stratton's yard.

Words didn't pass between them as the buggy
wheels rumbled along the road.

The road back to Harmony.

She didn't want him to leave. She couldn't imagine

her life without him. She loved him. More than anything. He had accepted her for who she was just as she had come to accept him for who he was.

He needed to know that.

"Matthew, stop the buggy," Meg said, putting a hand on his shoulder.

He reined the horses and pulled on the brake. Propping his foot onto the box, he turned to face her. The back of his arm rested on the seat back. So casual and relaxed. So unlike Matthew.

His fingers grazed her back and a delightful shiver ran across her skin.

She smiled at him. But her smile sobered. "Matthew, I have to tell you that I understand in your heart that you truly want to help people. Your articles do have good in them. I didn't want to see that before. If you've decided to go back to San Francisco . . ." She could say no more, her voice dimming like a flame flickering to darkness in the wind. For surely that's what her life would be like without him.

Darkness. Loneliness.

"Darling, I couldn't go back to San Francisco even if I wanted to." He stroked her hair and the nape of her neck. "I spent my return train ticket money, and then some, on something in Harmony." He reached into his trouser pocket and came out with a key. He handed it to her.

Bewilderment lifted her brows. "What's this?"

"The key to the new home of the *Harmony Advocate*. I sent my editor my termination letter this morning and I've asked him to ship a printing press and everything I'll need to start Harmony's first newspaper."

"Really?" she asked, surprised. "Does this mean you're not going to write the article about Wayne?"

"I already tried to write it. I had a draft, in fact. Two nights ago when you came to see me, but I knew something was missing. It had nothing to do with proof. You made me realize what. What was missing was my heart. It just wasn't in the right place. I'm never going to write another article like that one, or like any of the others I've written before. From now on, I'm going to write about good things." He tucked her hair behind her ear. "Like the first woman to win a fly-fishing tournament."

"Oh, Matthew. I don't know what to say."

"Say you think it's a good idea."

"I think it's a wonderful idea." She hugged him, pressing her lips against the warm side of his neck and clinging to this man she loved. Whispering at his ear, she said, "You asked me once if I'd marry you. Does the offer still stand?"

"Yes."

"Then I accept."

Matthew drew her away from him, searched her face, then kissed her. A soft and rewarding kiss. A sealing of their love. Promises. Of things to come. She reveled in his touch. The feel of him next to her. His mouth on hers.

At length, he broke away. "We can do things up your way. I know you want something big like your friend."

She shook her head. "I don't."

He gazed at her with a playful skepticism in his eyes. "Is this the Meg Brooks I love?"

"Yes. But she doesn't want to wait for invitations and bouquets and a wedding dress." She covered her mouth with her hand, as if to keep from busting out laughing. "Honestly, Matthew, it's you I want to marry. Not the bouquet or the wedding dress. I really don't care about that."

"Really?"

"Uh-huh."

"Then what would you say to eloping with me? Right now. Go on over to Alder and be man and wife before sunset. What do you think?" He kissed her quickly, as if to test her reaction to the idea.

She kissed him back. Smiling, laughing. "I think we're wasting time sitting here."

Matthew unhitched the buggy's brake, and set the team in motion with a holler.

They were married by the Alder court justice in a ceremony that lasted no more than ten minutes. Before they went to the courthouse, Matthew took Meg to the small town mercantile and bought her a wedding ring they picked out together. It wasn't a diamond like Johannah's, but that fact bore no consequence to Meg. She'd been thrilled with the four small rubies with a polished pearl in the center in a fancy setting of gold.

And with all the thoughtfulness she'd ever wanted in a husband, he gave her a bridal bouquet. It wasn't the ivy, snowdrops, and maiden's blush roses that she'd thought she'd have on her wedding day. It was better—a thick bunch of yellow daisies, pink azaleas, and lilacs with a long train of glossy ivy.

After the brief ceremony, they'd had a wedding supper at the only restaurant in town and then they'd checked into the Knotty Pine Hotel as man and wife. Their room was one of only two that had a fireplace.

Although the evening air had the promise of summer, Matthew had stoked a fire while Meg went to the bathroom down the hall and freshened up.

She hadn't thought about a change of clothes, or a nightgown, when she and Matthew had eloped. She hoped she didn't disappoint him. As she closed the bathroom door behind her and walked down the hallway to their room, her fears ebbed. She loved the man she married. He wouldn't think less of her for not having a silk wrapper to wear on their wedding night.

She opened the door to their room and saw her husband standing by the window, the sunset silhouetting his body.

As she shut the world out for the night, Matthew said, "I had the desk clerk send your grandmother the note you wrote."

Meg smiled. "Thank you."

She'd written a message to Grandma Nettie that said she was all right. And that she was with Matthew. Meg preferred to tell her grandmother in person that she'd married.

"I had the hotel send up champagne." Matthew motioned to the small table by the window. A bottle and two glasses sat beside one another. "They didn't have wineglasses."

Unbidden, a quake of shyness struck her as she nervously replied, "I'm sure it will taste the same."

"Have you ever had champagne?"

"No, just sherry. Once. On my sixteenth birthday." Why was she feeling so . . . giddy?

Matthew uncorked the bottle with a *pop* and poured a splash of the sparkling wine in their glasses. He handed her one, their fingers brushing, as he raised his glass to her. "To my wife. My love. I used to think I wasn't cut out to be a decent husband. You've changed my life for the better."

Blushing, she replied, "I love you."

She sipped the champagne, liking the taste and the tickle the bubbles made as they passed her throat.

"Do you like it?" Matthew asked.

"I think I may like it too much."

They drank the champagne, yet neither of them could take their eyes off the other and Meg's heartbeat thrummed in her ears. She glanced at the bed, the monstrous thing that seemed to take up the entire room. How did she tell him she wasn't afraid of that . . . of what they would do? If she came right out and said so, he'd think her brazen.

Yet, he hadn't thought her brazen for entering a fishing contest as a man. In fact, Matthew loved her for who she was. So there was no reason not to speak her mind, if she dared. But she did, after all, still have modesty.

She bit her lip, thinking Matthew the handsomest man in the world and marveling just how lucky she was to have found him, to have found a man who loved her just as much as she loved him.

She felt the potency of Mrs. Wolcott's words on love. Love wasn't something that could be forced. She could no more force herself out of love with Matthew as she could force herself to be in love with him. She'd fallen for Mr. Wilberforce, but it was the Matthew in Vernon that she'd loved.

Would always love.

Would make love to.

"I do believe it's warm in here," Meg remarked, fanning her face and looking toward the fireplace.

"Do you want me to put it out?" Matthew set his glass down.

"Oh, no. I like it. It's just that maybe we should take off our shoes." She hastily added. "To cool off."

He gave her a sly smile and patted the top of his thigh. "Put your foot up. One hand on my shoulder to steady yourself."

She put her glass next to his and rested her shoe on his leg. He undid the laces with deliberate slowness that had her shivering. His casual manner wrecked havoc on her senses, which seemed to be heightened even with what little champagne she'd had.

Her husband removed her shoe, then grazed his hand up her calf and gently massaged her muscles. She leaned her head back a little and closed her eyes. Heaven. His touch was heaven.

Then he brought his fingers higher, drawing her petticoats and skirt hem upward to her garter.

"Is this petticoat going to fall off?" he murmured.

"I don't know . . ." she said, her voice sounding throaty in her ears. "It would seem my petticoats have a mind of their own. I've bought some new ones."

"But you'll save the old ones for me and wear them around the house. I might just get lucky and watch one fall off."

She laughed, soft and full of love.

With a slow slide, he pulled her stocking down her leg and off her foot. She giggled when he ran his fingertip beneath her instep. "Ticklish, are you?"

"Not me."

"Liar."

She couldn't help laughing.

He lowered her right leg and pointed to her left. "Other foot, darling."

She complied, thinking this was the most romantic thing she had ever experienced in her whole life. The taking off of one's shoes and stockings by the man she loved.

Once she stood barefoot, she said, "I'll take off your shoes."

She felt wicked doing so. Delightfully wicked for undressing her husband. But it was empowering knowing that she could make him shudder just by drawing her fingertips over the knuckles on his toes. Toes she had fallen in love with from the first time she'd seen them while hiding under his bed.

When she finished, he gathered her into his arms and spoke two words that heated her skin: "Kiss me."

And she did.

Long and without restraint. Cherishing him. He tasted sweet like the champagne. She wanted to melt inside him—to be a part of him. To be his wife in every way.

"Am I really your wife?" she whispered.

"Yes," he replied against her mouth.

"Then show me what only a husband can show his wife."

Matthew lifted her off the floor in one swoop of his arm and brought her to the bed, laying down beside her.

While he stroked the contour of her cheek, he asked, "Do you want to talk about making love?"

Dismayed that she would blush over the subject, and with him, she replied with boldness, "I don't think we should talk about it. I think we should do it."

"All right, Meg . . . whatever you want. This night is yours."

"And yours," she returned.

Matthew brought his hands to the buttons of her shirtwaist and began to unfasten them. With each button that popped undone, she drew in a breath, her breasts straining against her corset. As soon as she wore only her corset and shimmy, she unfastened the buttons to Matthew's shirt and slid her hands inside across the taut planes of his chest.

He had very little chest hair; the slight ruffling of crispiness beneath her palm excited her. She explored him with her hands. Testing. Learning. Liking the way he sucked air into his lungs when she lowered her fingertips to the edge of his trousers.

With her barely being aware of it, he rolled her on to her back and raised himself over her, dipping his head down to kiss her fully on the mouth. Taking from her what she so freely gave: Her heart. Her love. Her desire.

She loved the warmth of his skin as she splayed her hands up the slope of his back and upward into his hair, so soft and silky. So masculine in its *El Soudan* fragrance. Coconuts. She remembered the first time she'd been aware of how he smelled. She'd been enamored by him. Intoxicated by him.

Meg made fists of her hands and rested them on his shoulders, thinking she'd go crazy if he didn't take off her skirt and corset. All this kissing. All this glorious and dizzy kissing was making her want things far more . . . heated.

Matthew lifted himself onto his elbows and sat up, holding the bulk of his weight on his knees as he slipped her shimmy up and over her head, then, with an ease that didn't escape her notice, he went for the hooks of her corset. They fell open with each snap of his wrist, and each bit of her skin that was exposed felt cool and dusted with moisture that made her nipples pucker.

Once she laid there without anything to bar her breasts from his view, that old self-consciousness befell her again. She almost couldn't look at him looking at her. She even began to turn her head. But he caught her chin and made her watch him, watching her.

Made her stay still as he lowered his mouth over her. As he took one nipple into his mouth . . . and loved her just the way she was.

That realization, that knowledge let her slip over the edge of humility and set herself free.

The sensations he evoked within her caused her blood to heat like that of the fire blazing in the hearth. With every way his hands touched her, felt her, excited her, she melted a little more. Her fingers opened, her palms flattened on his shoulders, bringing him closer to her.

Shameless. She was shameless and she didn't care.

Matthew breathed against her breast, "I love you."

"I love you," she whispered.

Her skirt and petticoat were discarded; cast over the bed's edge. As were Matthew's shirt, trousers, and underwear.

Naked. They laid next to one another naked. Meg never thought she could do such a thing with light in the room. But she could. She wanted to. Wanted to see her husband. And have him see her.

He kissed her once more. So passionately she thought she'd die from the long artful advances of his mouth over hers. Without breaking the kiss, he pressed her into the mattress. Her breasts ached for his touch. The light wedge of curls on his chest rasped across her taut nipples. A need for him to touch every inch of her made her entwine her legs with his. She wanted him to find the secret place that made her a woman and make her his own.

His fingers brushed the column of her neck, searing her, startling Meg in her desire to want him so. He raised his head, found her collarbone with his fingertip and traced it downward, to her breast, circling and deliberately staying away from the nipples that begged for him. Her back arched and she wanted more than this slow touch. This slow torment.

The quickening that had started deep inside her intensified as the heat of his tongue wrapped around her nipple once more. She writhed beneath him, unable to stay still. Twisting, she brought herself closer to him. His hand fondled her other breast and the combination of fingertips and tongue were almost too much for her senses to keen.

She shifted, wanting more. Needing more. She felt the length of him next to her thigh . . . then between her legs. He pulled himself tall on his arms and stared down at her. The sight of him, bare-chested, his hair in a cascade around his face, was pleasure of the purest degree.

Oh, how she loved him.

He kissed her again. This time with an urgency that bruised her lips and left her reeling. The pulse that beat at the juncture of her thighs felt wet and warm . . . empty and wanting.

As he stretched out fully on top of her, mindful of his weight over her body, and nudged her legs open, tingles ran down to her toes. She was in awe that he could evoke such power over her body. Such a quaking and beating of her heart.

Matthew brought his hand between her legs, teasing

her open, wider. With soft and gentle strokes, he touched her. That place that no one had ever touched. And he tormented. A sweet torment. His thumb circled and rubbed over a tiny part of her. A part that made her lose control and she was on the edge. The edge of something so rapturous and wonderful she wanted to call out her husband's name.

But before she could breathe, he entered her. Consumed the place his hand had just been. Her moistness enveloped him, sheathed him, took him. A slight pain, a moment of uncomfortableness, stilled her. Then he pushed deeper and the twinge died. And the pleasure began.

Such a pleasure she had never known existed. The movements. The thrusts. She seemed to know what to do. From some place within her soul, she knew. Each time Matthew pulled back, he buried himself deeper. The motion became faster, shorter, harder.

In perfect tempo with one another, Meg held Matthew close as she rocked in sync with him. Her body pulsated. Built with a need that had to be unleashed. A pleasure that burst upon her and showered her with a heat and rush of sensuality she reeled from.

Matthew pushed into her, one last time. His murmur of fulfillment mingling with her own. He laid softly atop her, her breasts a cushion for his body. She felt him throb inside her. Her legs still wrapped around his, and their breathing matching in tempo and gasps.

They stayed that way for a long while. Holding one another. Spent and damp.

In rapture.

In love.

❧ Epilogue ❧

"How does it feel to be the president?"

Meg laughed at her husband as she removed her hat and set it on the mantel of their apartment. "Quite good, thank you."

"I'm going to lock up downstairs and I'll be up in a minute." Matthew bussed a quick kiss on her cheek. She smiled at him as he left through the door of their residence, which was located above the newspaper office.

They'd just returned home from a meeting of the Woolly Buggers club where Meg had been elected as the new president. Gus Gushurst had lost by a margin of two votes to one. Ever since Meg had won the fly-fishing contest nearly a month ago, the Woolly Buggers had changed their tune about who could enter— much to Gus Gushurst's protests.

Matthew had run an article in the *Harmony Advocate* about the business of equality and fairness. His well-crafted words had sparked a debate in Harmony

among men and women alike, and it seemed as if
boundaries were more open to closing.

Grandma Nettie had been delighted by the changes.
Meg fully agreed with her grandmother that it was
glorious to be able to do and say what one wanted
without any restrictions from society.

However, there was still one restriction. And that
was the secret she and Grandma Nettie shared about
Wayne. Meg had confided in her grandmother and
they both thought it best the matter be laid to rest.
Her brother had left for Europe for an extended tour
and had told the family he didn't know when he'd
return. When he did, Meg hoped she would be able
to look him in the eyes and not think ill of him. Time
would heal . . . at least, she wanted it to.

Telling Grandma Nettie she'd married Matthew in
a private ceremony hadn't been difficult. After everything that had happened, her grandmother had
changed her mind about Matthew and thought he was
the perfect man for her. But Meg and Matthew's marriage wasn't the only one to surprise the citizens of
Harmony.

Blushing newlyweds themselves, Grandma Nettie
and Mr. Finch had left for Washington, D.C., three
days ago for the White House campaign when Meg's
parents had returned home from their anniversary
trip.

The shock of coming home and being informed that
her only daughter had married caused Iris Brooks to
faint in the family home's parlor. Meg and Matthew
helped rouse her while her father brought a glass of
water. When her mother batted her lashes and came
to, Meg reiterated that she had married and was blissfully happy that the man beside her was indeed her

legal husband. Iris had looked at Matthew, then at Meg, then smiled before fainting once more.

Meg's father had congratulated them and so had Meg's mother when she came to a second time and collected herself while sitting on the sofa. As soon as her mother realized that her daughter truly had married and missed out on a wedding ceremony with all the trimmings, she'd lamented that it wasn't to be tolerated. That at least a bridal party was in order.

So, a week ago, Meg had had a bridal shower. Hildegarde and Ruth had taken her aside and said they wanted men of their own and figured becoming members of the Woolly Buggers club would be the place to start. It had, after all, helped Meg find her man.

Tonight Meg's friends had shown up at the meeting with several other town ladies interested in becoming members. Hildegarde and Ruth were allowed to join and even had gained the attentions of two gentlemen. Ruth wished Meg the very best with her Mr. Gage and hoped Meg wouldn't think she still sought his affections. And Hildegarde said she was sorry for not realizing that Mr. Bascomb was Meg.

Meg sighed with contentment and stared at the mantel. Hanging above it were four framed items:

Their wedding certificate.

Meg's graduation diploma from Mrs. Wolcott's school—her last essay had been on women coming into their own.

Matthew's Silver Press award plaque.

And the first page printed by the *Harmony Advocate*. The headline read: *A Woman's Place Is Where She Makes It*. The article was all about Nettie Rothman, woman extraordinaire.

In the center, on the mantelpiece itself, was Meg's fishing trophy.

Meg crossed the room's red rose–patterned tobacco-colored carpet. She'd done the decorating herself, having papered the walls with pale green flocking. She went to the corner table, which displayed mementos that she and Matthew had collected, and put a recording on the Victrola. Merriebell Smith began to sing sweet sentiments that had Meg humming.

Her gaze fell on the notepad that belonged to her husband, the Williams Rightwriter typewriter, the unlit cigar, the hair combs she'd taken from her hair the other day, the bouquet of dried flowers beneath a glass dome.

Her wedding bouquet. She'd cherish it always.

Matthew came inside, a curious expression on his face. His arms were behind his back, as if he were hiding something.

She went to him with a raise of her brows. "What's the matter?"

He showed her what he had.

Her diary.

She tried to take it from him but he wouldn't give it to her.

"A friend just gave this to me," he said, his smile crooked.

"What friend?"

"Barkly."

"Barkly?"

"I found him on the boardwalk in front of the newspaper. He had this in his mouth and when I went to go see what it was, he dropped it and ran." Matthew lifted the charred book with muddy edges—as if it had been buried for a while—and began to skim the pages.

"Why, I'll bet that dog was the one who stole my petticoat. That's how Clovis Lester found it. Discarded who knows where," Meg mused. Then she sobered and held her hand out. "Give me that silly thing. You don't want to read it."

Matthew gave her a lazy smile and pulled the diary out of her reach.

Meg knew darn well he'd read most of it downstairs, because he knew what page to go to. One on which she'd written all sorts of fabrications. She flinched as her husband began to read her foolish ramblings about kissing and being in love.

Matthew lifted his eyes to hers, a grin on his mouth. "I think I'm going to have to punch this Mr. Wilberforce in the nose. He's had his hands all over you and he's kissed you in ways that I haven't. *Yet.*" He put the diary down on the chair and took Meg into his arms.

She laughed as he nuzzled the crook of her neck and kissed her over and over behind her ear, tickling her. Then he kissed her mouth. "I don't remember Wilberforce ever kissing you like this."

Lingering and long. The kiss was timeless. She swayed into Matthew, savoring the feel of his lips over hers. The feel of his warm, strong hands on her back as he held her close.

"Or kissing you like this," he said, deepening the meeting of their mouths. "And this . . ." he murmured as he grazed the tender skin about her lips, then delving his tongue softly into her mouth and kissing her with an intimacy that shook her clear to her toes.

In a single motion, Matthew swept her into his arms. Meg gave a little scream of deviltry as he walked toward the bedroom. Once inside, he kicked the door closed with the heel of his boot. Then he tumbled them sideways on the bed, arms encircling one another.

"Ah, Meg . . ." he said, teasing a curl at her brow around his fingertip. "How I love you."

"I love you, too." She reached out with her hand and traced the fullness of his mouth.

Then they kissed. Softly. Passionately. Madly.

They'd been hooked.

Dear Readers:

I hope you found *Hooked* enjoyable reading. I began the book in Idaho and finished it in Washington. I now live in the beautiful Seattle area. My office window looks out at forty acres of woods. When I'm stuck on my plot, I can lean back in my chair and watch the bluejays and a variety of birds that swoop through the yard to get at the bird feeders.

It's difficult for a writer to pick which character she's penned that she likes the best. I'd like to think that every hero and heroine I've written has somehow touched a reader. However, I have to say Meg Brooks is the closest to my heart. From the moment she lost her petticoat, I was cheering for her. I think everyone wants to fit in and say, "Like me for who I am." But it's a difficult statement to make. I was delighted when Meg declared she was who she was. And as her author, I've got a good mind to cut my hair, too.

As to a few historical events: Yes, there really was a Princess Bust Cream manufactured by the Seroco Chemical laboratory. You could buy a jar for a $1.36 from the Sears, Roebuck and Co. catalogue.

Thanks to my friend, Carmel Thomaston, for answering my questions about reporters. You can visit my homepage at her website, Painted Rock. The address is:

http://www.paintedrock.com/authors/holm.htm

Next up to bat—literally—is a dark and sexy hero, Alex Cordova, who will heat things up in *Honey,* book three of the Brides for All Seasons series, which returns to Harmony, Montana. Camille Kennison has become the new manager of Kennison's Keystones and is bound and determined to turn the losing ball club into league champions. Along the way, she discovers loyalty and love. Alex finds a place in his heart that's never been touched.

And for those of you who've wondered if Hildegarde Plunkett will ever find her man, she finally does in *Honey:* a gentle soul named Captain, who has a past that only Alex understands.

You can e-mail me at **stefholm@eskimo.com** or snail mail me at my post office box. As always, a self-addressed, stamped envelope is appreciated for a prompt response.

Best,

Stef Ann Holm
P.O. Box 5727
Kent, WA 98064-5727

LINDA HOWARD

With more than five million books in print and eight awards—including the Silver Pen from *Affaire de Coeur*—to her credit, Linda Howard has truly captured the hearts and minds of readers and critics alike. Her bestselling romances have set a new standard for steamy, sensuous storytelling.

- ☐ Angel Creek   66081-0/$6.99
- ☐ Dream Man   79935-5/$6.99
- ☐ Heart of Fire   72859-8/$6.99
- ☐ A Lady of the West   66080-2/$6.99
- ☐ The Touch of Fire   72858-X/$6.99
- ☐ After the Night   79936-3/$6.99
- ☐ Shades of Twilight   79937-1/$6.99
- ☐ Kill and Tell   56883-3/$6.99
- ☐ Now You See Her   03405-7/$6.99
- ☐ Son of the Morning   79938-X/$6.99

SONNET BOOKS
PROUDLY PRESENTS
Book Three in the
"Brides for All Seasons"
Series

HONEY

STEF ANN HOLM

Coming Soon
from Sonnet Books

The following is a preview of
Honey. . . .

Alex Cordova had an appreciation for wood.

Most of his life, he'd earned his living from it. In his early youth, by carving scythe handles for cutting tobacco in Cuban fields. At nineteen, by swinging a bat at baseballs; a career that had lasted six years. And now, at twenty-eight, by designing and creating furniture.

To Alex, wood defined who he'd become, where he'd been.

He skimmed a jack plane across the hinged top of the bride's chest he was finishing for Grant Calhoon's daughter. The tool seemed dwarfed in his grasp and, to an observer, would look ineffectual in his large hand. But Alex was always in control, passing the blade with a fluid motion over the wood's surface.

The wood felt warm and smooth beneath his touch. He caressed it like he would a woman, slowly sliding his hand over the grained surface, feeling every sensation in his fingertips, every imperfection. Sometimes he'd leave a dimple on the finished surface—much like that of a barely discernible mole on a woman's inner thigh. Small blemishes lent certain furniture character. Alex saw beauty in what appeared to be perfect, yet was marked with an individual distinction.

Inside the wood shop, the mellow scent of old wax and boiled linseed oil hung in the air. They mingled with the woodsy definition of ash. He'd left the barn-sized doors open so the fresh smell of that particular wood wouldn't trigger memories. But it did.

It stirred in him the overwhelming desire to once more become a part of the American pastime: baseball. To go . . . home. Home to the sport he'd loved with its speed and grace, failure and loss, imperishable hope, and that defining moment that can override every sensory feeling ever known to man: winning the game.

That surging emotion, that indescribable passion to play that came with the arrival of springtime and ended with onset of autumn, could still grip Alex three years after he'd quit.

But now, spring and autumn were merely two seasons in a calendar of four. Alex no longer allowed himself to anticipate either: Because he'd sworn never to pitch another ball or swing another bat for as long as he lived.

Pensive thoughts clouded his gaze, and he set the jack plane down. He left the bride's chest and went to his workbench where he placed both hands on the side rest and leaned forward. Eyes closed, a suffocating feeling pulled the air from his lungs.

He couldn't afford to let baseball haunt him now.

Pitching sliders was a shadow in his past. Only the present mattered.

Holy Christ . . . a big problem weighed on him.

Money.

He needed a lot of it. Close to four thousand.

Opening his eyes, Alex reached for the door handle on one of the wall cabinets above the bench. Hidden behind the boxes of cut nails and cans of varnish was an envelope. Alex slid it from its niche and held on to it as if it were thin glass. He read the typeface in the left corner.

Silas Denton Sanatorium for Nervous Diseases
209 Niagra St., cor. Main
Buffalo, N.Y.

A heaviness centered in his chest. Alex didn't know why he felt he had to look at the envelope. By memory, he knew what was typed on the outside and printed on the inside.

Silas Denton was renowned for his treatment of brain disorders. None of those docs who had Captain going through hell in the Baltimore Hospital for the Public had made any progress. The doctors had scared Cap senseless. Shaving his head and rubbing it nightly with mercurial ointment that blistered the back of his neck. Cap had nearly lost what was left of his mind in there.

Three years later, the memories of what they'd done to Cap purged his dreams into nightmares and he'd wake in a sweating terror.

Alex didn't know everything that had gone on in those two weeks that Cap had been alone. Cap had been in a real bad way for the first several months, but he'd gradually come into his own after Alex had gotten him out. A simple-minded, kindhearted man. If that side of Cap's personality had been with Cap before, Alex had never seen it. This Captain was an entirely different person from the man Alex had known before the accident.

Unable to accept the physicians' practice of routinely taking blood from Cap's feet by opening a vein, Alex had demanded he be released in his care since Cap had no family. Alex hoped that twenty-four-hour attention with a kinder hand would make a difference.

Now Alex wondered if he'd done the right thing.

Cap wasn't getting better. In fact, he seemed to be getting worse.

He had his good days and his bad days. Sometimes a spark of memory would ignite in his head and he'd become petrified. It was growing more and more difficult for Alex to reassure Cap he'd be all right. What had happened yesterday in Plunkett's mercantile had been the deciding factor for Alex.

Captain had to see the best doctor there was.

And that was Silas Denton.

But for that to happen, Alex needed four thousand to put Cap's demons to rest.

The Buffalo, New York, hospital was by the water. Captain liked the ocean. In fact, he was preoccupied by the Chesapeake Bay and catching crabs with nets— a fragment of that memory which floated inside his head like that of a fishing cork.

Alex had no intention of abandoning Cap to the hospital. He'd already inquired about rents close to the sanatorium and found several buildings with two-bedroom apartments for let. They were close

nough that Alex could walk Cap to the facilities
each day.

Everything would work out.

If only he could come up with four thousand.

Tucking the letter in is place, Alex closed the cupboard and went back to the bride's chest. As he
smoothed the jack plane across the wood, he went
through his options.

He could sell the wood shop. But he'd barely make
squat. Whoever bought it would have to know what
to do with it. The tools were of no value to somebody
who didn't understand wood.

He would advertise his skills in nearby Waverly or
Alder. But it would be a hell of a long haul to save
enough on the extra income. The bride's chest he was
finishing sold for twenty-eight dollars. He'd have to
make hundreds of them, and more, to come even close
to the four thousand.

He could borrow the money. But who to ask? He
had nobody. Nobody but Captain.

But that was another story. A time and place Alex
didn't like to go to.

He forced his attention back to the issue at hand:
How to come up with four thousand dollars. And of
course he knew the answer. In truth he understood
what he would have to do—a sad, gaping irony that
only Captain would understand—if only he could.

"Mr. Cordova?"

Alex swung around, his body tight, his thoughts
vaporating into the thin summer air. He hadn't heard
anyone approach the shop. A woman stood in the
double-wide doorway. Sunlight spilled over her.
Christ . . . she looked like an angel—blonde, tall. She

was wearing pale colors, the light fabric of her skir
doing a soft dance around her ankles.

Eyes narrowing, Alex slowly relaxed his stance
"Who wants to know?"

She took a few steps forward, her walk assured. H
liked the way she held her shoulders. The way he
hair looked soft tucked beneath her hat.

Then she did something that surprised him. She ex
tended her hand.

He didn't readily take it. Merely stared at the whit
silk of her gloves. The slenderness of her fingers. Th
tiny pearl buttons that ran up the inside of her wris
He swore he could almost see her pulse point; tha
muted beat of her heart beneath her delicate ski
and glove.

The awkward moment dragged on until he graspe
her outstretched hand. He was unprepared for the jo
of heat that shot up his arm brought on by her touch

"Mr. Cordova, I'm Camille Kennison. And I've go
a proposition for you."

Cool disappointment took over the searing warmt
in his body. Alex let her hand slide from his finger
"Your family owns the hardware store."

"My father, yes."

Turning away from her, Alex walked to the ches
and began to work on it again. Crouching to sit on
crate, he tried to put her out of his mind. He knev
what her proposition was all about and he wanted he
to leave. What galled him was, he didn't think Kenn
son would stoop so low as to have his daughter com
to do his bidding.

Alex hadn't even been aware Kennison had
daughter. Socializing in town wasn't something Ale

id. He preferred to stay at the shop and work on his projects. Trips to Harmony were made when necessity dictated it, and without undo conversation.

"Mr. Cordova." She came to stand beside him, the sheer layer of lace on her skirt nearly brushing his elbow as he moved his arm. "I'd like you to play baseball for the Harmony Keystones."

Even before she'd said it, a cold sweat broke out on his brow. He couldn't. He'd sworn he wouldn't.

"Not interested.'

"I know my father's asked you before, but this is different. I'm asking now and I—"

"Not interested." He looked up, glaring at her.

The ice blue of her eyes didn't flicker in alarm. Or fear. Or show any other kind of emotion but set determination.

"I can understand your reluctance to talk with me, but I can assure you that I don't have my father's temperament. I'm quite level-headed and never raise my voice to get my point across."

A light draft of air stirred the fine curls of wood shavings littered over the dirt floor. He lowered his gaze to watch them as they tumbled over one another, skittering across the tips of Camille's tan shoes. On the breeze, the fragrance of lavender perfume intruded in his male sanctuary.

"There is no point to make." Alex quit using the jack plane and rubbed his thumb over a small nub in the grain. He liked it. He'd leave it.

"Oh, but you're wrong," she said.

The conviction in her voice had him looking at her once more.

A skein of golden blonde hair touched her ear and, unbidden, Alex grew mesmerized by it as she spoke.

"I have an offer for your consideration. One I'm sure my father has never brought you."

Snapping out of the fog that held him, Alex gave her a hard stare. "I don't play baseball."

"So you've said. But as you might know, the Keystones have faltered miserably. Most especially this season."

"I wouldn't know. I don't follow the game any more."

"Then you aren't aware of the American League."

He said nothing.

"They're newly formed this year. Clean ball is their main platform. No profanity on the playing field and the umpires are legitimate agents of the league. Even your old club, the Orioles, are now in the American League. Things are quite different from the National League. The motto is 'a fair game and a good time.' "

"I don't give a bag of peanuts, honey."

That got her. She seemed to stand a little taller—as if to show him she wasn't weak. The soft-spoken Camille Kennison may not raise her voice, but she had a thread of stubbornness that lay hidden beneath the cool, white surface.

"I do think you'll *give a bag of peanuts* when you hear me out." The bit of edginess vanished, replaced by a calm exterior. "We're prepared to give you a contract of two thousand five hundred for the season. We can't legally offer you any more by way of salary. The American League has imposed a salary cap. But we can give you a bonus of three thousand five hundred for the exclusive use of your photograph and signature."

He went still. Six thousand. Two thousand more than he needed.

He pinned her with a dark frown.

"Let me assure you," she continued, "this is on the up and up."

For an instant, he thought about getting all that money. Then cursed himself. He couldn't play ball. Not for six thousand. Not for sixty thousand.

"When you left the National League, you were batting two-twenty-one."

She needn't tell him about his baseball career. He knew what he had and hadn't accomplished.

"Did you know Cy Young is averaging two-sixteen? And, so far this year, he's given up two home runs. You could beat his record, Mr. Cordova. Pitch against him."

Alex wondered just how much digging she had done on him. Stats were a matter of public record. No secret there.

Cy Young . . . hell. A ghost from the past. The last time he'd pitched against the right-hander, Young had been playing for the Cleveland Spiders. Kicked Alex's ass, too. The son-of-a-bitch didn't play fair. He loved to spike players. Alex would like to get a piece of him.

Six grand. Hell.

Alex stood. "Young's in the National League—I couldn't very well play against him now, could I, honey?"

"He left the National League for a better offer. This year he signed with the Boston Somersets. American League."

Conflict raged in Alex. The chance to go up against

Young was staring him in the face. She'd put the offer on the table. He was hungry. But he couldn't take the fare. Not without . . .

But holy Christ—six thousand.

He needed the money.

Alex rose from the crate.

Camille worried her lip, clearly refusing to give up. "I can also offer you your own hotel room on road games and—"

"Never mind. You had me with the six thou, Miss Kennison. I'll do it."

And as soon as he earned out his six thousand, he'd be on a train to Buffalo with Captain.

Alex watched as Camille's face lit up with relief. Her mouth remained open. Half from the words left unspoken, half from astonishment.

"You better close your mouth, honey, and get that contract written up before I change my mind."

And he just might.

"Oh . . . oh, well!" She extended her hand for him to shake.

He did so. Only this time without any emotions involved. This was a business transaction, cut and dry.

"Welcome aboard, Mr. Cordova," she breathed eagerly. "The Keystones are happy to have you."

"Yeah. Sure."

"I'll have my father's lawyer, Mr. Stykem, draw up the contract and we can meet at his office tomorrow. Shall we say eleven o'clock?"

Alex nodded.

"Eleven o'clock, then." She was walking backward when she said it, as if she felt she needed to make a quick getaway before he did indeed change his mind.

He let her go with a warning not to set him up in

the future. "I can be bought, honey, but I can't be had. Cy Young's only given up one home run this year. To Roscoe Miller of the Detroit Tigers."

Her cheeks paled, then she turned in a swirl of skirts and left the wood shop.

Camille walked as gracefully as she could, but she could barely keep one foot in front of the other. Barely think, barely breathe.

Heavens, he was still watching her. She could feel his gaze on her back, hot and level.

She was wrong about Alex Cordova. He could intimidate her. Put a little trip in her step. She quickly regained the smoothness of her walk so he wouldn't think she was bothered by him staring after her. And she shouldn't have been.

But prior to today, she'd only seen him from afar and had never taken a really good look at him.

His eyes were the soul of his face, dark and fathomless—keepers of the enigma that surrounded Alex Cordova. His hair was the color of pitch and fell over his brows as he smoothed the wood with a big caressing hand. For a moment, she'd imagined what it would be like for those large hands to skim over her.

A shimmer of something she wasn't interested in naming ran through her. She pushed it away.

The man was oblivious to her. No feelings at all. She hadn't shaken him up a bit. Cool. He'd been so cool. As cool as an Evergreen Creek in the springtime. But clearly she'd been cooler. Although, it had been hard when she'd looked at him to keep her thoughts in order.

His jet black hair had fallen in a part down the center of his head, just shy of being long enough to tuck behind his ears. He probably thought the wild untamed image suited him. It kept people at bay.

Well, it hadn't kept Camille Kennison at bay. She'd gotten him.

Look for
HONEY
Coming soon
from Sonnet Books